LYDIA SHARP

Entangled Publishing, LLC
644 Shrewsbury Commons Ave., STE 181
Shrewsbury, PA 17361
rights@entangledpublishing.com

Entangled Teen is an imprint of Entangled Publishing, LLC.

Visit our website at www.entangledpublishing.com.

Edited by Stacy Abrams and Liz Pelletier
Cover illustration and design by Elizabeth Turner Stokes
Interior design by Toni Kerr

ISBN 978-1-64937-409-7
Ebook ISBN 978-1-64937-427-1

Manufactured in the United States of America

First Edition August 2023

10 9 8 7 6 5 4 3 2 1

entangled teen
an imprint of Entangled Publishing LLC

ALSO BY LYDIA SHARP

Whenever I'm with You
The Night of Your Life

For Liz

At Entangled, we want our readers to be well-informed. If you would like to know if this book contains any elements that might be of concern for you, please check the back of the book for details.

Author's note

It is one thing to write a book, and it is quite another to publish it. After completing the original draft of *Frenemies with Benefits*, I wasn't sure what to do with it. But then I thought about my young self, my teen self, and my young adult self, and realized that this is exactly the kind of book I needed at that age.

I knew my peers were having sex in high school. Some days, that was all they talked about. They played made-up games to try to guess who in class was still a virgin. Girls openly described what their first time was like. Boys would make their "achievements" public to anyone in hearing distance. Even before high school, I was curious about sex. Turns out this is totally normal! But I didn't know it then.

The Internet was still an infant. There was no Google. All I had were books. And for me, *reading* about sex was much less awkward than *talking* about it. My mother was a registered nurse and had kept all her college textbooks on anatomy and how the body functions. There was an entire section about the reproductive system. And then there was my mother's hidden stash of romance novels that she didn't know I found…

Romance novels back then were pure fantasy. They were unrealistic to the point of ridiculousness. To be honest, I liked reading them but I also didn't. The men in those books were always so dominating and harsh. The women would always surrender. There was no such thing as "asking for consent." You either did what the man wanted or you did nothing. It was unusual for a woman to take control in the bedroom.

So my choices were either a cold, clinical textbook description of vaginal intercourse—and no other kind of sex—or something so unrealistic, it couldn't be trusted. But there was one book that was different. Literally only one book. *Forever* by Judy Blume.

The first time I saw this book was in middle school, in the cafeteria at lunch, when all the girls were passing it around to read a particular passage that included ejaculation. I read it, too—of course I did—but I didn't know how to react. The other girls acted like this was something scandalous, giggling, their cheeks turning red, and I just thought...why? Someone is finally telling it like it is. Clear. Frank. Just, *this is what happens* and no personal agenda behind it.

Sex was simply part of the story, part of the experience of being a teenager. I felt like I could understand what the characters were going through. And I never forgot that book.

There have been other books like it since then, more so in the last fifteen years than ever before, but it is still rare today, decades later. When I was a teen, I wanted to know what happens before, during, and after—and I wanted to see it from a teen perspective. Someone my own age.

In *Frenemies with Benefits*, I chose to show different kinds of sex on the page, either in action or discussed or both. I chose to show that sex can be enjoyable even when you don't always know what you're doing. I chose to show the importance of safe sex. I chose to show characters who respect consent. I chose to show the ability to control your own actions, make your own decisions, and not be ashamed of any of it. Virgin, not-virgin, whatever you identify as, wherever you are in life, the only person in control of how you feel about you is you.

I wasn't consciously aware of it at the time I was writing, but later I realized that I chose to show all those things because those are all the things I needed to see as a teen. And today, there are teens who need to see it, too. Whether you choose to have sex or not, and no matter what kind of sex you choose to have, *you* should be the one making your own choices about it. That, in the end, is what this book is all about.

You're in control. Always.

With love,
Lydia

Nine months ago…

Rayna: *what the hell was that all about???!!!??!!*
Me: *Benjamin Oliver is an asshole. End of story.*

Rayna: *he's usually a super nice guy! everyone i know likes him!!!!*

Me: *Except me. You know me and I don't like him.*

Me: *In fact I hate him.*

Rayna: *what am i supposed to do!! he's jeremy's best friend!*

Me: *And I'm your best friend.*

Rayna: *but i can't just ask ben to sit at another table because you had a fight with him!! he's not there for you he's there for jeremy!! and jeremy is there for me! and i'm not asking my boyfriend to leave because of this!!!!!*

Me: *That was not just a fight. Are you asking ME to leave?*
Rayna: *NO ONE is leaving!!!!!!!!!!!!!*

Me: *Your exclamation points are drilling holes into my brain.*

Rayna: *your drama is drilling holes into my LIFE!!!!*
Rayna: *!!!*

Chapter One

On the last day of school for the year, it's every person for themselves. The teachers have given up at this point. They've done all they can do—we will either graduate or we won't. There is no such thing as detention anymore or failing an assignment that's worth half your grade.

It's all behind us now. We just have to sit through the boredom of a nothing school day. Funny how the only day of the year we're not expected to use our brains is when people get the most creative.

Some guy in the room across the hall starts belching in Latin—*amo, amare, amavi, amatum*—and even my boomer English teacher is laughing along with everyone else here. I'd be laughing, too, if I wasn't so hungry. This is my last class before lunch.

Fourteen minutes.

I just have to get through fourteen more minutes, and then I can eat. Who knew being this bored out of your goddamn mind would give you such a raging appetite?

For the next fourteen minutes, I focus on playing solitaire on my phone instead of on my gurgling gut, and I only lose every time, so my pristine record still stands.

Finally, the fifth-period bell buzzes overhead, but I've

officially ventured into hangry territory now, and I practically run to the cafeteria. As fast as I can, anyway, with so many bodies crowding the halls. It's the last day of school—more people should be skipping out early. But I have to weave my way around people and accidentally bump into some girl with a "teacher's aide" badge hanging from a lanyard.

"Hey!" she squeals and grabs me by the elbow. "No running in the halls!"

"I wasn't running." My voice comes out breathy, which is *not* helping. I read the name on her badge. "Tiffany…hi. Can you please let go of me?"

She doesn't. This has to be in violation of at least seven different student codes of conduct. She's a walking hypocrisy.

"Promise you won't run again," she says. "You're a danger to yourself and others."

"This is the last day of school—" I start, but she cuts me off.

"The rules still apply!"

For fuck's sake. I'm getting lightheaded now. I'm a senior. I should be able to stand up to this freshman goody-goody with something to prove. But all I get out is a weak, "I promise I won't run again."

She gives me a smug little smile and removes her iron grip from my arm.

And I immediately take off in a jog. Technically not running! Tiffany's shrieks from behind me apparently disagree. I grin.

I really don't want anyone to get hurt, but if I don't get something to eat soon, I will either pass out or eviscerate someone. Or, more likely, pass out while I'm eviscerating someone. And if I don't get to the cafeteria before the rush, the line for the vending machines will have a wait time that could result in me going Godzilla on the entire population of our fifth-period lunch. Just before I die.

Thankfully, when I get to the cafeteria, my favorite vending machine has no line yet. I jog over to it and punch in the same thing I get every day—half a turkey sandwich, a tiny carton of chocolate milk, and a bag of Doritos, Cool Ranch flavor.

Within half a minute, I've got my sandwich. I've got my chocolate milk. I've almost got my Doritos, but when I search my pocket for another dime, I come up empty.

No...what? I'm short by *ten* cents?

There's a line behind me now as I frantically try to hold my sandwich and milk in one hand while digging through pockets with the other. All of them are empty.

Besides feeding myself—which is pretty damn vital—I also need to *not* press the change return in front of all these people and make it abundantly clear that I can't even afford my whole skimpy lunch.

"Move!" some guy shouts from far behind me. "Quit holding up the line, bitch."

I pound on the vending machine and then kick it, hoping it might rattle something out of place enough to drop.

"Is it stuck?" the girl directly behind me says. She sounds like she wants to help, like she feels sorry for me, and that's just the worst thing for me to hear right now.

I turn to face her. Swear to god, she could pass for twelve. And yet, according to my brain, speaking to her—a total stranger—is scarier than going hungry. I swallow hard and awkwardly force out the words. "Hi. Uh. You got a dime I could borrow?"

"I..." She looks up at me, an apology written all over her face. "All I have is a card."

The twelve-year-old has a credit card. I try not to let my frustration show. It isn't her fault her parents are probably filthy rich and she lives in a—mostly—filthy rich town. It isn't her fault that I'm part of the zero-point-five percent of students at Trinity High who use cash at lunch. She was only trying to help.

I turn back around with a "thanks anyway."

"What's the problem, Jess?" a new voice says. A voice that's warm and deep and makes me want to—

"Fuck off, Benjamin," I say without looking at him.

"It's Ben."

"It's 'I don't fucking care.' *Benjamin*."

He tsks, and in my side vision I catch him shaking his head. "Such language," he says. "You're gonna eat your lunch with that mouth?"

My heart does a thump-*thump* so hard I feel it in my throat. I still can't look at him—especially now, when he's using that fake-scolding tone that's somehow both annoying and *sexy as hell*.

I thrust my middle finger up in the general direction of his voice.

There's a moment of silence around me, just a quick beat, before the whispers start. Things like "wait for it," and "what's it gonna be this time," and "ten bucks says she kicks him in the nuts."

I'll take that bet. I need the money—getting to kick him in the nuts is just a bonus.

"Half a turkey sandwich," Ben mutters, "elementary school chocolate milk… What's missing here?"

I cast a sideways glance at him. He's got his hand to his chin, eyes squinted, like he's thinking. Asshole.

Then he snaps his fingers. "I got it. Doritos. Cool Ranch, right?" He wedges himself between the machine and me, and not a single person behind us is complaining now. Of course not. He's Benjamin Oliver. The mayor's son. Star quarterback.

King of Trinity High.

This whole Pittsburgh suburb's pride and joy.

Ben pushes the coin return, then scoops up all my change. Is there a hidden portal somewhere that I can crawl into? This is even more embarrassing than if I'd done it myself.

His warm fingers graze my palm as he hands me the money, and my breath hitches. Then he swipes his card and punches a few buttons. A blue bag of Doritos drops, and I purposely keep my eyes trained on the vending machine, rather than his *ass* in those *jeans* as he bends over to get the chips. The scowl on my face doesn't move, either, even though my heart is racing now.

What's worse than ogling the person you hate most? Letting anyone know you enjoy the view—especially him.

Ben pops back up, rising to his full height, which puts him several inches above me, looking down. With that annoying, sexy smirk. "Special delivery for Jessica Webster," he says, locking his rich brown gaze on mine. "Is there a Jessica Webster here?"

I refuse to look away, and remind myself people are watching. Remind myself he just bought me food out of pity. "Maybe I don't want your charity. Maybe I'd rather starve."

Someone calls me a bitch again, a girl this time. She probably has a crush on Ben—so many of them do. I've never denied the boy is hot, but the difference between me and the other girls is that all they want is the privilege of being called his girlfriend. I'd rather snort Pop Rocks than be his girlfriend. I can barely get through lunch every day without murdering him.

Something flickers across his face, and the "cocky jerk" expression falters. He leans closer to me and whispers, "Just take the chips and go eat. You look pallid."

What eighteen-year-old boy uses the word "pallid" in

everyday conversation? And why does he get to be jock-hot *and* nerd-hot? People should only be allowed one hot.

"Gee, thanks," I say, snatching the Doritos from him. "You sure know how to charm a girl." I turn on my heels and make a bee line for the table where my best friend, Rayna, and her boyfriend, Jeremy, are sitting with the rest of our...clique.

I hate that word, but it is what it is.

I can't help that my best friend is captain of Trinity High's champion gymnastics team, and ever since she joined the varsity cheer squad junior year, she's created a gravitational pull around her that sent certain people into her orbit. Jocks—that's how she and Jeremy got together. Cheerleaders—like our mutual friend, Kamy, along with her boyfriend, Todd, who is also—*shocker*—on the football team. They're all people who stand above the masses.

Then there's me, the anomaly. I'm not into sports. I'm not in any clubs or school politics. I don't even write for the paper or play in the band. The only thing attaching me to the most popular of the popular crowd is the fact that Rayna and me are a package deal.

And that's how Benjamin Oliver came into my life. Because Ben and Rayna's boyfriend, Jeremy, are also best friends, a package deal.

As soon as I sit, I shake up the milk and down the whole thing in one go, then tear open the bag of Doritos.

"Hey," Rayna says, "you okay?"

"She's fine," Ben says as he sits across from me with his own bag of Doritos—red bag, cheese flavor. Plus, a couple of *whole* sandwiches, a super XL protein bar, a six-pack of mini chocolate donuts, a banana, and a giant bottle of purple Gatorade. He's going to eat all of that in the next ten minutes and still have the flattest abs this side of Hollywood.

Athletes. They're the real anomalies here.

He cracks the lid off his Gatorade and guzzles, and for a few seconds I'm hypnotized by the rhythm of his throat bobbing up and down as he swallows.

It really isn't fair. His reputation as a sex god is one thousand percent valid. He can't even drink Gatorade without sending out pheromones.

"She doesn't look fine," Rayna says, then turns to me, her voluminous, fresh-from-the-salon-red hair swishing as she moves. "You don't look fine."

Ben lowers the Gatorade bottle from his mouth to the table and says to Rayna, "You're just not used to seeing her without her big pointy witch hat. Without it, the green tint to her skin is more noticeable."

"Try to burn me at the stake, scarecrow, and see if you survive it," I snipe.

He raises a brow. "Are you asking me to tie you up?"

"Are you asking me to castrate you with a rusty fork?"

"Guys, come on," Rayna says, even though the others sitting with us are laughing, including her boyfriend. "We're trying to eat here." She sends Ben and me a *behave yourself* look, then kicks Jeremy under the table and hisses, "Stop encouraging them."

Ben blows me a kiss, and I roll my eyes. I go back to eating my lunch, and for about seven seconds, we all sit in blissful silence, with only the sounds of chewing and slurping and a hundred other people making noise around us.

But then Jeremy and Todd start talking to Ben about a baseball game that went into extra innings last night and how the Bucs could make the playoffs this year, their voices so loud and enthusiastic and *male* that any other conversation at this table has become impossible.

It doesn't prevent me from feeling my phone vibrate in my back pocket, though. I pull it out and wake up the screen.

It's a text from my older brother.

Chris: *hey bad news*

My stomach sinks. The milk-and-Doritos combination in there goes sour.

Chris: *going to miss your graduation*

Me: *Are you serious?*

Chris: *won't be home for another month*

Dammit. Chris is my only brother, my only sibling, and I hardly ever see him anymore. Now I just lost a whole month of summer break with him? And he's going to miss one of the biggest days of my life? He'd better be stranded on a deserted island somewhere…that still somehow has cell service…

Me: *Why??*

Chris: *got accepted into the volunteer program*

Chris: *leaving for Cambodia soon*

I sit up straighter, my fingers flying over the screen.

Me: *OH MY GOD*

Me: *WHAT!!!!!!*

Me: *AAAHHHH CONGRATS!*

Chris: *thank you*

Chris: *there's more*

Me: *More bad news that's actually good?*

Chris: *that depends*

Chris: *remember my friend Andrew from Brazil*

Do I remember Andrew? Come on. I haven't stopped thinking about him since we met last summer, after Chris's second year at Florida International University. Florida is a long way from Pennsylvania, and me and my parents all went down there to surprise Chris, who also had a surprise for us — his hot new roommate. I hated the trip, but the destination made it all worth it.

Me: *Yeah I remember Andrew*

Chris: *he got into the program too so we're going out*

there together then he's coming back home with me until next semester starts

Chris: *he needed a place to stay so he's staying at our house*

Chris: *hope that's okay*

"Oh my god!"

I don't realize that was me who just squealed like a twelve-year-old at a Taylor Swift concert until I notice everyone at our table looking at me.

"What is it, what is it!" Rayna is so excited she's wiggling in her seat. "Who texted you?"

"Chris," I say, still staring at my phone. He's typing another message. There's more?

"Your brother Chris?" Rayna says, her enthusiasm dying fast.

"Yeah, but that's not—"

His next text comes through.

Chris: *did I lose you*

Me: *Still here. Sorry. Yes that's okay. I'm so happy for both of you!*

Chris: *yay!*

Chris: *gotta go now so much to do before we leave*

Chris: *see you in a month!*

"Hey." Rayna shakes my shoulder. "Tell me what's going on right now. I haven't seen you smile this much since…never. I have never seen you smile this much. Spill it."

"Andrew," I say. My hands are shaking. "Chris is bringing Andrew back with him this summer. To stay at our house. I can't—" I swallow, my mouth suddenly dry. *"Oh my god."*

It takes Rayna a minute to remember why this is a big deal. "*The* Andrew? As in, your brother's hot friend from Brazil? With the sexy accent? And the sexy bod? And the"— she gestures around her head—"sexy hair?"

"Yes, yes, and yes." Hair is not usually a thing for me, but Andrew's hair? It's perfect, long spirals springing from his head, messy but not messy, with streaks of natural blond through the darker shades of brown. I swear, he could be a model. He probably *is* a model.

But how would I know? He's never really talked to me — actually, reverse that. I've never really talked to him. I can't. I've had opportunities, and just like with anyone I don't know, I get all tongue-tied and fumble so badly I need a translator. The last time Andrew saw me, I was blushing so hard, he asked if I had a sunburn and recommended his favorite aloe vera gel.

But now…now, I'll have half a summer with him *in my house*. It's a chance to get to know him better, be more comfortable around him, have a real conversation, and maybe then he won't see me as just his best friend's shy little sister anymore.

"Rayna," I say, trying to tone down the desperation in my voice, "what do I do? He'll be right there in my house — what if he still doesn't notice me? How do I get him to notice me?"

She shrugs. "Just be you."

Across the table, Ben starts laughing. "Bad idea. Very bad idea."

Well, shit. I thought he wasn't paying attention. "Something funny, Benjamin?"

"Just imagining how this will go down — you, in all your frumpy glory, trying to seduce a 'sexy' dude in college."

If he's trying to rile me up, it's a weak attempt. I've told him seventeen hundred and twelve times that I take "frumpy" as a compliment, no matter how much he thinks it's an insult.

"He's what?" Ben asks. "Twenty-one? Twenty-two?"

"Twenty," I say. "So what? I'm eighteen. We're both adults."

"Jess, you just turned eighteen last month." He gives me a look.

I shoot that same look right back at him. "The age of consent is sixteen in Pennsylvania, so stuff it, Benjamin."

"Okay." He smirks. "Exactly where would you like me to—"

"Shut *up*."

Of course, he just keeps talking.

"You're right, though. Age isn't what really matters here. You have worse things to worry about, like the fact that you're more innocent than a Teletubby."

My face heats. "That has nothing to do with—"

"That has *everything* to do with it," he says. "You want this Andrew guy to notice you, you have to give him something to notice."

"What does that even mean?" I snap back.

He hesitates. But only for a second. "It means it's obvious you're a virgin just by looking at you."

I roll my eyes. "No it isn't—"

"What's wrong with being a virgin?" Rayna jumps in.

Sigh. I love her for trying. But everyone here knows she and Jeremy have been boinking since last Christmas. She can scream "V is for Victory" all she wants and no one will take it seriously.

"Nothing," I answer Rayna's question, keeping my eyes on Ben. "I'm not trying to hide it, either. Sex isn't everything in a relationship—unless it's a relationship with you."

He doesn't even flinch.

"I never said virginity is wrong or something to be ashamed of," Ben clarifies, as if he's an expert on the subject. *Pfft*. "But you're talking about a twenty-year-old male surrounded by horny college girls every day. Why would he leave the fun and excitement of the high dive to go sit in the kiddie pool?"

I want to tell him to shut up again. To stop being an

asshole. To stop…making sense.

"Fuck you, Benjamin."

His grin spreads wide. He knows I know he's right.

Seriously, though. Fuck him. No one asked for his opinion.

"I also never said this was hopeless, Jess. He'll be here in a month? That's plenty of time."

"For what?" I ask, realizing too late that I took his bait. Hook, line, and sinker.

"Sex is like any other skill," he says. "You get better with practice. All you need to do is practice with someone willing to teach you, then show Andrew what you can do."

Rayna's jaw drops. Even Jeremy gives Ben a look like *what the hell are you on.*

But I think that's exactly what Ben wants—a reaction.

"You're just teasing me," I tell him. Like he's been doing since the day we met.

He spreads his arms out, palms up. "Maybe I am, maybe I'm not."

That's all I can take of him. Of this. He's making a joke out of my feelings for someone perfectly decent, someone Ben could never measure up to except maybe in looks. Nothing about this is serious—nothing about him is *ever* serious. And I may have trouble talking to Andrew or anyone else I don't know, but I've been sitting with Ben at lunch for the last nine months. I know him well enough—I know him *too* well. I have no hesitance when it comes to calling him out on his own bullshit.

"Let me get this straight," I say. "You want me to ask someone to have sex with me—not just once, but so many times it would be considered *practice*—and then say 'thanks, that was fun, bye,' and this will somehow magically make Andrew want me?"

"Yes."

"Okay." I practically snort. "What kind of sex-crazed Neanderthal would be willing to do all that? Wait, let me guess—you?"

His face goes hard for a second, and he swallows, but just when I think I've caught him, that cocky smirk reappears. He leans forward on his elbows, folding his hands together. Interlocking those long, nimble, *skillful* fingers. "Only if you admit that I'm the best choice."

Whatever retort I might have said gets stuck in my throat.

He *would* be the best choice, if he was actually offering. And if I was considering such a thing. But I'm not. Hell no freaking way. Also? We both know he isn't actually offering.

This isn't about the offer at all, really. This is about the same thing it's been about with me and Ben since the very first day we sat at this table. We go back and forth until one of us "wins" and one of us "loses."

I'm not going to let him win. Every day for nine months, I've had to sit across from him and his stupid-hot face. It's the last day of school in our last year of high school, the last time I'll ever have one of these nonsense arguments with him at lunch. As if I would let him get the last word now.

He's still got those gorgeous brown eyes on mine, his perfect, pillowy lips set in a bring-it-on smirk. I refuse to get distracted by what he is on the outside. I have to remind myself of who he is on the inside—an asshole through and through. A player. Both on and off the football field. This is all just a game to him.

"Benjamin," I say.

"It's Ben—"

"How can I admit you're the best at anything, when all you've ever shown me is your worst?"

He laughs, but it sounds cold. "That sounds like you want me to show you my best."

Come on.

Is he high?

I mean…seriously. Is he?

It wouldn't be the first time he had "special" snacks in his lunch. In fact, those mini chocolate donuts look highly suspect.

"The answer is no," I say.

"The answer to what?" he counters. "I didn't ask you anything, Jessie."

True. He didn't, just heavily implied it. All he really did was tell me about a dumb fucking idea that he knew I would disagree with. No matter how badly I want Andrew to notice me.

"Ask me, then," I say in challenge.

The bell rings through the speakers above us, loud and obnoxious, followed by the sea of sound created by a hundred students making a mass exodus from the cafeteria. Ben stands up, then leans over the table toward me, his face closer to mine than it's ever been. I can see every shade of brown sparkling in his eyes, every little curve in his pillowy lips, the tautness of his smooth light-brown skin over sharp cheekbones…

Suddenly there isn't enough air. I'm having a hard time finding my next breath.

"I would never disrespect a girl by asking her to do that," he says. "But if she was the one doing the asking?"

Then he just turns and walks off, leaving me staring after him.

Chapter Two

"*I*s it a crush if all you want is to have sex with someone?" I ask Rayna, sitting on her very large bed in her very large bedroom, then scoop up another very large spoonful of salted caramel ice cream.

Her head pops out from her walk-in closet all the way across the room. "What?"

I debate repeating myself. It was just a passing thought, because I haven't been able to get Benjamin Oliver's ridiculous suggestion out of my head since lunch. "Never mind," I mutter.

She rushes out of the closet, holding a scrap of pink fabric she thinks passes for a bikini. "Try this one on, Jessie. You would look so cute in it!"

"What's the point of looking cute if you're hiding in a dark corner, counting the seconds until you can get the hell out of there with no one seeing?"

She rolls her eyes with a smile. "Fine. That one is too skimpy for your taste. But at least let me find you something that has color. This is a party, not a funeral."

With our last day of school officially done, along with our last year of high school, I only have two more things to get through with these bozos I've been bumping elbows with in the halls for the last four years. The first one—Rayna is throwing an end-of-the-year pool party tonight. The second one, of course, is our graduation ceremony in a few days. But now, as I sit in my bestie's bedroom, devouring my second bowl of ice cream while she rummages through her walk-in closet that is roughly the size of my entire bedroom at home, she's trying everything she can think of to get me to change my usual tack tonight.

My usual tack being a very simple, solid black tankini with boy shorts. No frills. No nonsense. Which has never bothered Rayna before...so what's her deal today?

It's our last big school party, and she's hosting. I get it. This is important to her.

But still. What does that have to do with me "looking cute"?

I scoop up my last, melty bite of ice cream, then set the empty bowl on her nightstand and walk over to her closet.

"Why do you suddenly hate my choice of swimwear?"

"I don't *hate* it," she insists, flicking through a rack of floral-patterned cover-ups one by one. "I just think you should try something different tonight. You know, show a little skin, get a little attention. Just admit you have a nice body, Jessie, and show it off for once. Be bold."

I'll ignore the "nice body" comment coming from someone as athletic and toned and somehow still curvy for miles as Rayna—it's an argument we've had seven thousand times; I might be passably pretty, but she is drop-dead gorgeous and therefore gets no vote on this—but only because something else she just said is even more ridiculous.

"Show it off to who?" I ask.

"To whoever sees it." She shrugs, eyes still on the gauzy, floral tornado before her. "It doesn't matter who it is. All that matters is that you look good and you know you look good. Confidence is just as much an accessory as hair clips or jewelry. And that makes you look good to everyone else."

Confidence is an accessory. Okay. Sure. Tell me where I can try some on and buy it.

I lean against the doorframe, slide all the way down until my butt hits the floor, and blow out a sigh. "Why do I have to 'look good' for other people? I like how I look and feel in my boring black tankini. Isn't that good enough?"

I've never been one for fashion, like Rayna. Clothing is more about efficiency than style for me—partially because that's just the way I am, and partially out of necessity. My family has never had money to blow on clothes, or anything else, beyond the basics. My brother going to school all the way out in Florida is a perfect example—they gave him a full-ride scholarship.

"It *is* good enough," Rayna says, sitting on the floor now, too, so she can go through the bottom rack. "Most of the time," she adds. "I mean, look at it this way—if Andrew was going to be here tonight, wouldn't you want to show a little more skin? Get his attention?"

My heartbeat kicks up just at the thought. Me. Andrew. *Skin.*

I shake my head back into reality.

"But he's *not* going to be here. He's on the other side of the world right now."

"That is so not the point!" Rayna shrieks. "And you know it!"

"Geez, Ray, I'm sitting right here. You don't need to use your cheerleader voice." I hold out both of my pale, lanky arms. "Who would want to see more of this pasty skin anyway? Look, I can see all my veins. It's disgusting."

"Nothing about you is disgusting," she argues. "Stop being dramatic."

If I had Rayna's olive-toned skin or Jeremy's dark-brown skin or Kamy's soft-white skin with warm undertones, rather than this literal white porcelain doll shit, maybe I wouldn't be so determined to hide it. None of them has their arm veins on display like I do.

"Listen," she says, undeterred, "all I'm saying is I think you should put a little more effort into it tonight. Let people see on the outside how beautiful you are on the inside."

"Thanks, Hallmark."

She rolls her eyes again.

"Why is tonight so vital for me, anyway? This is *your* party, not mine."

And suddenly, she's too quiet. Which is never good.

"Are you setting me up with someone? Because *no*."

"I'm not setting you up with anyone. We really don't need a repeat of that disaster." She gives up on whatever she was searching for and sits back, shoots me a serious look. "I know Ben was just trying to get a rise out of you today at lunch, but he did have a point."

"Why. Why did you have to bring up Benjamin Oliver and his ridiculous sex plan. I just had ice cream, and I'd like it to stay inside my stomach, but now that's feeling pretty iffy."

She ignores all that. "Maybe you *should* hook up with someone—not Ben, because obviously—just have a fling to get in some practice before Andrew is living in your house. Maybe you could meet that someone tonight."

I laugh, but it's not even funny. "I can barely talk to a boy I've just met, let alone get naked with him and do naked-person things. You know this. You know I can't control whatever malfunction my brain has when I don't know someone well enough to have natural conversation. My tongue literally feels like it gets tied up in knots. When you have knot tongue, words don't come too easily. Not if you want them to make sense. The only reason me and you got along so well at first was because *you* did all the talking, remember?"

Rayna just stares back at me, her big blue eyes full of… something. Concern? Pity?

"Don't look at me like that."

"Like what?"

"Like you feel sorry for me."

"I don't feel sorry for you at all. I was just thinking… maybe you don't have to do any talking. Your body can do the talking for you."

"For fuck's sake, Rayna." I shake my head, and this time my laugh is real. Because I know her just as well as she knows me. "You're not going to give up on this until I give in."

She smiles big. "Please? Let me have some fun doing you up—clothes, makeup, the works. Just this once? It's our last high school party!"

I drop my face into my hands and groan. "All right. Just this once." I pop my head back up. "But don't expect me to go falling at anyone's feet tonight. If something happens, it happens. I'm not going looking for it, and neither are you. Okay?"

"Yes, yes, okay!" she squeals, clapping her hands together, then springs up to a standing position the way only a flexible little sprite like her can. "Stay right where you are. I'll handle everything. This is gonna be life-changing, just wait, you'll see! You won't even recognize yourself."

"Yeah," I say, though I don't think she can hear me over the flurry of clothing and accessories and makeup bags she's pulling down from racks and shelves. "That's what I'm afraid of."

Chapter Three

This is a mistake.

It's a huge, colossal mistake, but I promised Rayna, and I can't stay in the house all night, locked up in her bedroom like a socially allergic hamster. One of the myths about being shy is people think you don't like being around people — that's not true at all. I like people. I like being in a group. I even like going to parties. I just can't control my tongue, or my lungs, or my heart, or my hands when trying to talk to someone new one-on-one. My whole body revolts against it.

I sneak a peek through the slats of the blinds on Rayna's bedroom window and take in the chaos of the backyard. The party's been going for an hour already. People are everywhere. *Skin* is everywhere. The pool is so crowded, it's probably becoming a cesspool of disease.

Okay, *not* going swimming. And if I don't go swimming, then I don't have to take off this coverup. This…very sheer coverup that hides next to nothing anyway.

I blow out a long sigh. I'm probably overreacting. My long blond hair is fully down, for once, rather than pulled up into a bun, and it's been fluffed into waves. Rayna insisted my dull gray eyes seem brighter now, with just a little liner, mascara, and highlights. And since the blue of this bikini is bold but not dark, my skin doesn't seem quite so translucent.

I still look like me, just not a me I've ever seen before. A me that no one has seen before.

Rayna's plan was to give me more confidence, but now I'm less confident than ever. Drawing attention to myself just makes me *more* self-conscious.

Stop.

Over.

Thinking.

It.

Okay. Here I go. Just breathe.

I tug the coverup tighter around me as I head downstairs and then onto the back deck that overlooks the yard. People nearby snap their heads toward me, like I'm under a spotlight, and I rush down the steps and across the grass. *Don't look at me, don't look at me, don't look at me—*

"Cannonball!" a deep voice *booms*. That has to be Todd. One glance at the diving board proves I'm right. No one else is that big and broad and completely without dignity.

He jumps off the board, and the magnificent splash that follows reaches all the way to the people lounging poolside. Several screeches ring out.

I haven't seen Ben yet, but he's got to be here. He's always the guest of honor at any party. It could be someone else's birthday and people would go there to see *him*. And god, I want to see him, but I don't want to see him. I hate that he's got this kind of control over me.

"Jessie!" Rayna yells from inside the pool, her arms resting on the tiled edge. Her normally voluminous red hair is wet and slicked back straight against her scalp, making her big, round eyes seem even bigger and rounder on her face.

I step closer to her, keeping one eye on Todd, in case he decides to do another dive bomb, then squat in front of her.

"You need to get in here," she says. "This water is soooo nice. Feels like a bath."

Yeah, a communal bath. Not happening. "Have you seen Ben?"

"He was here a minute ago…" She looks around. "Maybe he had to pee?"

Okay, good. *Just stay away from him.* I straighten to stand.

"Hey, wait a minute," Rayna says. "Why do you need Ben?"

"I didn't say I need him."

"You're looking for him." Her lips spread in a devious grin. "So if you don't need him, then you must want him."

"Get that mischievous-monkey look off your face. I just wanted to know where he is so I know where not to go."

"Right. Sure, Jess. Okay." She laughs so hard she snorts. "Keep telling yourself that."

Why is she suddenly teasing me about the one person she knows I hate with the rage of a thousand suns… "Are you drunk?"

"Since when don't I drink at parties?" she says instead of answering.

Yeah, I know she drinks, but she's smart about it. Usually. "Get out of the pool, Ray. Come on, that's not safe."

"Why don't you make me," she says, then pushes off the wall and knocks right into Todd. Thankfully, Todd has pretty good reflexes and catches her on the fly, keeps her from going under. She laughs again, and Todd shouts to Jeremy, who is across the pool, "Jameson! I got something for you!" He lifts Rayna above his head, and she squeals.

"Todd," I warn, and he just glances at me with that shit-eating grin on his face. Jeremy has made his way over now, but he stays a good five or six feet away, holding his long arms out like he's ready to catch her. He plays wide receiver, so he knows how to catch. But there is no such professional sport called Toss My Drunk Best Friend Around for a reason.

This is all very typical of these jocks, and so far, no one has been maimed. Still, it makes me nervous. The pool is crowded. If he throws her, she could land on someone and they could *both* get hurt.

"Come on, guys, knock it off," I say, raising my voice. "She's not a football."

"Says you!" the red-haired football shouts. "I can be whatever I want, I don't need your permission."

"Not helping, Ray."

"Get in here and play with us, you grump!" Rayna yells, and several people turn to see who she's talking about, their eyes all landing on me at once. "Show us that hot bod!"

"Take it off!" some guy yells. No clue who that is. Then he starts a chant—"Strip, strip, strip, strip!"—and the other guys around him, also strangers to me, quickly join in. Do these people even go to our school?

"Come on in, Jessie," Todd says. "You just gonna stand by the pool all night?"

I blow out a breath. "If I take off this coverup, will you put her down?"

"Of course." He grins.

Part of me was hoping he'd say no. But dutifully, I slide the sheer coverup off my shoulders and down my arms, then toss it over a lounge chair. It's near eighty degrees out here, but goose bumps pop up all over me and I can't help shuddering. I cross my arms over my chest, so at least my nipples won't be visible, even if the rest of me is...completely exposed.

Several wolf whistles pierce the air. They all feel sarcastic, like I'm a joke.

"One..." Todd says. "Two..."

"Todd, don't!" I shout, dropping my arms and rushing toward the pool. "You said you would—"

"Three!" Rayna says for him, and then she's flying through the air.

"Oh fuck," Jeremy says, his eyes widening as he backs up. He gets into the correct position at the last second and catches her with ease. She's squealing and laughing and then sloppily making out with Jeremy right there in the middle of the pool.

The breath of relief that whooshes out of me is so strong, I double over, leaning into my thighs until my heartbeat starts to drop back to a normal rate.

"Well, hello there," someone says behind me.

No, not someone. *Ben.* I'd know that annoying, sexy voice anywhere.

The goose bumps are back.

I straighten quickly, turning to face him, and his gaze pops up to meet my eyes.

"Jessie?"

"Were you just staring at my ass?"

"Yes," he admits without an ounce of shame, "but I didn't know it was *your* ass." Then his face changes from slightly shocked, slightly awed, and slightly intrigued to something outright devious. He looks me up and down, a slow grin spreading his lips wide until he's showing teeth. "So that's what you've been hiding under all those frumpy clothes."

You know what? It's bad enough he was making fun of me before, just because I've never had sex with anyone and he's had sex with practically everyone. Now he's standing there in all his golden-boy glory, his black hair wet and curling, water dripping down his chest and over those rock-hard abs, and his soaked swim trunks clinging to *everything.* And he's rubbing it in my face that he's been blessed by the divine, and I'm...me.

"If that's your way of charming me into your pants, Benjamin, I'm not that desperate."

He raises his hands in surrender, which is highly suspicious—Ben *never* gives in—and he's still smiling. It's all a joke. Everything is a joke to him.

I turn away, but where am I going? Am I really considering going into that cesspool just to get away from Ben?

Yes. Yes, I am.

I step down onto the built-in stairs on the shallow end and slowly sink into the warm water. Rayna was right, it does feel like a bath. With fifty other people.

And who knows what all their hands and other body parts are doing below the surface.

If only this were a swimming pool full of sanitizer. I'd gladly bathe in that now, even dunk my head under.

"You're here!" Rayna shouts, pulling me in for a wet hug. "You're my favorite."

There's beer on her breath and she's squeezing too hard. I gently push her off me. "So, what are we playing?"

"Chicken," Ben says as he comes up beside me. "Jess, you're with me."

Internally, I groan. Externally, I flip him off. "Don't you have some new vagina to investigate?"

"Always," he says. Then he takes both my hands, lifts them, and turns, so I'm standing behind him with my arms over his shoulders. "But right now, we need to beat these losers."

"I heard that!" Rayna shouts.

She's already up on Jeremy's shoulders, and Todd is lifting Kamy up and over his head. She's petite anyway, but next to him, she looks like an infant. And I know they have sex, but what I don't know is how he doesn't break her while they're doing it.

Aaron Fowler and his boyfriend decide to join, too, so we have even teams, and they're all looking at me and Ben now. Waiting.

Ben's still holding my hands, but I don't pull away. I'm so close to him I can smell his skin. I don't even know what to call this scent, it's just...*him*. Mixed with chlorine.

"Put your hands on my shoulders," he says, "and push up while I grab your legs."

What—

His hands move behind him and find my thighs, then slide to the backs of my knees to pull them up. The feel of his fingers slipping along my bare skin... I don't hate it.

"Push yourself up," Ben says. "You gotta help me out here, Jess."

Right. Because I'm not tiny like Kamy, and I'm not a gymnast like Rayna, who can climb Jeremy like a tree.

Awkwardly—and who knows why I'm even doing this—I push down onto his shoulders while at the same time jumping up onto his back. Graceful as a hippo doing ballet. "Now what?"

Ben doesn't answer. Well, he doesn't answer with words. His hands slide back up my thighs until they're just below my ass and he's pushing me up farther. If his fingers slip even one centimeter, they'll be inside my bikini bottom.

My brain can't keep up with this. I feel like I should either punch him in the throat or cradle my whole body around him and never let go. Or maybe one, then the other.

Ben says, "Get your legs up there."

"I'm not that flexible, Benjamin. What if I pull a muscle and fall and drown?"

"Don't worry, Jessie, I know mouth-to-mouth resuscitation."

I glare at his back. "And I know foot-to-mouth retaliation

if you even try it."

After a few failed attempts, I manage to climb high enough that I'm sitting on top of his shoulders. His arms are wrapped snug around my legs so I don't fall, but still, I feel like I could go at any moment, and the first step he takes has me grabbing his hair to keep myself in place. He doesn't even flinch, so I keep holding on until he stops us about three feet in front of Rayna and Jeremy, face-to-face. I shift around to find my balance again…and realize that I'm holding his hair while pretty much grinding myself on his head between my legs.

Oh, sweet Jesus—

There's nothing but a scrap of blue fabric between one of my most sensitive parts and the base of his skull, and it's doing nothing to keep me from feeling all the friction. My face bursts into flames, and the hot flush creeps down my neck. Down my back. Over my whole body. I'm on fire. Everyone is watching us, of course, because everyone is always watching Ben. And now everyone knows what I was just thinking.

Some girl says, "Lucky bitch."

Lucky, right. Because this is exactly how that online quiz I took predicted I would die.

"You good up there?" Ben says.

"Yeah." My voice comes out a little shaky. "All good."

"You have to let go of me to play. I won't let you fall, trust me."

"*Trust* you? There are a lot of things I'd like to do to you, Benjamin, and less than zero of them involve trust."

"Oh really?" He turns his head around just enough that I catch the twinkle in his eye. "What kind of things?"

"The slow and painful kind." I give his hair a tug to let him know I'm serious, then let go, and we're suddenly rushing toward Jeremy and Rayna. She grabs at me with absolutely no technique whatsoever. Unless "drunk girl flailing" is an actual technique, because I can barely get a move in. She's wild. And I am zero percent athletic.

"Isn't this fun?!" Rayna squeals.

That's not the F-word I was thinking.

"I get to choose the next game," I say.

"Only if you survive this one!"

Below us, Jeremy and Ben are talking smack and laughing and splashing. Aaron is somehow still standing, with his boyfriend in a hand-lock with Kamy, as Todd creates tidal waves in the pool just from kicking his legs up. Everyone is having fun but me. I keep trying to get a hold of Rayna or even knock her off-balance, and every time Ben moves, I instinctively grab his hair to anchor myself in place. And *every time* I grab his hair…my mind goes into fantasy land.

I lose my focus. I struggle to breathe normally. I'm still hot all over but somehow also covered in goose bumps again. My nipples seem to have forgotten that I hate Benjamin Oliver. It's like they're reaching out for him, the traitorous wenches.

This just proves how inexperienced I am. Rayna and Kamy aren't having the same trouble. They're not virgins. Sitting up on a boy's shoulders like this doesn't faze them, because they've already done way more with those boys with way less clothing. I can't even blame any of this on Ben, either. It's not his fault that I'm innocent, or that being this close to him, skin touching skin, turns my brain to goo.

So who is left to blame for the way my body is reacting to him? Only myself.

Pathetic. I can't even hate someone properly. It isn't normal to want to boink a guy you hate. I drop my arms, let my body go slack.

"What's wrong?" Ben says.

"I'm done playing. Let me down."

"But we're in the middle of battle!" Rayna shouts. "No forfeiting! We fight to the end!"

She thrusts her arms forward, and Jeremy charges toward us. Ben easily moves us out of the way, and—I guess?—he trips Jeremy in the process, because both he and Rayna go down fast.

"And that's the end," Ben says as the two of them splutter and splash. Then he tells me to climb down while he pulls me around to the front of him, forcing my chest and abdomen to slide slowly over *his* chest and abdomen.

I swallow, hard.

God. What is wrong with me?

Once my feet touch the pool floor, Ben releases my hands, and for a breathless moment, we just stand there with our wet bodies pressed together. Then I look up, and with a grin, he leans down closer to whisper, "Feeling desperate now, Jess?"

My jaw drops, and for the second time today, I don't have a witty comeback.

He turns and wades away, leaving people clambering for his attention in his wake. My hands clench into fists. My jaw clenches, too, grinding my teeth together.

That *asshole*. He knew exactly what he was doing to me the whole time.

Chapter Four

The morning of graduation, Chris calls me for a video chat. And Andrew is with him.

Holy. Shit.

I swallow my tongue and make some kind of gurgling, choking noise. He's even hotter now than I remembered. In a cotton T-shirt and khaki shorts, his springy curls pulled back on his head, sweat dripping down his temples—

"Hello, Jessica," he says, and he smiles.

His smile puts me into cardiac arrest. "H… Hi."

Aaaaaaaand that's all I got.

Thankfully, Chris starts talking. More like shouting. "Jessie! You're graduating today! Woohoo! Hurray for not flunking!"

I let out a breathy laugh. My brother has always had this magical ability to cheer me up in even the worst circumstances. He also knows what my shyness does to me, so he steps in with exaggerated gestures and loud exclamations to distract anyone from noticing I'm dying inside.

"I feel really awful that I can't be there in person," he says, "so I asked Mom to FaceTime me when you get your diploma. I want to see it happen in real time."

He goes on for a while then, telling me all about

Cambodia and how the volunteer program works and the amazing doctors he's met and everything he's done in the few days since he got there. Something is different about him. He's just so happy. Happier than I've ever seen him, I think.

Of course he is, he's living his dream.

While he's talking, I keep darting glances at Andrew, who's just sitting there calmly, listening to my brother go on and on. Their friendship seems to work for the same reason my friendship with Rayna works—she does most of the talking, and I don't mind listening. With Andrew and Chris, it's my brother who's the motormouth.

It's just one more thing Andrew and I have in common. We're both the listeners.

That isn't all we have in common, either. When I met Andrew last summer, it wasn't love at first sight. I don't believe in the idea of that anyway. Of course, I was attracted to him physically at first sight, and that drew my initial interest. That, and the fact my brother is good friends with him. Chris may be nice to everyone he meets and give off a happy-go-lucky vibe, but he's careful about who he lets get close to him. He's been used and burned by so-called friends in the past.

My parents and I stayed in Florida for a week to visit with Chris, and during that week, I could count on one hand how many words I said to Andrew. But I paid attention to everything *he* did and said. He isn't shy like I am, he's just not chatty like my brother. When he did join a conversation, I hung on every word, and there was one thing in particular that stuck with me.

He's a conservationist. He hates waste, especially plastics, and he does whatever he can to repurpose things so they don't end up in landfills. Since I hadn't said much more than "hi" and "bye" to him then, he couldn't have known that I do the same thing. Not at the time he said it. But it's possible

Chris told him about my projects later, after we left.

"Are you still working at the library on the weekends?" Chris asks.

"Yeah." I nod. "And in summer, I'll get shifts during the week. I'm working on some new craft ideas for the kids' programs, too."

I have to keep my focus on Chris as I'm talking, and block Andrew out so I can speak. And still, I feel like I'm choking on every word.

"Well, hopefully you won't be working *too* much. I can't wait to see you again. We should be there in time for the Fourth of July fireworks and the summer fair."

Right, so. Either I figure out how to act seductively around Andrew on my own before he gets here, or I have sex with someone for four weeks and hope that gives me the confidence I need to act seductively around Andrew.

God, that sounds so messed up.

No, I have to do this on my own.

"Oh, that's right," I say casually, though I can still hear a tremor in my voice. I clear my throat, try to make myself sound...I don't know, something other than terrified. "Andrew, you're staying with us?"

"Yep."

"H-how's that going to work, Chris?" *Breathe.* "We don't have an extra bed."

"We have a couch," my brother says.

"You're making him sleep on the lumpy couch?" My voice is warbled now, mixed with the blood pounding so hard in my ears. That's all it is, right? I don't actually sound like that?

"It's okay," Andrew says. "After sleeping on stiff cots here in blistering heat for a month, a lumpy couch and air conditioning will feel divine." There's that smile again.

My breath stutters. Audibly. Chris shoots me a look I've

seen too many times. His eyes say, "Are you okay?" Which is a sure sign he knows I'm not. I love my brother, but I'm tired of people pitying me for being shy. The only way to stop it is to *not* be shy. Be bold.

As flirty as I can, I say, "Andrew, you can sleep in *my* bed."

My heart thunders, and I break out in a cold sweat all over—even my elbows are sweating—waiting for someone, anyone, to respond to that.

Andrew's brow wrinkles. He looks at Chris, then quickly back at me. "So...*you* would sleep on the couch?"

No...

What?

Am I really so bad at this that he can't even imagine sharing a bed with me?

"Okay, forget it," Chris says with a laugh. "No one is sleeping on the couch. Doesn't Mom still have that old trundle in the attic?"

I nod on autopilot, a million things besides sleeping arrangements going through my head.

"We can just put that in my room. There. Problem solved."

"Perfect," Andrew says, then looks at someone off camera and nods, his face suddenly serious. "Time to go." He stands. "Christopher. It's urgent."

"See you soon, Jessie James!" My brother waves to me, and then the call ends.

I fall backward onto my bed, staring at the ceiling. What the hell just happened? Andrew didn't even say goodbye to me. I'm practically invisible to him.

It's like my innocence is a mile-high fence around me that he can't see through. If I don't break down this barrier, I'll never have a chance with him.

Dammit.

Ben was right. I *do* need help. I *am* that desperate.

He also said he's the best choice. And he is, but…

Come on, there has to be someone else I can do this with. Well, there is, technically, but it's not anyone I know. And it's the "I don't know them" part that has me seriously considering Ben. I may not like him, but I do know him. He's not a stranger.

He's the only person I have a physical attraction to besides Andrew, and he's the only person I'd have no trouble leaving after it's finished. I have zero emotional attachment to him. He made sure of that on the day we met by showing just how little I mean to him.

Ben said he'd never ask a girl to do what he told me I need to do.

But if she was the one doing the asking…

He didn't have to finish his sentence for me to know what he was implying.

No-strings sex is on-brand for him. But it's not something I'd ever considered doing myself. Could I really ask him to do this? Without him laughing in my face?

I'll see him later today, at graduation.

Okay then, Benjamin Oliver. I push myself up and blow out a sigh. *Let's see if you really mean it.*

Chapter Five

My gown is itchy, and my graduation cap is making me hot. Sweat drips down the back of my neck. "Rayna, do you have a tissue?"

"No," she answers from the bathroom stall. "All I have is a tampon, and you can't borrow it to wipe your sweaty face."

Thankfully, it's just the two of us in here, so no one else heard her. Rayna hates changing tampons around strangers, and since all of the restrooms available at this college auditorium are public, we had to sneak past a barricade in the hallway to find something unoccupied. It's just me, my best friend, and seventeen empty stalls.

"Never mind," I say. "I can use toilet paper. Why is it so hot in this thing?"

The toilet flushes. "Be glad all you have to worry about is perspiration," Rayna says, heading to the sink, and I can tell there's a rant coming. She's got that Debate Team Captain tone in her voice. "Here I am wearing a white gown, about to walk out in front of millions of people, and just praying to Jesus that I don't look like I sat on a packet of ketchup when I do it."

She rinses the soap from her hands and starts the dryer, raising her voice. "You know, it's really archaic that they make boys and girls wear different colored gowns, and the girls have to wear white, like we're what? Virgin sacrifices? And what about nonbinary people? What color were they offered for this? I bet they had to choose either blue or white, boy or girl, which is all kinds of fucked up." She shakes her head. "The whole system is stuck in the twentieth century."

By the time she's done with her closing argument, I've patted myself dry and stepped up next to her in front of a mirror. "You look good, though."

She smiles. "*We* look good."

"We did it, Ray. We survived high school." I smile back at her through the mirror. "Let's go graduate!"

Rayna links her billowy-sleeved arm with mine, and we practically skip down the empty hall like a couple of Kindergarteners until we hit the makeshift barricade. It's just some metal-frame, plastic-seat chairs lined up from wall to wall. Once we're through that and back to the auditorium, we head to the sea of blue and white caps and gowns on the stage, still blocked from the audience—our families—by a heavy-looking purple velvet curtain with twisted gold ropes.

There's bleacher seating set up, and we're all supposed to go to our assigned place, but next to no one remembers where to sit. We had a rehearsal for this a few days ago, but it might as well have been never.

Principal Ruiz and Vice Principal Johnson are up to their eyeballs in confused people slinging questions at them faster than they can answer. It's chaos.

Well, that's what they get for not making it easy for us, like using alphabetical order.

One by one, they call out each name—in alphabetical order—then direct that person to their nonalphabetical seat. My last name starts with W. This is going to take a while, so I move away from the crowd and find a wall to lean against.

Rayna must have gotten caught up in the swarm somewhere. I just stand there, silent, minding my own business—

And that's when Benjamin Oliver walks in. Hard to miss the person everyone starts clambering for as soon as they arrive. Normally, I'd just roll my eyes and ignore it, but now...

The back of my neck is sweating again. So are my pits and palms. I need to talk to him.

With a deep breath, I move back into the crowd, get right up next to him.

"Nice outfit," he says, that characteristic smirk firmly in place. "I expected your gown to be black, though. And your hat to be more triangular than square."

I'm not here to spar with him, even if it is physically painful to hold back a scarecrow retort to his witch jab. It's been a running insult between us since last fall. Instead, I look him dead-on and say, "Were you being serious about your offer? If I'm the one who asks?"

Ben's eyes widen, but only a fraction, before his face goes neutral again. "It's hard to hear with all this noise," he says. "Can we go out to the hall?" He doesn't wait for me to answer, just starts walking to the stage exit. Expecting me to follow him like a lost puppy, no doubt.

And I do.

The exit door is still swinging closed when I reach it and push it back open, and I find Ben a few feet away, wearing a look I've never seen on him before. It's almost like...if a growl had a face, that would be it.

Is he mad? Swear to god, I will never understand this boy.

"I need to know exactly what you're asking me, Jessica," he says, his voice low.

Oh...it's never good when he uses my full name in that tone. But I can't back out of this now without making a complete fool of myself. Or worse, *continue* making a complete fool of myself in front of Andrew every time I see him.

"All right." I glance around quickly to make sure we're alone. "Would you really be okay with having sex with a girl just so she can have a chance with the guy she *really* wants?"

"Are you *really* willing to do this?" he counters.

Answering a question with a question. Fantastic. Apparently the being-clear-with-your-intentions thing only applies to me.

"Of course I am," I say firmly. But it's all just false bravado. As subtly as I can, I wipe my sweaty palms on the sides of my gown. Try to take a deep breath instead of a deep *gulp*. Then I throw the ball back into his court without mercy. "And if you are, too, then convince me. Tell me how serious you are about it, or…" I blow out some of my tension with a sigh. "Or forget the whole thing. I'll never bring it up again. But it's your choice, Benjamin."

"It's Ben—"

"Just answer me," I snap. *"Please."*

"Jess—" he starts, but then the stage door opens behind me and Vice Principal Johnson yells, "Oliver! Benjamin Oliv—oh, there you are. Get in here, both of you!"

Ben casually walks past me and through the door as if he wasn't just about to make or break my entire world. What was he going to say?

"Miss Webster, sometime today, please." Vice Principal Johnson gestures toward the door she's holding open.

"Sorry," I mumble, and scuttle back onto the stage to find Principal Ruiz pointing at my seat, telling me to *sit down and don't move, we can't get you all mixed up again.*

I barely hear him, though. I don't even register who I'm sitting by, all I know is it isn't Ben or Rayna or Jeremy or Kamy or even Todd—and I've never felt so alone in such a huge crowd of people. My mind is whirling in every direction, with one question ringing loud and clear in the center of the vortex.

What was he going to say?

The commencement ceremony goes on for roughly nine thousand years before we finally get to the part where we officially graduate. For all nine thousand of those years, I've been thinking of Ben, wondering what almost came out of his mouth. Something good? Something bad?

Something neither?

What if it was, "Jess, we should probably get back in there now"?

This must be what death feels like. Melting in a polyester gown under hot stage lights, sweaty bodies pressed against you on all sides, waiting to be called up and singled out in front of a thousand people you don't know and will never meet and who will all see your pit stains, while wondering if the guy you just propositioned in the hall will say yes. Wondering why you want him to say yes more than you want your next breath, as long as we're being dramatic here.

God, my brother is going to see this. Chris will never let me live it down if I trip or do something equally embarrassing. Then my stomach does a nauseating *flip-flop* when I realize… Andrew is probably also going to see this. They could be watching it together.

I'm gonna be sick.

Vice Principal Johnson gestures for everyone in my row to stand and move to the side—*don't step out of order!*—where we'll wait until our names are called. Just as we're getting into position, stage left, Principal Ruiz booms through the mic, "Benjamin! Gabriel! Oliver!"

Gabriel?

Huh. That actually suits him.

The auditorium erupts into a standing ovation with thunderous applause. There goes Trinity's golden boy. And even as I'm criticizing it all in my head, my heartbeat kicks up just watching him stride across the stage, oozing charisma and confidence. If I had only an ounce of that, my life would be so different.

God. I really want him to say yes.

Now that he knows I'm willing to go through with this ridiculous plan, if he says *no, I was only messing with you…*

"Jessica Florence Webster," Principal Ruiz says with noticeably less enthusiasm. I was so caught up in my thoughts of Ben, I didn't realize he'd called up fifteen other people since then. My heels clack across the stage—I can hear every step clearly because there isn't much else making noise. There is courtesy applause and the sound of my father cheering too loudly for me. I take my diploma as Principal Ruiz shakes my hand with a perfunctory "congratulations."

"Thanks," I mutter and keep walking. At the other end of the stage, someone calls me Florence and a bunch of other someones snicker behind their hands. Assholes. We can't all have suave middle names like *Gabriel.*

I ignore them and sit back down, staring at my diploma. I made it. I graduated. But now what? I'm not headed to college in the fall, because I couldn't decide on where to go or what career to even pursue. There are so many options, it's overwhelming. I just don't have it all figured out like everyone else does.

The only thing I know for sure right now is that Andrew is going to be living in my house in four weeks, and I want to spend those four weeks learning how to be a sexier, more confident version of myself. Even if that means learning it from Benjamin Gabriel Oliver.

But there's still a chance he'll say no. Which makes no sense at all, because he's the one who suggested it in the first place.

The rest of the ceremony moves fast. Everyone gets a diploma. We're announced as graduates. Then we all move our tassels from one side of the cap to the other and cheer for ourselves. We're not supposed to throw our caps into the air—it's dangerous, we've been told a few trillion times—but there are some idiots who do it anyway, then go scrambling to find where they landed before someone accidentally stomps on them.

Chaos surrounds me almost immediately as giddy people rush around the stage, some of them jumping off the stage to see their families. I try to find Rayna and Kamy, but suddenly someone grabs me by the hand—*Ben?*—and pulls me through the crowd.

Pulls me out the door, into the hallway.

And keeps pulling me down the hall, until we reach an alcove tucked under a stairwell.

"What the *hell* are you doing—"

"Giving you my answer." He sweeps me up in his arms and brings my mouth right up against his. I have a fleeting thought to push him away, but then I remember—this is exactly what I wanted.

Because if this is his answer, then his answer is a big "fuck yes."

Benjamin Oliver…is *kissing* me.

But to call this a kiss doesn't seem right. This is unlike any kiss I've ever had. It's like his lips and tongue are dancing with mine, like it's something they've practiced together over and over again. Every little motion is perfect. How can he know exactly what to do with me?

Well. I guess that's why I need to learn from him, isn't it?

He pulls away, and we both gasp for air. My head is spinning, and I can't really see straight. I'm literally *dizzy* from that kiss.

"Was that convincing enough?" Ben says, then steps back, putting an arm's length of space between us. "Do you still think I might not be serious about this?"

It takes me a second to understand what he means. My mind had totally blanked. I study his face, now that I can see again—he's still the same-old, cocky, smirking Benjamin Oliver who thinks he holds the world in his hands. Because everyone treats him that way, so why wouldn't he believe it?

He's calm, collected. Cool and confident.

Kissing me didn't affect him at all.

While I'm over here ready to collapse from it.

That stings.

But what did I expect? He's a sex god, and I'm a virgin; he's experienced, and I'm a newbie; and he hates me as much as I hate him. Of course he can turn it off as easily as he turned it on. And that's actually what I *need* him to do.

"Haven't you ever heard of asking for consent?" I say, which is ridiculous considering I invited his tongue into my mouth and asked it to stay for dinner. But this is Ben. I don't know how to talk to him if it's not a fight. "Or are you so used to every girl falling ass over ankles for you that you think you're exempt from the rules of common decency?"

"Jessie." He gives me a look. "You asked me to have sex with you. Are you saying now you don't want to?"

"No."

"No you don't want to, or no you're not saying you don't want to?"

I shake my head. Let me try this again. "I still want you

to…for us to… Do you?"

"Yes."

"All right, then. We're doing this." I start nodding and fidgeting, unsure what to do now. I didn't think this far ahead. "I guess I'll…see you tomorrow?"

I go to move past him.

"Jessie, wait," he says. "I'm helping you here. But what am I getting out of this?"

"A month of sex isn't enough for you?"

He smirks. "I'd be getting that anyway, just not with you."

That's a fair point.

But what could I possibly give him that he doesn't already have? The Olivers are the wealthiest family in a city full of wealthy families, and Ben is pretty much a local celebrity. A strand of his hair is probably worth more than my house.

"I'm not paying for sex," I say.

"I'd never ask you to." He raises a brow like he can't believe I even thought it. "I do something for you, and you do something for me — otherwise, you're just using me. I mean… you wouldn't sleep with me for the fun of it, right?"

I hesitate. Would I?

"Right," he says before my mind can turn his rhetorical question into something much more complex than it really is. "I'm only asking for a fair deal, Jess. Put us on equal ground."

I almost laugh out loud. As if I could ever be considered "equal" to him in anything.

"Okay, Benjamin."

"It's Ben—"

"What do you want me to do?"

He grins. "A favor."

I wait for him to explain, but he doesn't. "You'll have to be more specific," I tell him. "What's the favor?"

"I'll let you know as soon as I know," he says.

I'm thoroughly unamused by this. "You want me to agree to do some undetermined favor for you at some undetermined time."

"Exactly."

"You're *exactly* high as a kite."

He shrugs. "That's the deal, Jess. Take it or leave it."

This could be very, very bad. Or it could all be a joke. There's nothing he would ever need that I could give him. *Nothing.* The asshole is just testing me. He must not think I'm actually serious about any of this.

Before I can overthink myself out of it, I thrust my hand toward him, offering to shake. "All right, Benjamin Oliver. You got a deal."

Chapter Six

*T*he only reason I have Ben's number is because we're both on the same group chat with our mutual friends. Before today, I hadn't even added him as a contact yet, so whenever he sent a message in the chat, his number was with it instead of his name. Big mistake. Because now I have his number *memorized*.

I quickly add his name to my contacts and send him a text the morning after graduation, while I'm getting ready for my shift at the library. My lips are still tingling from that kiss, and it's still playing on repeat in my head. I've never felt so equally awkward and eager about something in all my life.

Me: *We need to set some ground rules.*

His reply doesn't come until I've finished eating breakfast.

Ben: *it's six am let's do this later*

Me: *Actually it's eight am and I'll be working later so let's do this now.*

Ben: *...*

Ben: *fine*

Ben: *rule number one is we start tonight*

That's not really a rule, but...

Me: *Okay. My parents have their bowling league on Mondays so they'll be out for a few hours.*

God. I'm going to be useless at work today, thinking about tonight, tonight, tonight...

Me: *Rule number two is no one else can know about this. Not even Rayna and Jeremy.*

Ben: *why*

Me: *Because*

I pause, my fingers hovering over the screen. The truth is, because it's embarrassing. For me. Who else has to go to such lengths to lose their virginity?

Me: *Because no one means no one.*

Ben: *brilliant*

Me: *Rule number three is we start slow and I let you know when we can level up.*

Ben: *fair*

He's being entirely too compliant about all this. Is this really Ben texting me?

Me: *Rule number four is this ends after four weeks no matter what.*

Ben: *but if either of us wants to end it sooner we can*

Ah, there he is. That's the Ben I know.

Me: *Trying to bail already?*

Ben: *rule 4 A*

Me: *That isn't funny.*

Ben: *...*

Ben: *...*

Me: *Whatever you're taking forever to type isn't funny either.*

Ben: *...*

Ben: *at any point if you want me to stop what I'm doing or you want to stop what you're doing all you have to say is stop and we stop immediately no questions asked*

I stare at my phone, my foamy toothbrush hanging from my mouth. I spit. Rinse. Reread his text a few more times. No matter how I look at it, I can't find any sarcasm. He means every word of it. And I didn't know just how much I needed him to say that until I blow out a long breath and feel my shoulders drop. What we're doing here is risky—especially for me. I'm putting myself in a really vulnerable position with a boy I don't even like. Knowing I can stay safe just by saying one little word makes all the difference.

I have to admit, it's a good rule, even if it does feel a little *Fifty Shades*.

Me: *Okay.*

Me: *Anything else?*

Ben: *no*

Ben: *can I go back to sleep now*

Me: *Not yet.*

Me: *There's one more thing we need to agree on first.*

Chapter Seven

*O*ur first time—*my* first time—doing anything is going to be in my own room, on my own bed. On *my* turf. It's the only way I'll be comfortable, and Ben agreed to it, so as soon as my parents have left for their bowling night and I hear the car backing out of the driveway and heading down the street, I text him. Before sending it, though, I check through my bedroom window to watch their taillights until they turn off onto another street.

Me: *All clear.*
Ben: *knock knock*
Me: *?????*
Ben: *I'm here let me in*
He's here?
Oh god.
He's here!

I rush out of my room and nearly tumble headfirst down the stairs, then trip over my own feet on my way to the front door. And open it.

Ben looks me up and down, his big brown eyes burning through every inch of me as he grins. "Why are you so out of breath? Did you get started without me?"

"Shut up and get inside before someone sees you." I swing

the door open wide, and he walks in, shaking his head. "How did you get here so fast?" I say. He lives on the complete opposite side of town. The *nice* side of town.

"I parked down the street and waited until I saw your parents leave, then walked over."

"Oh." That's actually smart of him. No one will see his car in my driveway. Benjamin Oliver has a brain in his skull, who knew? All this time, I thought it was in his pants.

I shut the door, lock the bolt, then turn. "So, um. Yeah, this is my house." And it looks like a mangy mutt hut compared to his shining purebred mansion. "The kitchen is over that way, if you need a drink or something. Bathroom is upstairs if you…need to do bathroom things."

He nods. "I should wash my hands before we start anything."

My gaze instantly goes to his hands. His fingers. And my mind instantly goes to all the things he can do to me with those hands—and will do, at some point. Tonight. That's all part of what we agreed to, I know, it's just suddenly…very *real* now. I thought about it all day and decided to go as far as letting him touch my bare skin tonight. Hands only. Anywhere. By the time he leaves here, he'll have touched me in places I've never let any guy touch me before.

Not only the obvious places, either. Like, what if he gets a face-full of my armpit? I have no idea how that would happen, but *what if it does*?

I thought I was ready for this. But now my heart is beating out of control and it's getting hard to breathe. Is it just from nerves, or is my gut telling me to end this before it starts?

"Okay, then," Ben says, as if all of this is normal, everyday conversation. "I'll go do that and meet you…" His tone rises at the end like a question.

I give myself a mental shake. "My room. It's right across

the hall from the bathroom, and the bathroom is the second door on the left."

"Got it." He kicks his sandals off by the front door, then heads up stairs in his bare feet, like this isn't the first time he's ever been here and he isn't about to teach me all about sex.

How has my life come to this.

I run my hands down my face, then go back up to my room and wait on my bed with the door open. From here, I can see just enough of the hall to know the bathroom door is shut. I can hear water running, and when it stops, I expect Ben to come bounding out, boner at the ready, but nothing happens. The door doesn't open. And I can't hear him doing a damn thing.

I wait and listen some more.

Nothing.

What the hell is he doing in there?

More waiting, and listening, and waiting, and listening, and now I'm getting annoyed. It's been ten minutes—just to wash his hands and, I don't know, mime at himself in the mirror? Who knows. Maybe he's just staring at how beautiful he is and accidentally got entranced.

I blow out a breath and fall back onto my bed with a sigh. After what seems like another hour has passed, I finally hear the bathroom door click open, and I only have enough time to sit up before he's standing there in my room, looking down at me. Still fully dressed and no tent in his shorts.

But that isn't what makes my mouth forget how to form words.

Benjamin Oliver is in my bedroom. And I'm not chasing him out with a bat. This is just too weird.

"Hi," I say too softly, like this is the first time we've met. We really don't need to relive *that* scenario. What is wrong with my mouth?

He gives me a look that says he's thinking the same thing. "Hi. Should I join you on the bed or sit on the floor?"

"Bed. You're here for the bed, right?"

"That is correct, Miss Webster," he says very formally, and when he sits on the bed, it creaks a little. Okay, we definitely need to have an empty house whenever he comes over. He pulls his phone out of his back pocket. "But first, I need to ask you some questions."

My defenses go up instantly. "About what?"

"About you." He's opening an app on his phone. It looks like...a notes app? He's taking *notes*. Aren't I the one who's supposed to be studying here?

"What about me?" I hedge.

His gaze pops up from his phone to me. He's so...damn... *close* I can see the different shades of brown in his eyes, spreading out around his pupil in a starburst. I will never admit this to him, not in a million lifetimes, but his eyes are my favorite part of him. They always have been.

"I need a baseline," Ben says, "so I know how much you've done and not done."

"Oh." Relief rushes out of me in a breathy *whoosh*. "That's easy. I've done nothing."

"Nothing at all?" he challenges. "I know you've been kissed. *I've* even kissed you once— Oh... Was that your first-ever kiss?"

I roll my eyes. "I meant no sex."

"Right, okay. What about a hand job, then?" He says it so casually, it jars me for a second. How can he be so calm and cool about this? I know he's experienced, but he's...him. I expected him to be cracking jokes the whole time, and telling me to get naked as quickly as possible so he can show off his skills. But he's not. He's stoic, serious. I hardly recognize him right now.

I take in a breath, reminding myself this is what he's here for, and say evenly, "No."

"Not even a *solo* hand job?"

"Come on." I shoot him a look. "I'm a virgin, not dead."

He's tapping away on his phone. "I need you to state your answer clearly, please, ma'am. So there are no misunderstandings between us."

Ma'am?

Okay. I get it now. He's purposely not being his usual snarky self in an attempt to put me at ease. Or to draw this out in case I change my mind, giving me plenty of time to say "forget it." I should be grateful for that, not complaining about it. Also, it's kind of hot.

If he pulls out a "pardon me," this lesson is going to be over in zero-point-zero seconds flat. There's only so much of his hotness I can take before I spontaneously combust.

"Fine." I enunciate every syllable as I say, "I have masturbated."

"What about orgasms?"

"Seriously?" I pull my knees up until my legs are folded in front of me on the bed, and hug them. This is the opposite of what I'm supposed to be doing. I'm closing myself up instead of opening. But talking about this is somehow more uncomfortable than the thought of actually doing it.

In fact, the images running through my head *because* we're talking about this have set my cheeks on fire, and I'm sure Ben has noticed even if he hasn't made that obvious.

He just looks at me, expressionless, not even a twitch of a smile. "Have you ever had an orgasm, Jess?"

An entire flock of butterflies has taken flight in my gut, as I realize…he's going to see my O face.

Oh. My. God.

That settles it. We're doing this with the lights off.

"Jess?" he prods.

"Yes," I snap. "I have had an orgasm."

"How many times?"

"Jesus—I don't know!" My glare at him is so hot, I swear my eyes just burst into flames. "It's not like I'm keeping track in some jack-off journal on my nightstand."

Finally—*finally*—he shows me more of the Ben I know, laughing and glancing at my nightstand as if he has to make sure there really isn't a notebook there. I wasn't trying to make him laugh, but seeing it now, hearing it…somehow that relaxes me. It's familiar, while the rest of this situation is anything but.

I'm still annoyed, though. And still glaring at him.

He gets himself under control. "Okay, okay. Sorry, I was just curious," he says and clears his throat. "I'll strike that question from the record."

"I'll strike something else if you don't hurry up and finish this already."

"Wow." He shakes his head, tapping on the phone screen. "Hope I never hear *that* line when we're—"

"Benjamin," I cut him off, then blow out a sharp sigh.

"Right," he says, more serious now. "Okay. Next question. Have you ever given or received oral sex?"

Thank god my knees are up, covering the front of me, because my nipples just hardened into tingling rocks. Arousal hits me so hard and fast it's like I just sat spread eagle on a pile of hot coals. It takes every ounce of strength I have to resist squirming and giving myself away. If he can be cool about this, dammit, then so can I.

"I already told you, no sex. Ever."

He shrugs. "Some people don't really consider that sex. I wanted to be clear."

"Fine. I have never given a blow job, or… What's it called when you give oral to a girl?"

"Heaven," Ben says, the corners of his mouth lifting.

That *mouth*.

My throat has gone completely dry.

That mouth could be all over me.

I didn't think about this when I said "I don't want to be a virgin anymore." I didn't think about all the things that fall under the umbrella of "sex." I know about all these things, but I just didn't *think*. I really am too naive. But now that I'm thinking about it, I can't stop. What if we—

He brings his gaze up to mine, brows coming together. "You have a question for me."

"No," I say quickly, squeezing my legs to relieve some of this sudden tension in me.

"Jess." He sets his phone down on the bed and looks at me squarely. "This isn't going to work unless we're completely honest with each other. I wasn't asking. I can see it on your face. You want to ask me something. So, ask me."

I nod. "Okay." *Deep breath.* "I was just wondering, are we…going to…you know, do that? What you just said?"

"Only if you want to," he says. "Do you?"

Be honest. "Yes?"

"Is that a question or an answer?"

"It's an answer," I say firmly. "*Yes*. But just…not right away? I feel like I need to work up to that. Having your face that close to…"

Well. My brain stopped working halfway through that sentence. Maybe if I pretend I never started it, he'll forget he ever heard it.

He picks up his phone again. "Just let me know when. I'll be ready and waiting."

Then he waggles his eyebrows at me. *Waggles*.

"If you ever give me those eyebrows again, I swear to god this is over and you'll be leaving with one less nut," I tell him. "That's, like, old man creepy."

"Oh, my bad. I thought 'old man creepy' was your thing. Since you're going after an old college dude."

"Not old. Old*er*." Why am I even debating this? He wasn't serious about any of it. I just walk right into his traps—every time. I grab my pillow, smash it over my face, and let out a groan as I fall back onto the bed.

"What was that?" Ben says. "I can't hear you over the sound of that cat dying under your pillow. Do we need to call a vet?"

"Har. Har." I pull the pillow away from my face. "Are we done with the interrogation now? What's my baseline score? Less than zero?"

"No. Like you said, you're not dead." He tosses me a grin over his shoulder, and it's hard not to notice how his eyes linger over me as he draws his gaze slowly back to the notes on his phone.

Does he like what he sees? Or is he just mentally preparing himself for something awful?

Whatever. This is Benjamin Oliver. It doesn't matter if he likes my body or not. I mean, I like his body, but I don't like *him*. So either way, I don't care. Knowing what he thinks of me physically is not going to change anything.

"On a scale of one to ten," he goes on, "I'd say you're somewhere between a one and a two. Where do you want to be at the end of the next four weeks?"

"A ten," I blurt, then realize that's probably not realistic. But Andrew is in college, and I have a lot of catching up to do. "Or a nine, or…close to it. Is that possible?"

Ben puts on a serious face. "That's a *lot* for one month. And you're assuming I'm already at a ten, or else how would

I get you there?"

Yeah, I did assume. It never crossed my mind that he'd be anything less than that. Even with him calling me out on it, I still can't imagine.

"Aren't you?"

That damn sexy smirk is back. "Guess you'll have to find out."

"Smart-ass," I say, sitting up. Dizziness hits me, and the room blurs a little. Either because I sat up too fast or because things are about to get really real in here. Probably both. "I'm done with the questions now, Benjamin. Except this last one. How do we start?"

Chapter Eight

"Step one," Ben says, "is making out and seeing where it goes."

I laugh, but it's not even funny. This is his great sex advice? See where it goes?

"We know exactly where we want this to go," I tell him, "so let's just get there already."

"Jessie." He shakes his head and makes a tsking sound, like I've misbehaved. "There is no 'just getting there' with this. Unless you want the whole experience to be awful. I don't want that. Do you?"

"No." I blow out a breath. "Fine. Let's…make out."

His grin spreads slowly, like a cat planning to pounce. "You start."

"Okay…" I swallow. Lick my lips. Stare at his, while moving a little closer. I'm about to kiss Benjamin Oliver. On purpose.

I should be repulsed, but my heart, my lungs, my hands, my mouth, every part of me is pushing me toward him. When I finally touch my lips to his, it's barely a whisper of a kiss. And then I just…stay there, like our mouths have been stuck together with glue.

Malfunction. Red alert.

I've forgotten how to kiss.

Then I feel his lips moving. But not with a kiss—he's smiling.

He doesn't speak, though. He doesn't move, either. I'm completely in control of what happens here, and realizing that puts my body back in motion. As soon as I've applied more pressure—firm but not hard—and softened my mouth, letting it mold against his, Ben kisses me back. This is nothing like the blazing kiss he gave me after graduation, though. This is softer, slower, and a thousand times more sensual. It makes me want to fall back onto the bed because I can barely keep my head up.

As if reading my mind, Ben breaks away from my mouth and starts moving his lips over my jawline, then down my neck—gah, that tickles! I squeal and squirm away, laughing without meaning to, then immediately start apologizing, because Ben looks hella confused. Like he doesn't know if he should be looking for a spider or running out the door.

But then he relaxes and says, "You're ticklish."

"Yes."

"So…I'm guessing you don't want me to do that?"

"I don't know," I admit, and insecurity has me stiffening up again, unsure what to do. And yeah, I'm a little embarrassed. We were finally getting somewhere, and I scared the shit out of him. We're off to a solid start.

"Let's try again," Ben says and swoops down on me so fast, I don't realize we're kissing again until I hear myself let out a little noise of…I don't even know. Surprise? Gratitude?

And that just reminds me, once again, that Ben is going to see and hear things from me that no one else ever has. But isn't that the point of this? To get all this awkwardness out of the way now, so I'm not behaving like a drunk turtle when— assuming this insana-banana plan actually works—I'm doing this with Andrew?

Still, I can't shake it. Ben is doing his best to massage my lips with his, but they just won't relax. He's warm, he smells faintly of pizza—probably what he had for dinner—and these are two things that should make me feel better, and they just aren't. I like being warm. I like pizza. I even like kissing Ben, if I'm being honest. But my mind keeps fixating on what comes next and what comes next and what comes next and—

"Stop," I say, and gently push him away, then take in a few breaths. My heart is thudding hard against my chest, I can actually hear it pumping blood through my ears.

Ben looks at me, probably trying to figure out what he did wrong. He did nothing wrong, though. This is all my stupid fault. I can't stop thinking and just let this happen.

I need to stop thinking.

Go all the way, right now, and do the thinking later.

"What is it?" he finally says.

I quickly lift my tank top up and over my head, toss it aside, onto the floor, then do the same with my shorts, leaving me in nothing but a cotton bra and panties. Then I lay back on my pillow, presenting myself like I'm a sacrifice on an altar, and say, "That's enough kissing. Do more now."

His face has gone hard, every angle sharp. "No."

"What—"

He's up and off my bed in a blink, and in two long steps, he's at the door, but then he stops. "I can't do this if you're not going to take it seriously."

"Did you really just say that?" I push myself up so I'm sitting. "You think *I'm* not taking this seriously, Mr. How Many Orgasms? Asking me all these questions and taking notes like I'm a goddamn science experiment or a college entrance exam— You know what? No. Stop talking. This is the dumbest argument we've ever had. Get your jerk ass back over here so you can see how serious I am."

He fucking smiles at that, but at least he's moving toward me, away from the exit. And I am *lit up* now, so as soon as he's within reach, I grab his hand and pull him down onto the bed, then climb on top of him, holding his hands down on either side of his head, and kiss the hell out of him. It's not a nice kiss. There is nothing soft or gentle between us now. This is a "let me show you what I'm made of" kiss—and Ben totally succumbs to it.

He doesn't fight me at all. He doesn't try to take over. He doesn't *not* like this.

I don't *not* like it, either.

Eventually, regretfully, I have to breathe. I pull away, our lips making a loud suction-pop noise as I do. That sound is… oddly satisfying.

We're both breathing harder now. I'm still holding myself up over him, still in just a bra and panties and not feeling at all uncomfortable that he's still fully clothed. He's seen me in a bikini. It's no different.

I've never been on top of him like this before, though, straddling him, pinning him, and that's seventeen thousand percent different. He's looking at me like he can't figure me out. Like I'm not me.

But I *am* me. I'm just a me he hasn't seen until this moment. And I feel like I could lift a building with my bare hands right now and throw it all the way to the moon.

"Damn," Ben finally says. "That's more like it."

I smile down at him, and it feels wicked. "Now what? Tell me what's next before I lose this high."

"Actually, I think we do better without talking." In one swift move, he grips my hands more firmly and pulls me down next to him. He props himself up on his side with one arm, then uses his free hand to pull his shirt off.

On my next breath I nearly swallow my tongue. Am I ever going to not have that reaction when I see his bare chest? It's so goddamn annoying.

His shorts come off next, and now I know what brand of boxer briefs he wears.

And just how much he liked that kiss.

It's very, *very* obvious.

He catches me staring. "Should I take this off, too?" he says, touching the waistband of his underwear.

Yes. "I thought you said no talking."

"Right. No more talking unless it's to say 'stop.' Agreed?"

I nod—because no talking. He gets it, and he smiles, also not talking now. His fingers are still on his boxer briefs, and while he keeps his eyes locked on me to watch for my reaction, he slowly starts pushing the cotton fabric down. Down. Down.

Damn.

I kind of hate that all the rumors about him being a well-endowed demigod are true. It's just one more thing he gets to brag about. But I can't hate it too much, because…well, it's me with him now, not a cheerleader or the class president or a nice pair of boobs he met at a party. Just me.

Just us.

No words.

Only touch.

The first time my hand wraps around him and he hisses like he's just been poked with a hot curling wand, the first time I catch myself tunneling my fingers through his thick, wavy hair, the first time he hooks a finger under my bra strap and tugs, the first time he slips a hand down the back of my panties and kneads my bare ass while he's kissing me— through every first with him, there are no words. Only touch.

He's absolutely right. It's much better when we don't talk.

Maybe that's our problem. Maybe all we need to do is shut up and we wouldn't hate each other.

We don't do everything tonight—not even close—but it's more than I ever did with anyone before, and just having the experience of it in my memory now makes me feel a little bit more like the person I want to be at the end of this. I feel stronger, in a way. More sure of myself.

Ben leaves once I've said it's enough. He walks out my front door with his hair disheveled and his shorts on crooked, and he has the loose swagger of a boy who just rubbed a girl off then showed that girl how to rub him off, too.

And I didn't even think about what my face looked like at any point.

I close the door, lock the deadbolt, turn around, and head up the stairs in a daze.

That was…unexpected.

I didn't expect to go back to my room with a smile so big it hurts. I didn't expect to hug my pillow and breathe in his lingering scent. I didn't expect a lot of what happened in the last two hours.

Mostly, though, I didn't expect to like it all so much. Or to be counting down the seconds until we can do it again.

Chapter Nine

I haven't seen Ben in two days, and instead of relishing my sudden Ben-free existence, I'm thinking about how I can get my parents out of the house tonight so he can come over. Which is distracting me from whatever Rayna is trying to tell me while we shop at some fancy boutique for some overpriced who-knows-what. Really, only one of us is shopping, and it isn't me.

Rayna holds up a soft, fuzzy, delicate-looking ivory sweater. "What do you think?"

"I think buying a sweater in June is dumb," I say, scrolling through TikTok on my phone, debating whether to ask Ben how we're supposed to get anything done together after I insisted it has to be done only at my house. I wasn't thinking about my parents when I made him agree to that. I was thinking about *not* losing my virginity somewhere sketchy like…a fitting room at a clothing store, or a public restroom. I've heard the stories.

Rayna scrunches her nose. "It's a summer sweater."

"Still a sweater. You'll roast. I'm sweating just looking at all that fuzz."

"Fine," she grumbles and moves to a rack of silky, lace-bottom tank tops.

"Those look like pajamas."

"Jessie—"

"Can I ask you something?" I say. "About sex?"

The pajama tops trying to pass as fancy tank tops are quickly forgotten, and Rayna's attention is laser-focused on me. "You can always ask me anything."

"Okay." I look around, make sure no one is standing too close to us. "Do your parents know? Do Jeremy's?"

"Oh." Rayna's face falls. "That's not really *about* sex."

"It's related," I counter. "So, do they know?"

"They do now, but they didn't at first. Not for a while." She pauses. "Why?"

"Just wondering how you got around that. Like, did he go to your house only when your parents weren't home? Did you have to make up excuses for why he was there if they *were* home? Just…I don't know. I'm not good at lying. And I'm eighteen now, it's not like I'm doing anything illegal here, but I could be thirty-five and it would still be awkward to know my parents are in the same house when I'm…"

Her eyes light up, big and round. "Is this about Andrew?"

Well, it *will* be about Andrew eventually. So this isn't lying when I say, "Yes."

Rayna lets out a little squeal. "You're really gonna go for it with him?"

"I'm gonna try, yeah." I smile just thinking about it, but before I can go any further, my phone dings with a new text message.

Ben: *are we on for tonight*

Oh shit. I can't talk to Ben in front of Rayna.

"What's that face for?" she says.

"What face?"

"The face of either abject horror or guilt." Her eyes narrow. "Who texted you?"

"Nothing— I mean no one. It was spam. I um, I need to use the bathroom. Emergency." I start fast-walking toward the back of the store and don't turn to see if she followed until I reach the restroom.

She didn't. I blow out a breath, my shoulders dropping. That was close.

Inside the restroom dressed up like a nineteenth-century debutante ball, complete with a fainting couch, I sit on the shiny brocade cushion and text Ben as fast as I can.

Me: *Parents.*

Me: *Ideas?*

Ben: *are you at work*

Me: *No.*

Ben: *are your parents*

Me: *Yes.*

Ben: *be there in 30*

Thirty? As in, thirty minutes from now?

During the day...

That's actually brilliant. Why did I think we had to do this only at night? God, that's such a virgin thing to think. The only problem is, I'm out with Rayna, and I can't just say "sorry, I need to go hook up with Ben now, catch you later." My stomach churns for real this time.

Rayna's my best friend. If I was able to explain this to her, she would understand. Right?

I shoot a quick "Okay" to Ben, then leave the restroom, slipping my phone into my back pocket. When I find Rayna, she's in the shoe section, trying on a pair of yellow suede pumps.

"That was fast," she says.

"Yep. Fast and furious."

"Ew."

"Very ew," I agree. "I'm sorry, I'm not feeling very well."

It isn't a lie. But it's not the full truth, either. There's a little pang in my chest when I say, "Can you take me home before my stomach revolts again?"

"Ew!" She throws her hands up, then grumbles, "Fine. But do *not* make a mess in my car." Then she puts her own shoes back on and tosses me a smile. "Come on, Mount Vesuvius, I got you."

I send her a smile right back, but it's weak. She's being a friend, even if she is totally grossed out by me right now, and she doesn't know what I'm really up to. This *sucks*.

And it's my own damn fault for making the rule about not telling anyone. What did I think would happen if Rayna knew? Would her knowing really be so terrible? Is it worth our friendship to keep secrets like this from her? When she lost her virginity, it was a big freaking deal. She called me and Kamy over to her house for ice cream and alcohol and spilling all the details. What am I going to do when it's my turn...sit alone in my room, shake my own hand, and say *congrats, Jessie, you're the only one who knows. Go, you.*

For the entire ride home, I can't look at her. I stare out the window and mentally kick myself over and over and over again. By the time she parks in front of my house, I've decided to tell her *something*. Give her some kind of hint.

And in the side mirror, I see Ben's car approaching.

Fuuuuuuuuuck.

It's only been twenty-five minutes!

Rayna does a double take at the rearview mirror. "Is that Ben?"

"What?"

"What is right," she says. "What is he doing on a little side street on this end of town?" She watches the mirror intently, and I'm afraid to look. I squeeze my eyes shut. This is it. We've been found out.

"Oh, Jessie, I'm sorry." Rayna unlocks the doors. "You look awful. Go inside and lie down. Call me when you're feeling better, okay?"

I crack one eye open, then the other. Ben is gone. He must have seen Rayna's car and decided to keep driving around until she leaves. I blow out a long breath. "Okay. Thanks, Ray."

I'm out of the car, up my driveway, and into my house with record speed. That was brutal.

Ben and I need to have a talk about this. I can't keep something so huge from my best friend. How is he doing the same thing with Jeremy?

At thirty minutes on the nose, Ben texts me.

Ben: *knock knock*

My reply this time is to just open the front door, and there he is, his hair wet, sleek, and curling, his whole aura giving off the smell of *clean*. He… Wait a minute. He showered for me?

He showered for me.

I don't know why that makes me feel all bubbly inside, but it does.

Get a grip, Jessie, it's just basic hygiene. Maybe he was out mud-hopping in a four-wheeler before this. It did rain pretty hard last night.

Ben steps in, kicks off his shoes, and closes the door. Then, without a word, he sweeps me up into a blazing kiss. *Sweet Jesus —*

The world spins for a few dizzying moments before he pulls away with a grin and says, "Hi."

"Hi. Um —" I take a second to catch my breath. "We need to talk."

"No we don't." He starts for the stairs, and I have to rush to keep up with him.

"Yes, actually, we do."

"Is someone dead or dying?" he says, still plundering up

the stairs.

"No, but—"

He reaches the top and whirls around to face me. "Then it can wait."

And he's off and moving again, heading straight for my bedroom like he lives here, tearing his shirt off as he goes. *Hell.* The sight of his bare back makes me just as awestruck and speechless as the sight of his bare chest. The boy has *back muscles*. I didn't even know that was a thing.

Inside my room, he turns to face me, then wriggles out of his shorts. "You're wearing too many clothes, Jess. Catch up."

"Benjamin…" I close the door behind me and just look at him. Stare at him. Drink him in from top to bottom and up again. My whole body has some kind of Pavlovic response to his presence now. I'm hot all over and also shivering. I already know what he looks like completely naked, yet I need—*need*, in some primal, visceral way—to see it again. All that's left of his clothing to remove are his boxer briefs, and it's still too much.

He's right. Whatever I needed to tell him, it can wait.

I take a step toward him and hold both my arms straight above my head.

He grabs the hem of my shirt and lifts it up and off, keeping his eyes on mine the whole time. "Kiss me," he says. "Take control."

"No talking—"

His mouth is on mine in a flash, his arms bracing around me, and then, I don't know how, I'm suddenly bouncing backward onto the mattress with him on top of me. I let out a squeak. I'm not a squeaker; what is this? Our legs tangle together, and I can't figure out what part of him my left knee is pressing against. His thigh? The back of his knee? His appendix?

"Don't let me do this unless you want it," Ben says against my ear, one hand trailing down my bare side, over my ribs, and into the waistband of my shorts. "You're the one in control. Always."

Yes, I am.

Always.

I grab his hand, stopping him. "I said no talking, Benjamin."

He goes silent and still, just watching me for direction.

And I get that high feeling again, like I'm invincible. Like I could climb a mountain and not even break a sweat. If this is confidence, I'm already addicted. *Give me more.*

With both hands, I push up against his chest until he's kneeling on the bed, and then I pull myself onto my knees in front of him and make a twirling motion with my finger. He raises a brow but does as I ask, turning around, so his back is fully facing me. I never thought I'd be turned on by someone's back before, but here I am, running my fingertips over every line and angle, like I'm memorizing each and every inch of him. If I'm tested on what his back looks and feels like later, I'll ace that test. Benjamin Oliver 101.

He shivers under my touch, but he doesn't stop me. He doesn't question me.

As quickly as I can, I remove my bra and toss it aside. Then I scoot up close behind him, press my chest to his back—instantly melt from his warmth—and wrap my arms around him, fingertips brushing over every ridge of his ribs.

He takes in a sharp breath but says nothing.

Just like he did a minute before, I slide my hand down his torso and into the front of his underwear. It took us an hour to get to this point last time, though. Am I moving too fast?

He still hasn't stopped me.

I slow down my silent exploration of him, and he lets out

a breathy hiss. I remember this. That sound means he likes it. And knowing he likes it just makes me want to do it more, find more ways to get a reaction out of him.

I've already learned that some of his strongest reactions happen when *he's* doing things to *me*.

"Benjamin," I whisper against his skin. "Touch me—"

"No talking unless the word is 'stop.'"

"But—"

"Don't tell me, Jessie." He's still kneeling with my body pressed against his back, my arms wrapped around his middle. Every breath tastes like his skin. "Show me."

The confidence I had a minute ago is fading fast. I know what I want. How do I tell him without words?

Slowly, I walk on my knees around him until we're facing each other. He's so tall I have to reach up, not just out, to take his head in my hands—can he feel them shaking?—and pull him down to me. Not to my mouth or my neck or to do that thing I never imagined I would like when he takes little nibbles from my shoulder down to my elbow. I plant his mouth right over my left nipple.

Go on, Benjamin, you know what this means.

He obeys my command so thoroughly that our "no talking" rule is no longer a choice. Because what are words? The only thing going through my head is *nnnnnnngggggghhhh…*

"*G*ood morning, sleepyhead," Ben says.

Morning?

My bleary eyes spring wide open, and I shoot up to a sitting position. "What time is it?"

"Three."

"In the morning?" I jump off the bed, snatch my clothes up from the floor, and get dressed as fast as I can without falling over.

On the other side of the room, Ben's laughing. He's also fully dressed and flipping through one of my old Dr. Seuss books. Fantastic. I can only imagine what he thinks of my literature collection. Though, to be fair, he likely doesn't read above that level anyway.

"It's afternoon," he says.

"Then why would you say 'good morning'?"

He shrugs. "You were asleep, and then you woke up. It seemed appropriate."

"It was completely *in*appropriate, you gave me a heart attack—" Something clicks in my brain. "How long was I out?"

"An hour...ish."

Oh god. He's been in my room, unsupervised. Sure, he looks totally innocent now, reading *Horton Hears a Who!* but... "What have you been doing for the past hour?"

"Listening to you snore," he says.

"I do *not* snore—"

"I can take a video of it next time if you want proof."

"No! No videos of me doing anything at any time ever. I mean it. Say you won't do it."

"Okay, Jess, I won't do it. Not at 'any time ever.'" He turns a page, smiling. "When do your parents get home?"

I blow out a sigh and grab the brush off the top of my dresser, then pull the elastic band off its handle and tie my hair up in a quick bun. "My dad goes to the gym after work. He won't be here before dinner. And my mom..."

Ben looks up from the book. "Your mom what?"

"If she comes straight home from her office, she'll be here around four thirty."

I wait for him to ask what time it'll be if she doesn't come straight home or what she's doing after work. But I'm not going to tell him even if he asks. Mostly because I don't know.

He nods, closes the book, then slides it back into its spot on my little bookshelf I've had since I was three. "I should probably get going, then." He scratches the back of his neck and looks around, like he isn't sure what to do.

It's weird seeing him like this, so out of his element. But he could have left anytime. He didn't have to stick around while I slept off the spell he put me under. Now it's awkward.

He hasn't moved. Does he need me to give him the okay to leave?

"Yeah, sure, that's fine," I say.

"Okay." He nods but still doesn't move.

"Um. Thanks. Today was…educational," I say, then press my lips together and stare down at my feet, at the chipped blue nail polish on my toes.

"Wasn't there something you wanted to talk about?"

Was there? What on earth would I need to talk about with Benjamin Oliver—

"Oh, right! Yes. Yes, there is." *Duh.* "Jeremy."

His expression turns confused. "You mean Jeremy my best friend and your best friend's boyfriend Jeremy?"

"Yeah. But it's about Rayna, too. And me. And you. And Kamy and Todd. The six of us, I guess. It's… Isn't this hard for you? Keeping us a secret from Jeremy and Todd, I mean. I feel like I should tell Rayna and Kamy."

"Why?"

My mouth twists. "I don't know. When you texted me earlier, I was out shopping with Rayna, and I had to lie to get away from her so I could text you back without her knowing. It felt wrong."

He thinks about that for a minute. "We made a rule,

Jessie. No telling anyone, including our best friends."

"Then we can unmake the rule," I say.

"But it's a good rule." He turns his head to the side, blows out a breath, and turns back toward me again. "The less people who know, the better. For both of our sakes."

What is he talking about?

Is he…embarrassed to be doing this with me?

It was *his* idea.

And I certainly didn't hear him complaining while we were—

Oh.

Of course I didn't hear him complaining. I didn't hear him saying *anything* because of our no-talking rule. I really didn't think this through. All my dumb rules are working against me.

"It's only a month, Jessie. Then you don't have to worry about it anymore." He reaches for the doorknob. "When are we meeting up again?"

Good question.

"You're right, it's only a month," I say, "and the first week of that month is almost over already. We can't skip days anymore. We'll just have to find a way to see each other every day unless one of us is sick or something. Do you have anything going on that we'll have to work around? Like a job, maybe?"

He smirks. "No. I'm free just about any time."

Right. Why would the son of the mayor, the richest man in Trinity, need a job?

"Okay, well. We can do what we did today on the days I don't work. The days I do work, I can only meet in the evening, and my parents are hit or miss with their social calendars. They might be here, they might not."

"And we can't meet at my place," he says.

"Why not?"

He just looks at me, his face suddenly hard, his eyes locked on mine. "It's not an option."

I throw my hands up. "Well, then, we're screwed three to five days a week."

"You mean not screwed."

"Shut *up*," I say through a laugh.

He gives me another look, but this time his eyes are soft, his brow relaxed. His mouth turns up at the corners, just a bit. "I'll figure something out."

"Like what?"

"You'll just have to trust me, Jess." He smiles fully then, before he opens the door and steps out. I follow him down the hall and down the stairs, catching up to him at the front door, where he slips his bare feet into his shoes.

"We've been through this before. I don't trust you at all, Benjamin."

"Right." He laughs. "You want to believe you don't, but you do. We wouldn't be here if you didn't."

And with that cocky grin of his that I know too well, he walks out of my house, leaving me alone with my imagination and seventeen levels of anxiety. What the hell kind of plan is he going to cook up next?

Chapter Ten

The Trinity Public Library is just as fancy schmancy as the rest of this town. I guess we're not a large enough city to have our own museum of history and fine art, so the good people of Trinity decided to combine that with our library. There are great big paintings on the walls and crystal chandeliers on the ceilings. A wide spiral staircase connects the two main floors. There are busts of Beethoven and other dead composers in the music section and old black-and-white movie posters in the film section. Everywhere you turn, there's a leather armchair to sit and read.

Even though it's a bit stuffy, I love working here. Of course I'm a reader, but it isn't really that I like books that much, and I definitely couldn't care less about the decor. It's the silence.

Sweet, beautiful silence.

The library is the only public place I can be myself without judgment. People aren't supposed to talk here. And if they do, it's at the information desk or the checkout, which I can easily avoid. My entire job description is to *shelve books*. I push my little cart around, up and down the aisles, filing away the returns or the books people so nicely leave scattered across the tables and displaced on the shelves. And it would be a horrid way to fill a six-hour shift if I didn't find something to keep my mind occupied.

Right now, I'm in the biography section, organizing everyone from Barack Obama to Genghis Khan. To have a biography written about you, you have to have done something with your life worth writing about. All these people… I envy them. They knew what they wanted and went for it. They had a talent in something and used it to their advantage.

I don't know what I want, and I have no talent.

My problem with Andrew is a perfect example. I know that I like him, like being around him, like the things he does and says, and I know he's the kind of person I want a relationship with. But beyond that, it gets muddy. I don't know what I want with someone—anyone—long-term. I can't even decide what I want for my own future, by myself, how can I know what I want for a future with a whole other person who has their own dreams and goals?

As for talent… My dad would say the things I make from repurposing plastics just to keep them out of landfills is a talent. But he's my dad. He's supposed to say things like that. It isn't really a talent, it's just a way to prevent boredom when your parents can't afford to buy you high-tech devices or take you on a family vacation. Ever.

It isn't talent to build a fire if you're stuck outside in the cold. It's survival. Anyone would do it. Talent is something you have that others don't, something that makes you special.

Sometimes I flip through these books to give myself ideas. But that usually just gives me more indecision. The more I learn about things, the more overwhelming it is to have to choose *one* thing in life and master it. I find the world of medicine incredibly fascinating. But I feel the same way about the world of geology. And the world of architecture. And the world of—

"Psst," someone says to my right.

I whip my head around so fast my neck cracks. It's some guy in a hoodie and sunglasses with mirror lenses, holding a book open, head bent down a little like he's reading. But then he opens his mouth again. *Please don't ask me for help.*

"What time is your shift over?"

As soon as he finishes the sentence, my whole body goes slack with relief. It's just Ben.

"What are you doing here?" I whisper-shout, then casually push my cart toward him until we're only about a foot from each other. I keep acting like I'm working, and he keeps acting like he's reading. With a performance like this, we could rule Hollywood.

"Looking for you," he says. "You didn't answer my texts."

"No phones allowed while working."

"Right." He nods at the book he's holding. "Do you get a break soon?"

"Why?" I say, then it hits me. "I'm not doing anything with you here!"

"Not even in the bathroom?"

"Especially not in the bathroom," I hiss.

He grins, still looking down at the book in his hands. "I was kidding, Jess. Public-bathroom sex is gross. Twelve out of ten do not recommend."

Well, then, at least that's one thing I won't have to worry about.

"My shift ends in an hour. What's your plan?"

He slaps the book closed, a loud *smack* echoing around us, then drops it onto my cart. "I'll be back in an hour. Meet me outside."

Without another word, he turns and walks off. I watch him until he disappears around a corner, then glance down at my cart... The book he left there is called *Sex for Dummies.*

Real subtle, Benjamin.

Whatever, joke's on him—I already read that one.

I grab another book, shaking my head, and slide it neatly into its place on the shelf. This is going to be the longest hour of my life.

After I clock out for the day, I check my texts—three from Ben asking different variations of "when are you free" before he decided to find me in person, and one from Rayna reminding me she and her family are leaving for their trip to Aruba today.

Just as I reply to Ben with "Walking out now," a text comes in from my mom.

Mom: *Call me*

Okay...

Then there's another text from Ben that tells me he's parked in the back.

I hit "call" on the chat screen with Mom and slow-walk through the parking lot. It rings three times on the other end before she picks up.

"Jessica," she says. "Can you do me a favor?"

Hello to you, too, Mother.

"Sure, what is it?"

"When you get home, check the mailbox and tell me if there's anything in there from Sweet Synthetics. I'm expecting a small package."

"Okay." I have no idea what Sweet Synthetics is. Probably something for her job. "And if it's there?"

"Hide it from your father until I get home," she says.

Great. That doesn't sound suspicious at all. But if she wasn't completely shrouded in mystery every time we talked, would she even be my mother?

I spot Ben's shiny black car and catch him watching me walk up to him in the side mirror. He's still wearing those shades, so I can't actually see his eyes, but what else would he be looking at through the mirror? He parked in No Man's Land.

"Okay, honey, I have to get back to work now," Mom says. "Thanks, love you, bye!"

Click.

Sigh.

I slide my phone in my back pocket and take the last few steps up to Ben's car. He leans across the passenger seat to open the door from the inside. "Get in."

"Such a gentleman," I say, then slide onto the seat and close the door. But the question "where are we going" never makes it past the tip of my tongue. This car...

This car smells like money.

Not literally, but oh my *hell*. I thought my mom's new-used Buick was cool because she could use her car to call people hands-free while she's driving. But if her car is considered cool, then Ben's car is a mile-wide glacier. This has everything anyone could think of putting in a car and everything no one would think of putting in a car—until now. It's like I've stepped into an honest-to-god spaceship. Or a time machine in a remake of *Back to the Future*. What are all these displays and buttons for? I turn to look at the back seat, and I'm actually surprised to not see a butler offering me a drink.

What I do see back there? *Room.* Lots of it.

I turn my gaze to Ben. "Are we about to get naked in your car?"

"No. Here, put these on." He hands me his shades and pulls out a baseball cap from the console between our seats.

I don't have to ask why. He's hiding my identity, because of course anyone who sees him driving will know who he is, and they wouldn't think twice about seeing some unidentified girl with him. That's what happens when you have vanity plates that say NOFKSGVN.

I tuck my bun up under the ball cap, then slide the shades onto my face. "These are huge on me."

Ben laughs. "You look like a *Saturday Night Live* skit gone wrong."

"Or very, very right." As he puts the car in gear, I buckle my seat belt. "So, where are we going? I have to be back before my dad gets home."

He shakes his head. "If we had time to do this before your dad gets home, we wouldn't be in my car. We'd be in your bed."

It really isn't fair how often he's right about things.

I blow out a sigh. "Then take me home for a minute first. I have to check something."

He doesn't ask what. He hasn't asked me who I was talking to on the phone before, either. He just says, "Okay," and drives.

Within a few minutes, we turn down my street, and even from here I can see my dad's car in the driveway.

Fuck me.

"Let me out here," I say quickly. "My dad's home early."

"What—"

"I have to look like I walked home." Because normally, I would have. I don't have a car of my own.

Ben slows to a stop about six houses from mine. I pull his giant sunglasses off my face, rip the hat off my head, and practically jump out of the car. Graceful as a gazelle on crack.

"Park somewhere until you see me come back out, then meet me at the corner."

"Yes, ma'am." He gives me a two-finger salute, and I slam the door shut.

Going from the ice-cold AC in that luxury sedan to the bog of heat and humidity outside almost puts me into anaphylactic shock. My pits are damp, my face is dripping, and my feet are sliding around inside my sandals by the time I reach my house. Instead of rushing inside, though, where it's cooler, I go right for the mailbox mounted next to the front door.

And it's empty. My stomach drops.

He picked it up already...

Maybe there's a chance he hasn't opened anything yet—

I push the door open. "Dad!"

He takes a step out from the kitchen, holding a small cardboard box, and smiles at me.

Oh no. That has to be the thing. It looks like he hasn't opened it yet, but clearly he was about to. How do I—? What do I do?

"You're home," I say.

"Yeah, we finished early for once. Nice, huh?" He steps back into the kitchen, and I run to catch up, only to find him using a knife to slice the box open.

"Dad, hey, I was wondering if—"

"What the jiminy cricket is this?" He pushes his glasses up onto his balding head, lifting something wrapped in plastic, then squints at a tiny pamphlet and leans in closer to read it.

I can't see what it is, not with it clutched in his hand like that.

God, Mom, what did you...?

Suddenly, a flush creeps up my dad's neck. He slowly turns his head toward me. "This is a sex toy."

OHMYGOD, MOM!

"Really?" I let out a nervous laugh. "How do you know?"

"Because there's instructions here on how to use it."

I can't see what kind of contraption he's still holding, I just know he's not supposed to have it or even know it exists. I'll ask my mother questions later. Right now, I have to think of something to tell my dad before he goes so red he starts melting.

"Um…sorry, Dad. That's mine." I take a quick step toward him and snatch the whole thing out of his hands, box and all. "You weren't supposed to see that."

Now I'm turning red.

Which must make him believe I'm telling the truth, because he blows out a breath and starts opening the other mail he'd left on the kitchen table. "Be careful, okay?"

"I know how to follow an instruction manual—"

"I mean in general, Jessie. Just…*be careful*."

"Oh, right. Yeah. I am. Nothing to worry about."

Literally nothing. I don't even know what I'm holding, and I don't *want* to know.

Dad shakes his head, still not looking at me. "What did you expect, Dale?" he mutters to himself. "She's eighteen. She can't be your innocent little girl forever."

"Dad—"

My phone buzzes in my back pocket, so I pull it out to see who's texting.

Ben: *did you die*

Yes. From embarrassment.

Me: *One minute.*

"I'm going out tonight," I say, backing up toward the stairs, clutching this…whatever this is to my chest. "I just, um, came home to change out of these clothes."

I hustle upstairs and into my room, then tuck that little gift into the far corner of my closet. I'll deal with it later. And since I really am sweaty and need to change, I grab a light-yellow sleeveless sundress. The skirt is a little short for me, but when it's this hot, I choose not to care. Besides, I can wear short-shorts underneath, so even with a breeze, I'm good.

I freshen up and change in record time, then fix my hair and run back downstairs, tossing Dad a "see you later!" on my way out.

Speed-walking to the corner and waiting for Ben to pick me up takes seventeen years. I open the door myself this time and hop inside, then aim every single vent at my face, closing my eyes because even my eyelids are sweating. "I've never been more thankful for air conditioning in all my life. It feels like you're breathing water out there."

It takes me a second to realize the car isn't moving. And Ben isn't talking.

Dead. Silence.

"Benjamin?" I turn to look at him.

He's just staring at me. "You're wearing a dress."

"Yes…"

"I've never seen you wear a dress before."

I roll my eyes and turn back toward the blast of cool air. "That doesn't mean I've never worn one before. And there's nothing special about this. It's just a plain cotton summer dress."

"Right," he says. "Just a plain dress. It's very you."

I'll take that as a compliment even if he didn't mean it to be. "Can you tell me where we're going now?"

"Put the hat and sunglasses back on." He pulls away from the curb, then crosses onto the main street that runs through the center of Trinity. "Are you hungry?"

"Starving."

"Good. I'll get you anything you want for dinner, as long as you promise to eat what I pick out for dessert."

I snort. "Let me guess. You're the dessert."

He flashes a grin but keeps his eyes on the road. "Not exactly."

Chapter Eleven

We've been driving for at least thirty minutes now. We've driven right out of Trinity and into the boonies of western Pennsylvania. And then beyond that, into some little town named Dover.

Ben picked up drive-thru burgers and fries—at my request—and said we had to eat in the car on our way to dessert. Now I know why; it's too far to wait until we're stopped. At least I could take the hat and sunglasses off as soon as we left Trinity city limits.

I assume he's just taking me as far away from knowing eyes as he can, but when he pulls into the cracked-asphalt parking lot of an ice cream shack surrounded by picnic tables, it feels too specific to be random. It's also not at all the kind of place I'd imagine Ben taking...anyone.

I read the sign out loud. "Nut Hut? Really?"

"Don't knock it till you try it," Ben says.

"How do you even know about this place?"

"We had a game out here once." He shrugs, then cuts the engine and opens his door. "Come on, we gotta get it before the sun sets. It's best when it's melty."

"Okay, weirdo." We still have a few *hours* of light left.

I open my own door and step out. It's not quite as hot

as it was before, but it's still hot enough to complain about. It's crowded here, too. Sweaty, stinky bodies everywhere. The picnic tables are full of people of all ages, shapes, colors, and sizes. "Where are we going to sit?" I say to Ben as we get in line for the order window.

"Somewhere over there." He points to an open grassy field behind the Nut Hut. "We don't want any kids around for this. Or anyone, really."

What the cinnamon toast fuck is he talking about?

Wait a minute… What are we going to do with this ice cream!

Damn my curiosity, because now I have to know. Even if I end up hating it.

Try anything once, right?

Even though the line is long, it moves fast, and *bless the dairy lord*, they have my favorite flavor here. "A small bowl of salted caramel for me," I tell Ben.

"A woman of taste." He grins, then says to the girl behind the window, "Waffle cone, salted caramel, three scoops. Actually, can you do four?"

"That's not what I—"

"I know," he says.

I cross my arms and blow out a breath. While we're waiting for my caramel tower, Ben pays—with a fifty-dollar bill. The poor girl at the register practically empties her whole till giving him the change.

"No credit card?" I say. He used his plastic at the burger joint.

"This place is cash only."

"Really? Is that even allowed?"

He shakes his head. "You need to get out of Trinity more often."

"Yeah," I say under my breath. I know I do. There's only

so much you can learn from reading about people and places and things. You have to *experience* them.

If I had a few extra thousand dollars lying around, I'd buy my own wheels and be gone. But such is my life. My parents can't even gift me a car, and they both work full-time.

The Nut Hut girl hands me a wobbling tower of salted caramel on a waffle cone.

"I need two hands for this," I say.

Ben laughs.

"It isn't funny."

"It's extremely funny," he says. "Don't trip." He starts walking toward the field.

"Wait, where's yours? Didn't you get something?"

"Nope."

I step as carefully as I can behind him, keeping one hand at the side of the ice cream so I can catch it if it falls. This is so ridiculous.

"Well, I'm not sharing this. You could have gotten your own."

He glances over his shoulder at me. "I'm not asking you to share."

"Then *what* are you asking me? It's already melting. And something tells me I can't just eat it without your permission—"

I clamp my mouth shut.

I just answered my own question. I'm going to eat phallus-shaped food, the kind of food that requires a lot of licking, while he sits there and tells me how to do it.

Unless I'm wrong…

Do I even want to be wrong?

Ben turns to face me but keeps walking. Backward. Hands in pockets. Stupid-hot grin.

"How much farther?" I say. We're closer to the woods now

than the Nut Hut.

"Don't let it drip onto the cone."

"That's not an answer." Still, I place my tongue where the ice cream meets the cone and twirl it around, licking up all the drips in one horizontal sweep.

"Not like that," Ben says, then stops. Finally. "We can sit here."

"In the grass."

He squats, then sits cross-legged and reaches out toward me. "Need a hand?"

"Yes." I give him the ice cream cone and a smug smile, letting my skirt flare around me as I sit a few inches in front of him. Our knees bump.

"Here, it's melting again." He hands it over to me, and I grab it with both hands.

"Now what?"

"Don't let the ice cream drip onto the cone," he says. "But don't lick it horizontally. Lick it vertically. From bottom to top."

"Okay…" So, I wasn't wrong. He's using perfectly innocent ice cream to show me how to give head. I can't even be mad at him for it, either, because I'd rather practice on this first before doing it for real. Somehow, he knew that. Maybe this isn't the first time…

"How many other girls have you brought here?" I say, then start a slow lick upward. The heady mix of salty and sweet coats my tongue. "Holy crap…this is really good."

"Perfect, just like that," Ben says, then goes quiet until I've made my licks all the way around. "Zero."

"What?"

"Zero other girls."

I dart a glance at him. He's not smiling or smirking. He's totally neutral.

He's telling the truth.

"Keep catching the drips," he says. "So, where would you go?"

I pause, my tongue plastered against the side of the tower of ice cream. I pull it back in, swallow, and lick my lips. "You lost me."

"If you could get out of Trinity, where would you go?"

"Oh." *Hmm.* I'd love to go to Brazil and see where Andrew grew up, learn about his native culture. I would only go if it were Andrew taking me, though, and I'm pretty sure that isn't what Ben is asking. I take another lick, then say, "Anywhere, I guess. I'm not picky. Um, should I be licking this faster?"

"Not yet."

"How will I know when to speed up?"

"You won't at first. But don't worry, the ice cream will tell you what it wants. Then, when you have more experience, you just know." He watches me for another couple of seconds. "If you had to pick a specific place, what would it be? You're at an airport—"

"I've never been on a plane."

"Doesn't matter," he says. "This is just a for instance. Don't overthink it."

Easy for him to say. He's not the Queen of Overthinking It.

"You're at an airport," he starts again, "and every flight will take you to a different place in the world. Which plane do you board?"

Liiiiiiick. "Can you narrow it down for me? The world is big."

"Okay, sure." He thinks for a minute, tilting his head back to squint at the sky. Some clouds have rolled in since we got here. "All right, I'll make it easy—three choices, and they're all in English-speaking countries. New York City, London, or Sydney?"

That's a tough one. I've been to none of those places, but I've read about all of them. And I'd love to visit any of them. Each has its own appeal in a different way. In Sydney, you're close to the Great Barrier Reef. Scuba diving would be so much fun. In London, you have all that history. Castles. Buckingham Palace. The Tower of London, where people were *tortured*.

And in New York City, you have…pretty much the whole world in one spot. That would be a good place to start, then. Like a sampler of other destinations. Just see which ones I like and go from there.

"New York," I say, eyeing him for a reaction from behind my ice cream.

He raises a brow. "A flight from Pittsburgh to New York is only like an hour and a half. You could go there in the morning, spend all day there, and be back home that night." He bumps his knee gently against mine. "You should do it."

Sure, if I had money for a plane ticket. And money to buy literally anything at New York City prices. *Keep dreaming.*

"If I'm going to New York," I say instead, "it'll be for more than a day. Even more than a month. There's so much to see and do. I could spend a year there, at the least. I'd have to plan it out, save up for it, all that." I shrug. "Someday, maybe."

Ben doesn't say anything, and when I look at him, his face is all pensive, like he's deep in thought. Maybe I'm revealing too much about myself. It's just supposed to be physical with us, and he was probably only asking me where I'd go to make chitchat, not to get all serious and emotive.

I hold the ice cream cone out so it's hovering between us. The salted caramel tower is still huge, but I've shaved a few layers off with all this licking. Not one drop made it to the cone, thank you very much. "I know there's more to it than this. Let's get on with it before there's nothing left for me to practice on."

His eyes glint, and…yep, there's the smirk. "You'll always have something to practice on, Jess. All you have to do is tell me where and when."

"Benjamin." I give him my hardest glare. "Today it's about the ice cream. Can we just focus on that?"

He throws his hands up, palms out. "Okay, okay, fine." He clears his throat, and when he talks again, he's got that "teacher tone" in his voice that makes my stomach do flip-flops. "You can satisfactorily eat an entire ice cream cone just by licking it until it's finished. But you also have the option of using your lips and the inside of your mouth—*if you want to*."

"I want to," I say automatically, then do a mental facepalm. He didn't ask me that.

Well, whatever. Now he knows.

"All right, then," he says. "Hold the ice cream cone in place, don't let it move. Keep it *right. There.* Now, open your mouth, then lower it over the ice cream. *You* go to *it*, not the other way around. If it's the other way around, you're not the one in control. Okay?"

"Yeah, got it. The ice cream doesn't move, only I do." I lick my lips and swallow, then do just as he said. As soon as my mouth touches the ice cream, he continues.

"Keep your lips touching it as you move, but keep your teeth away from it. Only use your teeth if the ice cream wants you to. Slower," he adds. "You move too fast and it's over too soon and then all you have is a mess." He mimes an explosion. "Ice cream everywhere."

If I ever look at melted ice cream again after this and don't think *premature ejaculation*, it'll be a goddamn miracle.

I'm about halfway down when the top scoop touches the back of the roof of my mouth, and I'm hit with a massive brain freeze. "Aghyow!" The cone goes flying out of my hand before I realize I've thrown it. Then my head falls forward, both hands pressing against it, all the way down to the ground. "Aaaaaaaaghhh."

"What happened?" Ben says. He sounds a little panicky. But that's just my frozen brain not working right, because Benjamin Oliver does not get panicky over *anything*. Least of all me.

"Too cold," I say to the ground. "Brain...hurts..."

There's a moment of total silence around me. It's so quiet I can hear birds chirping in the distance and kids squealing at the picnic tables that are at least a hundred yards away.

It's only a moment, but it's so crystal clear it feels like the world has stopped.

Then Ben pushes it all back into motion with hysterical laughter.

At first I'm annoyed—that's just my default reaction to anything this boy does—but once the icicles spiking through my head have faded, my other default reaction around Ben takes over.

My need for revenge.

"You think this is funny?" My lips and tongue and mouth are so cold, the words get a little slurred, which just makes Ben laugh harder. I push myself up from the ground and walk on my knees toward him, then crawl up into his lap and straddle him. "That was a waste of perfectly good salted caramel ice cream. Probably the best I've ever had."

"Don't get mad at *me*." He's still laughing. "I didn't know that would happen. You're the first person in the history of humanity to get a brain freeze from giving a blow job."

Asshole. "You know, suddenly I'm in the mood to share."

I grab the back of his head and bring his mouth to mine, making sure to use lots of icy tongue. He lasts about half a second before pulling away.

"You're freezing!"

"I know! Isn't it funny?" I tease.

His eyes go dark, like a challenge, and he wraps his arms around me, pulling my whole body closer. Despite the furnace of heat enveloping me, I shudder. *Anticipate.*

Because I know that look. I know what it leads to with him.

"You won't win this, Jessie."

"Win what?" I say sweetly.

"This game of wits you like to play with me."

"I don't know what you mean." I keep playing innocent. "My mouth was so cold, Benjamin. I was just trying to warm it up with yours."

"Oh, really?" He sweeps me up and into him, in a kiss so hot the Nut Hut will have to shut down for the night. Everything in a fifty-mile radius has been melted.

Warming my mouth with yours…your hot mouth…

We're beyond warm. We're sizzling.

Ben lowers me to the grass, keeping one hand behind my head like a pillow, never breaking the kiss. It's getting hard to breathe, but that doesn't make me stop. Right now, breathing is secondary. *Everything* is secondary to the sensations coursing through me. Ben's hand trails down my side, tickling my ribs, and I start to squirm. But his hand keeps going, past my hips, down my leg to the hem of my dress…and then under my skirt and up again. *God, yes.* But—

"Not out here," I say, gasping for breath. "Someone might see us."

Ben turns his head, his chest heaving over mine, his brow creasing.

"What is it?"

"No one's going to see us," he says. "Everyone's gone."

I look around as well as I can from underneath him. It does seem darker now...and colder...

Was it this breezy before?

I shoot my gaze straight up to the sky.

"Uh, Benjamin. We need to go."

"What?" His face snaps back to mine. "Why?"

"Storm clouds—"

Lightning flashes, followed quickly by a crack and rumble of thunder.

"Shit." Ben scrambles to his feet, then helps me up.

And we run.

I keep hold of his hand with every pounding step. Even when the rain dumps on us and we slide and stumble our way back to his car, I never let go. Neither does he.

When we finally reach his car and I have to get inside and release my hand, it's the only part of me that's still warm.

Ben rushes into the driver's seat and slams the door. It isn't long before the windows are fogging up. The visibility is nil. "I can't drive you home in this," he says. "It's not safe."

He's soaked. His cotton T-shirt is plastered to his skin. Droplets of water keep dripping off the ends of his hair and down his face. He's still breathing hard from the run, and so am I, my heartbeat thrumming along with no signs of slowing.

It feels like I had something important and lost it. Like I need to find it again or it'll be lost forever.

"Now what?" I say.

"Summer storms move fast. Once it lightens up, we can go."

I nod slowly. He lit me on fire in that field, and now he's stamping out the flames. But damn it, I want to keep burning. "How long, do you think?"

He shrugs and starts the car. The main display on the dashboard lights up. With a few taps, Ben has turned the heat on and pulled up the minute-by-minute weather forecast for our exact location. "About ten minutes," he says.

"That should be enough time. Right?"

"For what?"

"More practice." I catch his gaze and hold it, silently saying, *I'm serious.* "Is that okay?"

His eyes never leave mine as he moves his seat back farther from the steering wheel and unzips his shorts. He doesn't say anything, and I don't need him to. His body language is clear.

Everything he just did screamed, *Yes, please.*

Chapter Twelve

*T*onight is the night. I'm ready.

I've been with Ben three days out of the past five. We're on day six now—Saturday—one week gone already. I've dipped my toes in the water with him, kicked and splashed and played, but I haven't taken the big plunge yet. Ben has been waiting for me to tell him when, and I've never been more sure of anything in my life. It's going to happen tonight.

So, of course my parents are taking their good old time about getting the hell out of here.

They have some kind of social function to go to for the company my mom works for in Pittsburgh, and they'll be gone most of the night.

The circumstances couldn't be more perfect.

It's all I've been thinking about all day.

I showered and deep conditioned my hair. I painted my nails—fingers *and* toes. I lathered up in body butter so every last speck of my skin is smooth and soft. None of that is for Ben, really, but for me. Pampering myself is how I kill stress. Now I'm sitting on the living room couch, pretending to watch TV, while my dad pretends to be busy in the kitchen as he waits for Mom to finish getting ready. He's been tiptoeing around me since he opened The Package.

Mom hasn't asked me about it, so I haven't said anything. Because how am I supposed to bring *that* up? Let her just keep assuming it hasn't arrived yet. Or better, it got lost in shipping.

"No big plans tonight?" Dad says awkwardly from behind me, walking in from the kitchen. He's wearing a suit and tie, which for him is just another day in the life.

"Nope." I give him a grin. "Just me, Netflix, and the leftover pizza."

"Where's your bestie?"

"Aruba." I turn back to the TV screen and continue browsing. "She's having a great time," I say. My voice comes out bitter.

Rayna called me last night and told me all about it, and… I don't know, it's not like she hasn't been filthy rich for as long as I've known her. But it was hard to hide my jealousy and fake being happy for her. Thank god we weren't on video. It shouldn't bother me—it usually doesn't. For some reason, this time was different.

Dad leans a shoulder against the archway between the kitchen and living room. "Do you want to go to Aruba?"

I shrug. "Not particularly."

"Then why do you sound upset about your friend being there having fun?"

"I don't know." Another shrug. "It would be nice to have the option to go if I wanted to."

When you don't have money, those choices are made for you. It *sucks*.

And I'm afraid this is going to be my life for the rest of my life.

"Honey—" Dad starts, but then Mom rushes down the stairs and breezes by, right between us, her flowy red dress billowing behind her.

"Let's go, Dale," she says and opens the front door. "If we leave right now, we can be fashionably late instead of embarrassingly late." She blows me a kiss and then disappears.

"Duty calls." Dad heads for the door and grabs the handle of the suitcase waiting there for him. "I plan on getting as drunk as your mother tonight, so we're staying overnight at the hotel. It's an open bar, free drinks," he says, like he needs to explain his behavior. "Anyway, don't wait up for us."

Don't worry, I won't. I'll be in a coma until morning.

As soon as I hear them drive away, I turn off the TV and pull out my phone, then tap out a text and hustle up the stairs to my room.

Me: *Are you here?*

Ben: *just parked*

Ben: *walking now*

Me: *Okay the door is open so just come in and lock it behind you.*

Me: *I'm upstairs.*

Ben: *what no escort today?*

Me: *You're a big boy, you can handle it.*

He doesn't reply to that, but I can hear him entering the house now. Another five seconds and he's in my bedroom.

"Hi," I say.

"Hi."

Ben looks the same as he always does—confident, grinning, hotter than the sun—but tonight will be different. I choke past the lump in my throat. "I want to do everything tonight."

"*Everything* everything?" He sits next to me on the bed.

"Well, no, not literally everything. I mean, the main thing people think of when they talk about someone losing their virginity. That everything."

"Okay…" He nods slowly. Rubs his palms down his thighs.

"You sure you're ready?"

"It's been a week, Benjamin. We only have three weeks left. It's time."

He shoots me a look. "That doesn't answer my question."

"*Yes*, I'm ready." I give him the biggest, toothiest smile possible without splitting my skin. "I swear I'm ready. Are you?" Oh no...what if— "Please tell me you brought condoms."

Ben smirks, reaching into his back pocket. He pulls out four square foil packets all connected to one another in a row, then tosses them onto the bed. They look like candy.

I shake my head and tsk. "Only four? I expected more from you."

"Only four in my pocket," he clarifies. "The rest of the box is in my car."

"*Jesus*, I was kidding—"

"But listen, Jess. This isn't a quick thing, we really need to take our time with this part. Do you know when your parents will be back?"

"Yep." I lean back on my elbows and playfully kick my feet out one at a time, up and down, up and down. "Tomorrow."

"Tomorrow..." His grin spreads slowly. Then he climbs on top of me and pulls his shirt off. And predictably, I go into cardiac arrest at the sight of him undressing. I can feel my heart beating in my throat. It's pounding and yet completely stopped at the same time. "New rule," he says. "It's important, especially for tonight."

God, this is really happening. I reach up and stroke his chest, sending tingles from the tips of my fingers to the tips of my toes. He hasn't even touched me yet and I'm ready to burst. "What's the rule?"

"We talk. The whole time. No more 'no talking' rule."

"Deal." I was starting to hate that rule, anyway. It was

nice at first, it kept me focused, but now…I wouldn't mind hearing him say he likes what I'm doing. You can't have too many confidence boosts when you start with as little as I did.

He dives for the crook of my neck and starts trailing kisses down to my collarbone. The room spins. "Fuck, you smell good. New shampoo?"

"No, it's lotion." *Breathe, Jessie.* "What are we going to talk about?"

"Anything you want," he says between kisses. "Tell me what you want me to do. With words. Tell me if something doesn't feel right. With words. Tell me whatever crosses your mind, even if you think it's dumb. Okay?"

"Okay." I grab his hair to keep myself steady because the goddamn room is spinning. I'm not even naked yet. "Take my shirt off."

"Yes, ma'am," he mumbles against my neck.

"Oh…don't *even* with the 'yes, ma'am' business. I won't last another minute."

He laughs, tugging my shirt up and off. "That turns you on? Why?"

"I don't know, it just does."

Ben freezes, his hands planted on either side of my head, staring down at me. "Nice bra."

"I found it on a clearance rack for only two bucks."

"I don't care where you got it or how much you spent. I like it."

"Here, then." I wriggle my way out of the lacy contraption and toss it up to him. "You can have it."

"Thanks." He throws it over his shoulder, and it lands with a soft *thump* on the floor.

I dart a glance at my own naked chest, then back up at him. Telling him to take my shirt off was no big deal. But telling him what I want him to do to my body…is the biggest of deals.

I'm sure he can guess, though. My nipples are out and jumping for joy.

"Say it," he tells me, his voice low. "What do you want?"

"Your mouth."

"My mouth what?" He leans down closer. Our noses are almost touching. His breath whispers across my lips.

He's really going to make me say it.

"Benjamin…" I cup my left breast. I don't know why, but the left one always wants to go first. "Put your mouth on me. Here."

He grins that grin that makes my breath stutter, and then he says, "Yes, ma'am," and lowers his head and starts suckling and I have legitimately lost the ability to breathe. For eternity.

Sweet. Jesus.

For a long time—or at least it seems like it—everything we do is all stuff we've done before, just with a lot of talking. Kissing. Touching. Licking. Nibbling. But instead of me finishing him off with a hand job after I've gone to oblivion and back, Ben grabs a condom and tears it open.

I'm lying on my back, my head still fuzzy and my insides still quivering with aftershocks, watching Ben roll a thin piece of latex over himself. Then he tells me to lift my hips and he places a towel under me. Things are about to get messy.

This is it. This is the whole reason I'm here with Ben in the first place, to get this done and then keep doing it until it's no longer some big unknown, it's just something I do. It's something a lot of people do. Every hour, every day, all around the world.

But as he lies down next to me, waiting for me to give him a green light, I suddenly feel something I haven't felt around Ben since the day we met, before we even had our first fight. And it comes on so strongly, I can't talk myself into believing it's as ridiculous as it actually is.

Shyness. It's like I don't know him anymore, but I do. I know him better than any other guy I've ever been with. I know him better than Andrew, and that's part of why I thought doing this with Ben first would work. Still, my cheeks are flaming, my hands are trembling…

I can't look at him. I can't speak. I can't wrap my head around the fact that this moment of my life that I've wanted for so long is finally here. None of this seems real.

"What are you thinking?" he says. More like whispers. Like he thinks that if he talks too loud I might break. "Do you want to stop?"

"No, I…I definitely don't want to stop."

How do I explain? This only happens once in a girl's life. I'll never be the same after this, not physically or even mentally. Part of me is sad about that. I'm crossing a bridge that will collapse when I reach the other side.

There's no going back.

"Jess…look at me."

I don't move.

Ben nudges my face toward him, and somehow I manage to look up and into his eyes. That snaps me out of it. If I can make eye contact, then I'm not shy. I'm the one in control.

I'm in control. And this is what I want.

I know it might hurt. Or it might not. My two closest friends have already done this, and they each had a different experience. Now…this is mine.

Ours.

He smiles like he knows what just went through my head. Except he couldn't know, not really, he's probably just trying to make me feel more comfortable. And it works.

"Okay," I tell him, then take a deep breath in and out. "I'm ready."

He kisses me, climbing on top of me, caging my body

under his. I look away again, I don't know why. *God.* When I imagined doing this, I wasn't such a chickenshit about it.

"Look at me," Ben says. "Keep your eyes on mine the whole time."

I do as he says, focusing on all the different shades of brown that swirl around his pupils. Every move, every minute, our eyes are connected. So everything else…I just feel.

I just feel.

I just feel.

I just feel.

Until I realize we're both breathing so hard it sounds too loud and ragged in my ears, and the wave is building inside me again, reaching toward a crest. "Benjamin…"

My voice sounds pleading and pained. But I'm not either of those.

"I know," he pants, his eyes still locked on mine. "I got you—"

"Fuck." The world explodes in bright white light around me…inside out…through me…and I'm vaguely aware of Ben saying words I can't understand, like he's really far away… underwater…

Then I realize Ben's about to join me—there's no other explanation for how his perfect rhythm has suddenly become erratic, almost aggressive, and just as suddenly, he's frozen in place, his whole body tightened into stone.

When he relaxes again, still breathing hard but rocking slow, like a carousel horse, I squeeze him closer to me. Squeeze with my arms *and* my legs. We're technically finished, but I don't want to end this yet. I just want to stay here for a moment and linger in the way it feels to be this connected with someone. Not just physically, but…I don't even know how to describe it.

He's done this with so many other girls—and I'd be

stupid to think I'm the first virgin he's been with—but is it weird that I don't care? It doesn't matter what he's done before or what I do with someone else later. What happened here tonight is something only Ben and I shared. We're the only two people who will have this exact memory.

He lifts his head up and looks down at me. "You're smiling."

"So are you," I accuse.

"So I am." He doesn't move, doesn't stop smiling. "You're okay, then?"

My heart is still thumping, and my throat feels a little raw, but the rest of me is...floating. "Yeah, I'm okay."

"Me too," he says, and I start to laugh, but he cuts it off with a quick kiss. Then he's pulling out—which feels really *strange*. No one ever talks about the pulling out, just the pushing in. For so long, I wondered what it was like to be full of someone that I never thought about what it's like to be empty when they go. He lifts himself up and off me, kneeling between my legs, then uses the end of the towel I'm lying on to wipe me clean. So gently.

I can do that myself, but if he wants to do the dirty work while I just lay here, I'm not going to argue.

This is the part that I know very little about. The *after*. This is the part that everyone skips—even my two best friends never mentioned it beyond saying "make sure you go pee" and their initial surprise that their boyfriends actually wanted to cuddle them.

Ben probably won't, though. Our relationship is different. This isn't love or even like with us. It's just sex.

He tugs the towel out from under me, folds it up, and tosses it into my laundry hamper. Then he walks out— completely naked. Another door clicks shut, and I hear the muffled sounds of him moving around in the bathroom.

What is he…

Oh. The condom.

I hear him washing his hands before he comes back to my room, holding a small, clear plastic bag with a rolled-up wad of toilet paper inside. He tosses it into the corner by the door after shutting it and says, "I'll take that with me when I go."

Ben snatches his underwear from the floor, tugs them on and up, then gets back into bed with me. He lies on his side because he has no choice—if he didn't, he'd be half hanging off the mattress. My head is starting to clear now, and my vagina feels like it's been turned inside out.

"I'll be right back," I say, then head to the bathroom.

"Yeah," he mumbles.

After a quick pee, I notice a streak of red on the toilet paper, and I suck in a breath. *This is normal,* I remind myself. *You bleed a hell of a lot more during your period. It's fine.*

I spend a few minutes giving myself a more thorough cleanup, then check my face in the mirror. My hair is an absolute mess. My lips are swollen. My cheeks are actually glowing pink. But it's not like I can see any real difference between Virgin Me and Not-Virgin Me.

So, I guess that's it, then. Now we just do everything we did this week on repeat for the next three weeks? This really wasn't such a big deal.

When I go back to my room, Ben is sleeping. Good. I didn't want things to get awkward. What would we even talk about? All of our conversations this past week have been about sex. We got that covered. There's nothing else in common between us.

I settle in next to him, under the quilt my grandma sent me as a graduation gift, and his bare body is so warm, and the smell of him is so relaxing, and…this is the most comfortable

I've ever been in my own bed. As I close my eyes, I can feel the smile forming on my face again.

It's dark outside when I wake. "What time is it?"

No response.

"Benjamin?" I shift to get a better look at him, trying not to knock him over the edge. He's squished up against me on this tiny mattress, still sleeping.

Correction: he's *snoring*.

Keeping that knowledge up my sleeve in case he ever tries to blackmail me.

I shake his shoulder. "Benjamin, wake up."

He groans but doesn't move. I reach over him and grab my phone off the nightstand.

"It's almost two a.m."

"Oh no," he mumbles into my pillow, then turns only his head. His hair is mussed up in every direction, and his eyes are a little puffy around the edges. "I turn into a gremlin at two a.m."

"You already look and act like a gremlin. I can't imagine you getting much worse."

Ben snatches the pillow up and slaps it at me. And since he's still lying down and still half asleep, it just lands softly at my side. "Wow," I say. "Look at those gremlin skills in action."

In a flash, he pushes himself up and then pounces on top of me. I've barely registered that he actually *moved* when I realize he's also kissing me. Hard.

"Didn't you get enough?" I say through a gasp for breath.

"No such thing."

I twist my mouth. "You really want more now?"

"We have all night, don't we?"

"Yes." I've seen my parents drink—they won't be home before noon tomorrow. But that isn't what made me pause. Even though it only felt like a pinch in the moment, now that some time has passed and all those feel-good hormones aren't flowing anymore, I'm a little sore.

"But you don't want to," Ben says. It's not a question or an accusation, just a statement. "Should I go?"

"Only if you—" I push myself up to sit, hiss out a breath, and immediately flop back down. Okay, I'm more than a little sore. Holy *hell*. Was that his dick inside me or a baseball bat?

"You're in pain."

"I'm—"

Ben is up and off the bed before I can argue. "Tylenol or Advil?"

Sigh. "Either, but we only have the store brand. It's in the bathroom cabinet."

He disappears and returns a minute later, holding two white pills out to me. Completely naked still except for his boxer briefs. He didn't even take a second to get dressed first. Is it sad that this is the nicest thing a boy has ever done for me? Give me some pain meds after pounding my brains out?

I take them, and he gets the water bottle off my nightstand. I take that, too.

"I'm not a toddler." I swallow the pills. "I can take care of myself."

He flashes his hands up, palms out. "Just trying to help."

I know he is, and it's really nice of him. Which is why it's throwing me off.

Ben gets dressed without another word, but before he steps out into the hall, he says, "Was it everything you hoped and dreamed it would be?"

He's looking at me with that fucking grin on his face. The one that says he's god's gift.

Just when I start to think that maybe there's a sweet guy in there somewhere, he pulls this cocky shit and shows me that, nope, he really is an asshole. What does he want me to do, give him a star rating? Is he keeping track of it for future reference in case anyone doubts him?

Ninety-nine out of a hundred teen girls agree: Benjamin Oliver lives up to the hype.

And I would agree, too, make it a solid 100 percent, but his head is big enough already.

"Eh, it was okay." I lift one shoulder in a *whatever* shrug. "But you have three more weeks to keep trying to live up to my fantasies."

As far as jabs go between us, that was less than minor. But I've never seen such a wounded-puppy look on Ben's face before. It's only a flash, but I see it, then his expression goes hard as granite. He walks out, down the stairs, and out the front door.

Great. Now I feel bad—because I didn't tell him the truth, and he thinks I did.

The truth? If I wasn't sore right now, I would have told him to stay all night. I would have told him to get the whole box of condoms from his car.

Because I've read a lot of books about sex, and read articles online from medical doctors and psychologists, and I've seen seven thousand videos about this or that, and absolutely nothing could give justice to the *experience* of it.

He was right. There is no such thing as "enough."

And if I want Ben to be honest with me while we're doing this, then I need to be honest with him, even if it does fuel his huge-gantic ego.

I pick up my phone and send him a text.

Me: *It was amazing, you big jerk.*

Chapter Thirteen

Rayna: *on layover in charlotte will be home in a few hours*

Me: *Woohoo! Girls night!* 🎉🍦🥂😈

Kamy: *Sorry guys I'm sick*

Me: *Ugh.* 😔 *Take care of yourself.* 🖤

Kamy: *Fill me in later?*

Rayna: *nah we'll facetime you*

Kamy: *Kk*

Me: *I can't see you tonight.*

Ben: *you ok*

Me: *Rayna's coming home today so we're having a girls night.*

Ben: *I'll be thinking of what we coulda been doing while I'm in the shower later*

Me: *Thanks now I'll be thinking of THAT while I'm with the girls.*

Ben: *what happens at a girls night anyway*

Me: *We have a contest to see who can give themselves the most orgasms.*

Ben: *are there prizes*
Me: *Participation is also the prize. Everybody wins.*
Ben: *time for my shower bye*

Our version of girls' night is actually just the three of us getting together at Rayna's place to eat ice cream—she keeps salted caramel on hand for me—drink whatever alcohol she happens to sneak from her parents, and bitch about whatever shit happens to be going on in our lives at the moment.

Except the shit happening in my life right now has to stay a secret. And it isn't shit at all.

It's been almost four days since I gave up the full V to Benjamin Oliver, and I've already lost track of how many times we've done it since then. To be fair, I haven't been counting, but still. He'll need a new box of condoms soon if he hasn't already.

Today I won't see him at all, after seeing him every day for over a week, sometimes two or three times in the same day. We've been going at it like wild rabbits. He even took me out to the park on my lunch break yesterday—we never left the car. Now, sitting with Rayna on her bed, eating a bowl of ice cream topped with whipped cream, I keep feeling like I forgot to do something important.

I did. I forgot to do Ben.

The salted caramel ice cream isn't helping, either. It's giving me flashbacks to the Nut Hut. God, was that only last week? Seems like years ago.

"What are you thinking about?" Rayna says. "Your face is all red."

It is?

"Nothing, I'm just a little warm." While eating ice cream

inside an ice-cold air-conditioned room. Totally believable.

Rayna reaches behind her and grabs the can of Reddi-Whip from the floor. There are maybe two bites of ice cream left in her bowl, but she doesn't refill it from the carton before adding a veritable mountain of spray-can whipped cream to it.

Kamy isn't drinking at all—she's had to hang up and call back a few times—and I'm barely halfway through one wine spritzer. But Rayna has been drinking enough for the three of us.

She also has enough shit going on in her life for the three of us, so she's been doing most of the talking.

"Where was I?" Rayna lays on her belly with her bowl of whipped cream, and her next bite hits her nose before she finds her mouth, leaving a blob of it behind, but she doesn't wipe it off. I could tell her, but what's the point in having a best friend who likes to drink if you don't have fun at their expense?

"You almost got caught having phone sex with Jeremy on the beach," I supply.

"Oh! Yes! Right. So the next day, the day before we're supposed to come back, my parents take us all out to a restaurant on the water, we had our own private deck, and it was so cool and the food was worth murdering someone for, and the sun was setting…it was so pretty."

She frowns into her bowl of whipped cream.

This can't be good. She never frowns when she's drunk.

"What happened?" Kamy asks from the tablet set up on the bed.

"It was all a scam," Rayna says. "Me and my little sisters fell right into their parent trap."

I take a sip from my glass. "What kind of parent trap?"

"The divorce kind."

Oh shit.

"I should have known something was up when Dad said 'hey, let's go to Aruba' out of the fucking blue." Rayna rolls her eyes and says, "They thought we wouldn't get upset if we were in a nice place with nice food. They waited until the end of the trip to tell us that was our last vacation together as a family. And that..." She sighs instead of finishing the sentence.

"I'm so sorry, Ray," I tell her. I always thought Rayna had this picture-perfect family. She adores her twin sisters even though they're half her age. I've never seen her parents fight, ever. They take vacations together, they have dinner together every night, they all go to church on Sundays, smiling and happy.

I guess you never really know what's going on with people if they don't show it.

"I'm sorry, too," Kamy says. Right before she hangs up and disappears again. I don't think Rayna notices.

"Thanks, guys." She sniffles. "They said it's going to take a while for the whole process to be done, I'll be in the middle of college before it's over, but it's already started. And I know, it's such a dumb thing to get upset over. It's a normal thing that happens all the time. Half the people in our school had divorced parents, and half the teachers were on their second or third marriage. It's dumb to cry over it."

"It's not dumb. You're not dumb." I lean across the bed and squeeze her into a hug. The blob of whipped cream on her nose smears against my cheek when she pulls back, and Rayna stares at it for a minute, her brows furrowed like she's confused.

Then she busts out laughing.

Then immediately scrunches up her face like she's gonna cry.

"I shouldn't be laughing when my family is..." She mimes

an explosion. "Kaput."

"Don't say kaput," I tell her. "No one says kaput anymore except my dad."

"It's a good word, Jessie." And now she's smiling again.

A devious smile. Like she's planning something nefarious.

She grabs the can of Reddi-Whip, shakes it up, and aims it at my face.

"Don't—"

A rocket of whipped cream launches toward me before I can get my hands up. It's in my eyes. It's up my nose. It's in my mouth. It's dripping off my chin in a slow *plop…plop…*

"Mrs. Doubtfire!" Rayna points at my face, laughing so hard she not only snorts like a donkey but also falls over onto her side, holding her stomach like she's in pain.

I shake my head at her. "You're an infant, you know that? A drunk little baby."

She just keeps squealing and snorting and ends up on her back, kicking her legs.

Which means she's in trouble.

I swipe the unexpected facial dessert off my eyes and snatch the can of whipped cream, then scoot up next to her, kneeling, looking down at her wide-open mouth.

Ready. Aim. *Fire.*

She splutters and screams and spits, and there is white stuff flying everywhere now.

I lick my lips. "Revenge is sweet."

"Oh yeah?" Rayna jumps up from the bed and runs over to her desk to get her phone. She holds it up and I hear a *click.*

"Did you just take a picture of me?"

"Yes! And I'm sending it to—"

"No one." I jump and charge toward her.

"Kamy," she finishes.

"Okay, fine, you can send it to Kamy. But no one else." I

turn and walk to her adjacent bathroom.

After splashing my face with water seventeen times, my phone chimes with a text.

Rayna: *guess who*

What? She sent that to our group chat with the guys. There's a picture downloading…

"Rayna, I'm going to murder you!" I run back out from the bathroom—and find her sleeping on the bed. I should leave her alone. She's dealing with a lot, and I can't really hold anything against her that she does or says when she's drunk.

The picture of me appears in the chat. Everything is covered in cream except my hair, my eyes, and an open space where my mouth would be. You can almost see my tongue inside.

Todd: *Only two people in this group are blonde and I'm one of them*

Jeremy: *Is that Jessie?*

Ben: *ofc it's Jessie it smells like blackmail*

Me: *DO NOT*

Jeremy: 🤣🤣🤣

Jeremy: *What's on your face Jess?*

Ben: *gotta be either whipped cream or a beauty mask*

Todd: *It could be jizz*

Ben: *it isn't*

Jeremy: *How would you know?*

Ben: *bc this is Jessie we're talking about*

Me: *FFS. This is girls night. No boys and their jizz allowed.*

Me: *You weren't supposed to see this!*

But they did.

I grab the Reddi-Whip again and use it to "draw" eyebrows onto Rayna's face. And a mustache. And a beard. Then I use her own phone to take a picture of her and send it.

Me: *Not even the most skilled boy could do this while ejaculating.*

Jeremy: *How would you know?*

Todd: *Are you guys drunk?*

Ben: *has Jess ever used the word ejaculating when she's sober*

Todd: *I didn't even think she knew that word.* 🤣

Me: 🖕 🖕 🖕

Ben: *knock knock*

Me: *WTF are you at my house? It's after midnight.*

Ben: *the correct response is who's there*

Me: 🙄 *I'm sleeping.*

Ben: *you're texting*

Me: *Fine. Who's there?*

Ben: *water*

Me: *Water who?*

Ben: *water you doing Friday night*

Me: *You.*

Ben: *the correct response is going to the movies*

Me: *With you?*

Ben: *me you Jeremy Rayna Kamy Todd*

Me: *Then no hooking up.*

Ben: *not exactly*

Me: *What does that mean?*

Me: *Benjamin?*

Me: *Stop ignoring me.*

Me: *I'm not dropping my pants in a movie theater!*

Ben: *wear a skirt*

Chapter Fourteen

*R*ayna picks me up around six p.m. on Friday. We're going to the next town over, where the biggest, most luxurious theater in the county is. They even have an app that lets you order refills on your drinks and popcorn during the movie, and they'll bring it to you.

The only thing missing is a piss bin built into the chairs.

"Hi, Jessie," Kamy says from the back seat of Rayna's car.

I turn to look at her. "I thought you were sick."

"Not anymore, thank fuck. My mom was this close to forcing her homemade herbal detox on me if I didn't get better."

"Yike," Rayna says. "Sounds like it was serious."

"Did you go to a doctor?" I ask.

"No doctor," she says. "My parents don't believe in doctors. Not the hospital kind, anyway."

"Do they believe in death? Because you could have died from puking so much."

Rayna snorts. "Feeling morbid tonight, Jessie?"

No, actually, I'm feeling sexually frustrated and anxious as fuck.

This whole trip to the movies has me on edge, which could have been partially avoided if I'd seen Ben yesterday, like we were supposed to. For the first time since we started this thing, he canceled. And when I asked him why, he said it was nothing. That means it's *something*. He just doesn't want to tell me.

If he was hooking up with another girl, I will draw and quarter him, starting with his balls. We have a deal. This is *my* time with him, no one else's.

He still hasn't called in the favor I owe him for this, though. I don't think he'd risk losing that to do something with another girl that he would have been doing with me anyway.

So not only am I trying to figure out what he's hiding, but also we've gone two full days without even a heated look between us. Plus, all of today. If we can't find a way to do something at the movies—I don't even care what it is at this point, I'll take anything that involves part of his body touching part of mine—then we've lost three perfectly good days.

Three days.

I've chewed my fingernails down to nubs. I'm a big-ass grump right now.

But I shouldn't take that out on Kamy just because her parents are weird.

"It was probably just food poisoning," she says. "My dad's been experimenting with new recipes again."

"Okay." I sigh. "Sorry for being overprotective and sensitive. I worry about you."

"Don't apologize for that, Jessie." She scoots up behind my seat and wraps her arms around it. And me. "I like that you care."

The rest of the drive is quiet, and when we finally get there and park, Rayna gives me a long, hard look instead of getting out of the car.

"What are you so nervous about?" she says.

"I'm not nervous."

"Your leg is bouncing, and you've been eating your fingertips like snacks since I picked you up. If that isn't nerves, then it's drugs. Are you high?"

"I'm not high, Ray." I'm starting to wish I was, though.

She throws her hands up. "Then what's going on?"

"Nothing, I'm just—"

Kamy opens the back door and trots out to meet Todd in the parking lot. He swallows her up in a bear hug, and she practically disappears behind his arms.

The guys are here. All three of them.

I catch Ben looking this way, all cool like he *isn't* devising some wackadoodle plan to get me naked here. He doesn't smile or even smirk. Alarm bells go off in my head.

Rayna follows my gaze across the parking lot. Fortunately, Jeremy is standing right by Ben, and she says, "We'll talk later," then hustles out of the car like Kamy did.

I take in a deep breath and let it out slowly. My fingernails look like shit.

I did wear a dress, though, like he suggested. A cotton summer dress like the one I wore to our ice cream escapade, but this one is baby blue gingham. When I get out of the car, the skirt swishes just below my knees.

I catch up to the group, and we head to the entrance.

"Nice dress, witch," Ben says. "Did you kill Dorothy for it?"

"Still searching for your brain, scarecrow?"

The running gag between us came out so naturally, I don't realize what we just said to each other until a few steps later, when he opens the door to the theater and holds it for everyone.

Except me. It closes right in my face.

He smirks at me through the glass, gives me a little finger-wave, and turns and walks off. Just leaving me out here alone while everyone else goes through the ticket check.

What the hell?

Ben hasn't acted like this much of a dick to me since our last day of school.

Why? Because we're with our friends now?

Oh…

Maybe he's just throwing them off so when we disappear later, they won't think we disappeared *together*.

If that's it, then I will gladly play this game.

I open the door, and the smell of buttery popcorn hits me like a punch. A really delicious, mouthwatering kick to the head. After checking my ticket, I find everyone else at the concession area, buying drinks and snacks.

"Is Ben messing with you already?" Rayna says.

"Do you really have to ask?"

She laughs. "Maybe he just misses you."

"Right," I snort. Not possible. We've been seeing more of each other in the last two weeks than we had in the last few months.

Rayna steps up to Jeremy at the counter to make sure he gets zero-sugar Coke and extra butter on their popcorn, the same thing she always gets. I hang back and wait for them all to finish taking for granted how easy it is for them to buy whatever they want without looking at the prices. I have a decent weekly paycheck, now that I'm working more hours at the library, but I still hate spending on myself when it's not a necessity. This is entertainment. What if I need that money for a future emergency?

Paying for the movie ticket alone was painful enough.

Jeremy and Rayna are sharing a tub of popcorn, Todd and Kamy are sharing a mega tub of popcorn—at least 90 percent of it will end up in Todd's gut. And Ben glances at me over his shoulder.

"Popcorn?" he says.

"I don't want your charity, Benjamin—"

"It's Ben—"

"I have my own money," I finish.

"I'm buying it whether you eat it or not. But if you are, I need to get the big bucket so you don't get your greasy little monkey hands all over mine."

Yeah, the same greasy little monkey hands that were all over his naked flesh three nights ago, and he didn't have one complaint. I bite my lip to keep from calling him out on it. He is such a shit.

"Fine," I say. "Not too much salt."

He grins. "I know, there's enough salt in you already."

"Only when I'm with you." I give him a wide, toothy, plastic smile.

He presses his hand to his chest, over his heart. "I'm touched."

This always happens when we're out with all six of us. Ben and I are forced to be civil and share things, because the other four are already paired up. I can count on one hand the number of times we've been out with the group and had our own dates to bring. Ben is rarely with the same girl long enough to include her on a friend date. And me...I'm rarely with anyone, period. Most of the time, we're like two third wheels. With rusty spikes.

At the movies, sharing popcorn requires us to sit right next to each other, which always creates tension. I usually focus on the movie and pretend he isn't there. Sitting in the dark helps.

Tonight? There's a different kind of tension. One that has my heart pounding and my palms sweating and concentrating really hard on making it seem like I'm breathing normal.

A few minutes later, we find our seats — all the way up in the back — and Ben whispers, "Sit next to the wall."

Next to the wall...not close to the aisle.

Why?

Fuck.

What is he planning on doing with me *in the seats*? I assumed we'd have to maneuver a way out of here to find a janitor's closet or something. He already made it clear that public-bathroom sex is a no. But he wants to do it *right here*? With our friends sitting *right there*?

I scoot past Rayna and Jeremy and go all the way to the opposite end, by the wall. Rayna gives me a quick "WTF are you doing" look, but I pretend I didn't see it and just sit down. The seats in this place are cushy recliners. It's more comfortable than if I watch something at home.

Usually.

Now, my whole body feels stretched taut as a drum, like my skin is too small. And I'm burning from the inside out.

Ben settles in next to me and puts the popcorn bucket on the arm rests between us. "Cozy."

"This isn't going to work," I whisper harshly.

"It will if we're quiet." He puts a finger to his lips. "Shhhhh."

"So we're back to the no-talking rule."

"Yes, but the 'say stop if you want to stop' rule still applies."

"Okay." I blow out a breath. At least he hasn't gone *completely* bananas.

He pulls a tiny bottle of hand sanitizer out of his pocket, squirts a blob into his palm, then holds it out to me and does the same. It's just because we're eating popcorn, I tell myself. He's not actually going to *touch* me here. Not like that.

No matter how much I want him to.

"What are you two whispering about over there?" Jeremy says.

Ben doesn't miss a beat. "World domination."

With a laugh, Jeremy shakes his head. "If you two ever really do join forces, the world is doomed."

"We'd be unstoppable," Ben says, then drops a handful of popcorn into his mouth.

"Unstoppable misery," I retort. "You're safe, Jeremy, don't worry. It'll never happen. I'd rather eat a dozen raw eggs, shells and all, and shit out a full-grown chicken than work together with Benjamin on anything."

Ben leans toward me without turning and whispers, "Liar, liar."

I flash my middle finger at him, and he says, "Exactly my point." Then he angles his body so his back is facing Jeremy, leans in, and sucks the tip of my finger into his mouth. One swirl of his hot tongue and then he's pulling back again, his face completely neutral. While I'm on the verge of hyperventilating.

My cheeks flush hot. The lights need to go out now, before I give us away. Thankfully, Ben starts talking to Jeremy about whatever—who cares, as long as it gets his attention off me for two seconds so I can breathe. I recline my chair back until I can easily see my feet in front of me, then Ben turns his head to take another handful of popcorn and does a double take when he sees my feet. I'm wearing open-toe wedge sandals from the thrift store and drugstore nail polish.

Red.

It's the first time I've worn fire-engine-red polish on my toes, but that can't be it.

He turns back to Jeremy without explaining what surprised him. Weird. It's not like he's never seen my feet before. It's not like he hasn't kissed them, even, or had them up on his shoulders while he's—

Stop that thought right there. I stuff a handful of popcorn into my mouth and *crunch, crunch, crunch* until the lights finally dim down and the movie previews start. The actual movie we came to see will start in about seventeen years. Roughly.

I'm not super invested in this movie, anyway. It's another superhero in the same mega-verse we've seen in movies since we were kids. I'm over it. But our resident comic book nerds, Jeremy and Todd, really wanted to see this one, and none of us could find anything better, so here we are.

Ben reclines his chair until it's even with mine, like we're lying down next to each other.

We're both fully clothed, and in public, and I've been in this position with him a thousand times before, except naked, skin touching skin. I shouldn't be so anxious. This is nothing compared to all we've done already, in only two weeks. But when Ben turns his head toward me in the dark, his eyes so full of heat he's going to set off the fire alarm if he doesn't quit it, and whispers, "Don't move; don't make a sound," I don't know the details of what he's about to do to me, but I do know one thing for sure.

I'm going to enjoy every second of it.

Chapter Fifteen

*T*wo hours later, the theater lights brighten and the credits roll. I adjust my seat from the reclining position until I'm sitting up straight, then give Ben a hard glare. "I hate you so much right now."

The asshole smiles at that.

"All you did was tease me!" I say as vehemently as I can without anyone else hearing. "It would have been better if we did nothing here."

No, actually, it would have been better if we'd sat on the aisle and then snuck out. Even if we couldn't find anywhere in the theater to do something, we could have gone to his car.

"The night is young," Ben says, then stands and exits down the aisle with everyone else.

It really isn't fair. He barely touched me, and it was somehow hotter than if he'd asked me to straddle him. He'd go for several minutes without so much as an "accidental" brush of his hand, knowing the torture it put me through to just sit there anticipating his next move.

Sweet torture.

"You coming, Jess?" Ben says from the aisle.

"I wish," I mutter, then raise my voice and add a note of sarcasm. "Yes, dear!"

When I catch up to him, I get close and whisper, "It isn't exactly easy to walk right now."

"You and me both," he says with zero shame, then adjusts his shorts.

"We really need to finish this—"

He stops and turns to face me. "We will."

"But we're leaving."

"Yep." He turns and walks ahead of me again.

I have to hustle to catch up, and when I get to the lobby, I'm the last one from our group. We exit to the parking lot en masse. Jeremy and Todd are already picking apart every detail of the movie that they liked or didn't like. I honest-to-Jesus can't even remember seeing any of it.

The sun isn't going down yet, but still, the air is cooler now, comfortable.

"It's a nice night," Ben says to no one in particular. "We should go to the park."

I shoot him a questioning look, but he's not turned this way.

"Why, what's at the park?" Rayna says.

Ben grins. "I brought edibles."

"Sold!" Todd shouts, and everyone else chimes in with agreement.

We're going to the park to get high. How this plays into Ben's plan, I have no clue. Especially when he can't even join us in the fun—he's one of our drivers tonight. We have a rule that whoever drives the carpool is agreeing to be the DD if we drink or anything else like that.

And somehow, as we head back to the cars, I end up in Ben's car with him. Alone. Todd literally never leaves Kamy's side when they're in sight of each other, and Jeremy hops into Rayna's car with the three of them without even asking me if he could take my spot. I'm just standing here in the aisle of the parking lot, arms crossed, wondering if this is a blessing or a curse. "Your chariot awaits," Ben says, leading me to his car.

Sigh.

Once we're inside, Ben starts the engine but doesn't go anywhere.

"What are you waiting for?" I say.

"For Rayna's car to disappear."

"Why— *Oh.*" I turn my head slowly and look to the back seat. "Should we get in the—"

Ben snatches my jaw with both hands and pulls me toward him, smothering me with his mouth as soon as my lips meet his. I instantly melt against him and lose myself in a dizzying mix of the scent of him, the *sound* of him, all those guttural noises he makes in the back of his throat, telling me *yes, more.* No matter how many times I've kissed this boy, every single one is better than the last.

I try to lean my body against him, but there's a reason why I prefer the back seat to the front. The gear shift, the drink console, all those buttons everywhere... Too much to work around up here. I pull back, my lips as swollen and sensitive as other parts of me now, and maneuver into the middle so I can crawl into the back seat.

Ben snatches my arm. "Not here. Not now."

"Please tell me you're joking."

He buckles his seat belt. "If we don't show up soon, they'll be suspicious. Even taking that extra minute was risky."

Dammit. "Then why did you do it?"

"I don't know," he says flatly. "Maybe because I just spent the last two hours feeling you up in the dark? I had to vent some of that frustration."

"I'm going to need medical attention if you don't stop all this teasing." I fall back into my seat and buckle up.

"I'll take that as a 'thank you.'" Ben eases us out of the lot. "Stop pouting."

"I'm not pouting."

"Yes, you are," he says with a laugh. "It's—"

"Don't you dare say it's adorable."

He mimes locking his lips and throwing away the key.

I blow out a breath. "Do you actually have a plan here? Because if this unending foreplay is all you had in mind for tonight, just take me home now and I'll finish it myself."

"Don't tempt me," he says. "I'll stick around and watch."

Thanks, jackass. Now I have that image in my head, and it is. *Not.* Helping.

You know what? I really don't have to put up with this torture. Not sober, anyway. I open the center console between us and—BINGO—find a small plastic jar of gummy bears. I pick it up and unscrew the cap, and Ben doesn't stop me, so I grab two gummies and pop them both into my mouth at once.

"Easy, Jess."

I swallow. "I'm fine, I know my limits." I turn in my seat to look at him. "Do you think we'll get caught?"

"It's always possible." He grins. "That's part of the fun of it."

Hell no it isn't. How can I enjoy myself if I'm terrified of being seen the whole time? At least in the movie theater we had darkness to hide us, and the fact that everyone was intently looking forward at a giant, colorful distraction.

And besides, any guy I would be in a serious relationship with, like Andrew, probably isn't going to want to do anything public. What is even the point of this lesson?

"In fact," he goes on, slowing as we turn onto the road into the park, "the more times you don't get caught, the more likely you'll get caught the next time. That's just the law of averages at work. It's a simple ratio of frequency and probability."

"If you say so." Does he even know how nerd-hot he is right now? I'm getting warm and flushed all over again. If he starts explaining quantum theory, I will combust.

Ben parks and snatches the jar of gummies from me. He's out of the car before I've even unbuckled my seat belt. What's the rush? It's not like we're going to have sex on the playground.

Actually, I don't know how we're going to have sex here at all...

I give up. Whatever happens, happens. I'm done mentally exhausting myself over it.

Ben is already with the group, sitting on a bench, and I've still got a little ways to go. He must have done that on purpose so we didn't walk up together. By the time I catch up, everyone is passing around the jar of gummies. Rayna doesn't take any because she's the other DD, but she hands the open jar to me next.

"No, I'm good," I tell her. "I had some on the way over."

"Lucky you." She hands the jar to Kamy, who doesn't take any, either, before holding it out to Todd. He takes the jar, tips his head back, and shakes a few gummies into his mouth. Rayna is oblivious to all of it. "Did Ben behave himself? I didn't even realize you weren't with us until we were halfway here."

"Gee, that's comforting."

She rolls her eyes. "I thought you were squished in the back with Kamy and Todd."

"It's fine, Ray. I survived. There's only so much havoc he can wreak when he's driving."

"You feeling okay?" Rayna says. "You look flushed."

I take in a deep breath and blow it out, smiling, then do a spin so my skirt flares out. "I feel awesome, actually."

"How many gummies did you eat?" She laughs.

"Only two, I swear." It's not the gummies—it's too soon—which means the effects of Benjamin Oliver's teasing are written all over me. I grab her hand. "Let's go on the swings!"

We take off, laughing too hard, stumbling too many times, and not caring one shit. There are only two swings left unoccupied, and they're right next to each other. Score. I plop down on the flexible seat. It squeezes my legs together. Then, holding onto the chains, I walk backward as far as I can until my feet leave the ground—and I launch forward.

"Wheee!"

I float backward, light as a feather, and someone pushes me from behind. I soar higher and higher.

"Who the fuck—"

"I got you, Jess," Ben says, giving me another strong push.

"Benjamin!" I squeal. "Not too high!"

"It's Ben." When my back meets his hands again, he shoves me even harder. My feet touch the clouds.

It's Ben...

He's said that to me twice tonight, but I've called him Benjamin more than two times. Why didn't he correct me *every* time like he used to?

I try to think as he continues pushing me steadily, keeping me high.

Whoosh. Push. Whoosh. Fly.

Every time I get close to him, his scent grabs onto me and I carry it back up.

I can't remember if Ben ever corrected me on his name while we were getting busy in my bedroom, or even just talking or texting privately. I called him Benjamin in the car on the way over here, and he didn't correct me. But now... and earlier, right before the movie...

It's happened so many times since we first met—the whole "Benjamin / It's Ben" line is what turned our meet-cute into a meet-hate—that it just became normal whenever we spoke around each other. Or at each other. After a while, it wasn't even worth acknowledging anymore.

What changed?

Whoosh. Push. Whoosh. Fly…

It's starting to get dark, and people are leaving. Technically, the park doesn't close until an hour after sunset, so we're not going anywhere yet.

Rayna and Jeremy are doing barrel rolls down a grassy hill, laughing their asses off. Kamy is sitting on Todd's lap on a bench farther away, talking about something I can't hear. I'm leaning up against a tree, watching everyone, and I could sit here all night just feeling the breeze whisper over my arms and legs. The air smells like honeysuckle.

My phone buzzes in my dress pocket, tingling the side of my leg. I must not have turned the sound back on after the movie. I pull my phone out and unlock it.

Ben: *can you get away without anyone noticing*

I look around, but the dwindling light makes it hard to clearly see much farther than maybe ten or fifteen feet. Where is he? Last I remember, he was doing handstands and his shirt kept falling down, exposing his bare chest. It was mesmerizing. When did he stop doing that and disappear?

Me: *I think so.*

Ben: *meet me at the pavilion*

What…? I push off from the tree and scan the area again, spinning. There are a lot of trees in this park, and a lot of buildings scattered around. The pavilion is hard to miss, though. It's the only thing with a roof but no walls. I can't see where Ben is from here, but I guess I have to trust him. Again.

It's been getting easier to do that lately.

I cast one more glance at the others to make sure they aren't looking my way, then step off as quietly as I can until I've gone what I think is ten feet. Then I run. As well as I can in wedge sandals, anyway.

It takes me about five seconds that feel like five years.

But when I reach the empty pavilion, I still don't see Ben anywhere. I pad around a few picnic tables, then pass a brick pillar. As soon as it's behind me, someone grabs my hand.

"Hey—"

"Shhh." Ben's eyes meet mine, and in that split second, an understanding passes between us with startling accuracy. He sweeps me in close to him and captures my mouth with his.

The kiss is rough and full of urgency and *god*, I don't want it to end. All I can smell now is Ben. All I can feel, hear, taste…

He pulls away quickly, releasing my lips with a sucking noise. "Follow me."

I nod even though it wasn't a question, and following him is as natural as breathing. He hasn't let go of my hand, so I keep a tight squeeze on his. He tugs me along the grass, weaving between the wide trunks of giant oak trees, until we reach a small brick building far from anything else.

"Inside?" I say.

"No, it's locked." He leads me around to the back. The only part of the park that's close on this side is a tall fence, so no one can see anything from there, but I still feel like we're out in the open. I need walls around me. "Here," Ben says.

We step around a little part of the building that juts out and creates a small, three-sided alcove with an opening just large enough to walk through. There's a showerhead near the top of one wall.

Well…if people feel safe enough to shower in here…

Ben lifts me by the hips, and I instinctively wrap my legs and arms around him so I won't fall. His hands move to hold me up by my ass. Then he's kissing me again. In another second, rough brick is pressing against my back. Every new sensation shoots me higher and higher. I can practically touch the moon.

And now I get what the point of this lesson is — confidence. The risk of getting caught makes every second that we haven't been caught more risky. The longer we get away with this, the stronger I feel. This is the biggest confidence boost Ben has given me so far.

"Right here?" I pant. "Like this?"

"Are you ready?" he says. "This is gonna be a quickie."

That didn't answer my question, but…

"Benjamin, I was ready three days ago. Quit stalling."

He smiles and says, "Yes, ma'am."

Sweet Jesus.

He sets me on the ground, pulls a condom out of his pocket, then drops his shorts and gloves himself in record time. He starts to lift the skirt of my dress.

"Wait," I say. "Let me get my underwear."

I hold myself up with my palm against the brick, then use my other hand to reach under my skirt and tug down my panties. I get as far as my knee when I need to lift up a leg. In these wedge sandals. And so dizzy from arousal that I wobble on one leg and my underwear gets tangled in my shoe — the one I'm holding up.

For a second I just stand there like a drunk flamingo, unsure what to do. Ben is more than ready to go, and I'm acting like this is the first time I've undressed myself.

What was I just thinking about a confidence boost? One dumb move and I'm plummeting into the pit of insecurity again.

"Help," I say. "I'm stuck."

Ben laughs, which makes me laugh, because I can only imagine what we look like right now. It takes him three attempts to detangle my panties, with me nearly falling over twice, before succeeding. He drops them on top of his own underwear and shorts, which are down at his ankles.

"You good?" he says, and I nod quickly.

He lifts me up against the wall again, holding my legs around him, but with just one push, I'm telling him, "Stop."

He freezes. "What is it?"

"The brick," I say. "It's going to take my skin off if we do it this way."

"Sorry." Ben lowers me slowly until my feet touch the ground.

"Is it always this difficult in a public place, or is it just the combination of you and me together that's taking the sexy out of it?"

Ben laughs at that. "There's plenty of sexy left, we'll figure it out. Maybe we could…" He gives me a wicked grin, then says, "Turn around."

"Um…okay." I turn so I'm facing the brick now, and Ben is behind me. He pulls me by the hip with one hand and gently presses my back down with the other, forcing me to bend over with my palms planted against the wall, my arms straight out on either side of my head.

Oh god. Is he doing what I think he's doing? We've only done it this way once before, and it was intense. I told him we had to space these out.

Well. It's been three days of nothing. That's spaced out enough.

"Ready?" he says.

"Ready."

Ben flips my skirt up onto my back and—

"Oh god!"

"Too much?" he asks, his voice breathy.

"No, it's…" It's like my entire body has been electrified all at once. I don't know if that's because he teased me for so long before this, or because of the position? Both? All I know is I want him to, "Keep going."

"Yes, ma'am."

The rest of it happens so fast, all I can do is surrender to it. To *him*. The world blurs and disappears. It's just us, in this moment.

It's just us…

And almost as quickly as we climbed, we're falling back down. My breaths come so hard that my throat feels raw. I taste…blood? My god, I bit my lip.

I'm boneless. If not for Ben's arms around my middle I'd be a puddle of goo on the concrete right now. His breath is hot and heavy on the back of my neck, sending chills down my spine even though I'm sweating. I blink my eyes open and see my red-painted toes, remember the look on his face when he noticed them.

Ben hasn't said a word. He hasn't moved.

"Are you okay?" I ask, glancing at him over my shoulder.

"Yeah," he says. "I just needed a minute."

He pulls away and drops my skirt back into place, then helps me get my underwear back on. I turn, lean against the wall, and watch him pull his shorts up then toss the condom into a trash can just outside the alcove.

Now what? I guess we need to go find our friends before they notice we're gone. But there's a slight problem.

"I don't think I can walk yet," I say.

Ben stands with his whole back against the brick, then tugs me over into his arms. I rest my head on his chest. Feel his heartbeat. *Thump-thump, thump-thump, thump-thump*. And my breathing finally slows. He strokes his fingers through my hair, rubs circles on my back, kisses the top of my head so softly, I almost missed it. I've never been treated like something precious before.

This is quite possibly the most romantic moment of my life.

And it shatters like overheated glass when both of our phones go off at the same time. Ben gets his out first. "It's Jeremy. He wants to know where the fuck I am."

"Say you just met a really hot girl and couldn't pass up the opportunity to get some."

He grins. "It's not a lie."

"Shut up," I tease, pulling my phone out from my pocket. "Rayna. Asking where the fuck I am." I look up at Ben. "What should we do?"

He's still smiling at me, then he laughs when he says, "I have no idea."

Chapter Sixteen

"Jessie!" Rayna shouts in the distance, followed by Todd's booming voice yelling from a different direction.

"OLIVER! You're my ride home, you fucker!"

Ben peeks around the wall of the alcove. "Jeremy and Rayna are to the left. Todd and Kamy are to the right. I think we can get past them using the trees as cover."

"I don't know…" I start, but then Ben is tugging me along by the hand, and I have to trot to keep up. I'm one misstep away from a trip to the emergency room. "Hey, some of us here are in extremely inappropriate footwear to play turbo hide-and-seek. *Slow down*."

"Sorry," he says. Then abruptly stops by a tree trunk wide enough to hide us both. As long as we're on top of each other. Ben squeezes me against him, then dares a peek around the tree. "Shit, Jeremy's right there."

"Maybe he's still high."

"Fingers crossed."

"And toes," I say.

"This isn't funny, Jessie!" Rayna shouts, and I tuck in closer to Ben's chest.

He looks down at me with a smirk. "Did I mention you're giving me a foot fetish with that toenail polish tonight?"

"Why? Because it's red?"

"Dear, sweet, innocent Jessica," he says with a tsk. "It's not just red. It's fuck-me red."

"Actually, it's red number 762, fire engine frenzy."

"I'll buy you a case of it," he says, and then we're off and running again.

I'm trying to keep from laughing on the outside as much as I am on the inside, with this warm, bubbly feeling in my gut and a smile so big my cheeks hurt. Sneaking around with Ben isn't terrifying at all, even though we can easily get caught at any moment. It's a thrill. It's…freeing.

He was right—this does make it fun.

And I can't imagine doing this with someone else, not even Andrew. It's just very *Ben* of him to turn a quickie in the park into a game.

Up ahead, between the trees, the sunset paints the sky in pink and purple hues that blend into midnight blue farther up. It's so pretty—

We stop again, panting hard. There's a sheen of sweat on Ben's forehead.

I lay my cheek on his chest and watch the sun sink down, down, down—

"Come on!" He pulls me into another run, and I let out a yelp.

"Did you hear that?" Jeremy says distantly, but no one replies. It's getting so dark now, I can't see anyone or anything that isn't right in front of us. But since Ben apparently has night-vision superpowers, I don't need to.

There's that trust thing again. It keeps creeping up on me.

"Okay," Ben says, "we have to split up now."

"What—"

"You stay here. I'll go to my car and then pull around, like I've been waiting for them all this time so we can go. Then you find Rayna and act like you've been looking for her and you've been so worried, blah blah blah. Make it believable."

I swallow back my arguments because there's no time to voice them. We are so screwed.

"Okay, go," I tell him, accepting my fate.

"Just one more thing." He holds both my hands with both of his and weaves our fingers together. "If this doesn't work and we get caught, was it worth it? Was...I worth it?"

My first thought is he wants me to stroke his ego again. But when I look in his eyes, I don't see the cocky boy I know he can be. Instead, I see a vulnerability that Benjamin Oliver has never shown before. At least not to me. Maybe not to anyone.

We're enemies who sometimes get along.

Or we're friends who just like to fight.

Either way, my answer is the same.

"You're worth it, Benjamin." I push up onto my toes and kiss him, maybe for the last time. "Now please get your sexy ass out of here."

"Yes, ma'am." He gives me that trademark grin, his teeth flashing white in the dark, and then he's gone. He's the same Ben he's always been, and I'm the same me. But the two of us together...sometime over the last two weeks...we've become something totally new.

Maybe that's a good thing. What we're doing now has an end date, but that doesn't mean our relationship has to end. Maybe we could still be friends.

Would it be weird? To be Andrew's girlfriend and still be friends with the guy who secretly taught me all the basics? What if they meet...

I wait until I can't see him anymore, then I head off in no particular direction and call for Rayna. I send her a text telling her where I am, and *oh, sorry, I must have lost my signal, I only just got your message.*

And it works.

I nearly give myself an aneurism from holding in all my excitement.

Hallefuckinglujah it worked!

Me: *I had fun tonight.*
Ben: *me too*
Me: *If anyone asks I'll deny it.*
Ben: *me too*

We're three weeks into my Sexology 101 with Professor Oliver now and still encountering new things. I got my period yesterday.

Because the first day is always the worst, I told him I wasn't feeling well and we couldn't meet up. Not even close to a lie. The cramps. The bloating. The bleeding. Did I mention the *cramps*? I actually called in sick to work.

But by the end of day two, it's already on the upswing and existing as a female human is bearable again. I told Ben I'm feeling better—because I am—so he's on his way over tonight, but I'm not sure how *he's* going to feel about meeting my Aunt Flo.

Not literally. Ew. I need to tell him, though, before he even thinks about putting on a condom. That kind of sex just isn't happening today.

And he could be one of those boys who doesn't even want to be in the same room with a girl on her period, let alone touch her. There's only one way to find out. I have to drop it on him without warning to see his instinctive, caught-off-guard, gut reaction.

My parents left five minutes ago, so Ben will be here any second now—

Ben: *knock knock*

Me: *It's open. I'm in the bathroom.*

There's his first hint that something is different tonight. I'm in the bathroom instead of waiting for him on the bed. New tampon in, a quick freshen-up, and I'll be ready. As soon as I hear Ben on the stairs, I give myself a last once-over in the mirror. Nothing out of place, nothing different than the usual—my hair is up in a bun, my cotton tee and shorts could pass for pajamas, and my face is as naked as the day I was born.

One thing I've learned from all this sex with Ben? You don't have to be all dolled up to get some—forgetting to shave your legs isn't a dealbreaker. You don't need special underwear—cotton is pulled off as easily as satin. You don't even have to be especially pretty—your face is involved but only one of several parts. You do have to be willing and able.

And you need that spark happening between you.

I step out of the bathroom and into my bedroom. Ben is lying back on my bed, flipping through another Dr. Seuss book. "What is your fascination with those?" I say.

"What's yours?" he counters. "You're the one with the collection here."

"Nostalgia." I snatch the book from his hands and put it back on the shelf.

Ben sits up. "You sure you're feeling better? You don't need another day to rest?"

"Yeah...about that." I sit next to him on the bed, turning my body to face him. "I wasn't sick in the way you probably thought I was sick. I'm feeling tons better today, but yesterday…I was on my period. I still am."

He doesn't flinch.

He doesn't speak.

He doesn't even blink.

"How do you feel about that?" I ask.

"About what? The fact you're a woman with a working uterus and this is totally normal? Or something else?"

So, my bleeding from his favorite orifice doesn't bother him. That's a relief.

"Something else," I say. "How do you feel about doing what we do here while I'm on my period?"

He nods slowly, like he's thinking, and rubs a palm down his thigh. "I'm not sure. I've never been in this situation before, so I don't really know what—"

"Wait, stop right there." I hold up my hand, palm out. "All the girls you've been with, and you've *never* come across this situation before? *How?*"

He shrugs. "I'm not usually with the same girl more than a week or two. So, I guess it was either a timing thing or they just didn't tell me. You're the first."

I'm the first.

I'm *his* first with something.

"This is amazing," I say through a laugh. "I can't believe it."

"Believe what?"

"That *I* get to teach *you* something now."

He rolls his eyes but with a smile. "You are such a dork."

"A dork." I snort. "Is that the worst you can do? You're off your game, Benjamin."

"No games tonight," he says. "I have questions. First, what can we do or not do?"

"I can't speak for other girls, but for me, there's only two things we really can't do. The rest is negotiable—"

I hear the front door open and close downstairs, followed by, "Jessica! Are you here?"

Both of us snap our heads to the closed door and freeze.

"Oh my god, that's my mom," I say to Ben. "You have to get out of here!"

"I thought you said your parents are out tonight."

"They are! I mean, they're supposed to be. They left and now they're back and I don't know why but—"

"Jessica?" Footsteps march up the stairs.

Oh fuck oh fuck oh fuck.

I pull Ben up and off my bed and shove him into my closet.

"Jess—"

"Don't. Move." I slam the door closed just as my mother opens the other door from the hallway. She's picture-perfect, as always. Not a hair out of place, not a wrinkle on her clothes.

"Mom? What are you— Is everything okay, do you need something?"

Breathe, Jessie.

She gives me a skeptical stare, and I literally *gulp*. But then her face relaxes and she says, "No, I just forgot something, but when I called and you didn't answer, I got worried. I know you're having a bad time of the month—"

Jesus, Mom. Ben can hear all of this! There's a huge difference between me telling him about my period and him hearing about it from my goddamn *mother*.

Also, for the record? There is no such thing as a good period. They're all bad.

"—and if there's anything you want us to pick up for you while we're out, just shoot me a text, okay?"

"Does a hysterectomy count as 'anything,'" I say.

She doesn't miss a beat. "Not before you're at least thirty years old and have had at least one pregnancy scare to let you know how you really feel about having kids. I'm sorry, we have to go, we're already late. Take it easy tonight, okay? Soak in the tub. Use the heating pad. Watch your favorite movies. Eat junk. Paint your nails—"

Why does she choose now, when I need her gone, to suddenly take interest in my self-care?

"Okay, Mom, I got it. Pampering is encouraged."

She gives me a quick kiss on the cheek, gifting me with a cloud of her floral perfume, and then leaves as fast as she arrived. The house goes quiet.

"Benjamin?" I rush to open the closet. "I'm sorry, I didn't know what else to do."

He's standing very still, holding a small cardboard box labeled Sweet Synthetics that was opened weeks ago, stashed into my closet, and forgotten. Until now.

"What is this?" he says, a slow grin spreading.

"Not yours." I try to snatch it from him, but he pulls it away and steps past me. "It's not mine, either."

He laughs. "Whose is it, then? It was in *your* closet."

"It's my mom's."

He drops his smile as quickly as he drops the box. It lands with a *thud* on the carpet.

I pick it up. "Geez, Benjamin, she hasn't *used* it. She doesn't even know I have it. And to be honest, I don't even know what it is—"

"It's a—" he starts, but I cut him off.

"I don't want to know! I repeat, it's my *mom's*. If you tell me what it is or what it does or what it's for, then I can't unknow it. And I really don't need those images of my parents…"

Wait a minute.

Dad was just as confused by that thing as I was, and Mom told me to hide it from him. Holy shit, is my mother having a kinky affair? Is that what she's been doing on the days she comes home late from work?

"Whoa, Jessie," Ben says, "I just saw every drop of blood drain from your face. What's going on?"

"Nothing, I…" I shake my head and set the box back down in my closet. "It's nothing you need to worry about."

"We don't have to do anything tonight," he says.

"I feel fine, really." I keep my voice light and force a smile. Force all those anxious thoughts out of my head. "Now… where were we?"

He grins. "You were about to play naughty schoolteacher and give me a lesson."

"Yes. Yes, I am." I pull my shirt off and climb into his lap.

Chapter Seventeen

*T*here are only a few days left in June now. Ben has been in my room so many times that it feels odd when he *isn't*. How messed up is that?

And even more strange is that we don't always spend all of our time getting freaky. Sometimes, we'll just sit and talk with some kissing and other things now and then. Ben actually cuddles with me, and I don't even have to initiate it. We've gotten more comfortable with each other, because we've gotten to know each other better. We've gotten to see who we are, separately and together, beyond the daily bickering at school.

Today has definitely been a "getting freaky" day, but we've got all afternoon to ourselves. We don't have to rush anything, and I kind of like that leisurely pace once in a while.

After round one, I freshen myself up in the bathroom, put on a T-shirt and cotton shorts, then return to my bedroom and find Ben sitting on the floor by my bookshelf, wearing only his underwear. Is he obsessing over those Dr. Seuss books again?

"What are you doing down there?" I ask, lying across my bed so my face is right by him.

"Just wondering why you have a tote bag full of empty pill

bottles hidden in the corner of your room." He turns to face me, giving me a grin. "Tell me you're a drug addict without telling me you're a drug addict."

"Stop it." I give his shoulder a playful shove. "Those aren't mine. I mean, not originally. I collect them from other people. My parents both have prescriptions that are refilled regularly. The rest, I get from neighbors or whoever."

"That still doesn't explain why you have them," he says, and he seems genuinely curious. Not like he's trying to set me up for a joke.

But telling him about this makes me feel more exposed and vulnerable than being completely naked in front of him. "It's, um... I make things out of them."

"Like what?"

"Anything?" My cheeks are getting hot. Why is this so hard?

Maybe it's a good thing, though. I want to be able to talk to Andrew about this, and he's going to be here—living here with me—so soon. Only a few days. Maybe talking about it with Ben now can be my practice.

"A lot can fall under 'anything,'" he says. "Do you have something you can show me?"

Yes. That I can do.

A month ago, I wouldn't have dared. I would have assumed Ben wanted to see it just to make fun of it. And me. But I guess things change between people once they've spent as much time alone together as we have. I don't question his every word anymore. I actually want to see his reaction to this, whether it's good or bad. I just want to know what he thinks.

"Over here." I get up off the bed and walk across the room to my dresser, and Ben follows me. On the top, there's a multi-purpose storage container made from pill bottles of all different sizes glued together into a kind of sculpture. I'm sure Ben has seen it already—it's hard to miss—but it isn't easy to see what it's made from because I've painted over and decorated it. As well as I can, anyway, being someone with zero artistic skill. You have to look closely, though, to know it's a bunch of plastic cylinders.

"This," I say, pointing to it.

Ben is quiet for a moment. He looks at me with his brows raised. "This?"

"Yeah."

"You made this?"

I laugh a little. "Yeah."

"Can I…" He gestures toward it.

"Sure. Just don't let anything fall out."

He places his fingers around one side of it, delicately, like he's afraid it might break. But it won't. That thing is sturdier than most things like it you can buy. And you definitely won't find anything on Amazon or a store shelf that's been hand-painted to change the look of the plastic and also to label each compartment.

One for hair ties, one for hair clips. One tall bottle near the back for my brush, and another for pens and markers. The short, wide ones are great for holding things like mints and M&M's, because I can easily get my fingers in there. The rest are a hodge-podge of random things, like my ear buds. Putting them in a pill bottle keeps the wires from getting tangled. I have several that hold spare change—one for quarters, one for dimes, one for nickels, one for pennies, one for dollars—so I can quickly and easily find what I need rather than rummaging through an all-in-one cash jar.

Ben is holding it in both hands now, slowly turning it this way and that, studying it. Then he sets it back down on my dresser and says, "You keep surprising me, Jessie."

I'm not sure how to take that. What else about me has surprised him?

"Have you made other stuff?"

I nod. "Yeah, lots of things. And it's not just pill bottles, it's anything plastic that would otherwise be tossed in the trash. Like milk jugs and water bottles."

"Where are they?"

I shrug one shoulder. "I give them away to family and friends, mostly. Right now, I'm trying to come up with a fun, easy project for kids in the library's summer programs. I need enough to supply the whole group—you found my stash for that."

Ben just stares at me, and I don't know what that look means. He's never stared at me so intensely before unless we were trying to outdo each other with creative insults. And even then, it was different than this, though I can't exactly say how. I just feel it.

"What—" I start, but then he's kissing me, sweeping me up in his arms, and I *do* know what that means.

He's done with this conversation. Time for round two.

*C*hris is coming home tomorrow. *Andrew* will be here *tomorrow.*

It seems like only yesterday that I was sitting at lunch on the last day of school, telling Ben how ridiculous his idea was. But it was a little more than four weeks ago, and so much has changed since then. Sometimes, when I think about it, I feel like a different person.

But a lot has also stayed the same. I'm still me, just a me with more experience.

More confidence, too. At least with Ben.

For our final rendezvous, my parents and our schedules just wouldn't behave, so I'm going to Ben's house for the first time ever. His actual house. Where he lives every day. Where he eats and sleeps. Where he jacks off. Where he brushes his teeth. And it's because all those things are so ordinary that being allowed to go there with him feels…extraordinary.

If I thought the inside of Ben's car smelled like money, then the inside of his house—also known as the mayor's mansion—smells like a goddamn bank vault full of gold bars.

I've never been in a house so huge. It could be its own city. Everywhere I look, my jaw keeps dropping. I've lost the ability to close my mouth. They give tours here occasionally, mostly for school field trips, and I can see why. But…this is where he and his family live. It's their house, not a museum.

"Hungry?" Ben says.

"No, not really." My appetite has been swallowed by my amazement at this place.

"Okay, well, if you need anything, the kitchen is that way." He points to our right, but all I see are walls full of artwork and what looks like a panoramic airplane-view photograph of Trinity in the 1950s. "Okay?" he says.

"Sure." I nod. "But I'm not much of a cook."

"No problem, I can make you whatever you want."

"You what?"

"Don't look so shocked." He laughs, then heads for a giant staircase. "I spent a lot of time with our chef in the kitchen when I was growing up. My parents were never around, so…"

The thought of him being all domestic is driving me wild. If he puts on an apron…*nothing* but an apron… *Oh god*. He needs to get naked and put on an apron and bake me some cookies.

I follow him up a sweeping, curved staircase with a

polished wood railing. I glide my palm up it as I climb, and suddenly I feel giddy like a little kid on Christmas morning.

I'm getting excited over stairs.

At the top, the hall is open on one side to the floor below, and the opposite wall has some mirrors. I catch a glimpse of my face as we walk past them. I look *happy*.

Happy, in a place I never thought I'd be. Happy, with a person I never thought I'd be.

Ben leads me into his bedroom, which is roughly the size of my living room at home, if you put three of them together. The decor is neutral and classy, nothing too bold or in your face, which immediately calms me. He has a walk-in closet— the door is open, and I'm pretty sure it will take you to Narnia, because I can't see the end of it—and there's a desk with a full computer setup and three monitors like he works for the fucking FBI, a huge flat-screen TV mounted on a wall, a cushy chair with an open book on the seat, bookshelves *everywhere*…and…a cello?

That's just for decoration, right?

And then there's the bed.

It's at least a queen. The blankets are neatly set, and the pillows look fluffed. Someone put forth effort to make that bed so perfectly. And I have zero qualms about messing it all up. I sit on the edge of the mattress—no squeaks, nice—and then lie all the way back.

Every ounce of tension in me loses its grip and flies out the door. I let out a long sigh.

"Does it meet your approval?" Ben says.

"I'm never getting out of this bed."

"You're shameless," he says with a laugh.

"Guilty." I roll onto my side to look at him. "Why haven't we been using this bed for the past month instead of my tiny, lumpy squeak machine?"

"Because I never bring anyone here."

Never? *Right.* "Come on, Benjamin."

"I'm not lying. You're the only girl who's ever been in this bed. Or even in this room. It never got that far with anyone else..."

No way.

No way am I the only girl who's ever been invited to his lair.

And what does he mean by "never got that far" if he doesn't mean sex?

Ben clears his throat. "I'm gonna start the shower."

He slips away into the adjacent bathroom, and soon I hear water running. I should join him—he's *expecting* me to. But I'm stuck here, frozen by the bomb he just dropped. I'm the only one who...has seen any of this? Slowly, I get up and wander around the room, looking even closer at it, and suddenly one thing stands out more than anything else.

It's not what I see that shocks me this time. It's what I *don't* see.

Benjamin Oliver was a star quarterback and captain of the Trinity Tigers varsity football team. They went all the way to the state championship last season—and nearly won it. Yet I see zero anything about football in this room. No trophies. No team photos. No jersey hanging on the wall, proudly displaying his name and his number. No game-winning football covered in signatures and encased in glass.

As far as I knew, football was Ben's life. And still is. It's no secret he's going to play with the Ohio State Buckeyes come fall, one of the best college teams in the country, according to my dad.

But in his private space, his sanctuary, it's a totally different story.

Even I know that Ben is a god-level football player. With

my two closest friends on the cheer squad, I went to just about every home game and a few of the away ones. As loath as I am to admit it, Benjamin Oliver really deserved all the praise he got on the field. And he's one of the most arrogant, cocky bastards I've ever met.

You wouldn't know it by looking at this room. This is solely the room of his nerd-hot side, with a dash of emo artist, not his jock-hot side at all.

"Jess!" he shouts from the bathroom. "You coming?"

There's more to Ben than I thought. Maybe more than what anyone thought. And I'd love to unravel this mystery, but clearly, he hasn't shared this part of him because he doesn't want to. I have to respect that.

Besides, this is our last time together. Tomorrow, it's over. Aside from going out with our friends, I won't see or hear from him again until he calls in that favor—if he ever does.

So, I put all of these new thoughts about him out of my mind, undress myself as I walk across the room, leaving a trail of clothing in my wake, and then join him in the steamy shower.

It doesn't take long for us to make a mess of ourselves after the shower, for round two or three or whatever number we're on now. Each one blurs right into the next. But there is one specific thing I want to do with him tonight, and I can't get it out of my mind.

It's now or never.

"I was thinking…" I start.

Ben continues devouring my chest. In between licks, he says, "I'm listening."

"There's only one thing we haven't done that I said in the

beginning I want to do."

His face pops up, his eyes meeting mine. His lips are swollen and red.

"I'm ready now. Do you remember what it is?"

He grins, wickedly, and says, "Yes, ma'am." Then dives headfirst between my legs.

*S*ometime in the middle of the night, I realize I'm the one who has to leave this time.

I stretch like a cat, rolling to my side and hugging the pillow. Everything feels soft against my bare skin. I'm on a cloud.

But I can't stay.

I grab my phone. It's 2:57 a.m. and Ben is sleeping—I should go. We've had plenty of very late nights together, but never an *overnight*. I'm sure he doesn't expect to see me in the morning, though the idea of walking across town, alone, in the middle of the night to get home isn't exactly appealing.

I could ask Rayna to pick me up. Except I can't. She'll have too many questions, and my brain has the IQ of a slug right now. Not a good combination.

I could call my parents—

Yeah, right.

Okay, then. I guess I'm calling Rayna and making up some weak excuse. But not until I've walked far enough from Ben's house for her not to connect the dots.

I ease out of his bed as quietly as I can—the cold air hits me all over at once; I'm one giant goose pimple—then I tiptoe around the room in search of my clothes. It's hard to see, but I find my underwear first and put it on. This isn't even the difficult part. Once I'm fully dressed, I still have to navigate my way out of this huge mansion.

Without waking anyone.

Hell, I don't even know who else is in the house. Security guards? His parents? Siblings? *Does* he have siblings—I don't know a damn thing.

I stumble into his desk on the other side of the room from his bed and stub my big toe. *"Dammit,"* I hiss, hopping on one foot.

Ben rolls over in bed. I freeze, holding on to his desk chair for support, until I hear him breathing deep again. That was close.

I shake my foot out and test my weight on it, still holding the chair, facing the desk. It's so neat. Everything in its place from the pen holder to the stapler. Which is why the one thing that isn't sticks out like a sore…toe. Heh.

It's a letter of some kind with crease marks that show it had at one time been folded into thirds—it must have come through the mail. I squint, trying to make out the letterhead…

The Juilliard School. In New York. And it's dated for October of last year.

What the actual Jesus lord?

Ben is going to Ohio State to play football, not New York to play music…to play that cello in the corner? No fucking way. I can't even visualize him doing such a thing.

I snatch the letter up from the desk and hold it close to my face, reading it in the dark. "We are pleased to inform you…" I whisper under my breath. Then blurt, *"No way."*

This is an acceptance letter.

He doesn't just play music. He got accepted into the best music school in the country.

"Stay," Ben mumbles from the bed, and I drop the paper onto the desk.

Shit. Did he see me snooping?

I do a slow spin to face him, but I can't tell if he's actually awake or talking in his sleep.

"Benjamin?" I whisper. "Did you say something?"

He blinks a few times. "If you leave the house, you'll trip the alarms," he says, his voice low and throaty from sleep. "Come back to bed. I'll drive you home in the morning."

"Oh. I didn't think you would."

"You were wrong."

"Thank *god*." I rush back to his bed, scramble over him to the other side, and bundle up under the comforter, then press my half-naked body against his.

"You're freezing," he accuses.

"Because your AC is set to arctic." I wriggle my bare feet in between his.

"Jesus, Jess—" he hisses.

"Shut up and hold me. I'll warm up faster."

He lets out a long, drawn-out, overly dramatic sigh, admitting defeat, then braces his arms around me and cocoons me against his chest. "Is Her Majesty satisfied?"

"Yes, peasant," I say, smiling. I'm melting already. "You may live another day."

For a while we just lay there, breathing in sync, and in the silence, my mind gets loud.

"You still awake?" Ben asks softly.

"Mm-hmm."

"Do you feel more confident about seeing your dream guy now?"

It takes me a second to get who he means. *Andrew.* I forgot Ben knows about him. And that's ridiculous, because Andrew is the whole reason Ben spent the past month with me.

Still, I haven't said a word about Andrew to Ben since

the last day of school. It takes me off guard. But...this is Benjamin Oliver. Him asking me this is his version of a customer survey attached to your receipt.

"Yeah," I say honestly. "You did great."

"I know." His chest hums with a sound of amusement.

"Ha. Ha." I roll my eyes. But what did I expect? He's still the same arrogant ass he was four weeks ago. Having sex with me wouldn't change that. If it wasn't me he was with, it would have been someone else. This is all same-same to him. A day in the life.

I'm the one who changed.

Because four weeks ago, I would never have admitted something like this to him. I would never have made myself even an ounce of vulnerable to him. But he's been saying since day one that I need to trust him...and I do.

"I feel like, maybe ninety-six percent confident," I tell him. "Not a hundred."

He lifts his hand to the top of my head and starts stroking my hair. I don't know if he means it to be comforting, but it is. "What's the other four percent?"

"Fear of rejection."

"Nonsense," he says. "This guy would have to be either gay or stupid to not want you."

I bite my lip to keep from smiling too big. "Was that a compliment, Benjamin?"

"Well..." He gives a little shrug. "Like you said, I did great."

"Jerkwad." I smack his chest, and he laughs out loud.

We go silent again, just breathing together and Ben stroking my hair.

Then he says, "What's so special about this Andrew guy that his opinion matters so much to you?"

I'm warm through and through now, so I pull back from

him enough to see his face when I look up. "You really wanna know?"

"Yeah," he says.

"Okay…well, besides the obvious that he's hot *and* mature. Unlike some people, who think being hot is a free pass to be insufferable."

Ben rolls his eyes but keeps any comments to himself.

I think for a moment. "Andrew is sweet, and kind, and… altruistic. I mean, he's been volunteering in Cambodia for the past month, helping kids get healthy in less-than-ideal conditions. He's getting a degree in medicine not to make a name for himself or to get rich or to be in charge of other people, but because he really cares about people—children especially—and wants to help them get better. I'm not seeing a downside here."

Ben's eyes go distant for a moment, and I can't even guess what he's thinking. "Sounds a lot like your brother," he says.

Not at all what I expected him to say. "How do you know anything about my brother?"

He looks down at me, smirking. "I sat across from you at lunch for nine straight months. I probably know a lot of things about you that you didn't think I heard. I know you'd rather take an F on an oral report than speak in front of a class. I know you're allergic to strawberries. And I know your brother goes to school in Florida and you wish you could see him more."

Oh…wow.

It's only been a month, but sitting across from him in the school cafeteria every day seems like it was a different life. Like it was ages ago.

Honestly? It felt huge at the time, but when I think of it now, I realize it was a stupid reason that we started fighting in the first place. He said something that just set me off, and he thought that was funny—always laughing at me. I was only ever a joke to him, someone to rile up and poke fun at. And he was always my verbal punching bag.

That isn't what we are anymore, though, unless we're in public, putting on a show. So, *what* are we, really? We aren't enemies. Not when we can lie next to each other in the middle of the night, baring our bodies and our souls.

Are we actually friends now? Yeah. I think we are.

Secret friends.

"I guess Andrew is a lot like my brother," I say finally. "Is that a bad thing?"

"No," he says. "If you got a thing for your brother, that's not my business."

"You *asshole*." I push off him with both hands and snatch the pillow out from under him, then beat him with it.

It's a soft, weak beating. Because I can't stop laughing.

Damn you, Benjamin, for bringing me to the Dark Side, where I actually enjoy being with you. This is not what nature intended for us.

He takes about four hits before he says, "Enough, witch." The pillow is out of my hand and I'm pinned to the mattress in a blink, staring up at his smiling face. It's so rare to see him smile fully like this, all his bright white teeth showing. Hell, before this past month, I didn't think he even knew how to do more than smirk.

And this is the last time.

This is the last time I'll ever be in this position with him, the last time I'll feel his body on mine. The last time…

As if he read my thoughts, he leans down and kisses me. My hands are still pinned on either side of my head, and I instinctively wrap my legs around him. Suddenly, the air between us feels charged, electric, like we both just realized—we're still here. We still have time. We can still do this if we want to.

God, I want to.

What started as a slow, sweet kiss soon turns into a hot, sweaty game of "Who Gets to Be on Top?"

Spoiler alert: we both win.

Chapter Eighteen

*T*he morning after.

The morning after it's done between us.

The morning after it's done between us, I should be eager to get home and get ready for Chris's homecoming with Andrew in tow.

Instead, I'm looking at the time stamp on my phone—six a.m.—like it betrayed me, and dragging my feet to Ben's car. I barely slept, though. I'm just tired.

Except being tired doesn't explain why I want to run back into his bed with him.

With *him*.

Not only have I gone bananas, but I've lost them all, too.

Is it because he's my first? My only sexual experience so far?

Or maybe I'm just nervous about seeing Andrew. I know it won't be the same with him as it was with Ben. Everyone is different. Maybe it's the unknown that's bothering me, rather than the known. I don't know.

I thought being less innocent would make me bolder by default. I have more confidence, but I still get butterflies in my stomach and sweaty palms and my mouth gets too dry and my face gets too hot and I don't know if anything I did with Ben will make a goddamn difference.

I don't know I don't know I don't know—

The car comes to an abrupt stop, jolting me out of my head. I must have zoned out.

"We're here," Ben says.

Yeah, I got that. What he's really saying is "you can go now."

"Okay, well… Thank you for…" I shake my head at myself. "You know what you did, never mind."

I open the passenger door, and Ben snatches my other hand, stopping me.

"One more thing," he says.

Now? Here?

We're in my driveway. I mean, it's barely sunrise on a Sunday morning. The entire neighborhood is asleep, including my parents. The chances of anyone seeing us are nil.

Still, it feels too risky to even be sitting here out in the open.

I wait for him to say something. Or do something. I wait for a year.

Then he licks his lips and says, "Just remember. You're in control. Always."

"Yeah…" I say. That's it? "Okay, uh. See you around."

"See you."

I get out of the car and take the five steps to my front porch. As soon as I unlock the door and open it, he's driving off.

Well. That *is* it. I'm on my own now.

Inside, the house is dark except for a glow from the kitchen. Dad must have been sleep-snacking again last night and forgotten to turn the light off.

Sigh. I wonder if either of them noticed I wasn't here.

I reach around the wall, feeling for the switch, and someone tall and male and *not* my dad jumps out in front of me, yelling, "Surprise!"

My flight instincts kick in—because I have no fight instinct, it's always flight—but as I turn away, whoever it is grabs me. Grabs my entire body and lifts me into the air, spinning.

"What the fuck!" I scream and kick, and the man starts laughing. "Who the—"

Oh my god…I know that laugh.

"Chris?" I wriggle in his bare, muscular arms, trying to get a look at him. All I can tell is that he's shirtless. "Is that you? That better be you and not a half-naked serial killer."

"Why can't it be me *and* a serial killer?" he says, laughing again, then finally sets me down. "You don't think I'd make a good psychopath, Jessie? I'm hurt."

I turn to face him, take in that face of his I missed so much. Those soft brown eyes and his messy, maple-syrup-brown mop of hair. It's weird, he could be the male version of our mother, his features are so like hers. And I could be the female version of our father. We don't even look like we're related.

But I love him more than either of my parents. Or myself. It's the goddamn truth.

"What are you doing here?" I squeal. My eyes sting… What? I'm *crying*. "I thought you weren't flying back until this afternoon." I swipe the tears off my cheeks and squeeze him as hard as I can. He's home. Everything's going to be good now.

"I wanted to surprise you." He squeezes me back.

"I think you're confusing the word 'surprise' with the word 'terrify.'"

"We actually got in late last night," he says, "but you

weren't here. Mom and Dad didn't know where you were, either." He looks down at me with a hard stare, lifting one brow. "If you hadn't shown up this morning, I would have gotten the authorities involved."

"Oh no," I say. "Not the authorities."

So, my parents knew I wasn't here, but they didn't know where I'd gone, and they didn't send me a text to make sure I was alive?

Is this their version of allowing me privacy and independence, or do they just suck?

It only takes a split second for my brain to bury that thought and my mouth to take over. "Why are you up so early if you got in late? Do you need to sleep, or can we talk now? I want to know everything! You look like you got a tan—how hot was it? What kind of animals—"

"Jessie, stop the inquisition," he laughs. That's my brother, always smiling. "I've been up since we got here, but I'm not tired. The time zone difference has me all messed up. You look like you were up all night, too." He pauses. "You were with someone, weren't you."

"*Chris.*" My whole head burns hot. "I was *not*—"

"Your flaming face says you're lying." With another laugh, he pulls me closer to him and scrubs the top of my head like I'm a third grader who did well on a homework assignment. "My little sister's all grown up."

"Oh my god, *stop.*"

"Am I wrong?"

"I..." Jesus, I really can't lie to him. He'll just keep harping on this until he gets it out of me, anyway. "You're not wrong."

"I knew it!" he says like a cheer.

"Shhhhh, you'll wake up Mom and Dad!"

"They don't know?" He turns to walk back into the

kitchen, and I follow.

"No, I'm sure they've assumed—*ggghhh*." I stop dead in my tracks.

Andrew is standing right there.

Well, it's more of a casual lean against the countertop, sipping from a mug. *My* mug, with a picture of Eeyore on it and his tail as the handle. He looks like a perfume ad for Disney.

And he's fully dressed in a T-shirt and shorts, but my breath is still stuttering and my heartbeat immediately speeding up. If he'd been shirtless like my brother, I'd be dead on the floor.

He was in here the whole time? Listening?

"Hello, Jessica," he says, and his voice wraps around me like a warm blanket.

"H-h-hi?" *Brilliant.* "Hi, Andrew."

"Coffee?" Chris asks, pouring himself a cup.

"No, thanks."

Silence drops all around us. Now what?

I know Chris just arrived, but I need to get out of here. This is not at all how I wanted to make an impression. If I stay in this room one more minute, the world is going to explode. My brother will understand, won't he? I'm just trying to save all those innocent lives.

Chris clears his throat. "So, who's the lucky guy?"

Jesus-H on a stick. How do I answer that? With Andrew standing right there? *Oh it was no one, because I want Andrew to be the lucky guy.* Aaagggh.

I can feel the Earth's core starting to boil. Explosion is imminent.

What would Ben tell me to do?

Four weeks with him did not prepare me for this.

"Benjamin..." I mutter under my breath, like a curse.

"Wait, did you say Ben?" Chris asks. "The same Ben you always complain about?" He smiles, shaking his head. "You two are really dating now?"

I'm sorry, world. I tried.

Think, Jessie. Would it be better for Andrew to believe I'm having casual sex or for him to think I'm in a relationship?

"Uh...yeah? I guess." I flick a glance at Andrew, but he's super interested in his coffee. "It's still pretty new," I fumble out a weak explanation. "We're just seeing where it goes."

Chris laughs. "Good for you, that's great. It's about time you admitted all that fighting with him was actually flirting."

"What—"

Andrew finally pipes up. "If he does anything to hurt you, though, you let us know." He nods toward Chris. Like they're *both* my big brothers.

That's the exact opposite of how I want him to see us. I've already been the kid sister. I want to be the cool, confident girlfriend now, who just happens to be his best friend's sister.

"Thanks," I say. "I'm gonna... I need to sleep, Chris, can we catch up later?" He nods, and I give him another hug. "I'm glad you're home."

"Me, too," he says. "I missed you, Jessie James."

I turn and head upstairs. I'm *exhausted*. But now my head won't stop shouting.

Inside my room, I lock the door behind me and fall back onto my bed, staring up at the ceiling. What the hell just happened down there?

If Andrew is feeling protective of me, that's either fantastic or horrible. And I have no idea which one it is. He's hard to read.

Not surprising, though. My ability to understand the

opposite sex is like a three-legged horse's ability to win the Triple Crown.

There's only one person who can help me with this. It's been at least fifteen minutes since Ben dropped me off, so he should be home now.

Me: *We need to talk.*

Ben: *miss me already*

Instead of replying, I call him. As soon as he picks up, I say, "This is all your fault, Benjamin, everything is screwed up—"

"Wait, wait," he says. "What happened in the five seconds it's been since I saw you?"

"My brother is here. With Andrew." I lower my voice. The last thing I need is anyone in this house overhearing anything I talk about with Ben. I can barely stand to hear it myself. "They got here last night—Chris wanted to surprise me—but I wasn't here, because I was with *you*—and now he thinks you and me are dating!"

There's a pause, and I can practically hear the gears in his brain clicking and turning. "You told him you were with *me* last night?"

"He asked! He could tell I was getting busy all night just by looking at me. What was I supposed to say? Me and Rayna had a wild night of pillow humping?"

"I always thought you two might have a thing on the side," he quips. "Does Jeremy know?"

"Shut up," I hiss. "Just shut the fuck up and tell me what to do!"

Another pause. This one goes on for too long.

"Benjamin, I'm freaking out right now. You always have a plan for everything, so *start talking*."

"You told me to shut up," he says. "Twice. I wasn't gonna risk it."

I blow out a breath that turns into a grumble of frustration.

"Jess, don't worry, okay? This could actually work in your favor."

"Really?"

"Really," he says.

"How?"

"Nothing makes a guy want something more than when they think they can't have it. Most guys, anyway. So if Andrew sees you with me, he'll want you. He probably already does, he just hasn't said it yet. Two things—he knows you're not a virgin now and he also believes you're my girlfriend. You got this in the bag, Jessie. Just let nature take its course."

What the hell kind of messed-up male logic is that?

"So, you're saying we should be dating?" I try to wrap my head around it. "Publicly?"

"Not for real," he says. "But yes."

"So everyone, even our friends, will believe we're a couple. Fat fucking chance."

"Why?" He has the gall to sound defensive.

"Have you met us?"

"Okay," he concedes, "it'll be hard to convince everyone at first. But I think we can pull it off. We managed to hook up for four weeks without anyone finding out. We can do this, easy."

"Your definition of 'easy' is seventeen thousand percent wrong."

"Poh-tay-toh, poh-tah-toh."

"All right," I say through an exasperated breath. "I'll do it, but if this doesn't work, you are dead to me, do you understand? I only have a six-week window here. They're going back to school on August fifteenth."

"That's plenty of time. And that's the same day I leave for OSU, so it has to be done by then anyway."

Another thought hits me. "We'll have to break up at some point. I mean fake break up. Andrew's not the kind of guy who would agree to me cheating on someone to be with him."

"You know that for a fact?"

It's more a feeling than direct knowledge. But, "Yes, I do."

Ben sighs. "We'll figure that out later. As of right now, I'm your boyfriend. And you owe me a second favor."

"The hell I do."

"Fake dating wasn't part of the original deal. We're making a new deal here, Jess, where it's still very much about *me* helping *you*."

God, he's right. When will he stop being right? It's fuck-all annoying.

"Okay, two favors," I say, "but on one condition."

"I'm listening."

"You have to call in both of them before you leave in August. I can't live the rest of my life wondering when you're going to show up demanding I train your cat to use the toilet or some other dumb-shit thing you've thought up just to put me through hell."

"That won't happen," he says. "I don't have a cat."

I use my free hand to rub my temple. "Do you agree to it or not?"

"Yeah, sure, I'll think of something for you to do before I leave." He yawns. "I'm going to bed now. My girlfriend kept me up all night, she thinks I'm a machine."

"Poor baby." I roll my eyes. "That must have been torture."

"She's insatiable, Jessie. I have scars."

I snort. "You're delirious. Go to sleep, Benjamin."

"Anything for you, dearest."

I blow a raspberry into the phone, then end the call.

My stomach sinks and churns and does all those things it does when something bad is coming. And something very bad is coming. I have to tell Rayna and Kamy that I'm dating the boy they think I still hate. I have to make up some reason why I'm with Ben that excludes the truth—that we've been seeing each other in secret for *weeks* already.

I can't possibly survive this. My friends are going to murder me.

Chapter Nineteen

Me: *I have news. How soon can you guys meet?*
Kamy: *I have news too*
Rayna: *is this good news?? bad news???*
Me: *I have to tell you in person.*
Kamy: *I have to tell you in person*
Rayna: *i hate you both*

Chris drops me off at Rayna's house, and I go straight to her room. Rayna is literally mixing drinks on her vanity, and Kamy is sitting in the middle of the floor, hugging a pillow, looking like she's going to throw up.

That could mean she has bad news. Is she sick again?

Maybe she should go first. Then my news won't seem so bad by comparison.

God, that's such a selfish thing to think. My friend could be dying, and I'm worried about being judged because of Benjamin freaking Oliver. *Get a grip.*

"Hey, Jessie," Kamy says. Even her voice sounds bad.

I sit down next to her and put my arm around her. Tears are coming before this is over, I can sense it. Rayna plops down on Kamy's other side, a wine spritzer in each hand. She gives one to me, and I take a sip.

Tingly. Tart. Perfection. She could have a side hustle as a barmaid.

"We're here," Rayna says. "Tell us what's going on so I don't have to guess anymore. All my guesses end with someone dying."

Kamy gives a weak smile. "The only thing that's dying is my life as I know it."

I blow out a breath. If she still *has* a life, that's all that matters. Whatever this is, we can help her through it. "What happened?" I ask.

"Todd…" Kamy starts.

Oh thank god, I'm not the only one with boy trouble. I should have known this was about boys. They are the root of all evil.

"Do I need to dismember him?" Rayna asks.

"No! He just…um…he kind of…proposed to me?"

"He what?" Rayna and I say at the same time.

Todd? *Marriage?* We're teenagers, for fuck's sake.

"Why the hell would he do something like that?" I ask her.

"Because…" Kamy starts, then stops to take a deep breath. "I told him…"

I lean into her, as if getting closer will help her say it.

"Oh my god," Rayna yelps. "No way!"

I look back and forth between them. "No way what? What did I miss?"

Rayna points an accusing finger at Kamy. "She's pregnant!"

"Pfft, no she isn't." I turn to Kamy. "Tell her she's overreacting."

Kamy looks at me, her mouth dropped open a little and eyes pleading. She shakes her head. "I'm pregnant."

My jaw hits the floor. This isn't just boy trouble; it's the *epitome* of boy trouble. Stupid sexy boys and their dumb baby-making dicks. Why can't we all be lesbians? Like that dinosaur movie where all of them were born female—they found a way to procreate without sperm, so could we.

"You're pregnant," I say. Even the word feels wrong. "With Todd's baby?"

Kamy glares at me. "Who else's would it be?"

"I'm sorry," I say, then rub my palm up and down her back, and she softens. "I'm just trying to wrap my head around this. Don't you guys use protection?"

"Only condoms," Kamy says.

"What do you mean *only* condoms?" That's all Ben and I were using.

"I mean I'm an idiot." She shakes her head. "I knew I should be on birth control, too, and I just kept putting it off because I would've had to convince my parents I needed a prescription from a gynecologist, not some herbal gel you squirt up your vagina that my mom cooked up in our basement next to the grow lights." She sniffles. "I didn't think…"

Now, the tears come. Her small, fragile frame shakes against me, and Rayna joins us with a firm hug.

"It's okay," I tell her. "You're not an idiot. And you're not alone. We're here for you."

Kamy's flat belly is right in my line of sight. I can't even imagine a tiny human in there. She looks the same as she always has, it's just…unreal.

"So, you're keeping it?" Rayna asks.

"Why would you assume that?" I shoot her a look over Kamy's head.

"Because why else would Todd propose?"

Kamy sniffles and swipes at her face. "He wants me to keep it. And I… I'm not sure. I got accepted into *Harvard*. I can't just throw that away because I made a mistake."

A mistake, yeah. One I made, too.

I'm gonna be sick.

Mom said I needed a pregnancy scare to know how I really felt about having kids. Would a friend's unplanned pregnancy count? Because when I leave here, I'm going straight to my gynecologist and demanding my own warehouse full of contraceptives.

It would be so much easier if I could just say, well, then, I guess I'm not having sex anymore. Lord help me, I can't. Now that I know what I've been missing...I need it like I need blood in my veins.

"I don't know what to do." Kamy's voice quivers. "What would you guys do?"

"Keep it," Rayna says at the same time I say, "Give it up."

"Clear as mud, thanks." Kamy laughs without humor, and then her analytical side kicks in. It always does eventually. "If I keep it, I have to tell my parents. And if they choose to spare my life, how am I supposed to juggle being a student *and* a mom *and* a wife? It feels like a lose-lose-lose."

"Keeping it doesn't mean you have to marry Todd," I say. "You have us to help."

"I know," Kamy says, "and I love you both for being the best friends I could ever have. But my whole life will be a twenty-four seven struggle from one thing to the next."

"But you'll have a *baby*," Rayna says. As if that cancels everything out.

"Todd's baby," I remind her, trying to lighten the mood. If she smiles, it won't feel like her whole world is tumbling down around her. At least, for that moment it won't. "Honestly, Kamy might not survive pregnancy and childbirth with a behemoth baby of his. I'm surprised she's not already showing."

"*Jessie.*" Kamy laughs. "You're the worst. Don't ever change."

Rayna gives me a skeptical look, like she just remembered something horrible I did to her in a past life and she's on a karma mission. "Didn't you say you have news, too?"

Here we go.

"It can wait," I say. "This is more important—"

"Nuh uh," Rayna cuts me off. "You're not getting off that easy. Spill it."

"Yes," Kamy says, sitting up taller, "let's change the topic to anything but babies. I can only talk about this so much without having a panic attack."

"Fine." I look back and forth at them.

Deep breath in… Deep breath out…

Just say it and get it over with. Just say it and get it over with. Just say it—

"I recently, um, started going out with Benjamin Oliver? Like, as a couple."

You could hear a pin drop, it's so quiet. And the floor in here is plush carpet.

"Ben?" they say in unison, then Rayna's eyes go big and wide.

"I knew something was going on with you two!"

"Since when?"

"Since that day at the park when you both mysteriously disappeared."

Damn. I really thought we'd gotten away with it that night.

"You've been with him since then, really?" Kamy says.

Since before then, actually, but let's not split hairs.

"How did this start?"

"Very suddenly," I admit, then shrug. "We haven't killed each other yet, so."

"That was two weeks ago," Rayna says. "Have you two…?"

Fuck.

If I say yes, she'll honest-to-Jesus hate me for not telling her right away. If I say no, I have to pretend like I haven't had my body wrapped around Ben's like a koala on a eucalyptus tree as many times as I have. Or ever.

Just thinking about everything we did last night—and all the other days and nights—has my face getting hot and my heart pumping hard. "We've…you know…we've made out a few times."

A few million and twelve.

"Good," Kamy says. "Make him take things slow with a girl for once."

Slow, right. Slow for us was waiting a week after our first kiss.

And technically, we were having naked time on day one. So, did we even wait at all?

"Are you sure about this?" Rayna says.

"Nope."

Kamy laughs at that, but Rayna talks over it. "I'm serious, Jessie."

"So am I."

"What happened to going for it with Andrew? Is he not coming?"

"Uh, no…he's here now." *Shit.* Just when I thought this couldn't get more complicated.

"I'm lost," Kamy says.

"Me too," Rayna chimes in. "And I'm worried. You know how Ben is with girls. You know this will never be serious with him. It won't last."

I shrug. "It doesn't have to. He's moving out of state at the end of summer, and I'm not interested in a long-distance relationship. It's probably just a fling. I'm not expecting much."

She studies me for a moment. "So…no Andrew?"

"Come on, Ray. You know that was such a long shot. I never really had a chance." *God, I hope this sounds believable.* I can't look her in the eye, so I take another sip of my drink. And if she says anything about my cheeks going red, I'll blame the alcohol.

"Well, I think it's great," Kamy jumps in. "I hope it works for you and Ben, I really do. You've always had a kind of chemistry with him."

Right, but usually, it's the kind that blows up the science lab. Now it's more like…

No, it's still the kind that blows up the science lab. But in a fun way.

"Just…don't make the same mistake I did," Kamy says. "Promise?"

"Yeah." I give her hand a squeeze. "I promise."

Me: *Good news I'm not pregnant.*

    Ben: …

    Ben: *did you think you were*

    Me: …

    Ben: *Jess*

    Me: …

    Ben: …

    Ben: *Jessica*

    Me: *I'm taking anti-baby drugs for the rest of my life.*

    Ben: *did you need me for something or just felt like scaring the shit out of me*

    Me: *Chris and Andrew and me and my parents are going to the Trinity summer fair on the fourth. Come with us?*

Ben: *like a date*

Me: *Like a chance to make Andrew jealous of you over me.*

Ben: 😈

Me: *You better behave yourself.*

Ben: *absolutely not*

Chapter Twenty

*T*he morning of July 4th a giant box is delivered to my house — and I have to sign for it.

This is for me?

"Have a good day, miss," the delivery guy says with a tip of his head, then goes back to his truck.

"Thanks," I mutter to no one. How do I get this inside, it weighs a ton. "Chris!" I shout as loud as I can. "I need help!"

Sometimes having an older brother who's really into health and fitness comes in handy. He has muscle for days.

Chris thunders down the stairs, panting, scrambling to get his shirt on. Sleep has turned his hair into a giant fluffball around his head. "What is it, what's wrong, are you hurt?"

Okay, *that* was an excessive response. I need to remind myself he's a doctor in training and will always assume the worst when someone yells for help.

I point to the giant cardboard box on the porch. "I just need a lift."

The wild look in his eyes fades, his shoulders drop, and he bends — at the knees, of course, never at the waist — and picks up the box as if it weighs nothing. It's wider than his chest and nearly as deep.

"What is this?" he says and sets it down on the floor by

the couch.

"No idea." I check the label. "It's addressed to me, but it came direct from a warehouse in Virginia. A late graduation gift, maybe?"

But from who?

I get my answer as soon as I cut the box tape and pull open the flaps. And I can't keep the smile from stretching into my cheeks. "Oh my god...*Benjamin*."

"Nail polish?" Chris says.

"Yep."

But it isn't just any nail polish. It's red number 762, fire engine frenzy. A whole case of it, just like he said he would get me. I thought he was only making a joke in the moment.

"I'm guessing he wants you to wear this," my brother says.

"Yep." I nod at the ridiculously huge box, still smiling. "That's what I get for dating the one boy in Trinity with unlimited expendable funds."

Chris laughs. "You say that like it's a bad thing. Enjoy it while it lasts, Jessie. And pray it lasts forever. You'll be set for life."

He heads back upstairs, unaware of the sucker punch he just hit me with.

I couldn't smile now if I tried. Is this what people are going to think when they see us together? That I'm with him for his *money*?

Of course they are. I'm the poor girl, he's the rich boy. Why else would I go out with a boy everyone knows I hate, if not to take advantage of his money? My own brother just flat-out told me that's a reason to stay with him, because he knows what my life is like. He's lived it, too.

I flop down on our lumpy couch with a sigh and pick up my phone from the end table.

Me: *I got your gift.*

Ben: *you're welcome*

Me: *Don't ever do that again.*

Ben: *don't do what*

Me: *Buy me things.*

Instead of a reply, my phone rings. I pick it up. "Why are you calling me?"

"Because I want to make sure my tone comes across correctly when I say what the ever-loving fuck are you talking about? Why can't I buy my girlfriend anything? Why can't I spoil her, even? And why can't you just appreciate a nice gesture when you see one?"

He's actually upset over me being upset over this. Is he really that clueless?

"First of all..." I take in a deep breath. I have so many words to get through to him. "I'm not actually your girlfriend, and I never will be. Second of all, we are going to one of the biggest annual events in all of Trinity later today, and I don't want to be paraded around on your arm, wearing, and I quote, 'fuck-me red' nail polish, just so you can feel good about yourself."

"Jess, that isn't—"

"And third," I say over him, "you have no idea what a 'nice gesture' means in my world. You have no fucking idea what it's like to not have a gazillion dollars at your beck and call. Tell me, Benjamin. Tell me how it feels to eat the same gross boxed dinners night after night after night. Tell me how it feels to watch my fridge get emptier and emptier, knowing it can't be filled until the weekend when my parents get paid. Tell me how it feels to be short ten fucking cents on lunch because all I have is cash I got from my part-time job doing grunt work at the library."

"Jessie—"

"You have everything you need and everything you want,

and you have no fucking clue what it's like to not. You're the goddamn Mayor of Trinity's son. You live in a fucking mansion. Your bedroom alone is bigger than my living room. You drive a spaceship for a car—hell, just to have a car of my own would be a luxury, even if it was junk. So don't judge me for making decisions based on something you don't understand—that you'll *never* understand. If I don't want to be given pity gifts by my 'rich boyfriend' that'll just make everyone think I'm fucking you for what your money can buy me, then don't tell me I'm the one who's wrong. You don't get to make that call."

There's a long pause. The silence feels dead. Heavy. Suffocating.

"Are you still there?" I snap.

"I...I can't believe you just said all that."

My jaw clenches. "God, Benjamin, your response is proof of what I said."

There's another pause, and I can only hope my words are beginning to sink in.

"Are we having a fight?" he says. "I mean a real one. Over...nail polish?" He laughs a little. Not a full-on belly laugh, but still. He's amused by this.

Why is everything a joke to him?

"Every fight I've had with you was real, Benjamin," I say. "And it's not about the nail polish, dumb ass. And you know what else? *Fuck you.*"

I end the call before he can argue, then stomp back up to my room.

And then stomp right back downstairs because I forgot something.

I grab a bottle from the huge-gantic box of nail polishes and bring it back up with me. But I'm not doing this for him. I'm *not*.

I'm doing it for me.

. . .

Ben: *I'm sorry*

Great. He's apologizing. Why do boys think all they have to do is say they're sorry and everything will be sparkling—

Another text comes through.

Ben: *I should have asked if you wanted that gift first*

Ben: *you're right I don't understand your world*

Ben: *but I want to*

Well, shit. Now I can't be mad at him anymore.

I point my phone at my freshly painted toes and snap a picture, then send it to him.

Me: *Thank you.*

I ride with my parents to the Trinity Summer Fair in Mom's car, and Chris and Andrew take Dad's car. We meet Ben at the gate.

This is the first time I've seen him in person since the last day we slept together. Saying just the sight of him makes we want to do a thousand naughty things with him would be the understatement of the century. He doesn't just look good. He looks *damn fine* with a side of hot sauce. And when he catches me ogling him, my internal physical response is downright nuclear.

I lick my lips. I'll take that meal to go, please.

Ben is giving me a look that says, *I know what you're thinking*, but when we get up close to him, he bypasses me and stretches a hand out to my father.

Dad flicks a glance at me. He knows this is "the boyfriend," and I told him that sex toy was mine. I don't even want to know what's going through his head right now.

He grabs Ben's hand and gives it a firm shake. "Dale Webster, Jessica's father."

"Nice to meet you, sir, I'm—"

"Ben Oliver." My dad's eyes suddenly go wide like he's meeting a celebrity crush. "I know exactly who you are, I've seen you on the local news. Football, right? Quarterback. You got scouted by the Buckeyes."

"Right, that's me," Ben says and withdraws his hand.

"*This* is your boyfriend?" Mom says. "Mayor Oliver's son?"

She sounds equal parts shocked and impressed, as if she never expected her dumpy daughter to make such a catch.

God, I hate this dating thing already.

Introductions are made all around, and when Ben gets to Andrew, I feel like someone is standing on my chest. I can't draw a full breath until I see what happens. I told Ben to behave…

They're both extremely polite, though, and Ben doesn't give anything away. Like the fact we aren't really a couple. Or that he knows I'd rather be with Andrew.

Then, out of the blue, they start speaking Spanish—I think?—to each other. Fuck me, I only took French in school, and I quit after a year of it. Ben is talking to Andrew as easily as if they grew up together. Now they're laughing—*laughing!*—and I have no idea what's so funny.

I'm trying not to stare. But Andrew is just as hot and sexy as Ben, and this is already the most time I've spent in his presence since he got here. It's been two days of me going off to work at the same time he's coming in from an early morning run, or Chris taking him out to his favorite health food store just as I'm coming back in. At night, he stays in Chris's room, with only a wall between us. I can barely sleep, knowing he's right there.

But he hasn't really noticed me. No accidentally brushing by me in the hallway or on the stairs. No talking other than a quick hello or goodbye.

I guess that's what Ben is here for, though, to get Andrew's attention on me. Show him that I'm someone to be desired. I take in a long breath and blow it out slowly, steadying myself. I really hope this works.

Finally, Ben steps over to my side, slides his hand into mine, and gives me a very chaste kiss on the cheek. "You look damn cute," he says.

Cute? Nothing between us has ever been *cute*.

And nothing Benjamin Oliver does could be considered chaste. One quick press of his lips against my skin, one inhale of his scent, one squeeze of his warm hand around mine... and I'm done. Dead. Deceased by the onslaught of sensual energy coming off of him.

I've always had a physical attraction to Ben, and I've never denied that—at least not to myself—but this is different. When we sat across from each other in the school cafeteria, I didn't feel like I would have a spontaneous orgasm just from being in spitting distance of him.

It was more like...a daily consideration of whether the jail time would be worth murdering him, then deciding to spare his life because I've never seen such beautiful brown eyes in all my life, and I get to see them looking back at me every day.

But now, I know too much. I have too many heart-pounding memories of him.

Maybe that's all this is.

"Well," Dad says, "you kids have fun. Us old folks will be chillin' at the bandstand if you need anything." He catches my eye and winks at me, then takes Mom's hand, and they walk off toward the live eighties band and free beer. Dad leans to whisper something in her ear, and she laughs out loud, then brings their hands up to her lips and kisses his.

If anyone is looking cute today, it's my parents. There has to be some other explanation for Mom's secret package. They're too happy together for one of them to be cheating.

"Did he really call us kids?" I say to Chris.

"Did he really say chillin'?" he replies with a laugh. "When will people who were born in a year starting with nineteen figure out that they aren't the younger generation anymore?"

"Your father's just a kid at heart," Andrew says lightly. "Nothing wrong with that."

Chris gives him a smile, stuffing his hands in his pockets, and they start walking off together, leaving me and Ben to follow like stray kittens.

It's the middle of the day, and it's roughly nine thousand degrees outside with seven hundred percent humidity. A typical summer day for western Pennsylvania. All we need is one good rainstorm to come through and there'll be a frost warning tonight. But for now, I'm wearing nothing but a plain cotton tank top and shorts with flip-flops. No makeup. Hair up in a bun. Sunglasses—the correct size and style for my face.

They aren't mirror shades like Ben's, though. If someone gets close enough, they can see my eyes. They can see who I am and what I'm wearing and how pretty I'm not. Not by Benjamin Oliver standards, anyway. Every girl I've ever seen him with was like a human Barbie.

Trinity has no shortage of Barbies.

"What do you guys want to do first?" Chris says over his shoulder. "Games, rides, food?"

"Games," Ben says.

"Or rides," I add. Andrew's ass is maybe two feet in front

of me, and I can't. Stop. Staring. "I'm fine with either of those, but it's too soon to eat." My voice is breathy by the end of my sentence, like I just took a casual run over here from the moon.

At least I didn't mess up my words or not finish the sentence. That's a win.

"Enjoying the view?" Ben whispers close to my ear.

My cheeks heat up—I've been caught, no sense in denying it. "Yes, I am."

He smiles like he's proud of me. "Don't lose that," he says. "That boldness. That I-don't-give-a-fuck-what-you-think tone. When a woman knows what she wants and goes after it—that kind of confidence is sexy."

"Hmm…" I give it a think.

"That kind of noise you just made is also sexy."

I snort.

"So is that one," he says with a laugh.

"You're so full of shit." I bump his shoulder with mine.

"What are you two whispering about back there?" Chris says.

"Nothing!" we say in unison.

Chris laughs at that. We *all* laugh. This day may have started in a garbage heap, but it's on the upswing now. I came here to have fun, and dammit, I'm going to have fun.

"Andrew's a good guy," Ben says, keeping his voice low. "I approve."

"And you know this how? You only talked to him for half a minute."

He shrugs. "That was all the time I needed. I didn't get any bad vibes from him."

"Mm-hmm. I heard you guys talking in Spanish. Did you form some kind of Brazilian bro code with him?"

"No," Ben says, "because I'm not Brazilian. My mom's

side of the family lives in Venezuela. I had to learn the language to keep up with all the talk whenever we visit."

Interesting.

"Andrew isn't actually Brazilian, either. He was born in Ecuador. If he was born in Brazil, more likely he'd speak Portuguese, anyway."

"Really?" I can't even tell the difference. I'm such a stereotypical American.

"Yeah, Brazil is just where he was living before he started school in Florida, so that's what he told people when they asked where he's from. He wasn't totally fluent in English yet, so he got a little mixed up. Now everyone thinks he's Brazilian."

"And you got all that from half a minute of talking to him?"

"That's all conversation is when you first meet someone, Jessie. Finding a common ground and then discussing it." He shrugs. "We're both Latino, so I brought it up."

Right. So what do you do when you can't get any words out to find a common ground?

And how did I sit with Ben at lunch for nine straight months and not know he's bilingual? Did I even know him at all? I'm starting to wonder…

"There it is," Chris says, pointing to the left, then starts walking backward so I can see his face. "Come on, Jessie, it's tradition."

"It's Skee-Ball," I correct. "And you always win."

"Maybe this year you'll get lucky." He shrugs. "Or maybe you already have."

He leaves that innuendo hanging in the air between us, then practically skips to the nearest token booth and loads up his pockets. Andrew is right with him at every step. He's new here, I get it. He's sticking close to the person he knows best.

But would it kill him to look at me now and then?

"We should be in front of them," I say. "Andrew can't see us."

Ben steps up to the token booth and hands them a twenty. "Sure. After I slaughter you at Skee-Ball, we'll lead the way."

"That won't be too difficult," I say with a laugh. "I really do suck at this game."

We stop at an empty lane next to Chris, who is already cha-chinging his way to victory. He never misses. I mean *never*. Even if a ball hits a rubber ring and bounces the other way, it lands in another hole — usually one with a higher point value.

"You want a real challenge, Benjamin? Play against the legend." I take a step back, giving the boys some room. "Go ahead. I'll watch."

Ben lifts a brow and nods toward something to my right, then starts his game. I turn to look — and Andrew is standing next to me less than a foot away.

"H-hi." I grab a stray piece of hair that had fallen out of my bun and twirl it around my finger. Around and around and around... I'm burning up all the way down to my toes.

If he asks me if I have a sunburn again, I might cry.

Ben and Chris go head-to-head, slinging balls faster than I can keep up with.

"Your brother's really good at this," Andrew says.

Oh my god. Is he talking to me? He's talking to me. He's actually saying something that could turn into a conversation. What do I — *Breathe*.

Speak, Jessie!

"Yeah." I can't look at him, but somehow, I get a few words out. "He's really good."

Inwardly, I cringe. Nothing like repeating an obvious fact that someone already pointed out to you a second ago to show them you care.

"He talks about you all the time, you know," Andrew says.

Okay…maybe I can redeem myself.

"Really, what does he say?"

Andrew laughs—he's laughing! Hopefully with me and not at me. "All good things, Jessica," he says. "All good things."

Instinctively, my smile spreads big and wide. He's smiling back at me. He laughed with me. He knows "good things" about me. "Well—" I start, but my brother interrupts me.

"Yeahehess!" Chris bellows. "Game over! You lose!" He points both fingers at Ben, who takes his loss like a champ. To be fair, though, his score was two points less. I'd call it a tie.

Andrew steps up next to Chris and tells him that was amazing. He starts asking about logistics of the game, like he's super interested in *Skee-Ball*. Aaaaaand I've lost him.

Ben turns around to face me, then jerks his head toward Andrew while he's walking. "Anything?"

"Almost." I grab his hand and hurry to get ahead of my brother and his not-Brazilian bestie. But in only three steps we get stopped by someone who recognizes Ben.

A couple of girls. Giggling, photo-ready-face girls with salon-perfect hair and nails.

Chris and Andrew continue on ahead of us, and my brother says, "We'll catch up with you later."

"Oh—"

"Hey, Benny," the brunette says, her voice low and sultry and clearly an act. My god, she has legs for miles, and her denim shorts are so short I can see the pockets hanging out the front.

Also…Benny?

"Will you be at the park later for fireworks?" she croons.

"My girlfriend and I were planning on it." He turns to me, keeping a firm hold on my hand. "Weren't we, Jessie?"

"Um—yeah. Yes. We were. Are."

She looks down her nose at me, then back at Ben. "You're kidding, right?"

"Kidding about what exactly?" He stretches his arm around my shoulders and tucks me in closer to him.

She rolls her eyes and hands him a slip of paper. "Find me tomorrow. Or in a few days. Or whenever you decide to dump this one." Then she turns on her heels and she and her crony walk off, disappearing into the crowd on the fairway.

"Sorry about that," Ben says and tears up the paper into confetti, then lets it blow away in the breeze.

What... "Why did you do that?"

"Because she's a bitch."

"Who was she, anyway?"

"No idea." He starts walking again, keeping his arm across my back. "I've never seen her before in my life."

Is he just trying to make me feel better? She acted like she knew him. "She called you Benny," I remind him.

"And for that," he says, "I will put in a word with the devil to make sure her hellfire is extra hot. Molten-lava hot. The kind of hot that peels the skin from your skull. If she lost her face, it would be an improvement."

Jesus. I've never heard him talk like that before. About anyone.

"That really bothered you," I say.

"Yeah," he agrees. "Every time it happens. Every time someone thinks they know me just because they've seen me or heard of me or..." He stops himself, then blows out a breath.

But I know what he was thinking. "You mean like my parents did."

"Forget it, Jessie, it's fine." He points ahead of us. "You see that giant stuffed unicorn up there? I'm gonna win that for you. Right now."

"Pfft. What would I do with that? You want to impress me, Benjamin? Win me a giant ice cream cone."

As soon as I've said it, my cheeks and neck flare with heat and my mouth waters. The last time I had an ice cream cone with him, I ended up with my face in his lap. I'm suddenly having an intense craving for sausage.

A smile tugs up the corners of his mouth. "Challenge accepted."

Chapter Twenty-One

*A*n hour later, Ben has spent at least a hundred dollars on tokens, trying to win me something. None of the booths have ice cream as a prize. Not real ice cream, anyway, just toys. But still, he's on this mission to win something outrageous so he can give it to his "girlfriend."

The problem is, he keeps losing. Apparently Skee-Ball is his only skill at fair games.

"Benjamin, come on. Let's go on one of the rides. I'm bored."

He throws another dart but misses the balloon he aimed for. "I'm gonna get it this time."

"The only thing you're gonna get here is bankruptcy. And for you, that's saying something." I finish the last bite of the Polish sausage he bought for me. I'm the one who stood in line and paid for it—but with his money. He wouldn't leave the ring toss until he won it, and I was starving. He owed me.

"How is it possible for Trinity High's star quarterback two years running to have such suck-ass aim?"

"I'm rusty," he says. "I haven't touched a football in months."

He...hasn't?

"I'm close, Jess. I only need one more and that fat purple hippo is all yours."

"Gee, I might faint if you keep making such romantic gestures."

He draws back his hand, ready to throw his last dart.

I put my hand on his elbow. "Can I see that?"

"The dart?"

"Yeah."

"What," he says, handing it over. "You think it's rigged?"

Ready. Aim. Fire.

POP!

"Nope," I tell him. "I think I'm tired of standing here doing nothing. Let's go."

I start walking, and he says, "Wait, you forgot your hippo."

"I don't want the damn hippo. And technically"—I turn to face him and find him carrying a stuffed obnoxious-purple hippo with a dopey smile stitched onto its face—"it's not my hippo. I won that hippo for *you*."

He catches up to me. The thing is so big, Ben has to hold it at his side to see me. "Fine," he says. "It can be *our* hippo."

I snort. He is such a doofus sometimes. Spending a hundred dollars to win a two-dollar stuffy. "You can call it whatever you want as long as you're the idiot carrying it."

"Wilbur, then."

"What?"

"You said I could call it whatever I want. I'm calling him Wilbur."

"Wilbur is a pig," I say.

He makes a face. "Does *Charlotte's Web* hold a monopoly on animals named Wilbur?"

"Okay, whatever. I hope you and Wilbur are very happy together— Oh! There's Andrew and Chris! They're getting in line for The Hurricane." I pick up my pace, walking as fast as I can in flip-flops without tripping and face-planting on the concrete. Why didn't I wear different shoes? Something with arch support and padded soles?

Oh, right. Because I wanted Andrew to see my "fuck-me red" toenail polish. Which he's done a fantastic job of ignoring.

"Jessie!" Ben calls from behind me, and I slow enough to turn my head. "Ice cream!" He points to an ice cream stand with a line a mile long.

"You know what I want!" I shout back to him.

He gives me a thumbs-up, and I catch up to Chris and Andrew just as they're handing over tickets to get in line for The Hurricane. It's one of those spinning rides that always makes me puke, but today is about making sacrifices.

"Hey, Jessie James, you having fun?" Chris shoots me a happy-go-lucky smile.

"Uh…yeah…" *Shit.* I don't have any tickets.

I can't get in line without them.

"Do you have any extra tickets on you?" I ask my brother. "Benjamin has all of ours. He's in line for ice cream."

He pats down his shorts pockets, reaches in, and comes out with nothing. "Those were my last ones. I'll get more after this."

They're already in line, though, with more people coming in behind them. Andrew is waiting patiently for my crisis to end so they can move. *God.* Now he chooses to look at me? When I'm flustered and flushed from running and don't know what to do?

I focus on my brother, but I can still feel Andrew's eyes on me. "It's okay, I'll just run over and get them from him real quick." I take off in the other direction.

"Hurry!" Chris yells.

I'm trying.

Fortunately, thanks to Wilbur, it's stupid easy to find Ben in the crowd. I follow that purple hippo like a beacon until I get close to Ben, and…

He's at the front of the line already?

I catch up to him, panting. "How did you get through so fast?"

He jacks a thumb at the people in line behind him. "Everyone told me I could go ahead of them and wouldn't let me refuse. Can't imagine why," he adds dryly.

When the older woman at the vendor window appears with a giant waffle cone filled with salted caramel ice cream, Ben nods toward me and says, "It's hers."

She hands the cone to me. My mouth is watering so much I might drown in my own saliva. We're done with our lessons—I can eat this whenever and however I want to.

I sweep my tongue along the bottom edge, going all the way around once.

So good.

"Did you get something for yourself this time?" I say.

"I did." He grins. "Me and Wilbur are going to share, though."

"Don't be silly, Benjamin. Hippos are lactose intolerant."

The older woman returns again and hands him his own giant cone—chocolate with chunks of fudge all through it.

"Are we going back to the ride?" Ben says.

Kind of pointless now, isn't it? I'll have to catch Andrew on the next one.

"No, let's sit. My feet are killing me."

We *miraculously* find an empty picnic table *just* as we're approaching the eating area. A family of four suddenly gets up, looking at Ben like he's a goddamn king, before they've even finished their funnel cakes. I fight not to roll my eyes. Ben was right. All this special treatment and people assuming you expect it is really fucking annoying.

Ben sits across from me and props Wilbur up on the seat

beside him. "By the way," he says. "You owe me eight dollars for the ice cream and a hundred and twelve dollars for the hippo. That's an even one-twenty."

I freeze in the middle of a lick. Pull my tongue in. Swallow. "Excuse me?"

"I distinctly remember you telling me this morning, very adamantly, not to buy you things. So you'll have to pay me back for this. But I'm willing to split the cost of Wilbur, since we have joint custody."

When I look in his eyes, they're sparkling with humor. *Asshole.* He doesn't expect me to give him a dime.

"This ice cream was really eight dollars? If I'd known that, I would have skipped it."

Ben studies me for a moment. "Is that too much?"

"It is for me."

He takes a few licks, and I watch his tongue swirl around, then he bites into the top scoop to pluck out an especially large chunk of fudge.

God, what a great day to be fudge.

My phone buzzes in my back pocket, startling me so much I let out a little yelp and nearly drop my cone. Ben gives me a questioning look. "My phone," I say and finagle it out and check the screen.

Chris: *i think we lost you*

Chris: *we're heading to the ferris wheel*

Chris: *where are you guys*

I hand my cone over to Ben so I can type a reply.

Me: *We'll meet you there.*

"Come on," I say to Ben, stuffing my phone into my pocket and taking my ice cream back from him. "They're going to the Ferris wheel. If we go now, we can catch them."

"That's on the whole other side of the lot," Ben protests. He gets up and walks with me anyway, tucking as much of

Wilbur under his arm as he can fit.

I speed-walk through the crowd while speed-eating my ice cream. I'm nearly finished with it when I can finally see the line for the Ferris wheel. But my flip-flops have had enough of all this walking. The inside band on both of them have been rubbing on my arches since we got here, and the pain has gone from a dull ache to a sharp sting.

"Jessie," Ben says, slowing. "You're limping."

"I'm fine. It's just these shoes giving me blisters. I shouldn't have worn them."

He slows even more and starts looking around. "We should go to First Aid and get you some Band-Aids."

"No," I insist. "We're almost there. I can rest my feet on the ride. I'll be fine."

Finally, *finally*, we reach the line, but I don't see Chris or Andrew anywhere. They must have got on already. I look up and up and up. It's impossible to see clearly who's in the baskets.

Dammit.

"We missed them." I turn to face Ben.

He's handing Wilbur to some stranger's kid, saying, "Take good care of him for me." The little girl just stares up at him in awe like she's been touched by the divine.

I know the feeling.

Then Ben comes back over and *lifts* me up into his arms. He starts walking, but we're moving away from the Ferris wheel.

Getting that pressure and sliding friction off my feet is heaven. But, "We can't leave. We need to be there when they get off the ride."

Ben just keeps walking. People are actually parting the way for him, like he's Moses crossing the Red Sea. Everyone is...*looking* at us.

"You're making a scene. Put me down."

"I draw the line at blood, Jess."

"I'm not—"

"Don't argue with me on this."

I angle my head so I can see at least one of my feet dangling from his bent arm under my legs. Oh, *shit*. That's a bloody massacre.

Goes great with my fire-engine-red toenail polish.

I close my eyes, lay my head on his shoulder, and try to block out everything that's happening around me. Ben's hurried steps and the stress lines in his brow. The entire city of Trinity watching me get carried like a pitiful, helpless baby. But I can still hear it. The talk.

They're calling him a hero.

Yes, look at that brave warrior, defender of fragile feet, obliterator of blister wounds.

When we're safely inside the little building labeled First Aid, it takes all of five minutes for the nurse to clean me up and put bandages on. Then she so helpfully suggests, "You should wear better shoes."

My flip-flops are half covered in blood, so they have to dispose of them like biohazardous waste. Now I'm barefoot and bandaged and Ben's going to have to carry me all the way across the fairway and out to the parking lot to his car. I don't know whether to laugh or cry.

Well. At least my toes look good.

"Hop on," he says, patting his back.

Do I have a choice? Nope.

Ben squats down by the cot I'm sitting on so I can just lean forward onto him, then he secures my legs with his arms, and I secure my arms around his neck, and he slowly, steadily, stands us up.

As soon as we're outside, the freak show stares are all

over us again.

"Get me out of this crowd," I say in Ben's ear.

"Working on it."

Don't look at me don't look at me don't look at me…

This thing with us worked better in secret, away from prying eyes. Why did I think that I, someone who avoids the spotlight at all costs, could be out in public with Benjamin Oliver?

He doesn't just have a spotlight on him in this town. He has all the stage lights, too.

It's inescapable.

Ben stops, and I look around. We're back at the Ferris wheel.

"What are you—"

He walks right up to the operator and says, "Let us on."

Let us on…ahead of everyone else in line.

Let us on…without any tickets.

Let us on…I'm not asking you. I'm telling you.

Like he owns the place.

Maybe he does. Because the operator lets us on.

He carries me into the big metal basket and sets me down on the seat inside, then sits down next to me with his arm protectively around me, and the operator locks us in.

"Better?" Ben says.

We go up. Slowly. But with every inch more between me and the crowd below, I can breathe a little easier.

"Much better," I say.

Then my phone buzzes, and I pull it out of my back pocket.

Chris: *what happened where are you*

Me: *On the Ferris wheel.*

Chris: *hahaha we just left there*

Yeah, it's hilarious that we keep missing each other. It's

fucking hilarious I thought I'd have a day of fun with my brother, who hasn't been around since Christmas, and a guy I'd really like to get to know, and I ended up having a day of hell with Ben. It's a scream.

Chris: *long story but we're leaving*

Chris: *ran into an ex girlfriend from high school*

Chris: *remember lindsey?*

Yes, unfortunately, I do. My jaw clenches. What did she do this time?

Chris: *she invited us to a party about an hour from here*

Okay, first of all, why would he do anything with Lindsey after their disastership? And second of all—

Me: *You're leaving NOW?*

Chris: *yes*

Chris: *have fun with your boy i'll be back tomorrow*

"Tomorrow?" I frown at his last text.

"What's tomorrow?" Ben says.

"My brother is ditching me for some party tonight."

"Wow."

"Right? I love my brother, but you know what? That's so typical of him, treating me like the 'baby sister' all the time. Maybe I want to go to a party, too. Is that so hard to believe?" I blow out a sigh, returning my phone to my pocket. "What a disaster today was. And it's not even over yet."

"He just got here, Jess," Ben says gently. "You'll have plenty of chances to spend time with him before he leaves." He pauses. "Plenty of chances to play sexy siren with Andrew, too."

"True." It's just hard not to feel like a failure when I keep failing so spectacularly.

Our basket reaches the top of the wheel and stops. I can see the whole town from up here. All the expensive houses with pools in the backyard and professional landscaping.

Boutique shops and little plazas. Trees…a lot of trees and green, open spaces.

But if I turn my head just slightly to the right, there's a clear divide, where the nice part of town ends and the not-so-great part of town begins. The houses are smaller and fit closer together. The yards are tiny. Postage-stamp lawns, my dad calls them. And the streets aren't as well-paved, full of cracks and potholes waiting to be patched.

It's a totally different world.

"Should I take you home?" Ben says.

"No, I've never missed the fireworks with Rayna, so I have to go. But…" I look down at my feet then back up at him. "I need shoes."

He nods like he's thinking. "Do I have your permission?"

"To what?"

"Buy you a new pair of shoes?"

"Oh…" Is he really asking me?

My heart melts, and my insides go mushy. He's been listening. He's *trying*.

"Benjamin," I say with a smile. "You can buy me all the shoes."

Chapter Twenty-Two

*A*fter our detour to the shoe boutique, Ben drives us to the biggest park in Trinity, where they hold the city fireworks every year. It's already dark, and there will be nowhere close to park the car, so these brand-new kicks I got are vital. So are the other six pairs of new shoes for me in the trunk. *Honest.*

Once I decided it was okay for Ben to spend whatever he wanted on me — for this specific thing only — I might have gone on a little shopping spree. I might have had fun doing it, too.

"I made us late," I say while Ben circles the car around yet another city block to find a spot. Where are his Trinity minions now, clearing the way when we need them?

"The show hasn't started yet," he says. "And Jeremy said they got a good spot on the lawn, so we're fine. You didn't make us late. You just gave us an opportunity to make a grand entrance."

Right. Because that's what I wanted.

This night is never going to end.

And now, I won't even get the benefit of Andrew seeing us. He's off galivanting who knows where with my brother and who knows what other girls, and Ben and I still have to act like we're Couple of the Year.

It was so much easier when we were just having sex.

We probably won't ever have sex again, either. What would be the point?

Besides the obvious.

I can't do it. I can't give in to my physical need for Ben when I should be focusing on Andrew. If this works, I'll be having plenty of sex again in no time.

You can get through this abstinence, Jessie. Stop thinking about his abs. And his shoulders. And his fingers. And his goddamn sexy mouth all over you. Be strong.

Ben finally parks the car and shuts off the engine. "What are you thinking about?"

"Nothing."

"Liar," he says. "You're blushing."

I roll my eyes and open the passenger door.

"Jessie, wait. I need to know how far you want to take us faking it."

"Not as far as you're thinking."

He smirks. "What *I'm* thinking or what *you're* thinking?"

"Come on, Benjamin. You know we're both thinking the same thing."

He laughs at that, putting his hands up in mock surrender.

I flash a smile, but it quickly fades into a sigh. "All right. Public displays of affection only, where other people will see us. That's the whole point, right? So, nothing private."

"You mean no sex," he says.

"I mean no sex, no kissing, no nothing unless someone else can see it."

His face goes hard. "Wait a minute, wait a minute. You're saying I can't have any kind of sex with anyone for possibly six weeks?"

"I didn't think of it like that, but yes. That is exactly what I'm saying." Because Ben may have a lot of faults, and he's been with a lot of girls, but I've never heard anyone say he cheated on them. If he was with someone else, he would look like he's cheating on me, even though our whole relationship is fake.

"Are you trying to kill me, Jessie?" he says, completely serious.

"Hey, I won't be getting any, either. We're in this together now, no backing out. Your pain is my pain—"

"There doesn't have to be any pain for either of us when, A, everyone already assumes we've started fucking, and B, they're *right*." He shakes his head like he's exasperated with me. "Four weeks, Jessie. Four weeks with you. That's longer than anyone else I've been with. Add another six, and it's the whole fucking summer. I'm spending my *entire summer* with you."

"Not if it works," I remind him. "So just…make sure it works."

He drops his head all the way to the steering wheel. "I should get a third favor for this, you witch."

"Don't push it, scarecrow." I get out of the car and wait for him to come around.

When he reaches me, he snatches my hand and keeps hold of it while we're walking to the park entrance. It's three hundred blocks from here.

"You don't have to do that yet," I say. "We're alone out here."

"We're in public. That's the deal. Besides, you never know who might be watching."

True.

"And maybe I don't mind holding your hand. Did you ever think of that?"

I snort. "What a glowing two-star review."

He blows out a breath, and we're quiet for a whole block.

Then he says, the edge to his voice gone now, "How are your feet holding up?"

"Good."

"Good."

It's past sunset, so his shades are gone, but the streetlamps are reflecting off his eyes, making them sparkle like gems. The closer we get to the park, the more people we see gathered or wandering about. Kids with glowing neon necklaces, bracelets, and headbands. Moms pushing strollers with American flags stuck into the top, flapping in the breeze. Dads making dad jokes over beer, their loud guffaws echoing down the streets.

We get a few looks, but only from people close enough to see Ben's face as we walk by, and they leave us alone. But all of that changes once we're inside the park, looking for Rayna and Jeremy on the crowded lawn. This is where I start recognizing faces I've seen in the halls of Trinity High.

Convincing my family that we're a couple? No problem.

Convincing random people we happen to see? Easy.

Convincing our peers? Doubtful.

So here goes nothing.

I grab Ben's upper arm with my other hand, hugging it against me, turning his body into my own personal shield.

"You okay?" he says.

I nod too rapidly, and my voice is extra high when I say, "Yeah, I'm fine."

"Hey, Oliver!" someone shouts from across the crowd. "Over here!"

That didn't sound like Jeremy, but Ben raises a hand toward whoever it is to let them know he saw them, and we turn in that direction. I release his hand so he can go say hi without me getting in the way. He must know them. Football buddy?

No. Make that plural. *Buddies.* An entire group of them with their boyfriends and girlfriends and one-night dates. I recognize some of their faces, but no names come to mind. I've seen some of them on the football field, though. These are Ben's friends that I've never met.

His life doesn't revolve around me, I know. It's still weird to see him bumping fists and giving bro hugs to these...strangers.

"Jessie, you made it!"

I turn toward the familiar voice, and there's Rayna's big red hair and big round eyes, arms out wide, coming in for a hug.

"Hey." I give her a huge, squeezy hug, and all my built-up tension from the day disappears. "You have no idea how happy I am to see you. This has been such a crazy day."

She gives me one more hard squeeze, then pulls away. And this girl has some kind of laser-precision fashion radar, because the first thing she sees are my new shoes.

"When did you get those? They're so cute!" She pauses, then looks me right in the eye. "Jessie, I know that brand. It's expensive, even for me."

"Yeah, um..." I fiddle with my hands. "Ben got them for me."

"Shut. Up." Her eyes get as big and white as goose eggs. "He's buying you gifts already? It won't be long now."

"Won't be long for what?"

"Giving you gifts means he wants to give you something else, too." She lifts a brow. "That's how it was with me and Jeremy."

Speak of the devil, Jeremy comes up behind Rayna, wraps his long, lean arms around her, and bends down to plant a wet kiss on her cheek. "Hi, Jessie," he says, lifting his head. "How was the fair?"

"Ask Benjamin. He had a better time than I did."

"Why, what happened?" Rayna says.

"What didn't happen is the easier thing to answer. Anyway, I got new shoes out of it." I flash her a smile, and she returns it tenfold. "Can we go sit now? I've been on my feet half the day already, and we had to park the car in China."

"Sure, we're right over there." She starts walking, and I turn to find Ben.

He's laughing about something with three of the guys, and more than a few of the girls are giving him rapt attention. Just another day in the life of Benjamin Oliver.

"Benjamin," I say as loudly as I can without sounding like I'm shouting.

He immediately stops whatever he was saying and smiles at me. "Ready to go now?"

I nod, and he steps away from the group, taking up my hand as soon as he reaches me.

"What the fuck," some guy says behind us. "Is that his new girl? *Really?* If he was that desperate, I could have hooked him up with one of my sister's friends."

Ben slows his steps.

"Nah, there's something going on there," another guy says. "He lost a bet, probably."

Everyone laughs. Literally *everyone.*

"Isn't that the weird chick who sat at his lunch table? I don't know how he could stand it."

Ben stops now, but he doesn't turn around.

I clench my teeth together and squeeze Ben's hand. Is he going to say anything? Or just let them keep making fun of me like this? I can think of a million things I'd say—a lot of them using some form of *fuck you*—if I could only get the words out. But my throat is closing up and my chest feels tight.

Rayna must have realized she got too far away from me and turned back, because she appears right next to me again. "Don't listen to them," she says. "Come on, let's get away from these assholes."

"In a minute, Rayna," Ben says without looking at her. Then he turns to face me.

And sweeps me up in one of his signature blazing-hot kisses.

Sweet. Fucking. Jesus.

It's only been a few days since I felt his lips on mine, but it's like I was on the verge of dehydration and he just dropped me into an oasis. God, I missed this.

So much.

I should be embarrassed by the noises coming from both of us right now, but there's no room for me to be anything here but lost in sweet surrender. He's devouring me. In front of everyone. His hand is up on the back of my head, fingers threaded into my hair, giving it little tugs as we basically eat each other. He tastes so fucking good.

Then I feel both of his palms running down my back.

Oh god.

I know what he's about to do, and no way am I going to stop him.

His hands slide under the waistband of my knit shorts, inside my underwear, and grab my bare ass. One hand on each cheek. Squeezing and kneading them like stress balls. Pulling me closer against the front of him until there's not a molecule of space left between us. And he still hasn't stopped kissing me.

How long have we been at it? An hour? A year?

Finally, just when I'm about to collapse from lack of oxygen, Ben pulls away slowly. Only far enough for our lips to separate, and he stays that close for a minute, nose to nose, staring into my eyes and grinning.

I can't see straight I'm so dizzy. He's going to have to carry me again.

Ben takes my hand in his, clasping them together, and turns to face the small crowd around us. With his other hand, he raises his middle finger. At all of them.

And then walks away without a word, clutching me beside him.

As soon as my back is turned, the chatter starts.

"Well. Didn't see that coming."

"Who *is* that girl with him?"

"Why don't you kiss *me* like that?"

"Dude, that was practically porn."

Another minute and it would have been.

I smile to myself, following Rayna and Jeremy through the crowd sitting on blankets across the lawn. Ben doing that with me was seven thousand times more effective than anything he could have said to those fuckers.

When we get to our spot, Kamy and Todd give us all a wave and a "heyyyy." They're still together. They still haven't decided anything. They both look totally normal, like they aren't facing the biggest decision of their lives right now. If I didn't already know, I wouldn't even be able to guess.

As soon as I sit and cross my legs, Rayna and Kamy pounce on me like wildcats, leaving the three guys no choice but to talk among themselves.

Rayna hits me first. "You and Ben are so cute together!"

"I have to agree," Kamy says. "I wasn't sure what I'd think when I saw you together for the first time, but I can tell you now: You guys look super adorable holding hands."

"Thanks—"

"Kamy, you missed them kissing!" Rayna squeals, then tells her everything that happened a few minutes ago. The boys are maybe two feet away. Ben can hear all of this.

I can pick up on bits of what they're talking about, too. Jeremy is telling Todd about how changing diapers really isn't that bad once you get a system down.

He's the oldest of six kids. He knows his stuff.

If anyone around us is hearing this, they probably think we're all backward. The girls are discussing pornographic PDA and the boys are discussing proper baby care. Score one for crushing societal expectations.

"Damn," Kamy says when Rayna finishes her story, then she lowers her voice as she asks, "How far have you gone with him?"

"I..." I can't make eye contact with either of them.

How do I answer this? How long can I keep lying to my friends before the guilt makes me do something reckless, like tell them the truth?

"I really don't want to get into this out here in public," I say weakly. "Can we talk about something else?"

Rayna huffs, then gives me a long, dramatic "*fiiiiiiiine.*" She snaps her fingers at me. "But the minute you-know-what happens, you better be on the phone with me."

I snort. "You want me to call you as we're doing it? Why, so you can listen?"

"Stop it." She gives me a little shove. "You know what I mean!"

Thankfully, she and Kamy delve into other topics, and it isn't long before "The Star-Spangled Banner" is booming out of hidden speakers all throughout the park. That's the signal. The fireworks are about to start.

We split up and then pair up, spreading out on the blankets. Ben sits with his legs in a V and says, "Sit here," patting the spot directly in front of him. I settle in and nestle my ass up against his crotch—and it's like bolts of electricity are shooting through me, starting there and going out to my fingers, head, and toes.

We're supposed to be pretending, but the spark is real. You can't fake that.

I can't forget four weeks of naked time with him, either. No matter what happens from here, no matter what paths we take or how far apart we split, I will always have that memory. He will always be my first. Nothing and no one can take that away.

Ben gently wraps his arms around me. "Comfortable?"

"Mm-hmm." I hug my arms around his, lean back against his chest, smiling, and let out a long sigh. This is pure bliss.

If I close my eyes, I can imagine this thing with us being real. If there was a chance that Ben would ever really look at me like someone he wants to be with in every way. If there was a chance that where I come from and where he comes from didn't matter, and seeing the two of us together wouldn't make anyone question it. If there was a chance that we wouldn't fight all the time and we could be happy...

It's a fantasy, though. There's no chance of any of that being reality. At the end of summer, he'll be moving to another state, going to college and hooking up with whoever he wants to, whenever he wants to, and I'll be working out some kind of long-distance relationship with Andrew. Because that's what I want—someone who can commit. Someone who isn't just looking for the physical.

As long as I remember that, everything will be fine.

He leans his head down and brushes his lips across the side of my neck in a whisper of a kiss. And as the fireworks explode, crackle, and *boom* above us, my head falls back against him and his soft kisses find their way around to my jaw, then my mouth. I turn a little to get a better angle, and we're locked in now.

Forget the fireworks. Forget the whole damn world.

I know it won't last, but for these few moments, the fantasy is real.

Chapter Twenty-Three

*I*f Rayna asks me one more time if Ben and I have done the nasty yet, I'm going to crack. It's been a solid week of "did you have sex," "are you having sex now," "how about now?" Now? Now? *Now?!*

She's going to break me, and in my frustration, the truth will slip out—actually, no, now that we're dating, we're not having sex at all, and when we weren't dating, we had a daily hump-a-thon for a whole month. Because *that* makes sense.

I'm the reason we aren't getting naked now. I insisted we couldn't. Shouldn't. And I still stand by my decision, but the longer this goes on, the harder Ben is to resist. I get to hug him, snuggle him, hold his hand, breathe him in, kiss the hell out of him—but no further, because everything is in public. It's only been a week of abstinence, and what if I have to endure five more weeks of this torture?

Ben was right. We're both going to die if this doesn't end soon.

And I'm no closer to being with Andrew now than I was a week ago.

I clock out from my shift at the library and go to my locker to get my wallet and check my phone. I have several new texts from Rayna asking the same. Damn. Question. And one new cryptic text from Ben.

Ben: *need to talk I'll pick you up after work*

I hurry outside, and his car is idling by the curb. When he catches my eye, everything inside me lifts and floats, light as a feather. I hop into the passenger seat—no shades and ball cap needed—and buckle my seat belt.

"Hey, you," I say with a smile.

"Hey." He leans over and gives me a peck of a kiss. "Can we go somewhere and talk?"

His tone is all wrong. His body is all tense. His kiss was too quick.

"Yeah," I say. "What's going on?"

He starts driving, his hands on the wheel with a stranglehold. "Football moms doing what they do best," he says. "Meddling."

"This has to do with football?" In the five weeks we've been seeing each other, I can count on one hand how many times the word "football" was even mentioned between us.

"Indirectly," he answers. "Remember the night of the fireworks at the park?"

"Yes…"

His jaw clenches. "A lot of those guys played varsity with me."

I had assumed that. But I'm going to keep my mouth shut unless he asks me a question. He's never come to me with a problem before, and this is clearly a problem—a big one, if it's got him visibly bothered. This is foreign territory for us. I need to just sit back and see what course it takes.

Ben makes a turn onto a side street. I think we're heading to the park he took me to for lunch a few weeks ago. It's one of the more secluded ones, with less foot traffic.

"I didn't think about anything but what happened in the moment," he says. "I didn't think about anything but telling those guys off for treating you like garbage. I didn't think what would happen after…" He shakes his head. "I just didn't think. And now we both have a problem."

Oh *shit*. We're in trouble for something? For kissing at a park? People do that all the time. Though, to be fair, that wasn't your typical kiss.

We enter the tree-lined drive that leads to the little hidden park in the woods, and Ben pulls into a nearly empty lot. He parks the car. Cuts the engine. And stares out the windshield like the grass and trees and picnic benches might hold all the answers he seeks.

For what seems like an hour, he's quiet. I let him have his quiet, his time to gather himself and think about how to say what he has to say. If people did that for me, instead of expecting words to fill every second of time, I might not be so bad at conversing.

Finally, he half turns in his seat to look at me. "I know this is my fault. I know I don't have the best reputation as a boyfriend. To be honest, I never even considered myself anyone's boyfriend, not really. Not when the whole relationship was a week or two of nookie and done. But now, it's different. I'm calling you my girlfriend. I'm treating you seriously. And when I kissed you like that to make a point, it made a really good point, and you know…people talk."

Yeah, people talk. Myself included. Who *hasn't* talked about someone when that person wasn't there?

Ben runs a hand over his face then through his hair, roughing it up. "I need some air."

My chest tightens, and I have to clench my jaw to keep my expression from showing how worried I am. I've never seen him like this. Has anyone? It's not like him at all.

He gets out of the car, and I follow him around to the grass. As soon as I'm close, he snatches up my hand and we start walking down a path through the trees. The move is so natural, it's just what we do now. If he *didn't* hold my hand, it would feel off.

We walk for a while before he starts talking again. "So... word got around about us. It started with the guys and spread from there, and at some point, someone's mom or a lot of someones' moms overheard the story. And by then it had been exaggerated from the truth. Did you know we stripped naked right there in the park and did it doggy style in front of everyone?" He gives me a weak smile.

"I think I would remember that." God. People are just shit. Pure, steaming *shit*.

"Me too," he says. "Once the football moms had their version of the story, probably a different one for each of them, it all got back around to *my* mom, who told my dad."

"*Fuck.*" My breath hitches. "Now what?"

"Now...my parents want to meet this girl who's had such a powerful effect on me. You're officially invited to our family dinner."

"What?" I stop walking, and he stops and turns to face me. "Benjamin, no. I-I can't do that." My breaths come faster and faster, visions of me making an absolute wreck of myself in front of the most prestigious family in all of Trinity floating through my head. "You know how I am around people I don't know. It even happened with you the day we met."

My tongue getting tied up, my face catching fire, my breathing too fast—my stupid shyness was the start of everything bad between us. And every time I meet someone new, I can feel it's going to happen again. I'm going to ruin a relationship before it even exists.

"I know," Ben says. "I was there."

"Then tell him I can't."

He takes both of my hands now and holds them to his

chest, steadying me. "I tried, Jess. I swear, I tried. But my dad always gets his way. He makes sure of it."

Do I even want to know what that means?

No. I don't. If a mafia is coming for me, I'd rather be ignorant until it happens, because I can't stop it from happening either way.

And I *want* to help Ben. I just don't know if I *can*.

"When you say family, who's included in all that?"

He releases one of my hands, and we start walking again. The air here smells lush and green and earthy. I take in as deep a breath as I can, then blow it out. I do it again. And again.

"There's my parents, obviously," Ben says, "and I have two brothers, both of them married with kids. Dean has two, and Jake has two, with another girl on the way. My sister, Lori, who is closest in age to me but still pushing thirty, has a fiancé. And every single one of them will be at this dinner."

I do the count in my head—and panic.

"I can't," I repeat. "That's *twelve* people. Strangers. I *can't*."

"I know that…being around people you don't know is really hard for you. And my family being who they are will just make that ten times worse. But I…I wouldn't ask you to do this if it wasn't important or if I felt like I had any other choice. I'm desperate, Jessie. I need your help. So…I'm asking you to do this as a favor. One of two that you owe me."

I plant my feet, and he turns toward me, but I can't look at him right now.

He's serious with this. He's goddamned fucking *serious*.

When I made the deal with him to pay him with a favor, agreeing to put myself through one of the worst kinds of situations I can think of for me personally was *not* what I had in mind.

Ben puts his hands on either side of my face, gently

turning my head so I have no choice but to look at him. "Please, Jessie? Please…"

How can I look in those pleading eyes and say no? He's done so much for me over the last several weeks. We made a deal. So I can't go back on my word, even if it's hard to keep it.

"I…" I try to take in a breath, and it just feels like I'm hiccupping. "I'll do it."

The wrinkles in his brow soften and smooth out, his eyes still locked on mine. "You will? Really?"

I nod, afraid that if I speak, the words that come out will be "just kidding, bye."

"Thank you." He smiles so big he laughs, picking me up off the ground and swinging me around a full rotation before setting me back down. "Thank you, Jessie."

"Yeah." I nod again. Maybe if I keep nodding, I'll wake up and discover it was just a nightmare.

Ben turns around on the path, taking us back the way we came. "I better get you home now," he says, "so you'll have time to get ready."

What?

"Family dinner is always formal," he continues, "so wear something formal, but, you know, not prom formal. No taffeta or tiaras. But no pants or shorts, either."

I repeat, *what?*

"Your sundresses are nice," he says, "but if you have something maybe a step up in formality from that, it would be perfect." He pauses, looking at me. "Oh… Should I get you some new clothes?"

"No, no…" I shake my head. "I'm confused. When is this dinner?"

"Tonight," he says. "I'll pick you up at six."

The trees around us spin into a blur of green. *"Tonight?"*

· · ·

The first thing I do when I get home is go straight to my room and scream into my pillow.

I was so stupid to think that he would never need a real favor from me. That he would never *need* anything from me, period. And I can't even blame him for this being needed. If I hadn't come into this arrangement with him, none of this would be happening now. I agreed to it. Not only one favor, but two—I can't imagine what the next one will be, if this is the bar.

Past Me is a dumbass.

I pound my fist into my pillow. *Stupid. Stupid. Stupid!*

And the meeting-his-family drama and being picked apart by them like vultures on a carcass isn't the only thing I'm worried about.

I have nothing to wear.

Nothing.

Those plain cotton dresses? That's as fancy as it gets with me.

Ben offered to buy me something, which I would have said yes to if I had been thinking clearly. But I wasn't. And now here I am.

I push myself up and sit on the edge of my mattress.

I have a best friend who knows fashion. Rayna even has the money—aka a credit card she got from her parents—to purchase something really classy if I want it, and she would. She's never been against buying me things. She just knows I don't want her to. Most of the time.

This feels like an emergency, though.

I pull up my chat with her on my phone…and see three new texts just in the time between now and when I left work.

Rayna: *are you with ben right now?*

Rayna: *have you seen him naked?*

Rayna: *you aren't replying so you must be screwing*

Fuck. Fucking fuck on a fuck stick.

If I ask her to help me get all dolled up for some fancy dinner with Ben and his family, she'll be texting me through the whole thing asking if he's popping my cherry at that very moment. Every minute, on the minute. She'll find me something great to wear, but she'll be talking to me about sex the whole time she's doing it, thinking I need her to prepare me.

And I. Will. Crack.

Possibly crack her skull, but more likely, I'll have an explosive meltdown and tell her everything just so she'll stop. And then *she* will have an explosive meltdown and we *all* die.

I can't do that.

I value her friendship too much, and the general population of the human race.

Me: *Calm yourself.*

Me: *I was at work most of the day and now I'm home. We did nothing.*

I toss the phone onto my bed and stare at my closet, dread coiling tighter and tighter in my gut. Even if I had a "nice" dress, I don't know how to do anything with my hair other than a basic bun. I'll look ridiculous.

"Oh, hey, honey," my mom says from the hallway, pulling my attention. "I didn't know you were home yet. I was thinking of ordering some pizza, what toppings do you want?"

I blow out a sigh. There are so many things wrong with what she just said.

First, I came home late from my shift because I spent time with Ben at the park before coming home, and she didn't notice that she got home before me, which happens almost never. So I wasn't here...and she didn't know or care.

Also, she almost always gets pizza on Friday nights, because she gets paid on Fridays and wants to "indulge a little," so she doesn't have to say it like it's something new and different.

And she didn't ask if I wanted pizza, or maybe, just maybe, if I might want something else.

Finally, she knows what toppings I would want, because they're always the same. Pepperoni, Italian sausage, and banana peppers. One or all of those, or two in any combination.

This isn't hard.

"Actually, I won't be here for dinner," I tell her. "I'll be with Benjamin and his family."

Her eyes go big and round. "Oh my goodness, really?" She brings a fist to her mouth like she has to keep herself from screaming with joy. "You're going inside the mayor's mansion?"

I just blink at her. Part of me wants to say, you know what, Mom? If you were involved in literally any part of my life, you might know by now that not only have I already been inside that huge-gantic fortress, but I had sex all night in it, too.

But the other part of me, the sensible part, doesn't want her to die of a heart attack.

"Yes," I say instead. "And I have nothing to wear—"

Something hits me. My mother might not know me very well anymore, but I still know her. Extremely well. She has a knack for looking posh on a budget.

"Mom." I jump up from my bed and pull her inside from the hallway, closing the door behind her. "You can help me with this."

"With what?" she says.

"I'm having a fashion emergency."

She gives me a look. "*You* are?"

"Yes! Because I have no fashion!" *Duh.* "And I have to wear something"—air quotes—"'nice.' I don't have anything…"

Wait a minute. Yes, I do have something.

One of those frivolous pairs of shoes Ben got for me last week. Glittery baby-pink high heels. Like, it looks like they have actual glitter on them. The sparkle is outrageous.

And totally not my usual style, but I loved them too much to pass up. I told myself, even if I never wear these anywhere outside my own room, at least I'll have them, and that's more than I ever expected. When would I ever have the opportunity or the money to buy them again?

Now I do have a reason to wear them. Maybe Past Me wasn't so stupid after all.

I rush to open my closet door and drop to my knees, scrambling through all the shoe boxes I stacked in there.

"Where did you get all those shoes?" Mom asks, her voice breathy with disbelief.

"Benjamin."

"Good heavens, that boy must really like you…" She trails off, probably wondering why I'm suddenly acting like a rabid walrus.

I open every box, tear off every lid, until I find the one that sparkles like a jewel in the sun.

There you are, my pretties.

I lift them out of the box by their narrow heels, push myself up to stand, and turn toward my mother. "I just need something to go with these," I rush. "Do you have anything in your closet that might work?"

She just stares at me, silent, with a look on her face I can't figure out.

No…she isn't staring at me. She's staring at something behind me.

I turn to look and—*ohmyfuckinggod!*

Among the scattered shoe boxes and lids, there's a small, plain cardboard box with the flaps open, tipped on its side so the label is facing up.

The Package.

Her package.

"Is that…" she starts, sounding bewildered, then moves around me to pick it up. "It is." Her tone is curt now. "Explain."

"I…um…" I swallow hard. "Dad got home early that day, and he saw it before I did. I was there when he opened it."

My mother's eyebrows hit her hairline. "*He* opened it?"

"Yeah, and…I didn't know what it was? I mean I did, in general, once he opened it and told me. And you said to hide it from him, so I…told him it was mine, and…"

She shakes her head slowly, staring at the box. "I thought this got lost in the mail. I had them cancel the order and give me my money back. When they kept insisting their records indicated it had been delivered, I insisted that their records were shit." She pops her gaze up to mine. "You had it this whole time? Have you *used* it?"

"No!" I clutch the heels of my shoes harder, just to have something to squeeze instead of my mother's throat. This is *her* fault. "Mom, I don't even know what that is or what it does. I didn't know what else to do with it after that happened. I had to take it, Dad thought it was mine. So I hid it, like you told me to, and then…I didn't know how to tell you without both of us dying from the awkwardness, and eventually I just forgot about it."

She blows out an exasperated breath, rolling her eyes away from me like she can't stand to look at me right now.

"You can have it," I say. "I don't want it."

Her shoulders drop. "It was an impulse buy. I wanted you to hide it so I could return it without your father ever knowing I had it in the first place." She shakes her head at the thing. "When you've been with someone for as long as he and I have been together, sometimes you need to get creative."

T. M. I.

Finally, she looks at me, but then she stretches the box out toward me. "You might as well keep it now."

I take it from her hands gingerly, waiting for her to explain what this is and how it works. Waiting for her to ask me, *Since when did you start having sex?* Waiting for her to care.

Her version of The Talk that every parent is supposed to have with their child happened when I was fourteen. She scheduled me an appointment with a gynecologist, left it up to the doctor to tell me everything, and never said a word to me about it since.

Come on, Mom, sit down and talk to me. Let's have a real conversation for once. Give me the motherly advice I think I don't need but actually do.

But she doesn't. And I should have known better than to even hope she would.

"Thank you," I bite out, then toss it into the dark, cramped closet where it belongs.

When I turn back around, she says, "Those shoes are fab, Jessica. And I have just the thing for you to complete the look." She heads to the hall and makes a turn toward her bedroom. "Seems this boy is good for you," she says, raising her voice because I haven't moved yet. "You're already acting more like someone of class."

That shouldn't sting as much as it does. It's not the first time she's insinuated I'm one plaid shirt away from being a tomboy, or implied that being a tomboy would be unacceptable. But it stings so much, I feel it all the way up to my eyes, holding back the urge to let out my frustration and cry.

She wasn't always like this.

I glance at my Dr. Seuss collection across the room, then swallow back the tightness in my throat, take a deep, cleansing breath, and go to my mother so she can do what she's been hoping to do with me for the last ten years.

Pretty me up like I'm the daughter she really wanted.

Chapter Twenty-Four

Mom puts the finishing touches on my makeup, then steps away from her floor-length mirror, and I finally get a look at myself.

I blink a few times, like my eyes aren't working correctly. What am I seeing? Because that suave, gorgeous woman can't possibly be me.

She has luscious lips, doe eyes, *cheekbones*. Her hair is swept back in an elegant chignon with pearl clips at the crown—fake pearls that look real. Just like the earrings. And the necklace. And…oh my *god*, I have cleavage.

I don't know when Mom got this silky satin pink blouse and slim black skirt, because I can't remember ever seeing them before. She and I aren't the same shape or size, yet they fit me perfectly.

The shoes, though… The shoes just make everything come together like they were sold as a set. And my legs look really long and shapely. It's like I'm borrowing someone else's legs for the night.

The scariest thing? I look like someone who belongs in Trinity now.

I guess that's the point, though. I'm having dinner with the mayor.

"What do you think?" Mom says. When was the last time she smiled that big?

She's so damn proud of herself for transforming me into something I'm not.

I take a test walk in the heels and stumble a little, nearly rolling my ankle. "No, this is bad. I won't make it—"

"No, no, you'll be fine," Mom insists. "All you have to do is keep a hold of your man's arm whenever you walk; he'll keep you upright."

I give her a look. "Isn't that a little archaic? Relying on a man just to be able to walk?"

"No," she says. "You're not relying on him. You're allowing him the privilege of being your cane."

"Okay," I snort, then take a few deep breaths and twist back and forth, smoothing my hands down the skirt. "I guess I'm ready."

"Wait, one more thing." She rushes back to her closet and pulls something sparkly down from the top shelf. Then she hands it over to me.

"Mom…" My jaw drops. It's a clutch bag in the same baby-pink glitter as my shoes. She never left the house while I was getting ready. I was with her the whole time. And this is literally the exact same material. I open it up to find the label—same brand.

"What did you… How…"

How could she even afford this? Did she skip a few mortgage payments on the house? *Would* she do something like that for me? Obviously, she did *something*…

She smiles smugly, then goes to the closet again and pulls out a shoebox. Inside are the same shoes I'm wearing. Which she didn't have to give me, because I already got them for myself.

"Seriously, Mom. Are you a witch?"

"No," she says with a laugh. "I just know you. And I knew if you ever needed such an outfit, this would be the one. It's simple but still dazzles."

She knows me. Right. As hard as it is to believe, I can't argue it. She picked out exactly everything I would have if I'd done the shopping myself.

"To be honest," she says, "I thought it all might sit in my closet forever."

"That would have been a fair bet." I wobble over to her and pull her in for a hug. "Thank you. I love it so much."

I pull away, trying not to ruin my makeup with these misty eyes, and it feels like we're...having a moment. I should take advantage of it.

"Mom, if I, um—" This is harder to say than I thought it would be. This isn't even going to happen tonight, but I need to know. "If I don't come home until tomorrow morning, because I stayed the night with Benjamin, would you be worried?"

"Not at all," she says calmly. "I know you're smart and you can take care of yourself. I trust you."

She trusts me.

Now I really am going to ruin my makeup if I don't get out of here.

Mom helps me navigate down the tricky stairs in these heels, and when I get to the bottom, to the living room, Chris and Andrew are sitting on the couch with a giant bowl of popcorn between them.

"Whoa," Chris says. "Who are you, and what did you do with my baby sister?"

Thanks, jackass, did you have to say that in front of Andrew?

But Andrew must not have heard him, because his whole face lights up when he catches sight of me. I can see his eyes assessing me up and down. *Sweet lord*. My stomach is struck with an onslaught of butterflies so strong my hands start trembling.

"Jessica," Andrew says. "You look *stunning*."

My head.

My entire head.

Has gone up in flames.

This is a huge step in the right direction, just when I thought it would never happen.

I can't look at him, though. Or anyone. "Thank you."

"Too bad you're leaving," Chris says, grabbing a handful of popcorn. "We're about to start a John Hughes movie marathon. *The Breakfast Club* is up first."

"It would have been fun if you could stay with us," Andrew adds.

Oh...shit-fuck-damn.

Another missed opportunity to spend time with Andrew. And my brother, for that matter. He's only here for a few weeks, then he's gone again until Thanksgiving.

My clutch bag chimes, and I pull out my phone.

Ben: *I'm here do you want me to come in*

No, there's no reason for him to waste time with that. Everyone will want to make small talk until an awkward silence rolls in and we abruptly leave.

Me: *Meet me on the porch.*

I tuck my phone away in the bag, clasp it shut, then ask my mom to help me to the door. Already, it's getting easier to walk in these things. Maybe I just need practice.

"Have a lovely night," she says, then escorts me out the door and closes it.

Ben is standing on the porch, his hands in his suit pockets, and he does a double take when I step out. A slow smile creeps up into his cheeks as he takes in his fill of me.

I have to admit. I don't hate the feeling of a boy clearly liking what he sees.

And I am loving what I see in front of me, too. Ben in a T-shirt and jeans is breathtaking. Ben in a tailored suit and tie is lethal.

"Can you help me to the car, Benjamin?"

He gives me a questioning look but offers his arm anyway.

"Have you ever seen me walk in heels?" I ask. "Neither have I."

He laughs. "Don't worry. I got you."

Ben escorts me to his shiny black car, opens the door for me, and holds his hand out for support as I maneuver into the passenger seat. Then, before closing the door, he leans down close to my ear and says, "You look amazing, you big jerk."

Ben drives up to his house and stops by the entrance, where a valet is waiting for us to get out so they can park the car in an air hangar in the back or something. With the planes and blimps.

My hands are shaking again. There's so much adrenaline coursing through me I might literally pass out. "Benjamin, can we— Can we wait here a minute before going in?"

"Of course," he says, giving a hand signal to the valet. "Take all the time you need."

"I'm okay, just...feeling a little dizzy." I let out a nervous, breathy laugh that's not convincing anyone I'm okay. Not even myself.

I need a distraction. I need to talk.

"So...uh, I was wondering about something you said earlier."

"Yeah? What about?" Ben says.

"Your family. You and your siblings, mostly. There's a lot of years between you and your sister."

He nods. "Ten years."

"Are the others very far apart in age, too?"

"Uh, no, actually, they're all exactly two years apart. It was planned that way." He looks down, though I'm not sure at what. "I'm the only kid who wasn't planned. I'm the mistake."

"Don't you mean accident? Or surprise?"

"No, I mean mistake." He lifts his face and gives me a smile as unconvincing as what I said about myself a minute ago. He doesn't explain, and I'm not going to ask him to. If he wants me to know, he'll tell me. If he doesn't, he won't. It's not my call.

The look in his eyes guts me, though. Not because he looks sad, but because he's trying so hard to *not* look sad. He really believes his whole existence should have never happened.

I shouldn't have assumed.

I shouldn't have assumed that just because he was born into money that his life is perfect.

I shouldn't have assumed anything about him at all.

And taking my focus off myself and putting all my attention on Ben has cut loose the band of anxiety that was squeezing around my chest. The distraction worked.

But at what cost? His dignity?

I take his hand, take a deep breath, and say, "I'm ready now."

"Okay." He nods and flashes a smile. "Wait here, I'll come around."

When he gets out, he tosses the keys at the valet, then opens my door and helps me stand. It takes me a second to steady myself, to shake off the lightheadedness and get my bearings, and I squeeze Ben's arm like it's a life preserver.

Then we climb the front steps and walk through the front door, into the main foyer.

And stop. Right. There.

I've been here before, but the last time was under very different circumstances. The main one being we were alone. Now, I'm greeted by an army of Olivers who are all curious about Ben's mystery girl. Me. Like I'm the guest of honor.

Ben introduces me to each of them, one at a time and not too quickly, allowing me to absorb it at my own pace and have a moment to take a cleansing breath between this person and the next.

His siblings are all very nice and normal, they call him "the baby," and they make it easier to get through this gauntlet. His nieces and nephews are stinking adorable. I can't even imagine Ben being an uncle, though. It's just wild.

Almost as wild as imagining Kamy and Todd as parents.

Okay. That part's done. That wasn't so bad.

But then we get to his parents.

His mother is the picture of elegance. She's fucking *radiant*. Her salt-and-pepper hair is cut in a chic style that frames her face perfectly. There's barely a wrinkle on her smooth brown skin, but she has to be pushing sixty years old. She has a broad, brilliant smile and calm, confident manner that immediately puts me at ease. And even though she's shorter than I am, with delicate, bird-bone-thin fingers, I don't doubt she could pin me to the floor before I even knew what hit me.

"Mom," Ben says, "this is my girlfriend, Jessica Webster. Jessie, this is my mom, Daniela Oliver."

"Jessica. *Darling*," she says. "It's lovely to finally meet you in person. I've heard so much about you." She takes both my hands in hers, then gives me an air-kiss on each cheek.

It's not hard to see who Ben got his charisma from.

"Thank you, Mrs. Oliver." *Keep eye contact. Don't fidget. Breathe. Stop fidgeting!*

The only person left to meet is the Mayor of Trinity himself.

Ben's dad is tall, even taller than Ben, who stands at six-foot-something. Mr. Oliver commands the room with just a look. His white skin is a stark contrast to his thick, wavy, jet-black hair with graying temples, and his ice-blue eyes are so sharp they could cut diamonds. His large frame actually *looms* over me when we stop about a foot in front of him.

He's handsome. For an old guy.

"Dad," Ben says in the same formal voice he's been using since we got here. "This is Jessica Webster. Jessie, this is my caring and benevolent father, Gavin Oliver, and the best mayor of the great city of Trinity, Pennsylvania, who's ever served a term."

Wow. That sounded…sarcastic as fuck. Ben really is bitter about this whole thing we've been forced into tonight.

The glare Mr. Oliver gives Ben tells me his introduction language wasn't appreciated, but he doesn't call him out on it. "Pleasure to meet you, Miss Webster," he says and swallows my hand with his in a very firm handshake. *Jesus.* Any firmer and he'd dislocate my elbow.

"It's nice to meet you, too," I say.

He looks me up and down, making no attempt to hide the fact he's assessing me. What happens if I don't measure up to his standards? Will he kick me out?

Out of the mansion? Out of the city? Out of the *state*? He probably has that power.

But he must find something in me he approves of, because he turns away without a word and disappears into one of the many rooms coming off the foyer. Mrs. Oliver gives me a polite smile and makes her exit as well. Everyone else starts filtering out, too, and Ben heaves a long, slow sigh, dropping his shoulders and the weight of the world he had on them.

"You're doing great," he says.

I let out a skittish laugh. "Am I?"

He studies my face for a minute. "Is that lipstick smudge-proof?"

"I think so, why?"

"Because I don't want to make a mess when I do this." He leans down and kisses me full on the mouth, slowly, thoroughly, and without holding anything back.

Now I'm lightheaded again. I'm never going to be able to let go of this boy's arm.

He pulls away and checks my face. "Still looks perfect."

"What was that for?"

"My brothers are watching," he says and turns around.

Sure enough, Jake and Dean are hovering by the doorway, sneaking glances at us.

"Right. Good move." *Of course* it was only for show. What other reason would he have?

This isn't real, I remind myself. I'm only here to pay him back the favor I owe. This is not, and never will be, my life. This extravagance all around me, including the boy at my side—hell, including the outfit I'm wearing—is not my world. I'd never fit in here.

We start crossing the foyer to join everyone in what I can now see is a formal dining room with a long, polished table, a zillion chairs, and sparkling chandeliers overhead.

I'm walking into a lion's den. A very pretty lion's den, but still.

The rest of this night? Is about survival.

Chapter Twenty-Five

*T*wenty minutes.

That's how long I lasted, using my mouth only to eat and drink but not talk, before someone asked me a direct question that I have no clue how to answer. Something I can't respond to with a nod or a shake of my head.

Up until a moment ago, the only person talking at my corner of the table was Mayor Oliver. He went on and on and on about some fundraiser talent show he arranged to raise money for children's cancer research. It's coming up on August fifteenth, and for twenty minutes I sat here hoping he wouldn't ask me if I had any special talent so I could participate. But he didn't.

Twenty minutes. I know because I've been watching the clock.

Formal dinners don't normally last more than a half hour, maybe forty minutes, right? Ben told me the servers are bringing out dessert next—and he made a point of informing me it's some kind of strawberry layered cake thing I've never heard of so I don't eat it and die.

I was so close to getting through this dinner unscathed. And now this.

"Did you hear me, dear?" Mrs. Oliver says. She's sitting

across from me, and I have Ben at my left and Mr. Oliver kitty-corner to my right, at the head of this massive table like he's a king and we're his court. "I said what are your plans now that you've finished high school? Where will you be continuing your education?"

God, why. Why *this* question.

"I—" I clear my throat. "I'm not."

She blinks, as if waiting for me to go on, then says, "You're not what?"

I grab my glass and gulp down some water. "Um, I'm not going to college. At least not—um, not right now. Maybe someday. I haven't decided on a career path."

"Well," Mrs. Oliver says, "that's hardly a requirement for getting started. It takes years to earn a degree in anything. Why wait?"

"Mom, she doesn't—" Ben starts, but his father cuts him off.

"What business is your family in?" Mr. Oliver says. "Consider doing that first."

"Oh…my family…" *Lives paycheck to paycheck.* "I'm not really interested in that."

"What is it with kids these days? I've tried to get my sons into politics like their old man." He starts stabbing vegetables on his plate, collecting a stack of them on a fork. "But none of them went for it. Dean, over there"—he points his fork to the other end of the long table—"he has a knack for debate and public speaking. He could talk the ocean into buying water. Could have been the next president if he wanted to, but he became a lawyer instead. Now he owns one of the top law firms in the state."

"A friend of mine wants to be a lawyer—" I try, but he cuts me off again.

"And Jacob"—he points with his fork again—"is one of

the best problem-solvers I know. I thought, surely, he'd try for a seat in Congress. Use his skill for the good of democracy. But no. He started his own tech company and now he's a multimillionaire. Not a bad second choice, though."

Mr. Oliver shifts his gaze toward me…but not *at* me. Next to me.

"Then there's Benjamin—"

"It's Ben," Ben snaps, and I nearly choke on my next bite of stuffed chicken breast.

He just corrected his father on his name. The same way he used to do with me.

But he *doesn't* do that with me anymore. I can't even remember the last time he did.

"Benjamin," Mr. Oliver emphasizes, and I cringe. I used to do the same thing. "He's lucky he was born with a good throwing arm, or I don't know what he would have done with his life. He's not smart like his brothers or even his sister. Too interested in girls and fun and living for today instead of thinking about tomorrow."

I dart a glance at Ben's sister, Lori, who's sitting directly across from him. She's in hearing distance, but she's holding up a baby and cooing at him, completely oblivious to the conversation happening right next to her. They're all oblivious, talking among themselves. The only people paying attention are me and Ben and Mrs. Oliver, who keeps giving her husband a side-eye like she's bored and just waiting for him to finish so they can have dessert.

I expect Ben to pipe up and correct his father again, tell him he *is* smart. Tell him he's good at more than just football.

But Ben says nothing. He's suddenly very interested in the broccoli salad on his plate and starts inhaling it like if he does it fast enough, he'll win something.

"Then again," Mr. Oliver says, "Benjamin—"

"It's Ben—"

"—couldn't even get *that* right. Almost missed the submissions deadline and would have missed out on the best opportunity of his life. Probably the *only* opportunity of his life. Without a chance at playing pro, he's got nothing. He'll end up a bum like my brother." He pauses long enough to sip his drink. "One of those in every family, but I'll be damned if there's one in mine."

Beneath the table, my free hand—the one not holding a glass of water so tightly it might crack—clenches into a fist. Why is he saying these things? About his own son? With Ben sitting right there?

I try to catch Ben's eye, send him a silent message of *what the fuck is going on here*, but he only has eyes for his plate.

His father's onslaught continues. He's on a roll about how incompetent his youngest child is, and every new point he makes starts with, "Benjamin," and then Ben correcting him with, "It's Ben."

Soon, it's all I can hear.

Benjamin.

It's Ben.

Benjamin.

It's Ben.

Benjamin.

It's Ben—

"Stop," I say, but they must not have heard me. My voice is too soft and weak, because I'm afraid to speak up to people I've known for less than an hour. It's like the day I met Ben all over again, except this time, I should be speaking up to protect *him*, not myself.

Ben hasn't said anything but *it's Ben, it's Ben, it's Ben*, and that hasn't deterred his father from firing more and more bullets at him. Why doesn't he stand up for himself?

He isn't like me. He's silent now because he's choosing to be, not because his body is forcing him to be.

I look at Mrs. Oliver across the table for help, but it's clear I won't get any from her. She's just sitting there primly through this slaughter happening to one of her children, eyeing me over the rim of her wineglass as she drinks.

Why are you looking at me? I want to shout. *Can't you see what's right in front of you?*

Is this what Ben meant when he said he's a mistake? Do any of them care?

"He got the dates mixed up," Mr. Oliver is saying. "Almost cost me the election that year. And—"

"Stop," I say again, but he keeps going. *Come on, Jessie. Use your voice.*

I did it somehow the day I met Ben. I was so upset over what he said to me, what he'd so blatantly implied, that need to put him in his place overcame my inability to speak.

And what I said was cruel because it was the truth. He just couldn't handle it. He snapped back, and I snapped back again. From then on, we hated each other.

If I do that now, I'll be making an enemy of someone very powerful.

"Benjamin—"

"It's Ben—"

My jaw clenches so hard it feels like my teeth are about to crack.

"Benjamin—"

"Stop," I say.

"It's Ben—"

I pound both my fists on the table. "Stop!"

Everyone goes dead quiet, even the people a mile away at the other end of the table, and they all stare at me with varying expressions of shock. Even Ben. Even the *children*.

I just yelled at the freaking mayor, in his own house, sitting with his entire family.

My whole body tenses up with the urge to run out of here. Find a dark corner somewhere and curl up in it until the danger has passed. But I fight it with everything I've got.

I have to fight it. I have to say this because no one else will.

"Benjamin isn't—" I start, and my throat catches. Should I still call him that? "You're wrong. You don't know him at all."

"I beg your pardon?" Mr. Oliver says, his voice eerily calm.

"He's not stupid, he's incredibly smart. Intelligent—"

"Miss Webster—"

"He's sweet and generous and dedicated and loyal to those who deserve it. Absolutely nothing you said about him is true. Nothing—"

"Young lady, you're out of line—"

"Do you know how hard it is to be a quarterback? To make a split-second decision while a herd of buffalo is stampeding toward you with only one goal—to knock you down flat?"

"Jessie—" Ben says.

But I keep my eyes on Mr. Oliver, whose expression has remained cool and calculating, like a cobra about to strike. And just like my first fight with Ben, once I've started, I can't stop.

"Do you know how hard it is to do that again and again and again no matter how sore you are, or how numb you get in the cold—"

Ben gently covers my fist with his warm, comforting hand. "It's okay," he says.

"No, it's *not* okay." But now that he's thrown a rock into my gears, my verbal aggression comes to a grinding halt. The adrenaline rushes out of me so fast I feel faint. My hands start trembling, my lips quiver. My throat constricts, and my tongue feels too big.

My gaze falls downward, unable to look at anyone right now.

"I'm sorry," I say to my half-empty plate. "I'm sorry—I should go."

I push up out of the chair and storm from the room, miraculously with my ankles still intact. My heels clack against the polished marble floors in the foyer, echoing all around me.

But I don't even reach the door before I hear Ben call for me, stepping up behind me then snatching me by the elbow.

"You don't have to leave," he says.

"No. I think I really do. That was… I shouldn't have done that. I'm sorry I ruined your family dinner."

"You're not the one who ruined dinner, Jess."

That's true, I suppose. I was only reacting to what his father did that was far worse, in my opinion. "Why do you let him talk about you like that? Why don't you tell him he's wrong?"

Ben shoves his hands into his pockets and lets out a long, heavy breath. "No point," he says. "He'll only ever see me the way he wants to see me. Just like everyone else."

There's nothing to say to that. He's one thousand percent right. The minute someone forms an opinion of you, whoever you are, that's their version of the truth from then on. It's why Ben and I kept on hating each other for so long and felt completely justified in doing it.

"I'm sorry."

"Yeah, me too," he says, then gives me a long look. "You wanna go get high?"

Chapter Twenty-Six

*M*y second time in Benjamin Oliver's bed, we're both fully clothed, on top of the comforter, lying next to each other on our bellies, feet at the pillow end and heads at the foot end, with a plate of "special brownies" between us.

"That's enough for me," I say after finishing off brownie number two.

Ben moves the plate from the bed to the nightstand, then settles in next to me again. He's not wearing his suit jacket anymore, and his button-down shirt is only half buttoned now, with his tie hanging loose from his neck.

I'm feeling deeply relaxed, and the giggles haven't started yet, but the sensible part of my brain is on its way out. I slide Ben's tie from his neck, then wrap it around my head like a sweatband and tie it in a knot at the back. "What do you think?"

He laughs and snatches it off my head. "I think you should have stopped after one brownie."

"You really made those yourself?" I ask.

"I really did."

"They're so good. I would eat that whole plate if I didn't know they were full of weed. Where did you get the weed from, anyway?"

"Kamy," he says. "Her parents grow it in their greenhouse."

I snort. "They do not."

"Oh, you don't believe me?" Ben digs something out of his pocket—his phone—and sets it down in front of us. "Call Kamy right now and ask."

"No, I'm not bothering her." I flick his phone across the bed. "She has way more important things to worry about right now."

"Yeah…" Ben goes quiet, his head angled, then says, "Todd's excited about it, though."

"Todd isn't the brightest bulb in the box."

"Fair point. But he's gonna smother that kid with love."

Hopefully that's the only thing he smothers it with. "You know, that could have been us," I say. "We could have made a baby."

He shrugs. "That's always a risk when two people are fertile."

"No, no…listen." His voice repeats in my head, and I laugh. "Say fertile again."

"Ferrrrrtilllllle."

"Fertile turtle."

"A fertile turtle named Myrtle," he says, and now we're both laughing.

But I was talking about something important. *Concentrate.*

"Listen," I say again. "When we were sleeping together, I wasn't on birth control."

Ben looks at me like he's never seen me before. "We used condoms."

I shake my head. "It's not enough by itself. That's how Kamy ended up with Todd's monster baby. You need both. You need condoms to prevent disease and birth control to prevent babies. It's a fact. Unless you're Kamy's parents— then it's a myth."

"Maybe Todd just has really aggressive sperm." Ben makes an angry little sperm face. I've never seen an angry little sperm's face before, but it seems pretty accurate.

"Don't talk about Todd's sperm. Or anyone's. You're banned."

He mimes locking his lips and throwing away the key, and we just lay there for a few days, letting the world go on without us.

"I'm taking pills now," I say.

"But you don't need them now. Right?"

"Right..." I do a slow blink, processing this new information. "No sex, no baby."

He nods. "That's how it works."

"Yes—" I point a finger toward him. I don't know why. "No, that's wrong. You have to stay on the pills in case there's sex again. You have to be always ready. Like the Marines. Semper feee...Semper fyyy?...fo fum. *That's* how it works."

"Is it?"

"Yes, listen. I have a doctor, and her whole job is vaginas and uterus...uteruses? Uteri? She told me everything." I turn to lay on my side and prop my head up. "Go ahead. Ask me anything. I bet I know the answer."

"Okay." He puts a finger to his chin, thinking. All four of his heads are thinking. "Yes, I do have a question. I've been wondering this for a while."

Oooh fun. "Ask me, ask me."

"What's the story behind your Dr. Seuss collection?"

My mind goes blank. I roll back over onto my stomach, propped up by my elbows, and stare across the room at Ben's desk. His perfectly clean and organized desk.

"That has nothing to do with vaginas," I say. "You broke the rules."

He rolls his eyes. "Fine, I broke the rules. But I want to

know. What's the deal?"

"I don't know."

"Yes, you do." He sighs. "If you don't want to tell me, just say that."

I can't think of any good reason not to tell him, though. It's just that I haven't told *anyone* this, so I thought I couldn't. But I can tell him. I know stuff about him that no one else knows. It's only fair.

I run my palms over the bed in front of me, then kick my feet up behind me and cross my legs at the ankle. I'm still wearing my heels. "This bed…is so…soft…"

"I'm glad you like it," Ben says. He shrugs out of his button-down shirt, revealing a plain white tee underneath, and drops the other shirt to the floor. Then he starts on his pants.

"No naked time," I remind him.

"It's hot in here."

I wave him off. "You're always hot. That's just you. You're hot."

"Thank you."

"I mean warm," I clarify. "But the other hot, too. You're a lot of hots. You're so many hots I need sunscreen."

He laughs at that, which makes me laugh, too. God, I love when he smiles, my heart gets all fluttery. Fluttery buttery.

I stare at my fingers and pick at my nails. Ben rolls onto his back, clasping his hands behind his head, like he's splayed out on the grass on a lazy summer day, watching clouds. In his underwear. He's so cool and calm all the time. Why can't I be like that?

"When I was little," I say, "like, preschool, kindergarten. I had a different mom."

"The mom you have now isn't your first mom?"

"No…same person. I mean she was different. She spent

more time with me. She paid attention to me. We used to play together and go out and do things together, just the two of us. And she read me one of those books every night. *Every. Night.* Over and over and over again. It was my favorite part of the day, and…I miss that. I miss her. So I keep the books to remind me of that part of my life, when I had a different mother."

"Nostalgia," Ben says.

"Yeah." I take in a deep, shuddering breath. "I don't expect her to still be reading me Dr. Seuss books every night, but I don't want her total absence, either. There has to be a middle ground, you know?"

Ben turns his head toward me. His eyes are so fucking beautiful. Works of art.

"Have you told her this?" he says.

No. I haven't. But it can't be that easy.

"That's enough drama," I say. "My turn. I get to ask you something now."

He pulls his hands in front of him and rubs his palms together, then cracks his knuckles, like he's about to go out on the football field. "I'm ready. Hit me."

I give him a weak punch on his side, and he laughs.

"Ask me the question, Jessie."

"Okay, okay." I look around. What could I… *Oh.* Perfect.

I bring my hand up to my face, just under my eye, and squint, pointing at a far corner of the room. "That…big thing over there."

He turns to look. "The cello?"

"Right, the *cello*," I say. "Can you really play that thing?"

"Yes, I can play the cello," he says dryly. "Ask me something harder."

"Oh, a challenge? Okay…" I keep staring at the cello, and this vision comes to me. "I got it, I got it! Play it right now."

"I could be wrong," he says. "But I don't think that's a question."

I roll my eyes. "This isn't *Jeopardy!* but okay. A question. Can you go over there right now and play a song for me?"

"Yes." He starts to get up.

"Wait, wait!" I flash my hand up like a STOP sign. "You have to do it naked."

"I *have* to? Why?"

"Because I want to see you naked." *Duh*.

"*That* is an excellent point." He pulls his T-shirt up and off, then kicks off his socks and goes to the cello corner. I reach out to touch his smooth skin as he walks by, but he's farther away than I thought. Or my arms are shorter than I thought. One of those.

"Underwear too," I say.

"No." He laughs. "That chair is cold, and my ass is warm."

"You mean hot."

"You can't see most of this anyway with the cello in front of me." He picks up the instrument from its rack, grabs the bow, and then sits, lying the cello sideways on his lap. I'm not an expert on this, but I'm pretty sure that isn't how you play a cello. He twists something at the bottom and pulls out a long stick, and when he sets the cello upright in front of him, the whole thing rests on that thin, spindly leg.

He's right. With the instrument between his knees, only the fabric on his hips is visible. He runs the bow across each of the strings, one at a time, and fiddles with the pegs at the top. His face is so serious, looking down but clearly focused on listening. He's concentrating really hard.

And I start laughing hysterically.

Because he's doing it *naked*. And high.

This is a once-in-a-lifetime moment. I snatch my clutch bag up from the floor and take my phone out. "I'm recording you," I tell him.

"Oh no. I better not screw this up." He grins. "You ready?"

I aim the phone, hit the big red button, and raise my arm high with a thumbs-up.

He starts with something slow, kind of melancholy, and every low, somber note flows right through me. I can *feel* it vibrating in my veins. And now I can't laugh anymore.

This song is sad. Beautiful misery.

Then he goes into something faster and happier, like a jig. His fingertips are flying, and they hit every note with precision. He can't even see where he's putting them—he just knows. And the faster he moves the bow, the more it looks like it's dancing over the strings.

It's mesmerizing, and all I can do is watch in awe. He isn't just good at this. He's a fucking prodigy.

Well, what did you expect, Jessie? He did get accepted to Juilliard.

Why he decided not to go there is the real question.

Also—*Jesus*—I just realized he's doing all of this without sheet music in front of him. He's going by *memory*.

He changes the song again, and the notes come out like falling water. Fluid. They blend one into the other into the other. The tempo isn't fast or slow—it's right in the middle. This song…this song makes me feel like I'm flying. Floating. And he makes it look so effortless.

With one long, final stroke, the song is over, and the last note hangs in the air even after he's stopped moving. To call it amazing is an understatement.

This boy really has been touched by the divine.

He pops his face up to look at me. "Did you get it all?"

"I…" I tap the red button again to stop recording, then drop my phone. "I got it."

For a long moment, I just stare at him, slack-jawed.

He puts the cello and bow back to their stand, then stares back at me.

"You know..." he says. "You're lying there fully clothed, with only the tiniest peek of cleavage visible, and your lips parted, and your feet kicked up behind you in those heels... and you've never looked so goddamn sexy." He shakes his head. "It's taking all my strength to be a gentleman right now."

I heard every word, loved every word, but still, I can't shake off this shock.

"You okay over there?" he says with a hint of sarcasm.

"Yeah, I just... That was... Is there anything you *can't* do?"

A slow, mischievous grin spreads into his cheeks. I used to hate that grin. But I can't hate anything about Benjamin Oliver ever again. Not even his faults.

"Yes, there is something I can't do," he says. "I'm terrible at being a gentleman."

He rushes across the room and tackles me, somehow spinning me onto my back and climbing on top of me in the blink of an eye, all without snapping my neck. It happened so fast my brain needs a minute to catch up. How did we end up here again? In this room, in this bed, in this position.

It's only been a week since the last time. A week that felt like a century.

A little wrinkle of concern appears in his brow. "If you don't want to, tell me. You're in control, remember?"

There was a reason... There was some reason we weren't supposed to do this anymore. But I can't for the life of me remember what it is.

"No," I say, and he starts pulling back. *"Stop."*

"I am—"

"No," I grumble, frustrated. "I mean stop moving. Stay right there."

He freezes, waiting for my next command. But I don't want to be the one calling the shots this time. I just want to go along for the ride, not knowing what's around the next bend.

"What are you thinking?" he says.

"I'm thinking we've done this enough with me in control. Four weeks of you giving me whatever I asked for. Now it's my turn to give you what *you* want. I want *you* to take control."

His eyes search mine, but what he's trying to find, I don't know. The truth? I told him the truth. The next move now is his.

"I'm not sure if I heard you correctly or if I blacked out and dreamed it?" he says. "Tell me again. I need to hear it again so I'm clear."

I smile up at him. "I want you to take control this time. Starting right now."

He doesn't hesitate, going for my shirt first. "Knock, knock," he says, grinning.

Oh sweet lord, knock-knock jokes in bed? This could end me.

"Who's there."

"Tara." He tosses my blouse to the floor, then pulls down the side zipper on my skirt.

I wriggle as he tugs it down my legs. "Tara who?" I say.

"Tara McClosoff."

It takes a second, but when the joke clicks in my head, I laugh so hard my stomach cramps. "You are the"—*breathe*—"biggest, sexiest dork"—*breathe*—"I've ever met."

He holds one of my feet up, the sparkly shoes dotting little rainbows around the room, onto the walls and ceiling. "You're keeping the heels on."

Chapter Twenty-Seven

*B*ing.

I startle at the sound, then squint against the bright light. Where…?

I blink and blink and blink and rub my eyes.

Right. This is Ben's bed. Ben's room. We must have fallen asleep with the lights on.

I stretch and roll to my other side, landing on Ben's chest. "Hey," I whisper.

But he only responds with a snore. Oh, this is perfect. Another video to add to my collection—I just need my phone.

Bing.

My phone! That's what that noise was. Someone is texting me.

I sit up and push off the comforter as quietly as I can, my eyes better adjusted to the light now, and search for my phone. What time is it, anyway?

Bing.

Who the hell is texting me in the middle of the night—

There it is. Tucked under the heel of one of my sparkly shoes on the floor.

I snatch it up then climb back into bed, under the comforter with Ben, where it's warm and soft and safe, far away from anything and anyone that might bother us.

Bing.

Unless they're texting.

I unlock my phone and notice it's only a little after eleven, not as late as I thought.

Kamy: *Hey guys me and Todd have made our decision*
Rayna: *don't make me wait tell me right now*
Kamy: *We're keeping the baby*

"What?" I blurt, and Ben stirs beside me. *Shit.*

I watch him for a minute to see if he wakes up, but he just cuddles closer to me, draping his arm across my ribs, his head nestled against my shoulder.

Bing. Bing. Bing.

Dammit.

I turn the sound off on my phone, then go back to the chat.

Rayna: *OH MY GOD*
Rayna: *I GET TO BE AN AUNTIE*

Yes, Rayna, because it's all about you.

Rayna: *we need details*

Kamy: *Girls night tomorrow? I'm too tired right now. I spent the whole day with Todd and his parents and my parents working out arrangements for when the baby comes*

Rayna: *is everything good with everyone*

Kamy: *Yes and no. It's a lot. I'll explain it all tomorrow*

I send a bunch of emojis because I can't put into words how I feel about this. I'm not even sure how I feel about this, to be honest. I'm glad Kamy's parents are involved and not planning Todd's imminent execution. And vice versa. But this is going to change her whole life. She's my friend, and I'm worried—so many things can go wrong.

Me: *If we're having girls night tomorrow then I have news too.*

I hold the phone above me and Ben, who is still out cold, and take a pic of us, then send it to the girls-only chat.

Rayna: *OH MY GOD*

Rayna: *please tell me that's ben's bed*

Me: *Yes. I'm spending the night.*

Rayna: *OH MY GOD*

Kamy: *Aww you guys are adorable*

Rayna: *how am i supposed to wait until tomorrow for all this*

Rayna: *you two are the worst*

Me: *Love you too. Bye.*

I set my phone on the nightstand, and my whole body suddenly feels light and free. We're out, finally. We don't have a secret sex life to hide anymore.

Though I'm not sure what that means from here. We're still only fake dating. Was tonight a one-time thing? Will we go back to our abstinence oath tomorrow?

Do I want to?

I tuck myself back against him, skin to skin, soaking up his warmth. The truth is, I have no idea how Ben feels about me, other than as a friend. And that friendship is still new. We're discovering things about each other. What if I ask him to try this out for real and he says it had never crossed his mind? Or what if he goes along with it, only for us to have a horrible breakup later because we should have known it was doomed from the start?

Andrew is still an option, technically. But in a way, so is Ben, and I don't know what to do with that now. Both of them are leaving in August to go to out-of-state schools. Best-case scenario with either of them is a long-distance relationship. Worst-case scenario… What if neither one of them wants to be with me? They'll both be gone. All of this effort could be for absolutely nothing by the end of summer.

Ben stirs again, this time with a soft groan, like he's waking up.

"Benja—"

No. I can't call him that anymore. Not after what I witnessed at dinner tonight.

"Ben," I say, and it feels like a foreign language. "Ben, are you awake?"

He blinks at me, then rubs his eyes. I should have turned the lights off.

"What did you call me?" His voice is all low and raspy from sleep, but the tone of confusion is unmistakable.

"Ben," I say. "Isn't that what you've been telling me to call you since we met?"

"No."

"Yes, you have."

"Not anymore." He blinks a few more times, then gives up and closes his eyes again. "Call me Benjamin."

"But you always used to correct me. And tonight, you corrected your dad a gazillion times. I thought you didn't like hearing your full name."

"I do," he says groggily. "I do and I don't."

"Thanks, that explains everything." I laugh, cuddling up closer. "You're not really awake right now, are you?"

He's quiet again, his breathing slow and steady. He must have fallen asleep.

I tiptoe out of bed to turn off the lights, then go right back to his side. I don't know what's going to happen tomorrow or next week or next month, but right now, I know I'm happy and cozy here with him in this bed. In this moment, that's all that matters. I can worry about tomorrow, tomorrow.

Chapter Twenty-Eight

*B*en is still determined to spoil me, and I loved my mini shopping spree for shoes with him on July 4th so much that in a moment of weakness, I agree to go to the mall with him.

Then I remember…I hate the mall. Too many different things to see, too many choices to make, and I like a little sparkle now and then, but there is such a thing as too much sparkle. Everything at the mall fucking sparkles, even the floors. Thankfully, Rayna and Jeremy come with us, so all I have to do is follow my bestie from place to place, wherever she wants to go.

And with Kamy and Todd's shotgun wedding coming up in September, with all of us in the bridal party, Rayna only wants to go to fancy dress boutiques, jewelry shops, and the baby section of every department store.

"Jess, what do you think?" Ben says. He's strapping a baby carrier onto his chest.

"I think you're about three seconds away from getting your nose removed with my bare teeth if you don't explain why you're wearing that thing."

"Simmer down, witch." He grins. "I have a new niece on the way, remember?"

"Oh." That's right. I'm an idiot. Kamy's pregnancy bomb has given me baby PTSD. Any little hint that I might be next sends me into a near panic. I blow out a breath. "Okay then, I think you'd look better in the green one. Orange does nothing good for your complexion."

I have no idea if that's true. I'm just harassing him. Because it's fun.

"She's right, Ben," Rayna says, piling seventeen packages of onesies into an already full cart. "Go with green or go with god." She looks to Jeremy. "You think that's enough?"

"You can never have too many onesies," he says. "But in your case, I think there's an exception to that. I'm cutting you off. Leave some for the other people shopping, Ray."

She looks to the near-empty rack she pulled them from, like she's actually considering going back for more. But Jeremy takes her by the hand and starts pushing the cart toward the checkout with his other hand. "We're done here."

Ben removes the orange baby carrier, sliding the straps off his shoulders, but instead of picking up the green one to buy, he grabs a neon pink one.

"Pink because she's a girl?" I say.

"No. Pink because I like it." He takes it to the checkout, and I follow him, wondering what he's going to surprise me with next. Honestly, since when does he like pink?

Probably since I wore those baby-pink glitter heels two nights ago and he told me to keep them on.

Several years later, Rayna still hasn't finished her purchase, and there's no way she's carrying all of that through the mall, so she also has to load up Jeremy's trunk. I tell her we'll meet them at the bridal shop, her next destination, and to just text me when she gets there. Kamy said we could pick out our own bridesmaids' dresses, which basically means whatever Rayna wants because I don't really care one way or the other. And Rayna has better fashion sense.

Then Ben and I head to the food court.

All the different smells hit me at once, and instantly, my mouth waters.

"What are you in the mood for?" Ben says. "Pizza, subs, burgers and fries—"

"Yes."

"Which one?"

"Any of them," I say. "Just get what you want and I'll have some of yours."

He laughs. "I've been out with enough girls to know that never ends well."

I know he has. This isn't news. So why do I suddenly tense up at the thought of him with someone else?

And, Jesus, how hypocritical can I be? The only reason he's fake-dating me is so *I* can be with someone else.

But my brain isn't interested in being reasonable. I'm getting *possessive* over Benjamin Oliver. Like he's actually mine.

"I'm not really hungry," I say. "You get what you want, I'll find us a seat."

"You're sure? Not even ice cream?"

"Yes, I'm sure, just *go*."

Ben gives me a look, and I don't have to ask why. Every pair of ears in a sixty-mile radius heard the sharp edge in my voice.

"You only get snappy like this when you're hungry," he says calmly. "I'm getting you something to eat."

"Benjamin—"

He walks off before I've even finished saying his name.
Dammit.

I find a table that's empty and not sticky, and wait for him to come back with a seven-course meal.

What am I doing with him? I mean, really, what is this? Self-inflicted torture, that's what.

Ben has gotten under my skin, and I don't want him to get out of it. I'm the one who keeps putting myself in these situations with him like we're actually dating. I could have done the bare minimum to be convincing as a couple, but no. I have to spend all my free time with him, knowing I'm getting more and more attached while he remains steadily aloof.

Except when it's physical. There is nothing aloof about *that*.

I'm not one of those people who can separate it, though. I thought maybe I could be, but I'm so, so not. The deeper Ben burrows into my soul, the more I want him to stay there.

Permanently.

That just gives me more reason to make it work with Andrew. If I'm going to be with someone, I need to be with them fully. I can't do relationships half-assed. I'm either all in. Or I'm all out.

With Ben, that means all we'll ever be is friends.

Andrew hasn't outright shown he's interested in me, but he hasn't outright shown he's *dis*interested in me, either. Until he does, I'm in this hellish limbo, wishing Ben and I could be more yet knowing we can't...and we shouldn't. And *not* knowing if he even wants to.

He finds me at the table, carrying two full trays of food and drink. I rush up to grab one before he drops them both.

"Thanks," he says, then sits with his tray. "I got two of everything so we can share. Take whatever you want."

I snag a piping hot french fry from a basket, and one bite has my cheeks tingling. "Vinegar?"

"You don't like it?"

"No, I love it. But I've never had vinegar fries around you

before. How did you know?"

He shrugs. "Lucky guess."

"Really." I grab another fry. "You didn't have my house bugged?"

"No," he says. "Well, not for that reason, I didn't."

I roll my eyes. "You're hilarious."

"I know." He smiles and takes a giant bite out of a Philly cheesesteak. I'm halfway through my fries already.

"This probably wasn't the best idea. Eating all this food before trying on clothes. My stomach isn't normally this huge."

Ben wipes his mouth and swallows. "It's perfect. Get something that fits today, and then if you gain a little weight between now and Labor Day Weekend, you won't need alterations."

Um…how do I respond to that? A boy mentioning anything about a girl gaining weight, saying it right to that girl's face, is a really good way for said boy to end up murdered.

All boys know this. Us girls have made sure of it.

But he doesn't seem like he's trying to get a reaction out of me. He isn't smirking or even watching my face to see what I do. He's just enjoying the hell out of that cheesesteak.

"What if I did?" I say. "I mean gained weight while we're together. If I wasn't skinny anymore. Would you mind?"

He freezes, the sandwich halfway to his mouth for another bite, then looks up at me. "Is this a trap?"

"No trap. I just want to know your honest opinion."

He sets the cheesesteak down slowly, takes a sip of pop, and wipes his hands on a napkin. He's obviously stalling, choosing his words carefully. I can't fault him for that.

"So, first," he says.

Oh god, he has a list?

"You're not what I would call skinny, Jessie."

"What the *hell*—"

He holds a hand up, palm out. "Let me say everything before you pass judgment, okay? You're the one who asked me. Let me answer."

I fall back against my chair, crossing my arms. "All right. Answer."

"There is nothing wrong with being skinny, but a skinny girl feels like a skeleton to me," he says. "That isn't you. You're soft. When I grab your hips, I like that I have something to hold other than bone. I like that I have something to dig my fingers into without hurting you. I like the way your ass jiggles when I smack it. And I know you already know this, but I'll say it anyway just so we're clear—I like smashing my face between those two pillows on your chest."

Sweet Jesus, now I've got all of those memories living fresh in my head.

I pick up my cold drink and press it against my cheek.

"Second, just because I've been with skinny girls doesn't mean that's what I prefer. Do you see me with any of those girls now? If that was my measuring stick for the perfect girl, I wouldn't have let them go. And for some guys, having a skinny girlfriend *is* the only thing that matters. But I'm not one of those guys."

My mouth twists. Why did I have to ask? Why didn't I just keep my mouth shut? This boy is a charmer through and through, and with every word he's sucking me deeper and deeper into his vortex.

"Third," he says, "and this is the really important one, so I hope you're listening."

"I'm listening," I assure him.

"Third...you could be twice your current size *tomorrow* and not one thing would change between us. Nothing we've done, are doing, or might do in the future."

He thinks we have a future?

"And why is that?" I ask instead.

"Because you'd still be you, Jessie. Whether you're an extra-small or a double-X, you're still you, and I wouldn't want you to be anyone else."

He leaves that hanging in the air and goes back to eating his Philly cheesesteak. Once I'm sure he isn't looking, I let myself smile.

That was a damn good answer, Benjamin Oliver.

The bridal shop is giving me heart palpitations.

Ben and Jeremy are at the counter to pay for their tuxes so they can just pick them up the morning of the wedding, while Rayna and I search rack after rack of dresses. She's already found a few for me to try on, but I keep having to stop so I can step away and breathe.

I've hardly looked at any of the actual dresses because I can't get past the price tags. How is this five grand worth of fabric here? I'll tell you how—it isn't.

And I know I agreed to Ben buying things for me today, but several thousand dollars for a dress I'm going to wear one fucking day and then never again feels wrong. Like I'm *using* him.

When I turn the corner and go down a new aisle, the prices only get higher. I suck in a breath. "Rayna?"

"Yeah?" she says from somewhere inside this tulle-and-lace prison.

"I changed my mind. I don't want to try on dresses today, you already got yours, and the boys are done, so. We can leave."

There's the sound of feet rapidly padding across carpet

just before she appears at the other end of my aisle. "What changed your mind?"

I grab a dress—any dress, it won't matter—and hold out the price tag. "The fact that a person needs to sell an organ to afford a dress here."

She waves me off. "Don't worry about price, Jessie. Ben will take care of it for you."

Oh no... My own best friend thinks I'm a gold digger?

"Rayna." I step up closer to her, though she isn't looking at me anymore. She's back to the dress search. "Is that why you think I'm with him? For his money?"

"No," she insists. "I would never think that. I'm just saying, it's a perk."

"It's a perk because I'm poor, you mean."

She turns her head to face me. "Why would you say that?"

"Because it's true, Ray. No one looks at you and Jeremy and questions whether your feelings for each other are genuine based on your family's financial statuses."

"Jessie, I'm sure no one thinks that about you and Ben. And anyone who even insinuates it is only doing so because they wish they were with him instead of you."

I want to believe her. But growing up in a "haves" separated from "have nots" society as one of the "have nots" has made me extremely wary of other people's opinions of me. Especially if those people are rich.

"Are you in need of any assistance?" a posh female voice says, startling me. It's the shop clerk. I give Rayna the *look*, silently asking her to handle the speaking part of this.

"My friend here is ready to try these on," Rayna says and scoops up the dresses she'd laid on the floor. She grabs my arm and tugs me toward the clerk. "Can you open up a fitting room?"

The woman nods primly and leads the way.

Once we're inside the overly spacious and glitzy fitting room—the mirror even has a gilded, scrollwork frame—Rayna hangs up the four dresses she picked for me, then starts pulling the red one out of the plastic. It's long and slinky with a slit way up the side. "You can wear this kind of stuff, with your body," she says. "I'd never pull this off."

"Come on, Rayna. You're like a size two."

"Yeah, but I'm an athlete, so I have muscular thighs and a disproportionately huge ass and broad shoulders. I have to get every dress I own altered to fit me right. But you"—she shoves the dress toward me, and I grab it—"you can wear anything right off the rack and it looks like it was custom made for you."

She's really serious. And she sounds a teeny bit jealous. Of *me*. What the fuck.

"I'll be right outside the door if you need help with this." Rayna walks off, shutting the door behind her.

"Now what?" Jeremy says from the other side. "How long is this gonna take?"

I catch myself in the mirror rolling my eyes. What is it with guys and waiting? Like it's the end of their life if they have to sit for a few minutes. I should ask him to hold my purse, and I don't even have a purse. But I will find one and throw it at him.

"Let's go look at the accessories," Rayna says. "Ben, stay here in case Jessie needs help with something."

"Me and Jer can pick out the accessories," Ben says. "Rayna, you should stay. This is a girl thing."

"And picking out accessories isn't a girl thing?" Jeremy says. "What are accessories anyway?"

"Come, my friend," Ben says, "and I'll introduce you to the wild world of heels and handbags and hairclips."

Jeremy sounds like he just puked up a lung. "Let's get

this over with."

The red slinky dress is a no. Too low in the back, dropping almost all the way to my ass. I go for the green one next. It's got a big fluffy skirt and some kind of embroidery thing going on in the fabric. Does Rayna even know me? I set that aside.

The next one is banana yellow. That's a no based on the color alone.

The last one is blue…a perfect shade of blue in a matte fabric that's silky smooth. Not too bold, not too pale, and not one glittery, shimmery thing in sight. When I hold it up against me, it complements my eyes, which are normally more gray than blue. But now they are *blue*, picking up that beautiful hue and reflecting it right back.

I'm not sure about this style, the neckline is angled weird, but I'll give it a chance just because the color is so great. I slip it over my head and feel the cool fabric glide down my body. There's a zipper in the back that I can only get halfway up on my own.

"Rayna?"

Nothing.

I raise my voice. "Rayna Della Toscani!"

"She's not here," Ben says.

And he is? What happened out there in the last five minutes?

"Where'd she go?" I say.

"To deal with Jeremy. He's complaining about everything."

"You think they're making out somewhere? I bet that was his master plan all along."

He laughs. "No, I think they went to the Starbucks around the corner. Jeremy will be fine once he's caffeinated. You need help with something?"

"Zipper, yeah."

The door rattles. "Can you unlock this?"

"Is anyone going to see you? People get kicked out of stores for this. Fitting rooms are not a co-ed sport."

There's a pause. "No one's around. Let me in."

I unlock the door and open it as quickly as I can, and as soon as he's in, I close and lock it again fast. Then I stand facing the mirror. "I can't reach it all the way."

He steps up close behind me. "We're in private, Jess."

"Well, I'm not going to leave the fitting room half naked."

"Okay then…if I touch you now, to help with the dress, it doesn't break our deal?"

The way he says "touch you" is illegal in seventeen states. I keep my eyes on myself in the mirror, rather than the glimpses of him behind me. "It doesn't break our deal," I say.

The other night, after his family dinner…we were high. We haven't talked about it, but I don't think that counts. And if it doesn't count, then we aren't supposed to be…*touching*.

But this is different. He's just helping me take this dress off—

No, *on*. He's helping me put this dress on.

If I can stay focused, I won't cave. I won't take advantage of the fact we're alone in a locked fitting room and do exactly what people get kicked out for doing.

He sets his hand on the left side of my neck, then slowly sweeps my hair to the right and over that shoulder. His fingertips graze my back, and my hair tickles me along the way. Goose bumps break out all over, and I have to clamp my jaw hard to keep from shuddering. Then he places his left hand on my waist, bracing down against the curve of my hip, and tugs up the zipper with his right hand. He takes his time. *Zzzzzzzzzzzzzip*. His touch leaves a trail of sparks in its wake, and this time, I can't hold back the shudder.

The dress is absolutely stunning, because just like Rayna said, it fits me like it was custom-made. But I can't fully appreciate it when all the blood is rushing out of my brain.

I've still got my eyes on myself, on my mouth that has dropped open to allow shallower breaths to come through, on the blush of color in my cheeks, on my eyelids drooping as I struggle to keep from closing them, dropping my head back onto him, and letting him pull me back against him.

His breath warms the back of my neck, and then his face appears next to mine in the mirror, his eyes intent on my reflection. "You like it?" he says.

Fuck yes. But he means the dress. "Yeah."

"I like it, too."

"Yeah?" God, even my voice is...sultry.

"I'd like it even more if it was back on the hanger now."

He never takes his eyes off mine in the mirror, never changes his expression. Never expects me to do what he wants just because he voiced it. He's waiting for me to say it's okay.

I can't think of a single person in my life who has ever made me feel so...*worthy*. And goddammit if that doesn't make him a thousand percent sexier than usual.

How easy it would be to lift this skirt and bend over. The more I imagine it, the more willpower I lose. To be able to see both of us at the same time while we...

My fists clench on the fabric. I start pulling it up, millimeter by millimeter, giving myself every chance to stop. But I keep going, and it doesn't take Ben long to figure out what I'm doing.

He sucks in a breath, sounding like a hiss. Or a prayer for strength. "Jess."

Every cell in my body is about to snap out of my control.

"It's the mirror," I say. "I just keep seeing us..."

"*Fuck,*" he whispers.

"No one would know. I'll be quiet."

He's breathing hard. Breathing in and out, in and out, in and out for several seconds. There's no way he walks away from this opportunity. I can't even see straight I'm so aroused. My knees are going to buckle if he doesn't take care of this soon.

He pinches the zipper between his fingertips and tugs it down, all the way down. My entire back is exposed to him now, and my chest is heaving, even though it feels like I'm holding my breath. Like I can't breathe. I'm…I'm about to have sex in a public fitting room.

"This isn't part of the deal," he says. "If we do this, that part of the deal doesn't exist anymore. Not just right now, but ever. It's gone. Tell me you're okay with that."

"I'm okay with that." I shrug the dress off my shoulders and let it drop, then kick it aside on the floor. "Tell me you have a condom."

He digs into his pocket and pulls one out. "Like you said, we have to be like the Marines. Always ready."

Semper fucking fi.

"I'm ready, Benjamin."

His hand comes around to my face, gently placing a finger on my lips. "Shhhh…"

I thought this was going to be quick, like that day in the park, but I was so, so wrong. Maybe it's because he's trying to be silent, I don't know, but Ben has never moved so slowly with me before. And he's got his eyes locked on mine in the mirror the whole time.

Don't make any noise, stay quiet, don't make any noise—fuck!

Fuck…fuck fuck fuck…fuck fuck…

I brace a hand against the mirror and lean into it, breathing hard as quietly as I can, making little blobs of condensation appear and disappear with every breath, and wait for my head to clear. It's going to take a while after that. Good *god*. It's possible I might not be able to come down this time.

But eventually, I do. We both do.

Ben kisses me and holds me and then helps me get dressed. Somehow, we have to get out of here without anyone knowing we were together in here. Or what we did.

Did we really just do that?

I put the blue dress back on the hanger. "This is the one I want."

"Can I buy it for you?" he asks.

"Yes, please." I hand the dress to him. "If anyone sees you, tell them I was just giving this to you."

With a smile, he unlocks the door and says, "Yes, ma'am."

Once he's gone, the door closed and locked again, I slump down into the cushy, brocade chair in the corner. I still can't believe we did that. What were we thinking?

We broke our deal.

We're free to have sex now whenever we feel like it, no matter where we are or who we're with, apparently. And dammit if I'm not already thinking about "attacking" him as soon as we get into his car.

I push up from the chair—enough time has passed now to hopefully avoid questions—and catch myself smiling in the mirror. I can't lie to myself. This is what I want.

To be with Ben freely. To be myself with him, and for him to be himself with me.

To just be in this new situation and not have to worry what anyone thinks. To just enjoy ourselves even though we still bicker and banter every day. We wouldn't be us if we didn't.

Yes, this is *exactly* what I want with Benjamin Oliver. To just be us.

And maybe…

Maybe it's time I tell him that.

Chapter Twenty-Nine

*T*here's little more than a week of July left. Every day that passes without me having this Very Important Conversation™ with Ben is making it all feel bigger than it is, more stressful than it should be. I'm so afraid of him saying no...or worse, laughing at me. I can't get past it.

Probably because this scenario is so similar to what happened the day we met—except back then it was reversed. *Ben* was the one asking *me* out.

I turned him down, obviously, and he laughed and said he wasn't really serious.

What if he thinks I'm just trying to get back at him for that? As if the nine months of hatred between us that followed wasn't my version of getting back at him already.

I wonder...

I wonder if that's what's really holding me back. The fact that we've completely transformed our relationship over the last almost-two months and never talked about why we hated each other in the first place.

I wonder if that's where I need to start.

Because how can we really move forward if the bitter past between us is still bitter?

Yeah, that seems like a good idea, in theory, but I have no

idea how to go about this without upsetting *both* of us and making it worse. What if I send us back to hating each other?

Ben: *knock knock*

Me: *Door's open. I'm upstairs, almost ready.*

With a sigh, I stuff the last bag of craft supplies into my duffel and then zip it up. The kids at the library are going to love this—I need to just focus on positive things today. You can't be grumpy around children, they will call you out on it and then make up their own version of why you're in a bad mood, and you can do nothing to stop the chaos once that starts.

That might have happened to me once.

"Hey, Jessie."

I turn toward the voice that isn't Ben's. It's my brother's.

"Hey," I say back to him.

He steps inside my room, looking around at all the bags. "Going somewhere?"

"Just the library. It's kids' craft day. We're making things out of pill bottles."

Chris's face lights up. "Sounds fun. You need help with any of this?"

"Nope, I got it," Ben says, suddenly appearing at the door. He steps inside, gives me a quick kiss, then hefts the duffel bag onto his shoulder and picks up the tote with his other hand.

Chris smiles and heads out of the room. "See you guys later, then."

"Tell Andrew I said hi," Ben says casually, then focuses on me. "Is this everything?"

Andrew... I didn't even realize I haven't seen him at all today, but I have seen Chris. The two of them are usually together.

I give myself a mental shake. This is so not the time to be

thinking about Andrew. If he was interested, he would have done or said something by now. But still…if I don't ask, this will bother me all day, and I need him out of my head so I can focus on Ben.

Me: *Where's Andrew today?*

Chris: *not feeling great*

Chris: *quarantined in my bedroom*

Me: 😔

Me: *Tell him I hope he feels better!*

Chris: *will do* 🙂

"Jessie?" Ben says. "Is something wrong?"

"No, sorry." I put my phone away and flash a grin. "This is everything. Let's go."

I pick up the other tote and then lead the way out, down the stairs, through my living room, and out to his car parked in my driveway. We stuff everything into the back seat and then sit up front and buckle our seat belts.

Once Ben is on the road, he snatches my hand, weaving our fingers together, keeping his other hand on the steering wheel.

"You nervous?" he says.

"Why would I be nervous? I've done this before. I like doing this."

He shrugs one shoulder. "You're not usually this quiet when you're excited about doing something." He pauses long enough to turn a corner and change lanes. "Is it something else?"

"I'm fine," I insist. "Just thinking."

"About what?"

"Nothing."

He laughs. "Okay, Jess."

Clearly, he doesn't believe me. But one of the things I've learned about Ben this summer? He'll never push me on anything, and he'll never ask me to explain myself.

And this is definitely something I can't explain. I *am* nervous. About *him*.

Within a couple of minutes, we're at the library, and once Ben has parked the car, we unload the back seat and head inside. The kids won't be here for another half hour, and Ben helps me set everything up. Empty pill bottles in various colors and sizes. Non-toxic glue. Non-toxic paint and brushes. Colored construction paper—recycled, of course. Stencils of just about every shape or object you could imagine. Pencils, washable markers. Ribbons and string. All of it is organized into cardboard boxes I collected from things that were shipped to my house and then labeled with big bold letters. The age group is from five to seven years, so most of these kids are still learning to read.

Just as we finish setting up, the parents start trickling in with their kids. More than one adult does a double take when they see Ben. Then a little boy's jaw drops and he points at Ben from across the room. "That's the football guy!" he squeals, but his mother shushes him.

"I appreciate you helping, but you don't have to stay," I tell him. "I'll be done in a couple of hours if you want to leave now and then pick me up later."

He smiles. "I'd rather stay, if that's okay with you?"

My stomach goes all fluttery. He *wants* to stay?

"It's okay with me, but…" I nod toward the little boy who is still staring at Ben.

"They're just kids, Jessie." And with that, he puts himself right in the middle of the room and starts high-fiving all those chubby little hands, excitedly saying things like "who's ready for some fun!" and making the shy kids blush with just a smile and a wink.

I've never seen Ben act like this before, but I guess it

shouldn't surprise me. These kids are around the same age as his nieces and nephews. He's had practice. I would bet my last bra that Ben is the "fun uncle" in their family.

It's strange, though. At the start of summer, when I imagined this, it was Andrew here with me, not Ben. And now, I can't imagine Ben *not* being here with me. While Andrew is just one big question mark.

Two hours later, ten pairs of happy hands are carrying out their upcycled masterpieces—the starstruck little boy painted his in Trinity Tigers blue, of course—and the room has been absolutely destroyed. "I've never seen such a mess here before," I say with a laugh.

"The size of the mess is directly proportionate to the amount of fun that's been had," Ben says in his teacher voice. "In layman's terms—the bigger the mess, the bigger the fun."

I snort. "Okay, nerd."

He starts collecting markers and glue sticks, safety scissors and stencils, while I pick up all the trash and toss it in the bin.

As we're walking back to his car, I say, "Thank you for staying. It was way more fun with you there than when I do it alone."

"I know," he quips.

I roll my eyes and give his shoulder a playful shove. "You're such an ass."

"Excuse me, ma'am, you like this ass."

Well. He isn't wrong.

He unlocks his car, and we load the back seat, then sit up front and get buckled.

"Where to now?" Ben says, pumping up the AC on full blast.

Don't be a chicken shit, Jessie. The day is going great. Don't ruin it and say something dumb like "to your bed, please, so I can show you just how much I like your ass."

Do I want to do that? Hell yes. But if I keep putting off saying these things that need to be said, we will never be more than sex buddies for the summer...and then he'll move on.

"Jessie," Ben says. "You sure you're okay? You keep zoning out."

"Yeah, sorry." I shake my head. "Sorry. I love craft day, but it's really exhausting." Not a lie. "Can we go somewhere, just the two of us, and do...nothing? I don't have anything left in me after that. But I'm not ready to go back home yet, either." I shake my head again. "I don't even know what I'm saying, never mind. Where do you want to go? We can do whatever."

Ben smiles and leans across the center console toward me, then gives me a super-soft kiss on the lips. He starts to pull away, like that was all he'd intended to do, but then comes back for more, a little less soft this time but just as gentle. Kissing always leads to something with him, so I guess this is his answer. But when he pulls away for real, and my head is spinning, he says, "Doing nothing with you the rest of the day sounds absolutely perfect."

We go to Ben's house—I mean mansion. It's a big, *empty* mansion. I don't know where his parents are, or the house staff, and I don't care enough to ask. I'd rather be alone here than constantly worrying who might see us...or hear us.

Ben leads me to the kitchen first, where we stock up on cookies and popcorn and chips and chocolates and water bottles and anything else we can fit in a tote, then we take all of that up to his room and spread it out on the floor between the mounted television and small couch.

"Movie?" he says, opening up Netflix. "TV show? Comedy special? Or documentary?"

I tear open a bag of cheese popcorn, an idea coming to me. "Maybe later."

"Okay." Ben turns the TV off and tosses the remote aside, then grabs a giant chocolate-covered pretzel and joins me on the couch. "Did you have something else in mind?"

"Maybe," I say, purposely teasing him.

"Okay," he says with a smile this time. "In Jessica Land, maybe means yes but you want me to guess."

I shrug. "Maybe."

He gives me a look, then thinks for a minute, just chewing his pretzel. "Give me a hint."

"Guessing is part of it."

"Twenty questions?"

"Close!" I say. "But no."

He goes quiet again. Then, "Truth or Dare?"

"Almost," I say. "It's called Truth or Truth. I ask you a question, and you have to answer it honestly. Then you ask me something, and I have to answer it honestly. No secrets. No lies. Only truth. And you can't back out by doing a dare. The truth is your only choice."

"This sounds terrible," Ben says.

I raise a brow. "Sounds like you have something to hide, Benjamin Oliver."

His face goes hard for a second, but then he smiles and cracks open a bottle of water. "All right, I'm game. Hit me with your first question."

Oh wow. He's really going for it.

No backing out now. It's all or nothing.

God, I hope I don't regret this.

"You know I lost my virginity at eighteen," I start.

"You did?" He feigns shock. "With who?"

I throw a piece of popcorn at him, and he laughs. "So…" I continue. "I want to know how old you really were when you lost yours. Rumor says it was freshman year. Was it?"

"You're going right for the jugular, Jessie. Can't we ease into this?"

"Nope." I flash a smug grin.

"You might not like what I ask you if this is the bar," he says.

My stomach does a flip-flop—he's right. But it's only fair, isn't it? If I want to know what's really going on with him, then I have to be willing to do the same for him.

"Just answer the question," I tell him. "How old were you when your cherry popped?"

He laughs at that. "Do I need to explain to you how the male anatomy works?"

"No… I'm very familiar, thank you. Now quit stalling."

"Yes, ma'am," he says, then clears his throat. "Okay. The answer is sixteen."

What?

"Sixteen during sophomore year or sixteen during junior year—"

"Nuh uh." He holds up a hand. "You had your question. Now it's my turn."

Dammit. I clamp my mouth shut.

Ben leans over to pick up a stack of cookies from the package sleeve, then straightens again. He's down two cookies when he finally asks, "If you could only eat one thing for the rest of your life, what would it be?"

"*That's* your question?"

He nods, shoving another cookie into his mouth.

What the hell kind of dumb question is that? The answer is fresh-baked bread, but that is a boring answer to a boring question. No. I need to give him something unexpected.

I stare him dead in the eye and say, "You. And more specifically, your protein bar."

Ben's eyes go wide, and then there are cookie crumbs spewing from his mouth and he's coughing, choking, his face going red. I'm not even the least bit sorry. Though I do watch him for a minute to make sure he doesn't die.

"You're supposed to tell the truth," he wheezes.

"That's what you get for asking a dumb question," I say.

"No, you broke the rules—I didn't. I get an extra turn now."

What rules? We're making this up as we go.

"Fine," I say. "But if you ask what's my favorite color, I'm locking you out of your own room and eating all this junk myself."

"Fine," he echoes and gives me a heated look. "What's your favorite kind of porn?"

My jaw drops, and my face catches fire. "What makes you think I even watch porn?"

"No, no," he tsks. "You have to answer the question, Jessie. The truth this time."

"Benjamin—"

He tosses over the TV remote. "If you don't want to tell me, then show me."

"You can't be serious."

"I can be, and I am." He gulps down the last of his water bottle.

Fuck. I don't want to say it, but I don't want to see it on his huge-ass TV screen, either, because that will just lead to us reenacting it. And right now, I need to stay focused. We can have naked fun later. "Can I...write it down?" I say.

Ben laughs at that but agrees. "Paper and pen are on my desk."

I lick the cheese flavoring off my fingertips and go to the

desk, then try to confess in writing that I'm obsessed with something this kinky without my face burning so hot that my head turns to ash. I walk back over to Ben on the couch, show him the paper long enough for him to read it, then crumple it up and say, "You tell anyone about this and I will end you."

He stares at me, silent and expressionless.

"My turn now—"

"Wait." He raises a palm toward me. "Why are we still playing this game when we could be doing *that* instead?"

"Maybe I'm not in the mood," I say. I'm a damn liar.

"All right. But the minute you *are* in the mood? You better fucking tell me."

Oh...this could be my chance to steer us back to the conversation I actually wanted to have. "Well, okay, but what if I'm not in the mood until...say...September? You won't be around to do anything about it."

He gives me a hard look, then snatches my hand and pulls me down onto his lap. "Listen. Jessica. You are welcome to make a booty call anytime you want. A month from now. A year from now. I don't care. *Anytime*."

A booty call... That's the only future he sees for us?

"What if you're with someone else?"

"Is that your official question?" He raises a brow.

"No, forget the game. Just answer me."

He nods slowly, like he's thinking. "If I'm with someone else, and you want to hook up, then..." He grins. "Threesome?"

"Be serious."

"That was serious."

But he's still grinning, and all those bad feelings come rushing back to me, hitting me hard like a tsunami. This boy doesn't know how to be serious. Everything about me, since day one, has been a joke to him.

That's what I really wanted to talk to him about today,

though. What started it all—and why. I've been tiptoeing around it with this made-up game of questions, when I should be asking him outright—*what the hell were you thinking that day?*

. . .

"*This is my friend Ben,*" *Jeremy says.* "*Ben, this is Rayna's friend Jessie.*"

"*Hi.*" *My voice comes out barely audible, but when I normally meet someone for the first time, I can't make eye contact. With Benjamin Oliver…I can't seem to take my eyes off* his.

"*Jessie, hi,*" *Ben says. He looks me up and down, takes in my plain cotton tee and scuffed-up shoes, and smirks.* "*Will I see you at the after-game party on Friday?*"

"*Uh…*" *Is he hitting on me? No. This is Benjamin Oliver. He has a type, and it isn't Frump Extraordinaire. He likes his girls pretty and confident and experienced in naked sports.*

Ben's giving me a sexy smirk that annoys the hell out of me. Even more annoying is I can feel my cheeks burning up, and the longer I say nothing, and the redder I get, the more Ben keeps grinning like he knows he's the reason I'm flustered.

Worse? He's a thousand percent right.

"*I'm, uh, actually…*" *I tuck a stray piece of hair behind my ear.* "*I'm busy Friday. But, um…thanks. For the invite.*"

Ben stares at me, that smirk still in place, but the humor has left his eyes. Those goddamn beautiful eyes. "*What invite?*" *he says with a laugh, then turns and talks to Jeremy across the table from me.*

"*He's such an asshole,*" *I say under my breath to Rayna, opening my bag of Doritos.* "*What, is that the first time a girl hasn't swooned at the mere sight of him? Good fucking grief.*"

I take a swig of chocolate milk, and when I set the carton back down on the lunch table, Ben is facing me again, staring at me with murder in his eyes.

Oh shit. He heard me.

Well, whatever he's about to say, I'm sure I can handle it. He isn't the first person to make fun of me, and he definitely won't be the last. I have the thickest skin in Trinity High.

"Benjamin—" I start, and he cuts me off.

"It's Ben," he snaps. "You think I'm an asshole, Jessie? I've been called worse by better." The smirk is back. "Try again."

This boy is going to be the death of me. And if I'm going down, then so is he.

Try again, he said. With him, I don't even have to try. It just comes out naturally.

"Benjamin—"

"It's Ben—"

"You are the human equivalent of period cramps. If I take a Midol, will you disappear?"

"No, I won't disappear," he says, that cocky smirk still firmly in place. "But I can ignore you so hard you'll start to doubt your own existence."

・・・

"**W**hat if I had said yes?" I ask him, then hold my breath, waiting for the answer.

His brow wrinkles. "You lost me. Said yes to what?"

"Remember the day we met?"

"Yes…" Now he's frowning. "I still don't know what you mean."

I take in a deep breath, then let it out, dropping my shoulders, sagging my whole body against him. I can't look him in the eyes and say this, but it needs to be said. "You asked me if I'd be at the after-game party that Friday."

He's quiet for a moment. Then, "I did."

"Well...what if I had said yes? What were you planning to do with me at the party?"

Ben adjusts his seat, pushing me away from his chest with one hand while wrapping his other arm around my waist so I can't go too far. "What are you really asking me, Jessie?"

My cheeks heat, and I focus on my hands resting on his shoulders instead of his face. "Why did you pretend you weren't asking me out, when you obviously were? Did I hurt your ego so badly that you had to gaslight me? You made it seem like I was misunderstanding—"

"Because you were." He laughs. "I was *not* asking you out. Is that what you really thought? Is that why you called me an asshole?" He shakes his head. "This explains so much."

No, actually, it explains nothing. I only have more questions. "You gave me *the look*."

"What look?"

"You know..." I mimic it the best I can, scanning him from top to bottom and back up again. "*That* look."

He laughs again. "You mean the look anyone gives anyone the first time they see them? But with you it was probably more noticeable because I'd never seen Frump Chic before."

"Oh, shut up." Finally, I catch his gaze and lock it with mine. "Why can't you just admit you were hitting on me?"

"Because I wasn't," he insists. "I was dating Samantha Jarvis when you and I met. Why would I hit on you—or anyone? But especially someone who's not even my type?"

He means me. I'm not his type.

"If that's true, then why the fuck did we break our no-fuck deal?"

"Wait, wait... We're talking about the past, not the present." He pauses. "Aren't we?"

Yes. *No*. Both? I throw my hands up. "I don't know what I'm talking about anymore."

He laughs. "Then how do you expect me to know?"

God, I've been such an idiot. Thinking that any of this could be more than just sex. And now, finding out that I completely misread him the day we met and everything bad that happened after that was totally my fault.

I push myself off his lap and turn for the door. "I'm going home."

"What?" He jumps up off the couch and puts himself between me and the exit. "Jessie, wait. What's really bothering you?"

"Nothing, I just..."

"It's not nothing, Jess. You're getting mad at me for something I did and said almost a year ago? Why does it even matter anymore?"

He's right. It doesn't matter—or at least it shouldn't. And I can't explain why my feelings for him are different now. They just are. I don't know why I'm feeling like this, I just know that I am. I don't know why I want this to be real with him, I just know that I do.

But if I can't even sort out my own feelings, how do I think a relationship is going to work? Why am I so bad at this?

I turn away from him to walk back to the couch and land my bare foot onto a package of Hostess cupcakes. It smashes through the plastic wrapper and up between my toes. Fantastic.

I just look at it, look at my cupcake foot, and Ben starts laughing again, and...it breaks something inside me.

"You think this is funny," I say, eerily calm. I don't even recognize my voice.

He goes quiet for a second, then busts out laughing again. "I'm sorry. Yes! It's funny."

Only one of the two cupcakes has been smashed. The other is still perfect. I bend down and take the fully intact cupcake out of the plastic, then turn and smash the thing in Ben's face.

It happens so fast, he doesn't have a chance to close his mouth before I've filled it with chocolate cake and white cream, and on instinct, he's spitting it out immediately.

"Benja—aggh!" It landed on my chest, clumps of it now falling to my already cake-covered foot. Aaaaand he's laughing again.

What's worse? Stepping in cake, or getting smashed, spewed-up cake spit all over you?

There's only one thing I can do now. *Revenge.*

I slowly turn and see all the food and drinks on the floor. Every one of those can be a weapon. And this is war.

Ben must be thinking the same thing I am, because as soon as I move to pick something up, he's right there next to me, choosing his own ammo.

The next few minutes are a blur of cake and crumbs and cream filling and exploded bottles of pop sprayed all over the room. We're both covered in food, head to toe, and I'm laughing so hard I can barely get a breath. Because it's impossible to stay mad in a food fight. I should have thought of that before I started this.

"Wait, stop!" I wheeze. "That's enough. I have popcorn stuck in my hair."

Ben stops moving for the first time since this started and looks at me long and hard. "You are a mess."

"You're more of a mess."

"Well," he says, glancing at the bathroom, "we can fix that."

"Or..." I look at his bed. "We can make more of a mess."

He points a finger at me. "Don't you dare."

"I'm suddenly...so tired. I can't..." I drag myself toward his bed, leaving a trail of sticky things across the carpet. "I need to lie down."

"Jessie, stop—" He breaks out in a sprint, and in three long strides he catches me by the arm just before I'm about to fall onto his very clean duvet. "You're in trouble now, young lady."

"Oh no," I tease. "I'm scared. Big Bad Benjamin—aaaaaaaaahhh!"

He scoops me up into his arms so fast I have to grab him tight to keep from slipping. My initial scream transforms into a fit of giggles, all the way to the bathroom, until he deposits me, fully clothed, in the bathtub, then turns the water on full blast and drops in two large bath bombs.

"What the fuck are you doing!" I start stripping my wet, sloppy clothes off and throwing them at him. He dodges every piece easily, while at the same time taking his own clothes off. Soon, we're both naked in this behemoth bathtub quickly filling with steam and bubbles, and I think I've figured it out.

This is it.

This is the reason everything we do or say turns into a fight.

Because when we fight, we aren't really fighting at all.

Ben slides up next to me, steam rising all around his neck and shoulders. His face is wiped clean now, and he says quietly, "Are we good?"

I bite my lip, thinking. This *is* good. What I have with him, it's good. The only time I think it isn't is when I want it to be something it isn't. I need to just accept it—this is what we have, this is what we are...and it's good. Period.

"Yeah," I say, pulling him closer. "We're good."

As good as we'll ever be. And *good* will just have to be *good enough* until he says goodbye.

Chapter Thirty

*A*ugust is a couple of days away. Only a little more than two weeks left before Andrew leaves. And my brother leaves. And Ben leaves. Kamy and Todd are leaving, too, so she can get her classes started at Harvard. Todd decided to put off college and work for his dad remotely until Kamy is done with school. They're engaged. I still can't imagine them as husband and wife—even harder to imagine them as parents. But I have a lot more respect for Todd now than I ever thought I could. He put Kamy and the baby before himself.

The only people sticking around are Jeremy and Rayna, who are both going to Penn State, but that means Ben and Jeremy will be rivals on the football field now. Everything is upside down and backward and inside out. If Rayna was leaving me, too…I don't know what I'd do with myself. She's my lifeline.

I've spent the night at Ben's so often now that when I do sleep at home in my own bed, I'm hit with the worst insomnia. But just because I'm losing sleep doesn't mean I don't have to go to work. Sometimes early in the morning, like today.

At four a.m., I'm wide awake. I should stay here and try to sleep for another hour. Even if I stay awake, though, I'd still be resting if I lie down. I should stay in bed. I should.

But I can't. I'm antsy. I need to move.

In a tank top and sleep shorts, no bra, and bare feet, I head down to the kitchen. If I have any chance of making it through my shift later, I need to start consuming as much coffee as possible as soon as possible.

I set the coffeemaker to brew a whole pot, then lean against the countertop and wait. Within a minute, my head starts nodding like it's too heavy to hold up.

Jesus. *Now* I feel tired? I'm not letting that coffee go to waste—

Someone steps lightly down the stairs and into the kitchen.

"Jessica?"

I snap to attention.

It's Andrew, all bright-eyed and bushy-tailed at four freaking a.m. He's in athletic shorts and running shoes, his springy curls tied up high on his head.

"You're up early," he says. "Big plans today?"

My face and neck heat. "No—uh. No, just going to work."

He nods slowly like he's thinking, then flicks his eyes away quickly.

Oh god, I forgot I'm not wearing a bra. *Agh.* I cross my arms over my chest.

Andrew scratches the back of his neck, looking to the side. Like he's nervous.

Why would *he* be nervous?

Oh shit—I'm such a dumbass. This whole time…what if he hasn't made a move because he's nervous about it? Fear of rejection is a real thing, for pretty much everyone. I know that.

I just didn't think of it with him. I was too busy thinking of it with myself.

"Would you…" he starts, then clears his throat. "Would you be free to talk later? Alone?"

A…Alone?

Oh my Jesus lord in heaven.

Ben's plan actually worked?

Answer the man, Jessie!

"Y-yeah, sure," I stutter out. "I'm off at three."

He smiles big and bright, then lets out a rush of air like he's relieved. "Okay," he says. "Okay, see you then." He leaves the kitchen, and soon I hear the front door open and close.

What do I do now? I can't screw this up. It's my only chance.

Coffee forgotten, I run back upstairs to my room, get dressed, brush my teeth, brush my hair, and grab my phone.

Me: *I need you. Right now.*

Ben: *it's four am you minx*

Ben: *on my way*

He thinks I'm making a booty call. A booty text? He thinks I want sex.

I look back at my message. Yeah, I could have worded that better.

Whatever, I'll explain it all when he gets here.

I wait for him on the front porch, pacing back and forth and back and forth, chewing my nails and fingertips like they're granola bars and this is my breakfast.

Ben pulls into my driveway, and I run down the steps and jump into the car before he's even fully parked.

"Jesus—Jessie, be careful," he says. "I prefer you alive."

"Park," I snap. "I mean drive. To the park."

He backs out, and we're on our way. "What's going on?"

"Andrew." I massage both sides of my head, leaning forward. *Breathe.*

"Andrew," he says flatly. "What about him?"

"He wants to talk later today. Alone. He wants to talk to me alone, that can only mean one thing, right? What else could it mean?"

Ben doesn't say another word until we're in the empty lot of the park. He turns the car off. "I'm not following," he says. "How did this lead to you texting me at four a.m.?"

"That's when it happened!"

He shakes his head. "Start from the beginning, Jessie."

I take in a deep breath, then the words rush out in one long string of a sentence. "I was up early, because I can't sleep in my bed anymore, because I've been spoiled by sleeping in *your* bed, and Andrew was up early to go out running, because he always goes for a run early in the morning, and I wasn't wearing a bra, and he was acting all anxious and nervous, and he said he needs to talk to me later—*alone*."

"Why weren't you wearing a bra?"

"Because I had just gotten out of bed. I said that!"

His face turns hard, and a muscle in his jaw ticks. "You don't have to shout."

"Yes, I do, because I'm freaking out, Benjamin! Are you even listening to me? I know you think I wanted to hook up this morning, but can you please get your head out of the gutter for fucking once and *help* me." I open the car door and get out, then slam it shut and walk a few feet onto the grass. The sun is only just starting to rise, and there's a heavy mist in the air.

I'm not headed anywhere specific, though, I just need to move. What is his problem right now? He should be happy for me.

He should be happy for himself, even. This was all his idea—and it worked.

I hear the car door open and shut, then Ben comes up behind me and wraps his arms around me. "What do you need me to do?" he says gently.

My whole body relaxes in his embrace. I hug his arms against me and just breathe for a minute. Breathe him in…

Then I turn around within his arms so we're touching front to front. I lean my head back a little and look in his eyes. Those gorgeous, deep brown, soulful eyes that have been like an anchor for me whenever I feel like I'm drifting off course. They ground me again now and strengthen my resolve.

"Break up with me," I say.

His expression turns to granite, and for a long time he just looks down at me, silent.

Then, finally, he drops his arms, shakes his head, and turns away, toward the trees.

"Benjamin, talk to me. Tell me what you're thinking."

"I'm thinking…" he starts, then pauses. "I'm thinking this whole deal we made is absolute bullshit."

What? "It was your idea," I remind him, tempering my annoyance.

"And my idea was shit," he says. "How am I supposed to break up with you when we've been all over each other for the last two months? When we've been…" He presses the heel of his palm to his forehead like it hurts.

What does he mean? This was part of the plan, no matter when it happened. We were always going to break up. Fake break up our fake relationship.

"You're afraid no one will believe it?" I ask. "Because we've been pretending too well?"

"No, Jessie." He gives me a look like he can't understand why I'd say such a thing. "No," he repeats. "Fuck. This isn't going to work."

"What isn't going to work?"

"Nothing. Anything. *Everything.*"

"Benjamin." My head is spinning. "You're not making

any sense. This is exactly what we'd planned for. And I told you at the start of it that we would have to break up. Even if Andrew makes it clear he wants to be with me, he won't do it unless I'm single. We just need to think of something convincing that would split us up—"

"Like a fight?" he says, then gives me a sardonic smile. "We always fight. That wouldn't change anything."

"We always fight and then make up," I clarify. "So, we just don't make up this time."

His brows draw downward, giving me a stern glare.

And that just pushes me over the edge. "Why are you mad at me over this?"

"Unbelievable," he says. "Why do you even have to ask that?"

"I don't know, Benjamin! Explain it to me. I can't read your fucking mind."

"You shouldn't have to," he counters.

My frustration has reached a breaking point. I'm confused and angry, and I don't know what I'm supposed to know that he thinks I know. My cheeks hurt, and my eyes sting. My throat feels tight, and my nose tickles. I sniffle. But I will not cry in front of him. I refuse.

"I thought this is what you wanted," I say. "I thought you'd be happy for me. But you're just… Why does everything have to be difficult with you? Since the day we met, that's all it's ever been."

"Fuck, Jessie," he snaps. "Why can't you see what's right fucking in front of you? Why does everything have to be either this or that or it's nothing? Why does everyone have to fit into some perfect fantasy role you created in your head or they don't exist?"

What the flaming hell is going on here?

"The more you talk, Benjamin, the less I understand."

He drops his head, and when he lifts it again, he's got that sad-puppy look that I've only seen once or twice before. But I can't feel sorry for him this time. He's bringing it on himself.

"I can't explain this to you," he says. "You either know or you don't. And I was starting to think you knew, but…clearly you don't."

"That makes even *less* sense!" I bite the inside of my cheek and turn away from him. If I don't, I'll lose it. I'll cry, I'll scream, I'll beg for him to stop being an asshole all the damn time. Why now? Why does he choose now to drop this cryptic shit on me?

I thought we were doing so well. I thought we had a chance at a long-term friendship.

I sniffle and swipe at my eyes before turning back around. Then I say as evenly as I can, "All I did was ask you for help. I don't know what you think this is, but it's not help. I'll just… I'll figure it out myself if you're not interested in fulfilling your side of the deal."

I pull out my phone and send Rayna a text.

"What are you doing?" Ben says.

"Getting someone else to drive me home. I can't even look at you right now."

I turn away from him and wait for him to leave. But he doesn't. He doesn't move, he doesn't talk, he doesn't do anything. I turn back, just a little. Just enough to make sure he didn't die on the spot.

"Congratulations, Jessie," he says. "We just broke up. Go and get your dream guy."

His tone is low and steady, but every word hits me like a stinging slap.

Then he gets in his car but doesn't drive away until Rayna's car is pulling into the lot. Is that supposed to make me feel better? That he waited to make sure my ride showed up but can't explain to me what the fuck is going on in his head? He'd rather just leave me here wondering?

He'd rather just leave me, period.

He...*left* me. That wasn't a fake breakup. That was a very real "I'm done with you in every way we've ever known each other."

Two minutes ago, he was standing here holding me. What. Just. Happened?

As soon as I get into Rayna's car, I'm crying so hard I can't speak. It's a miracle I can even breathe. I get one word out, "Benjamin," and she doesn't ask me any questions. She knows.

The only thing that gets me through my shift at the library without having another breakdown over all that nonsense with Benjamin that I still don't understand is knowing that Andrew is waiting for me to get home so we can talk.

At least something good will come out of this shit pile.

As soon as I get home, I go to my room and check myself in the mirror hanging off my closet door. My eyes are red, my nose is swollen, my lips are dry. I look like I have the flu.

Other than that? Grand.

Someone knocks on my door. Then, "Jessica?"

Fuck, it's Andrew. I'm not ready!

"Can I come in?" he says.

He must really be eager to get on with this. I've been home for a minute.

"Y-yeah, come in." I sit on the bed, and when he walks in and sees me, he closes the door behind him and sits right next to me.

Oh sweet heavens. He's so close I can feel the heat

coming off him.

"H-hi," I say. "What's up?"

He looks at me with this nervous sort of smile, then opens his mouth like he's going to say something but raises the back of his hand to my forehead instead. "Are you feeling okay? You look like you might have a fever."

First my blushing is sunburn, and now my emotional crisis is a fever.

Smooth, Jessie. Real smooth.

"I'm fine, it's just been a rough day. Ben and I had a fight." I sniffle. *Do not turn the waterworks on again.* "We broke up."

"Oh, I'm so sorry," he says. "We can talk another day if this is a bad time?"

"It's fine." Or at least it will be, now that he knows I'm available. "I'd rather talk about something else than stew over it."

"Okay." He nods. Then rubs his palms down the front of his thighs. And says not a word.

"Is something wrong?" I ask.

"No, no," he assures me. "I just don't know where to start?"

This is torture. I want to shake him and say, "just spit it out!" But if people did that to me when I couldn't get my words out, it would crush me. Maybe Andrew has the same issue that I do. Maybe we actually have something in common and this crush isn't one-sided, he just didn't know what to say or how to say it.

"This summer with Christopher," he says, "has been...eye-opening. He's helped me see things about myself that I didn't know were there. He showed me things about myself that I didn't understand."

Okay...

"Before we came to stay here," Andrew says, "I didn't know what I really wanted. And now...I do. Thanks to your brother…I know." He flashes a smile, but it doesn't affect me the way it usually does. Something isn't right here. "I also know how close you are to him," he goes on. "I know that whatever your brother does, whoever he's with, it will affect you, too."

Whoever he's with…

"Y-you…and Chris?"

"Yes," he says.

"Together?"

"Yes," he says again.

A million thoughts swirl in my head. A million words.

Stupid.

Naive.

Dumb shit.

Jesus fuck.

Ben.

Is this what Ben was talking about when he said I can't see what's right in front of me?

"We didn't want to tell anyone until we were sure of our feelings ourselves," Andrew says. "And he thought it would be better coming from me, so you didn't think you had to tell him it's okay even if…" He swallows. "Even if it isn't."

Of course it's okay. I know my brother is bisexual. But it never crossed my mind that Andrew might be, too. Or gay. Or anything other than *straight.*

Why? Because I wanted him to be? So he could be with me?

I try to think back on the last several weeks since he and my brother arrived. They've spent a lot of time together, practically attached at the hip. They've snuck off together for mysterious overnight "parties" that very well could have been a room at a hotel so they could…

God. Is Ben right? Was it there and I just didn't see it? *Did he know and not tell me?*

"Jessica," Andrew says. "You mean the world to Christopher. You mean a lot to me, too, I feel I've gotten to know you better this summer. Like a real sister. So, before we tell anyone else, we wanted to make sure you knew first."

"I…"

I can't believe I didn't see it. It was right there, and I didn't see it.

It was there before I even agreed to Ben's plan to do *anything* with me.

When Chris called me the morning of my graduation, I knew there was something. He was so *happy*. I knew something big in his life had changed. I just didn't put together the pieces that were right in front of my face—because all this time, I've only been focused on myself. My own problems and how I thought I could solve them. And doesn't that just make me feel like the worst human being alive.

"Jessica?" Andrew sounds worried now. "Please say something."

I look at him, at the hope in his eyes. "Andrew, I… I couldn't imagine anyone better for him than you."

Andrew's face transforms from anguish to pure joy in half a second. "Thank you, Jessica. *Thank you*." He pulls me into a hug.

How fitting. I finally get the man to touch me and it's because he's in love with my brother. What is my life anymore.

Also, if I know my brother—and I do—I'm pretty sure he's been standing in the hall eavesdropping this whole time.

"You can come in now," I say to the door, pulling away from Andrew.

Chris peeks in slowly at first, giving me a sheepish look like he's done something wrong. But he's not the one who's wrong here. I am fully, nine thousand percent wrong in all of this.

"I'm sorry," Chris says, walking in.

"For what?"

He shrugs. "I don't like keeping secrets from you."

And that kicks me right in the gut. I've been keeping things from him, too. I've been keeping things from *everyone*.

I stand up and give Chris a big bear hug. "I love you. I'm so glad you're happy."

"I love you too, Jessie James." He gives me one more hard squeeze, then pulls away. "And I'm glad you're happy, too. You and Ben are like, the GOAT."

The greatest of all time.

Sure we are.

That's why we're back to hating each other now.

"Oh, not anymore," Andrew says. "They had a fight."

"They always fight," Chris says.

"No, a real one," I tell him. "A really bad one. I think he's done with me and I...I don't even know why."

Chris stays and talks to me for a while. They both do. And I really do think they're perfect for each other—they're both the best big brothers I could ask for.

But as soon as they leave, I lock the door behind them and fall face-first onto my bed, burying fresh tears in my pillow.

I really am a colossal dumbass.

Looking back now, it's easy to see that he isn't the right guy for me. We can be friends. We can be family. And nothing else. We have a connection, but we've never had chemistry—not like what I clearly see sparking between him and my brother now. That's probably part of why it was always so hard to talk to him before. I was trying to force us into a relationship that wasn't meant to be.

I ruined everything good I had with Ben for something I could never have with Andrew.

And there's no one to blame but myself.

Chapter Thirty-One

Rayna: *are you still at work or are you home now*
Rayna: *jeremy told me that ben told him that you guys definitely broke up and ben is pissed but he won't say what happened*
Rayna: *you need to talk about it*
Rayna: *not for me but for you*
Rayna: *i'll pick you up*
Me: *I'm never getting out of bed.*
Rayna: *fine then i'm coming to you*

Me: *Did you know?*
Ben: *know what*
Me: *About Andrew? Did you know and not tell me?*
Ben: *bye Jessie*
Me: *Can we talk?*
Me: *Please don't ignore me.*
Me: *I messed up.*
Me: *Benjamin come on.*
Me: *Why are you doing this!*

• • •

*R*ayna shows up with ice cream. A whole bucket of salted caramel and two spoons, no bowls. We're just going to eat it straight from the container. And this is why I love her.

"Jessie," she says, placing a hand on my shoulder. "I'm telling you this because I'm your friend. You look absolutely wrecked."

"I *am* wrecked." I shovel another spoonful of ice cream into my mouth, swirl it around until it melts enough to swallow. "I screwed up so bad, Rayna. I don't even know where to start."

"Really? I assumed it was something Ben did."

"Well, he's not totally innocent, but…it was mostly me."

She digs in for more ice cream. "Can you tell me what happened?"

"It's a long, sad story."

"I got time," she says. "Start at the beginning."

I swallow down another melty, delicious bite, then take a minute to think.

When *was* the beginning?

"You remember that thing Benjamin suggested at lunch on the last day of school?"

Rayna freezes. "The sex plan?"

"Yeah." I blow out a breath and lean back against the wall. "I met up with him after graduation and we, um, put that plan into action. Me and him."

"What?" She stabs her spoon into the ice cream, leaving it there like the sword in the stone, and crosses her arms. "When? Why? How? And…*what*?"

I tell her everything. Every step, every decision, every deal we made. Everything that happened from the first night to the quickie in the park to the fake dating that turned into real sex to whatever the fuck just happened this morning. And everything Andrew told me later.

Rayna doesn't say a word through it all. She just sits there, absorbing. I guess that's better than her screaming at me for being a liar and keeping huge secrets.

By the time I'm done, my throat is somehow sore *and* numb, and my voice sounds raw and ragged. The bucket of ice cream is half empty.

"And now he won't even talk to me," I say. "He won't answer my texts. I call, and it won't go through—he's declining it every time. And I just don't get it. Everything was going great. I was even starting to think that maybe..."

Rayna waits for me to continue. But saying this part is harder than anything else.

"Maybe what?" she presses.

"I don't know." I set my spoon down on the nightstand. All that ice cream is churning in my gut now. "Maybe me and Benjamin could...be something real."

Rayna just blinks at me. Another blink. "What do you mean?"

"What do you mean, what do I mean?"

"I mean you and Ben *were* real," she insists. "Everything you just told me? It doesn't get more real than what you two did. How much more real are you looking for, Jessie?"

Okay, now I'm lost.

"We weren't really dating. We were faking it," I remind her. "We were just putting on a show. And before that we were just having sex. No strings."

She laughs. "No, you weren't."

"Then why didn't he ever say it was real? Why didn't he ever say he cares?"

"I don't know," she says sarcastically. "Maybe because he

was *showing* you it was real and that he cares every damn day for two months straight."

I throw my hands up. "That's not what that was!"

"Why not!" She blows out an exasperated breath. "Did you ever think that, maybe, he came up with that whole ridiculous plan in the first place because he liked you? After graduation he wouldn't get to see you every day. I'm not saying it was a brilliant plan, but…" She looks me right in the eye. "Maybe the reason was simple. He just wanted to be with you."

I laugh at that. "Come on."

"Why can't that be true?"

"Because he hated me," I say. "He hated me since the day we met."

"You really believe that?"

No. Of course I don't believe that. I'd even come to that conclusion myself recently—that all of that fighting wasn't actually fighting. It's what drew us together…and kept us together.

But stubbornness and pride get the better of me. I don't want to be proven wrong about anything right now. I don't want her to argue with me. I just want her support.

"Rayna, you were there. You saw it. He fought with me *every day*."

She makes air quotes. "'Fought with you.'"

"I can't believe you're siding with him—"

"I'm siding with *both* of you. You're both my friends. And when you were together? It was like everything was the way it's supposed to be with the six of us."

"I thought that, too," I admit. "But it wasn't."

She lets out a long-suffering sigh. "Think about it, Jessie. I mean, really, just give it a hard think for a minute. Even if there was some actual hate between you in the beginning of the school year, by the end of it, you two were just playing games with each other. Everyone could see it except you. Ben wouldn't have put up with it for that long if he truly hated it. If he hated you. And you know what? Neither would you."

Everyone could see it except me.

Damn.

Isn't that what Ben said? That I couldn't see what's right in front of me?

I assumed that by "right in front of me," he meant that Andrew and Chris were a couple. But...what if it was this?

I shake my head. "That still doesn't explain why he got mad at me for asking him to help with—"

Oh fuck.

Rayna raises a brow. "Andrew?"

"Yeah." I drop my face in my hands.

"Of course he got upset over that. He was hoping you'd decide to let that go at some point and just stay with him."

I pop my head up. It makes sense, but it also doesn't. Ben has made it clear, over and over again, that he's not looking to make any commitment, not with me or anyone. He's not going to change who he is, and I shouldn't expect him to. But still, a little part of my brain thinks it was possible, even if the chance of it was tiny. "Then why wouldn't he *tell me*?"

"Have you told him about your feelings for him?" Rayna says.

"No, but..."

"Why not?"

I bite at my lip. "I was afraid he didn't feel the same way. I was afraid of being wrong and losing him. You even said yourself that he wouldn't do anything serious with me."

"That was before I knew everything I know now. Before I saw the way you two fit so perfectly together when you got rid of the drama." Rayna shuffles across the bed so she's sitting beside me, then pulls me against her in a side hug. "Do you think it's possible that Ben was afraid of the same thing you were? Honestly, Jessie, he had even more reason to think you wouldn't feel the same. You did all the things you did with Ben so you could be with someone else. And then this morning you confirmed that all his fear of rejection was valid. You were choosing Andrew. What was he supposed to think?"

I lean my head down on her shoulder, inhale the clean scent of her hair. "If what you're saying is true, then why did he help me with Andrew at all?"

"Because when you love someone," Rayna says, "that's the most important thing to you. That the person you love is happy, even if it isn't with you."

Now she's pushing it. Love? "Benjamin doesn't love me."

Rayna sighs. "Maybe he does, maybe he doesn't. How would I know? I'm just saying think about it. Think back on everything he did with you and said to you this summer. Look at it through the lens of 'he liked me' instead of 'he hated me.' If you find even one small thing that proves this theory wrong, then I'm wrong and he's just the asshole you always accused him of being. So…tell me you'll think about it?"

Why do boys have to be so complicated?

"Okay, Rayna," I concede and give her a squeeze. "I'll think about it."

"Good," she says. "Now, let's rewind for a minute, okay? Did you really have sex with him in the park?"

Chapter Thirty-Two

*F*or three whole days, I stay locked up in my room, only coming out to go to the bathroom or grab a quick snack. My dad and my brother and even Andrew have all come to check on me at one time or another to make sure I'm still alive. I haven't seen my mom at all.

And Ben hasn't sent me any rage-texts or, I don't know, thrown a flaming poo bag onto my front porch. At least I would know he was thinking of me if he did. But him having absolutely zero feelings for me anymore is worse than if he hated me.

Rayna says I'm being dramatic, like always, but it feels like I've lost everything.

To think that things were going well and then have this bomb dropped...

I'm in shell shock.

But all this lying around, staring at the ceiling, has given me time to do what I promised Rayna I would. To think back on what Ben did with me and said to me over the summer through a different lens. And I keep coming back to the same thing...

He had sex with me for four weeks straight.

Because he liked me.

He pretended to be my boyfriend for four more weeks.

Because he liked me.

He got in a dumb-shit argument with me and refused to explain and cut me out of his life.

Because he liked me?

It just doesn't make sense. None of it. It doesn't line up with Ben's reputation, either. He's a player, a sarcastic motherfucker, an ego trip, a golden boy. Except he's not only those things—I know that now. He's also super smart, and he took care of me when I was hurt, more than once. He's both fun and funny, and he's generous with his time, his money, and his attention. He makes mistakes but then learns from them rather than repeats them. He's so, *so* talented—I still hear him playing the cello in my dreams, still watch that video I took of him every day.

And he just…gets me.

That's the hardest thing in all this. It isn't easy for me to make friends, so when I do find someone I'm comfortable with and who doesn't pressure me to be something I'm not, I cling to that person like they're the matching side to my Velcro strip. I never thought Benjamin Oliver would be one of those people, but he is. Was.

Goddammit. I didn't think I had any tears left to cry.

My pillow is soaked again.

"Jessica?" Mom says through my closed door. "Can I come in?"

Am I delirious or is my mother actually talking to me?

"Yes," I say as loudly as I can, and it comes out all raw and scratchy.

The door opens slowly, and she peeks inside before walking in. She takes one look at me and sighs, then sits on my bed and takes my hand into her lap without a word, running her fingertips back and forth over my hand, my wrist, my arm.

I just lay there and focus on her touch. We had this rope connecting us that was so strong before, and over the last ten years it's withered and frayed, and now it's so close to snapping that I'm afraid anything I do or say will be the end of us. But now, with every stroke of her hand over mine, those broken threads start weaving back together, bit by bit.

I don't need her to be perfect. I don't even need her to be constantly available and involved. I just need this, to know that she understands. I don't want her to say "you'll get over him" or "you're better off without him." I don't want her to say *anything*. I just want to know that she knows what I need and what I want from her.

And right now, she's doing exactly that.

She stays with me until I fall asleep, and when I wake up, she's still here, sitting on the end of my bed now, silently reading a Dr. Seuss book.

I rub my eyes. "What are you doing?"

"Oh…just reminiscing," she says and turns another page.

Ben asked me once before if I told my mom the way I feel about her. About us. I didn't answer him, because I didn't think repairing anything this broken could be that easy. But maybe he was right. I should just tell her and see what happens.

"Mom." I sit up. "Do you miss it? Reading to me every night?"

She closes the book and sets it on her lap. "I do," she says. "I think about it all the time."

"Me too."

"Things were different then," she says. "The world was different. I was different. Your father's job was different—he had a much higher salary then. I didn't have to work overtime every week just to make ends meet. I didn't even have to work *full* time. And on the days I had off and Chris was in school, I got to spend more time with you."

That's what she's been doing on her late nights? She sometimes doesn't come home until after midnight. Then gets up early again to go right back to work the next day? I had no idea.

I feel like shit for even *thinking* it might be something underhanded.

"You know that saying." She looks at me now, her eyes glistening in the low light. "The only thing in life that stays the same is that things will always change. But you know what my mother used to tell me when I thought my life was over because a friend moved away or a boy broke my heart? She'd say, 'Just because something changes doesn't mean it's gone. It's still there, only different.'"

I nod and sniffle, grab a tissue from the box on my nightstand and blow my nose. Grab another and wipe my eyes. Grab another and hand it over to Mom.

Then I scoot over to her, snuggling as close as I can, and take the book, open it…and read to her.

Me: *Have you seen Benjamin? Is he okay?*
  Rayna: *no sorry i don't know*
  Me: *Ask Jeremy.*
  Rayna: *he doesn't know either*

*O*n day four, I feel a little more normal and clearheaded again. Emphasis on little.

But it's a start.

If Ben really is done with me forever, I have to respect his decision and accept it. I don't have to like it, but I also don't have to try to change his mind. And since I'm at the point where there is nothing left for me to lose, I should tell him.

I should tell him now all the things I should have told him before, so at least he knows the truth. I'm not doing this to convince him to give me a chance or to guilt him into revealing his own feelings. I'm doing it because he deserves to know. And that's it.

Having a plan and carrying it out are two different things, though. He won't talk to me, but I still have a way to talk to him. He's not answering my texts, but he's still reading them. He never turned off his read receipts or silenced his notifications on me. So, all I have to do is cut my heart open and spill it into our chat. No big deal.

Right.

I can't censor myself, this has to be genuine. No edits. Just draft and send and draft and send and draft and send until I'm out of words. Or until he blocks me.

I take a deep breath and start.

Me: *I miss you.*

Me: *But it isn't just you I miss. It's us.*

Me: *You don't have to reply to any of this.*

Me: *There are so many things I didn't tell you that I should have told you.*

Me: *From day one.*

Me: *I remember the first time I saw you. Jeremy said this is my friend Ben and I looked at you looking at me and it felt like someone kicked me in the chest. Seeing you for the first time was physically painful. You're so beautiful it hurt.*

Me: *I knew who you were before that day. Everyone knew who you were but that was the first time I saw you up* *close. Your eyes*

Me: *Your eyes looking straight into mine undid me.*

Me: *I didn't know what to say or do and I knew right then you were trouble.*

Me: *For me, I mean. You were trouble for me.*

Me: *I don't know when it happened or why, but something made me shrink from you when I wanted to reach out to you. Something made me put up walls instead of building a bridge.*

Me: *For months and months I told myself I hated you.*

Me: *Benjamin Gabriel Oliver*

Me: *I never hated you. I thought I did but when I look back*

Me: *I was lying to myself. Those lies were a shield. If I hated you then you could never have an effect on me. I could convince myself that I didn't care and the only thing I could feel around you was annoyance.*

I pause for a minute, emotions welling up inside me like lava, ready to erupt.

Me: *It almost worked. I almost got through and moved on and forgot you.*

Me: *But then you found a way to stay in my orbit. And I tried to tell myself run, run, run, but some part of me knew it was already too late. I was already too attached.*

Me: *This summer*

Me: *This summer was like nothing I could have expected or imagined.*

Me: *This summer was when I got to meet you again for the first time. Only to realize I've known you all along.*

Something snaps inside me, and suddenly I can't type the words fast enough.

…the first time you called me witch. It was Halloween and I said it must be so hard coming up with such clever comebacks

without a brain. And from then on I was your wicked witch and you were my brainless scarecrow…

…that game-winning touchdown that put you guys in the state championship. You ran all the way across the whole damn field while the rest of the team just cleared the way for you. It was fucking magical. I never cheered so loud in my life…

…Kamy's New Year's Eve party. I had no one to kiss at midnight. Every single girl in the place had their eyes on you hoping you'd choose them and when the countdown started I left the room because I couldn't stand to see everyone else so happy but me and you followed me out. I accused you of rubbing it in my face that I was alone and you had your pick of anyone and when the new year started we were fighting. It was so typical of us. I wasn't angry at you though. I was angry at myself for not having the guts to kiss you. We were alone. No one would have known. But still I couldn't…

…I lied. It wasn't because I didn't have a date or because I suddenly got sick. Rayna doesn't even know the real reason. I left prom early because I wanted my date to be you. I wanted that to be the night for me. My first time. And seeing you with someone else. Again. Especially on that night…

…when really it's been you all along. I just didn't see it. Just like you told me. You said I can't see what's right in front of me. But I see it now, all of it. I see you.

Me: *I see you*

Me: *I see you*

Me: *I see you*

Me: *And I see us too. When I think of you and me this is what I see.*

I attach the picture I took of us in his bed. My hair is a mess and my eye makeup is smudged and I'm smiling smugly up at the camera with a look of utter contentment. Ben is sleeping, smashed up against me, his arm coming up from under the blanket to hold my opposite shoulder. There's no agenda. This isn't putting on a show for anyone—this is real.

Me: *And whenever I think of you this is what I see.*

I attach the video I took of him playing the cello naked, and I watch it again as it uploads. I'll never get enough of this. The beauty of the whole package—his face and body, his hands and the music. I don't remember him doing it at the time, but every once in a while, he darts a glance up at me—at the camera—and smiles, then goes back to that trance-like state while he plays, sometimes closing his eyes, just listening to the music. Feeling it.

Me: *This is the you I see. The intelligent you. The talented you. The beautiful you. The strong you. The gentle you. The you that you showed to only me.*

Me: *And there's one more thing I never told you but I should have.*

Me: *I saw your acceptance letter from Juilliard. I was so confused. I thought football was your life. I thought you were going to OSU because it was a stepping stone to the NFL. Everyone thought that's what you wanted. But it isn't. I know that now.*

Me: *I put the pieces together.*

Me: *You said you hadn't touched a football in months. You said you were rusty. But when you picked up that cello and sat down to play, it was perfection. You play that thing every day, I know you do. And you do it because you love it, not because anyone expects you to.*

Me: *You think you have this reputation to live up to but I know your secret now Benjamin Oliver. I know it's all an act.*

Me: *Dinner with your family confirmed it. You didn't choose to go to OSU. You were expected to. You didn't choose to be a star quarterback or be wildly popular or go to all the parties or sleep with all the girls.*

Me: *You were expected to, simply because of your name.*

Me: *And once people had that idea of you in their head of what it means to be Benjamin Oliver, you couldn't change anyone's mind even if you tried. So you didn't. You lived up to everyone's expectations.*

Me: *But you let yourself down. You hid yourself. And the only one suffering is you.*

Me: *So if you're still reading this I have only one thing left to say.*

Me: *Go and live for yourself now Benjamin. It's time to do what YOU want and say fuck off to the rest of the world, even me, and take your own advice.*

Me: *You're in control. Always.*

Chapter Thirty-Three

The last thing Ben said to me was a text he sent a little more than two weeks ago, before I told him everything.

Ben: *bye Jessie*

At the time, I didn't think that he meant "goodbye forever," but apparently, he did.

And I want to believe his nonresponse to me pouring my heart out to him isn't soul-crushing, but it is. Some days the only thing that gets me through is focusing really hard on *not* focusing on Ben.

Some days even that doesn't work. I end up watching him playing the cello on my phone again and again and again until I physically can't stay awake anymore, wishing I could go back to that night when things were so, so good.

But I have to move on. I told him to go and live his life for himself, and I need to live my life for myself, too. I need to figure out what I even want.

Besides him. Us.

Because he's gone. Today is August fifteenth and he's probably halfway to Columbus, Ohio, by now, if he hasn't arrived already. It only takes three hours to drive there from here.

I keep imagining his car on the highway, loaded up with

boxes, moving farther and farther away—

"Jessie, we have to go," my brother says, pulling my gaze from some nonexistent point on the horizon to his face, sitting next to me on the porch swing. "You gonna be okay here?"

Chris is leaving. Andrew is leaving. Ben is leaving. Everyone is leaving or already gone. Kamy and Todd are moving into their new place in Cambridge, near the Harvard campus. Jeremy and Rayna are moving into their Penn State dorms. I'm left here alone with myself, stuck. I don't even have a car to go visit anyone if I wanted to, or money to buy a plane ticket.

"I'll be fine," I tell Chris.

"You will," he says. "Eventually. But until then, you can call me anytime, okay? Day, night, weekend, holiday, whenever you need it."

"Okay."

He wraps me up in a hug just as Andrew exits the house, and then they say goodbye and my dad drives them to the airport.

It's just me and my mom here now, and hell if I know where she is or what she's doing. She said something about working in the backyard garden this morning. That was six hours ago, but she might still be out there. She gets into these zoned-out work modes on the weekends where she loses track of time and forgets to eat or drink or take any breaks. And it's hot today.

Like, volcano erupting on the equator of the sun hot.

I go inside the house and pour a tall glass of cold lemonade, then another, and take both of them out the back door. Mom is kneeling on a foam pad in the dirt, picking tomatoes, the wide brim of her sunhat blocking most of her face. We've already eaten so many tomatoes by the end of summer, we end up giving them away to anyone who will take them.

"Aren't those tomato plants tired of having babies yet?" I say, and she turns toward me. I hand her the lemonade.

"Thanks." After downing half the glass in one go, she says, "I really needed that."

"You've been out here all day." I sit down cross-legged on the grass. "Chris is gone."

"I know," she says. "He came and said goodbye to me before he left."

"Everyone's gone."

"Feeling left behind?" she asks.

"No." I blow out a sigh. "It's more like… I don't know. Wishing I had something to do so I wouldn't have time to think about what everyone else is doing. Wishing I had a plan."

Mom goes quiet for a minute, then tugs off her floral garden gloves. "Some people need more time to figure it out than others. Maybe you need to get away from here for a while and see what you think of the world. If you could go anywhere, Jessica, where would you go?"

I laugh to myself. "Benjamin asked me that same thing a couple of months ago."

"And what did you tell him?"

"New York City. There's so much to do and see there, maybe I'll find myself somewhere inside all of it." I shrug. "But I *can't* just go anywhere."

She nods slowly. "What if I told you that you could?"

"I'd ask you when you started taking opiates."

"Jessica!" She gives me a playful smack. "You don't have to be crude."

"I'm sorry, have we met?" I tease. "I'm your daughter — you might remember birthing me — and I wear crude like a little black dress."

Mom laughs, and I nearly expire from shock. Her laughter

is so rare it's almost foreign. It's warm and soft and rolls over you and around you until you're consumed by it.

"I'm going to miss you," she says, then pushes herself up to stand and walks back to the house.

What? Why?

Is she going somewhere too?

I jump up from the grass and go after her, finding her washing her hands at the kitchen sink. "Why did you say that? What are you...talking about?"

She dries her hands and removes her sunhat. She's got this look on her face that I don't understand. Like she's happy but also sad. It makes no sense.

"When you were born," she says, "your father and I started a fund. We called it the 'Our Daughter Can Do Whatever She Wants' fund. We've been adding money to it every month since you turned one month old. That's some hefty pocket change now. And it's all yours."

"It's...what?" *I have money?* "Why?"

"Because we wanted you to make your own choices, Jessica. Use it to go to school. Or don't. Use it to travel. Or don't. Use it to buy a house. Or a car. Or literally anything you want. Or don't—it can stay in the bank and keep growing. Whatever you do with that money, though, it's completely up to you."

I repeat her words in my head, twice, three times, before they start to register. My parents planned for this, saving for *years*. They can't give me a credit card like all my friends' parents did. But they gave me something better. Cold, hard cash. No debt. No student loans to repay.

I can do whatever I want to do. I can do things that will help me *figure out* what I want to do. And I just told my mother where I would start—somewhere far away from here.

I'm going to miss you, she said.

"I know I haven't always been the best mother," she tells me. "And I haven't been there for you as often as you needed me. But I thought, at least I could give you this—the freedom to choose your own path."

"Mom..." My voice dissolves into nothing as I step over and hug her tight. "I don't know what to say."

She squeezes me back. "Say you'll come home and visit once in a while."

I nod against her shoulder. "I will. I promise, I will."

"Good," she says, pulling out of the hug. "Now, go. Make a plan. Your whole life is waiting for you."

When I get to my room, the first thing I do is get Rayna and Kamy on a video call. I spend at least an hour talking to them about what they think I should do, and after that, I pull up my chat with Ben.

He's my friend, too; I want to tell him. I'm so excited about this, my cheeks are sore from smiling, and he knows— he *knows*—traveling is a big deal for me. But the last thing he said to me was, "bye Jessie." And the last thing I said to him was, "You're in control. Always."

I'd be a hypocrite if I reached out to him now.

He has to make the next move, if he makes a move at all. *Bing.*

Ben: *you still owe me a favor*

What the—

I blink several times, rub my head, and stare at the phone. Is that text from him real? Did I just...think and hope and dream that into existence?

Only one way to find out.

Me: *I thought you were leaving today.*

Ben: *later*

He's talking to me... He's actually talking to me!

Ben: *I promised I'd call in both favors before I left*

Me: *So you want your second favor now?*

Ben: *right now*

God. This could be a disaster or it could be a *total* disaster. He's still mad at me, I bet. What's he going to make me do as punishment?

Me: *Okay what is it?*

Ben: *meet me at the grandstand in trinity square*

Me: *Why?*

Ben: *you'll see when you get here hurry up*

Dammit. He's already there waiting for me.

I run downstairs and out the back door, where Mom is pulling weeds from the flower bed. My words come out fast and breathy. "I need to borrow your car, it's an emergency."

She snorts. "Absolutely not."

"*What?* Mom—"

"When was the last time you were even behind the wheel?"

I have to think. "When I took my driver's test two years ago."

"That's why. And I like you and my car too much to let you crash it in a mad rush to—" She gives me a long look. "What's this sudden emergency?"

"Benjamin wants to meet me at—"

"I'll get my keys." She's up and fast-walking to the house before I can finish.

I rush to catch up. "You changed your mind? I can take your car?"

"No," she says over her shoulder. "I'm driving you there myself."

• • •

The grandstand in Trinity Square is basically a giant gazebo used like a 360-degree stage, with chairs set up on the lawns all around. We're a block away from it when I realize why there are so many people here and no place to park. This is the talent show fundraiser thing for children's cancer research that Ben's dad was boasting about at their family dinner.

What this has to do with me doing Ben a favor? I'm honestly afraid to ask.

He better not fucking ask me to go onstage.

"I'll just drop you off here, okay?" Mom says, pulling up alongside the south end of the square. "Call me if you need me to pick you up?"

"Yeah." I step out of the car and close the door in a daze. It's so…crowded. And the show has already started. There's a group of six people, paired up into three couples, currently on the gazebo stage, dancing some kind of…waltz? The women's skirts flow elegantly around them, and the men are dressed to the nines in tuxedoes.

This is the most hoity-toity talent show I've ever seen.

I'm wearing a spaghetti-strap tank top and knit shorts, flip-flops—because I never learn—and no makeup. My face is sweaty, and my hair is stringy and falling out of my bun.

If I'm doing anything here other than sitting my ass in a chair and watching, I will die.

But part of me knows that isn't what Ben called me out here for. That would be too easy.

I can feel my death creeping up on me already. It's squeezing around my neck and turning my arms and legs into adrenaline-flavored Jell-O.

He wouldn't be this cruel, would he? He knows how a spotlight affects me.

He knows *me*. He wouldn't…

I need to sit down before my legs give out. And there's

nowhere to sit.

"Jessie—"

I spin so fast toward the voice behind me that I stagger and nearly topple. It's Ben.

My god, how I missed that face. One look into his dark, soulful eyes and my stomach bottoms out like I'm in a freefall.

Then I realize he's wearing a full suit, collared shirt, necktie—how is he not sweltering?—and he's holding his cello by the neck, with the bow hanging by the crook of his forefinger on the same hand. Relief whooshes out of me so fast, I get dizzy. He's part of the show, that's all it is. He's going to show everyone he can play music, not just football, and for a moment I'm so excited for him and proud of him that I almost forget why I'm here.

How would that be *me* doing *him* a favor?

"Benjamin?" Anxiety builds inside me again like a burbling vat of rancid stew. I'm gonna be sick. "What... What do you want me to do?"

His face and body language are completely neutral. Not stiff like a statue, just...his typical cool, calm confidence but without the smirk. He isn't pleased to see me—even though he's the one who asked me to come.

Cause of death: aneurysm.

Cause of aneurysm: confusion.

Cause of confusion: Benjamin Oliver.

He's finally decided to murder me for real.

"You made it just in time," he says. And I have only a millisecond to appreciate the sound of his naturally deep, sensual voice gracing my ears again before he takes me by the elbow, guiding me around behind the rows and rows of filled seats. "We're on next."

Chapter Thirty-Four

No. Nooo no nononononononooooo. And furthermore, NO!

I plant my feet on the grass, forcing Ben to turn. "You can't."

"Yes, I can."

"*Don't*," I beg. "I'll do anything you want but this. *Anything*."

"We made a deal," he reminds me, then glances around. Everyone starts clapping for the dancers—because they're done now.

Oh god.

Mayor Oliver steps out onto the stage with a mic in his hand, thanking the group for their performance, and then he goes into stats about how much money they've raised so far and who has emptied their pockets. Sounds like a guilt trip for the people who have yet to cough up any cash, but that isn't what bothers me.

That's the mayor. His *father*.

"Does your dad know about this?" I gesture toward his cello.

Ben starts tugging me around the back of the chairs again. "Of course he does. Who do you think paid for my lessons since I was three years old?"

"I... But he said you're only good at football."

"No, actually, he said I'm lucky I'm good at football so I can make something of myself by playing pro. Paraphrased. He knows I could play music professionally, too, but to him, it isn't worth it. There's no money in it. At least not the kind of money he expects a son of his to make."

My head is spinning. I struggle to keep up with his story and his long legs. "So...he's okay with you playing cello in front of all of Trinity's high society?"

"Jessie," he says, like this is something I should know. "Remember that day I had to cancel our hookup? It's because I was helping him with this. We held the auditions that day, and he wanted my help deciding what acts to say yes to and which to say no to."

Here comes that aneurysm again. Not a single word of that made sense.

"Wait, wait..." I stop again. "You helped your father? He *wanted* your help?"

"Yes and yes," he says. "He's about to call me onto the stage."

"But he was so mean to you—"

"He's not an evil villain, Jess. He's very opinionated, and so am I, and once he gets going on something, he doesn't know when to stop. We butt heads a lot. But that doesn't mean we hate each other. You of all people should know that someone can feel like they're your enemy and your friend all at once." He raises a brow. "Am I wrong?"

"N-no," I say, still not understanding what any of this has to do with me.

Ben takes my hand. "He knows what I'm doing here; he approves of it, even. What he doesn't know...is that in the last couple of weeks I changed my act."

"How?"

"I added you."

What—*why?* Two weeks ago was when we "broke up." Has he been planning my demise since then? Is that why I haven't heard from him?

"No." I start walking backward, pulling at him to release my hand, but he just holds it tighter. "No, Benjamin. I can't go up there. *Please.*"

He pulls me in close, leaning down to whisper in my ear. "I know you're scared as fuck right now. But I wouldn't do anything to hurt you. Not now, not ever."

"Then what—"

"Do you trust me?" he says.

Do I? There was a time when I didn't know.

Now, the answer is so simple. "Yes. I trust you."

But acknowledging that doesn't make this any easier. Something very public is still about to happen to me. Even if it's good, I'm not sure I'll survive.

Ben smiles at me, finally, sending me to the brink of cardiac arrest. And that familiarity eases a little bit of my tension. But then he says, "Good. Because I insisted the show be televised, and then I told everyone I know to watch it today. Live."

Holy shit. If there are cameras here, they're hidden. Can this get any worse?

"And for our final act," Mayor Oliver says, "my very own son, Benjamin Oliver, will be playing his original solo composition for the cello called 'You Were the First.'"

No way. This has to be a joke.

You were the first? Come on. That's clearly about me being a virgin and—

Oh my Jesus, is he going to tell the entire town about our deal? *Aaaagh.*

"We're on," he says, and guides me up the side stairs onto the stage.

I trust you Benjamin I trust you Benjamin I trust you Benjamin I trust you…

His dad passes us on his way off, giving me a questioning look. He really doesn't know about me being part of this. What am I walking into?

"If you wanted to kill me, Benjamin," I whisper, "a guillotine would have been more humane."

He smiles at that. Yeah, he's definitely up to no good.

But I trust him. I do. I have to stop listening to my anxiety and remember I trust him.

There are two chairs set next to each other in the middle of the stage, only a few feet apart. Ben points to one and says, "All you have to do is sit there and listen."

I nod, taking my seat, but I'm shaking. My knees are bouncing, my hands are trembling. I can't get a full breath. I'm literally *surrounded* by people, all of them looking at me like they can't figure out what gutter I was pulled out of and why they have to see such a mess.

Ben attaches a small mic to his ear that comes around his jaw to the corner of his mouth, then unbuttons his suit jacket and sits with his cello in the other chair. He clears his throat, and the sound goes booming through the speakers.

"Hi, everyone," he says. "I wrote this song about six months ago, for a girl who I couldn't get out of my head." He jacks a thumb toward me. "She's the one. My original didn't have any lyrics, though"—he laughs a little—"and I'm not much of a singer. So I decided to turn this into a poetry reading set to music."

He wrote a song for me…six months ago? We were still in school then.

And a *poem*?

Ben starts playing with long, slow strokes. It's like his cello is singing. The music takes flight, vibrating the air around me, wrapping me up in it like a warm blanket on a cold day.

Then he softens it so it's more like background music, but never stops playing as he turns his head toward me and he says, "Jessica Florence Webster, you were the first."

Oh my god. With this, plus the heat of the day, I'll burn to ash in a matter of seconds.

"You were the first one to ignore me," he says. "You were the first one to insult me."

You asshole, I silently scream. *I trusted you—*

"You were the first brave soul to tell me the whole world isn't about me."

Um…what?

His music gets loud again, and the tempo picks up. The longer he plays, the more I'm getting lost in it, my body relaxing without any conscious effort. I can't look at the audience, though. I just keep staring down at my red-painted toes. I've tried to wear different colors, but this is the only one that feels right anymore. Plus, I have a lifetime supply of it.

Ben softens the tune, and in my side vision, I see him turn to look at me.

"You were the first to give me a thing for frumpy clothes," he says, and there's some muttering in the crowd, like they aren't sure what he means by that.

Except look at me. It's obvious.

So, more likely, they're shocked he just admitted to finding this dumpy look attractive.

But no one is more shocked than me. Is he serious? He can't be serious.

"You were the first to give me a thing for plain cotton

dresses," he goes on. "You were the first to be yourself around me, even when being yourself was messy."

His rhythm is off, but the music is perfection. He's giving his best and his not-so-great all at once. He isn't hiding anything…not anymore.

This is his response to me pouring my heart out. He wasn't ignoring me, he didn't block me. He was just waiting to show me how serious and sincere he really is about it. In public.

My heart pounds so hard I feel it in my throat. In my ears. Against my ribs. Against my spine. He isn't done yet—he's still playing. How much more of this can there be?

Suddenly my phone buzzes in my back pocket, vibrating my ass, and I do a full-body flinch. Ben snaps his face toward me again, never stopping his song, but I'm only vaguely aware of it as I take my phone out to find a text from my best friend who isn't here.

Rayna: *OH MY GOD OH MY GOD THIS IS THE MOST ROMANTIC THING I'VE EVER SEEN IN MY LIFE ARE YOU GOING TO PASS OUT I WOULD PASS OUT!!!!*

I forgot she's watching this. Live. All my friends are. All of Trinity. Maybe even the whole county—I'm going to be on the news later. *Shit on a barbed-wire fence.*

Ben's laughter crackles through the speakers, and he says, "You were the first person to ever interrupt my performance to check your phone."

Now *everyone* is laughing. God. I still can't look at them.

Rayna: *did you really just read my text on live tv you dingle butt*

Quickly, I turn my notifications off and put the phone back in my pocket. She's right. What the hell was I thinking? But now…it's like the weather has shifted. The mood. The atmosphere. Awkward tension and silence have drifted away, and in their place are a sunny sort of lightness and inquisitive murmuring. I dare a glance up and out. People are *smiling*.

I turn to face Ben, and he's downright beaming from ear to ear.

My stomach is doing somersaults, and the rest of me feels fizzy and bubbly. How can I look at that beautiful face, that beautiful smile that's meant for me, and not melt on the spot?

The song goes on and on, and he keeps piling on more and more "firsts" he had with me.

Not just over the summer—but since the day we met.

And it sounds less and less like a poem and more and more like a declaration.

"You were the first to call me whatever you wanted and not give a crap what anyone thought, including me.

"You were the first to make me like hearing my name again. Again and again.

"You were the first to tell me before every game that if I got sacked you'd never let me live it down. And the first I ever tried my hardest to please on the football field.

"You were the first to go out for ice cream with me at my favorite spot.

"You were the first to get caught in the rain with me.

"You were the first who made me make a damn fool of myself trying to win a giant stuffed animal at the fair.

"You were the first I ever held at the top of the Ferris wheel, on top of the world, wishing we could stay alone in that moment forever.

"You were the first I ever played a private show for, with an audience of one.

"You were the first to make me wonder what the hell I was doing with my life.

"You were the first to dare me to hope for something different.

"You're the only thing I think about before I fall asleep, and the only thing I think about as soon as I wake up. And when I dream, it's all about you. And when I have nightmares, it's because you aren't there."

The more he says, the more the audience engages, like they're *rooting* for us. People start saying "ohhh" and "aww" like they're watching a cute-as-all-get-out fireworks display.

In a way, I guess they are. Because I'm bursting with emotions right now. I can't even keep up with what I'm feeling from one moment to the next.

"You were the first to tear down my walls.

"You were the first to build me back up."

I don't know how long we've been up here, but I'm done. I am *finished*. There is nothing left to see here but a puddle of blond-haired goo.

"You were the first to see the real me," he says. "You were the first to *see* me.

"You were the first to show me what it really means to be happy."

The cello music slows, and soon he's playing one long, final note.

Then he drops his bow hand and turns to me. The air goes quiet and still, like every last person here is on the edge of their seat to see how this ends. There are rivers running down my face. I can't stop sniffling. How am I still breathing?

Without any music now, just his strong voice, he says, "You're the first girl I ever fell in love with. I love you, Jessica Florence Webster. I've loved you since the day we met, and I'm sorry it took so long for me to understand it. I love you more than football, more than music, more than anything I've ever loved in my entire life. And I can't imagine my life without you."

Ben sets his cello down on its side and lays the bow next

to it, then comes around in front of me and takes my hand, pulling me up to stand. His expression turns worried, that little wrinkle forming between his brows.

He takes off the mic, sets it on his empty chair, and says to me, "Why are you crying?"

Why am I crying? *Why am I crying?*

How do I explain that he's the reason I'm happy and sad and eager and hesitant and agitated and blissful and all the other conflicting emotions that exist? All of them, always.

How do I explain he's the reason for *everything*?

I look long and hard into his deep, dark eyes that have been a source of comfort more times than I can count, and only one thing comes to mind.

"Because I love you, you big jerk."

His face splits with a big, toothy smile, then he places one hand on the side of my face and one hand behind my head, gently pulling me closer to him until our lips meet in a kiss.

A kiss I've been hoping for and honestly believed I'd never get.

A scorching, devouring, hold-nothing-back kiss *in front of everyone*.

And he just keeps kissing me like he can't get enough. The feeling is fucking mutual.

All around us, the crowd erupts into thunderous applause and cheers.

Finally, he pulls away, but keeps his face close to mine.

"I'm going to New York," he says, and my jaw drops. "I switched schools. The paperwork was a disaster and my dad wasn't too thrilled, but I did it. I'm going to be a professional musician. It's what I want, Jessie, and you helped me figure out how to get it."

"You're..." Did I hear him correctly? "You're going to *New York*? Now?"

He searches my eyes. "You don't think I should?"

"No, no, you should. You definitely should. I just—" I just can't believe this is happening. "Benjamin...there's something I need to tell you."

Three months later…

This is my first time having dinner with Ben's family since I told off his father in the middle of a meal over the summer. I've seen his parents once or twice before today, when they came to visit us at our apartment in New York. But sitting back at their mansion again on Thanksgiving, even knowing they're okay with me, no grudges, no judgment, and they're so glad me and Ben are happy together, I can't stop thinking about what happened the last time.

How embarrassed I was. How rude I was. How angry I was.

And I can't help wondering if there's going to be another argument.

Mr. Oliver is currently giving us all a lecture about his new plan to "clean up" the east end of the city. The area where I grew up and where my parents still live. It's about damn time.

"Have I mentioned you look ravishing tonight," Ben whispers, leaning close to my ear.

I swallow a bite of gravy-covered turkey. "You might have. Seventeen hundred times."

"Forget the Thanksgiving feast, I'd rather see you spread out on this table."

I elbow him in the ribs, holding back a smile. "Shut your filthy mouth."

"Make me, witch," he teases and scoops up a forkful of sweet potato casserole.

"Don't tempt me, scarecrow—"

"Benjamin, Jessica," Mr. Oliver says, "do you have something more important to discuss? Please speak up so the rest of us can join the deliberation."

Dammit, Benjamin.

"We were, um, saying how…" My voice trails off. I got nothing.

"How fast time is flying by," Ben adds. "Our married-couple friends are expecting a baby soon. Sorry for the interruption, Dad—they just texted us sonogram pictures and we couldn't wait to see them." He pulls out his phone.

I chug a few gulps of ice-cold water to keep my quickly heating face from giving away his lie. We got those pictures from Kamy and Todd a few weeks ago.

Ben pulls up the black-and-white pic, expands it to fit the whole screen, then hands his phone across the table to his mom. Good call, going for her first.

"Oh, how wonderful," Mrs. Oliver says, then shows it to her husband. "I just love babies. Looks like they're having a boy?"

"Yes," I say. "Due in February."

And I have to admit, the closer we get to seeing and holding that chubby little bundle of joy, the more excited I am. Rayna isn't the only one who gets to be an auntie. After their wedding, I started buying gifts…lots of them. Stacks and piles of them.

If anyone saw the spare bedroom in my apartment,

they'd think it was me who was pregnant here. But no, not for a while. If ever.

"They're so cute at that age," Mr. Oliver says, a smirk on his face that I usually see on Ben's. He hands the phone back to Ben, nodding toward his own new grandbaby at the other end of the table, who's sleeping peacefully in a sling around Jake's chest. "You know, before they learn how to talk. Once that happens, it's all downhill."

Mrs. Oliver playfully smacks his arm. "You love babies, too, and children," she reminds him. "Don't pretend like you don't." She shoots a sly look across the table at me, then Ben. "Plenty of room for more here…"

"Mom," Ben says. "Let me finish school and start a career before you make wedding plans and buy a crib."

"I'm just saying." She raises her hands in surrender, her tone overly innocent. "Whenever you're ready."

Enjoy the ones you've got, Mama Oliver, because they could be all you get.

"What about you, Jessica?" Mr. Oliver says. "Have you chosen which one of your options you'd like to pursue yet?"

"No," I answer confidently. "I'm still working on that." And I'm not afraid to say it anymore. I'm not afraid of my own indecision—I'm embracing it, trying out as much as I can with whatever I can, then on to a new thing. And whether it's by spoken word or a thought in my head, I thank my parents every day for their gift that made it possible.

A gift I had all along, I just didn't know it. Kind of like Ben.

Below the table, I squeeze his hand.

"Actually," I say, "living in New York for the last three months has only given me *more* options to consider. A lot to see and do."

A lot of expense, too. Even with Ben splitting the cost with me, living in New York is a good way to go broke. It didn't take me long to figure out I'd run out of money sooner rather than later, so for the last couple of months I've been learning how to make my money grow on its own with investments. I didn't think I'd like something that involved so much math, but I do. It's weird. And I never would have discovered that about myself if my life hadn't been exactly what it's been, leading me to exactly where I am today.

Mr. Oliver nods then says, "If one of those options is politics, you let me know. It can be hard to break into, but I can share a few tricks I learned that'll give you a leg up."

"Oh, uh..." Did he really just offer to help me? "Thank you."

My face is burning up, but thankfully Mr. Oliver takes the spotlight off me, bringing up a new topic. The rest of the dinner goes by in a blur.

At the end of the night, Ben and I go to his old room. It looks exactly the same as he left it. Exactly as it should be, the way I still see it in my memories.

"Can you imagine me being a politician?" I say with a laugh, plopping down onto his bed. "Your dad's a comedian."

Ben wrestles the knot out of his tie, tilting his head in thought. "I could, actually. I think you'd be a great politician."

I snort. "Because I'm so good at public speaking and debate."

"Maybe you aren't now, but you could be," Ben says. "I don't know anyone as passionate and determined as you are when you put your mind to something you think is important."

"Passionate and determined, huh?" I raise a brow, then kick my heels off, staring him down. "Why don't you come over here. I'll show you passionate and determined."

"Yes, ma'am." He gives me that heart-stopping grin, then starts across the room, shedding articles of clothing with every step.

A year ago, I hated this boy. Or at least I thought I did.

Six months ago, I cried over this boy, when I realized I wanted him and believed it could never happen.

Three months ago, I moved in with this boy. Because somehow our paths aligned in just the right place at just the right time, and we looked Fate in the face and said "bring it on."

Today, I'm so in love with this boy. I didn't even know what love was before him.

Love isn't perfection—it's the opposite. It's two imperfect people making mistakes together and memories together and learning and growing from each other and leaning on each other. Trusting each other. And I can't wait to see where our love takes us next.

Acknowledgments

Every book is a unique journey, and every book has a team of people working on it behind the scenes, but this one has been really special because that team of people is also my family of coworkers at Entangled. I love every single one of you, but my first note of gratitude has to go to Liz Pelletier for bringing this story to life in a way that I couldn't have on my own. Your genius knows no bounds. And I count myself lucky every day because I get to work with you side by side and see your brilliance shining in everything you do. You believed in this story when it was just a silly idea in my head three years ago, and I thought no one would ever want to publish something for teens with so much sex on the page. But you saw the potential in it, and you saw the importance of it, and you gave me a chance to show it to the world. For this, I can't ever thank you enough!

Thanks also to Stacy Abrams, who read this story without knowing I wrote it and fell in love with it without any bias. You've been my mentor, you've been my boss, you've been my colleague, you've been my friend. And now you've also been my editor. It's been almost ten years since we met, and I hope we'll have (at least) another ten more together!

Thanks to my agent, Laura Bradford, for your patience

and kindness and intelligence and all your hard work on my behalf. This one in particular was an atypical project, and you just rolled with it and found a way to make it work. I'm so lucky to have you on my team!

Thanks to Jen Bouvier for the daily laughs, the daily support, the creative memes, and the weenie jokes that I refused to use in this book. You are the weeniest weenie ever to weenie!

Thanks to Elizabeth Turner Stokes for the most beautiful cover art. You created something even better than I could have imagined, and I honestly cried the first time I saw it. And then I couldn't stop staring at it. You are so talented, and I feel privileged to not only see your art on a regular basis, through working together, but also to have had you as the designer for the cover of my book. You are truly one of the greats!

Thanks to Hannah Lindsey for your brilliant copy edits!

Thanks also to the rest of my Entangled family who helped me with this project in one way or another, either directly or indirectly. I love you all!

Thanks to my sister, my son, my mother, and my two emotional-support dogs. All of you have helped me on this author journey in different ways, and all of you are so important to me. I can't do it without you!

And finally, thanks to every teenager who reads this book when you could be doing literally anything else. You are the reason I write what I write, and I'm so glad I got to share this story and these characters with you!

Frenemies with Benefits is a playful and sexy teen romance that will keep you smiling. However, the story includes elements that might not be suitable for all readers. Divorce, infidelity, masturbation, and sexual devices are mentioned or discussed but not shown on the page. Underage alcohol consumption and drunkenness, recreational use of marijuana, teen pregnancy, sexual innuendo, and sexual intimacy in both private and public settings are shown in the novel. Readers who may be sensitive to these elements, please take note.

Let's be friends!

@EntangledTeen

@EntangledTeen

@EntangledTeen

@EntangledTeen

bit.ly/TeenNewsletter

entangled teen

an imprint of Entangled Publishing LLC